To Barbara
a dream of a niece
Dreams are our passports to
the stars. May your dreams
bring you joy in the year a... bring
and these stories
smile to your face
love
Gail

Mountain Dreams

by

Gail Kennedy

Laughing Owl Publishing, Inc.

MOUNTAIN DREAMS

This is a work of fiction. Any references to real people, events, establishments, organizations, or locations are intended only to give the fiction a sense of reality and authenticity. Other names, characters and incidents are either a product of the author's imagination or are used fictitiously.

Laughing Owl is committed to our Authors and their Work. For this reason, we do not permit our covers to be "stripped" for returns, but instead require that the whole book be returned, allowing us to resell it.

Library of Congress Cataloging-in Publication Data

Kennedy, Gail P., 1936 -
Mountain Dreams / by Gail P. Kennedy. - – 1st ed.
p. cm.
Contents: Five steps to flirting – Sunday school and the secret agent.
ISBN 0-9659701-0-8
1. Love stories, American. I. Title.
PS3561.E42635M68 1998
813'.54 - - dc21 98-41734
CIP

FIRST EDITION First Printing, 1998

Cover art by Kristen Anlage

Laughing Owl Publishing, Inc.
12610 Hwy 90 West
Grand Bay, AL 36541
www.laughingowl.com

ACKNOWLEDGMENTS

I owe my development as a writer and the fruition of this book to *many, many* supportive friends and fellow writers, too numerous to mention...after all I'm no spring chicken. Your encouragement and words of wisdom live with me each time I sit down to write. You know who you are, and I will personally thank each and every one of you.

First and foremost, thanks to my daughter, Robin. If she hadn't introduced me to the romance genre, these stories would never have been born. I am also indebted to Carolyn Haines and her courses on writing. And who could have a better mentor than Vicki Hinze. Hat's off to her and to Ginger McSween for their guidance and support.

A word of appreciation to two pilots, John Foster and Charles Pittinger, and to retired F.B.I. Agent Ray Phelps for their technical input. Thanks guys. And I'm deeply indebted to Hannah Monsimer for her background information on Las Cruces and to Ted Hoagland for his Spanish Lessons.

A special thanks to Judith Bland, cheerleader, friend, and critiquer extrodinaire; and to all the staff of Laughing Owl: Aleta, Muriel, Hamilton, Steve, no writer could ask for more author-friendly publishers.

As this is my first published novel, I'd like to dedicate it to my very own hero, who's been there for me—my husband and best friend, Roy.

God bless our children and their families—Pam, Kevin, (Ashley, Kelsey), Robin, John, Doug, and Janie—for living with their mother's passion for writing.

And last but far from least, thanks be to the Lord for any talents he bestowed on me.

In addition I have received in-the-trenches help from the following cast of characters. Jan Zimlich, Claudine Rushing, Lucille Badger, Susan Tanner, Sharon Irby, Carol Stringer, Libby Sydes, Lisa Brooks, Diana Jernigan, Kathy Carmichael, Sherry Cobb South, Melanie O'Hare, Doris Roeder, Joan Hauser, Pat Gordon, Betty Mabrey, Grace Harron, Caroline Philpot and Arlene Wadsworth.

Mountain Dreams

Two Novels

by

Gail Kennedy

FIVE STEPS TO FLIRTING

SUNDAY SCHOOL AND THE SECRET AGENT

FIVE STEPS TO FLIRTING

Prologue

No if's, and's, or but's!

She wanted a divorce—FROM HER FAMILY!

And not just any mealy-mouthed one, but an ironclad document with all the i's dotted and t's crossed. Most of all she wanted sole custody of her lovelife.

Regina Citrano dashed from the garden reception into the house, murmuring apologies to those she nudged along the way. Heads turned as her lavender skirt billowed and swirled and her matching heels pounded up the oak stairs. Her face flushed, her newly-permed hair flying, she sought sanctuary in her cousin's bedroom.

Once inside, she locked the door and marched to the open window. The May breeze ushered in the fragrance of lilacs but failed to cool her temper. Muted conversations, mixed with strains of romantic music, floated upward as she peered down on the idyllic scene.

Idyllic?

No gathering of the Citrano clan could be labeled idyllic, let alone idle.

Especially this wedding reception.

Her cousin Melva's marriage left Regina the only remaining single Citrano female in her generation. A state her family zealously pledged to rectify.

She sat down on the hope chest, conveniently

perched beneath the window. A collection of stuffed animals, once prized possessions of her cousin, sat atop it, propped against the bottom rim of the window. Preoccupied with her thoughts, Regina picked up a Teddy Bear, then spied a magazine wedged between the chest and the wall. She tugged at it, tossing the worn replica of Pooh onto the bed.

She'd had a premonition she'd regret coming today.

Too late now!

Come to think of it, divorcing her family might not be drastic enough, especially her three meddlesome aunts. Sure they had her welfare at heart, but today they'd stepped over the line. She had half a mind to put out a contract on them.

And how do you propose to do that when you're too shy to find your own dates?

Good point, she admitted, fanning herself with the magazine. A mutiny might prove easier. In spite of her anger, Regina chuckled, savoring the vision of her conniving aunts walking the plank. Just her luck, they'd cast a hex on her from their watery graves.

Too soft-hearted for her own good, she sighed. How could she stay angry with them? A good crew, they meant well. But heavens, this very moment three totally unsuitable men cruised the reception searching for her, each under the assumption she was their date and each escorted by one of her aunts. As a result, the aunts weren't speaking to each other, and family members had chosen sides.

World War Three, Citrano-style, was imminent.

Mortally embarrassed, Regina had beat a hasty retreat.

Don't blame them, her conscience chided. *They know how shy you are. They know you haven't had a serious relationship since you broke up with Paul four years ago.*

Regina chewed her lip and thumbed through the pages of the magazine. With three older siblings and a dozen older cousins doting on her, she'd hardly uttered a word till she was three—hadn't needed to. Her family's boisterous and argumentative nature had overwhelmed her. Yet she'd quietly observed and absorbed their antics, even managing to adopt them now and then. Once past her initial shyness with a person, her Citrano pizzazz shone through.

Of course, her disappointing relationship with Paul could be responsible for her shyness, too. It had lasted all through college and kept her out of circulation. That, combined with attending a Catholic woman's college hadn't provided many opportunities to interact with men.

But men weren't her problem.

Bless their ever-loving hearts, she was rather fond of them.

It was the seeking out and meeting them that defeated her.

If left to her own devices, taking her time to get to know a man, she did very well. Trouble was, it took her forever to break the ice and none of the men lit a spark, especially the ones her aunts pushed on her. And her aunts were growing increasingly impatient.

Regina stared blankly at the magazine. She could sit in this room stewing about her family's interference until she turned sixty, or she could do something about it. Something to convince them to stop. Something desperate... like...

Fighting fire with fire. But how?

Mutiny, murder, and divorce weren't the answers.

Suddenly, the magazine headline, FLIRTING IS FUN, stood out in bold red letters. *Not if you're shy. Not if your bottom lip quivers and your mouth turns dry.* Tingles spread through her fingers as she flipped through the pages, then scanned the article.

"Bull's eye!" This could be the answer to her prayers.

Hone your skills it said. Search for romance with the same determination you would hunt for a job. Practice makes perfect.

Hmm... maybe by using the article as her Bible, she could finally master the art of flirting. Wouldn't that just put a crimp in her aunts' matchmaking?

Practice makes perfect.

She liked the sound of that.

She'd give it a shot.

Chapter One

I can do this!

In a daze amid the hustle and bustle of Greater Cincinnati's Airport, Regina Citrano plunged her hand into her black and tan portfolio and retrieved her magazine. Ignoring the horde of people who walked by, she flipped to the article that had obsessed her for the past two weeks. "Five Easy Steps to Flirting."

Lord, she hoped so.

She skimmed the piece, then slipped it back in her case. According to the info, men succumbed to flirting no matter what their condition. Age or marital status didn't matter. A crowded airport was recommended as a fertile hunting ground for beginners.

And she was about to begin the hunt.

So why was she hyperventilating?

A Citrano never wavered but as the baby of the family, somehow she'd missed out on her allotted dose of Citrano Confidence.

Though stage fright contributed to her shakiness, she knew the root cause—a pathological aversion to airplanes acquired during childhood. Considering her phobia for them, she deserved nothing short of a medal for even setting foot in the terminal. Of course, the article mentioned several other promising venues besides the airport, and she planned to cover them all. Eventually. Next weekend she'd scout the mall.

Practice makes perfect.

And she intended to acquire plenty of it.

But for now, the airport seemed the least threatening—a place where people frustrated by long delays would be receptive to conversations, a place where it didn't matter whether the man was married or not as she'd surely never see him again, a place where if the flirting got out of hand, she could vanish into the crowd on a moment's notice.

A balding but attractive man sat down next to her. Regina studied him out of the corner of her eye. Well dressed, with a dark suit and red tie, and a fatherly appearance to his face, he looked harmless enough. She scanned his left hand for a ring. One thing she'd never do was intentionally flirt with a married man. Yet, the article stressed not to be concerned about that. Short, objective, practice runs were supposed to be preludes to the main event—a more serious interaction with the guy you wanted to get to know.

Do it, her conscience ordered. *Say something. Start a conversation. You want to get married, don't you?*

Regina nodded. Twenty-five years and counting, she saw her life slipping away before her eyes. Being a teller in a bank for the rest of her life didn't exactly fit what she had in mind. Out of style though it might be, she wanted a husband and children to fuss over. And judging from her family's zealous interest, they wanted it even more than she did.

You don't want your family to foist your future husband on you, do you?

Regina groaned. Not if it meant marrying Johnny Barbato, the man her Aunt Sophia and Uncle Guido were currently pushing on her. Bless her family's interfering hearts, every single one of them had been matchmaking for more than three years now. Not one of the candidates had stirred her heart. If Prince Charming was out there, she preferred to find him herself, and to do that she needed to overcome her chronic shyness.

For an extra boost she fished her compact from her purse, then snapped it open. Apprehensive, dark brown eyes peered back at her. An auburn wig covered her blah-brown tresses. The wig insured her anonymity. If someone she knew caught her hanging out at the airport and flirting with strange men, she'd die. Admiring the sexy aura the wig gave her, she considered changing the color permanently. She'd always wanted to be a redhead.

She winked at her image in the compact and snapped it shut. Crossing her fingers, she took a deep breath and peeked at the news magazine the man next to her was reading. As if sensing her scrutiny, the man turned and faced her.

Show time.

Regina swallowed then squared her shoulders. "I couldn't help but notice the article you were reading on Bosnia. Tragic circumstances, don't you agree?"

★★★

Tyler Novak leaned against the wall of the airport corridor and scanned the crowd with more than mild curiosity, his mind absorbing everything around him with rapid-fire ease.

"Whadda you think?" Jake, his stocky companion, asked him.

"I think it's him." Tyler reached into his jeans pocket and withdrew a snapshot.

He lifted his gaze to compare the man in question to the snapshot when a redhead walked by. The blazing color of her hair and her spectacular legs caught his attention. She wore a navy blazer and matching, short, split skirt. A very short skirt, and with her incredibly shaped legs, she'd chosen wisely. It'd be a shame to hide them.

Paying particular attention to the seductive sway of her hips, he let his gaze drift up and down in calm appraisal as she continued to walk across his line of vision. With one eye locked on her and the other on their target, he saw her sit down next to a bald-headed guy. Tyler immediately shifted his full attention back to their suspected quarry.

"Some dame, huh?" Jake, his partner commented, then softly whistled.

"What?"

"The redhead. Choice, wouldn't you say?"

That she was. He'd always been a sucker for redheads. "Yeah," Tyler agreed. She and the bald guy were engaged in an animated conversation. Hell. Probably her husband, lucky guy.

Regina released a deep breath and walked away from the third man as she surveyed the crowd. Her flirtatious conversations with the three men had gone well. She'd selected them and thought she'd improved her line of patter. The bald man had been a businessman, the soldier, on leave, and the overweight man, married with three children. Apparently flattered by her interest, the latter had even showed her snapshots of his kids. Maybe she'd try one more man before moving on to another gate.

The flight delay had caused the waiting area to fill up with people. The article had been explicit about not spending more than ten or fifteen minutes with each subject. More time tended to lead to something more serious—a level she wasn't yet ready to tackle.

She'd certainly hit pay dirt here. Plenty of men appeared headed to Chicago, and many promised to be good candidates. Especially the man across the corridor. More than once she'd caught him staring at her. If he'd been alone, she might have been inclined to approach him.

Not a good idea, Regina.

The article specifically warned against trying the routine out on someone who attracted you, and the man across the way definitely attracted her. One was supposed to hone the techniques on uninteresting strangers before applying them to someone you hoped to engage in a relationship. She'd probably get tongue-tied talking to the handsome hunk.

Less than twenty feet away he lounged against the wall in a sexy stance. There was a general toughness about him, sort of a rough-around-the-edges-look. Along with a strong pronounced chin and thin lips, a hint of a frown punctuated his face. She couldn't tell for sure as he watched her through slitted eyes, but she sensed his eyes were brown. His hair was the shade of golden sand and had a wiry curl to it, a curl she imagined would feel soft and springy to the touch.

As if in need of a crutch, Regina slipped her hand into her portfolio and fingered the magazine. No sense digging it out. The man was clearly off limits, and rereading the article wouldn't change it. When she dared look over at him again, he was still watching her. He sent her a smile.

Glory be! The tables had turned. He seemed to be flirting with her, and she'd barely had a chance to put anything into action.

Flirting couldn't be this easy, could it? Smiles and eye contact were important components, but before today she'd been too shy to practice them on strangers. Of course once she knew a man well enough to befriend and trust him, it was a different story. The realization that this man might be trying to get her attention sparked a funny tightening in her chest. The last thing in the world she wanted was to flirt with him.

Not true!

Okay, so it wasn't true. She did secretly want to meet him, and the sweat building on her palms verified it.

Go on, take advantage of the situation. So what if you're attracted to him. Don't let the article spook you. You can't wait for men to come down your chimney like Santa Claus.

Maybe they didn't slide down her chimney, but the pickings around here put Santa's warehouse to shame. Men came across her path like snowflakes in the North Pole. Had she suddenly acquired some magical ability to attract them? And to think of all the time she'd wasted by not hanging out in airports.

Darn, she needed to remember something the article said. Regina furrowed her brow, trying to reel the errant memory in—something to do with body language—not that the man across the way needed to be concerned about it. His body translated easily into any language. Now, she remembered. It mentioned giving the man a signal you were approachable by catching his eye, and when you did, to give him the most inviting, receptive look you could and hold it for three whole seconds. Or was is five?

Regina shrugged. Judging from his interest, she may have overdone it a bit and stretched it to ten.

Unable to resist the urge a moment longer, she pulled the magazine from her portfolio. Not only did she want to check the article again, but she wanted to note the author. Uncannily on target, the woman knew what she was writing about. Regina smiled. If her future excursions proved this successful, the author deserved a nomination for the Pulitzer prize.

"Ma'am."

Regina jumped, then wheeled around in the direction of the voice. Her gaze came eye to eye with the soldier with whom she'd just chatted. "Yes," she answered tentatively, masking a slight tremor in her voice.

"You left your umbrella on the seat next to me. I just noticed it."

"Thanks. I'm always losing it." She took the stubby, pink umbrella from him, slipped it into her portfolio, and watched him return to his seat.

The umbrella industry owed her a debt of gratitude. Single-handedly, she kept them in business. All over the country, possibly the world, people inherited umbrellas courtesy of her. Her umbrellas saw more exotic locales than she could hope to visit in a lifetime. They had a disturbing habit of disappearing on her, and it wasn't unusual for her to misplace five or six of them a year.

Regina debated sneaking another glimpse at the handsome

hunk. A split second later, when he fixed his gaze on some distant point, the debate ended. She took advantage of the moment to admire his profile and rangy physique. Less than a second later, he turned in her direction and his answering smile spelled, 'Gotcha'.

Okay, so he'd caught her staring at him, but he'd been staring at her, too. She'd do well to remember frogs were the ones more likely to turn out to be princes, whereas good-looking princes who looked like this man more often than not turned out to be toads. Still...

As she pondered approaching the two men, another came into view, a man far better suited to becoming candidate number four. Looking humdrum and decidedly safer, he sat apart from everyone else, not far away from the sexy man leaning against the wall. She was a woman on a mission, and the handsome devil with the extra dose of testosterone was mission impossible. Still... She hesitated, then resolutely turned aside the temptation.

As she walked in the direction of her new subject, the handsome hunk met her gaze straight on and smiled again. Deep wrinkles creased the corners of his light brown eyes.

His eyes *were* brown.

And sexy!

They reached out like magnets and held her in place for countless seconds. Regina felt a quickening in the pit of her stomach. A bemused look graced his face, a look that said he'd been watching her the whole time. Just her luck he'd turn out to be a security agent and tell her to move on. No. Dressed as scruffily as he was in faded jeans, dusty boots and a blue shirt, he couldn't be in a position of authority. All the same, she'd strike up a conversation with this other man in the smoking section and then move on to another gate.

"Excuse me," she said, sitting down next to the man, "I don't suppose you have the correct time."

Tyler grinned.

The bald guy sure as hell wasn't her husband. Nor the soldier. And now, to his amazement, she sat down next to their target. What the devil was Red up to? In the past thirty minutes she'd flitted from one man to another like a butterfly. Selling something? Herself, perhaps?

"Interesting development," Jake said. "Think she knows him?"

"Have you seen her in action?" Tyler stuffed his hands into his jeans' pockets. "She seems to know everyone."

"Yeah, I've been watching, along with every guy over fifteen. She sure is a sociable bunny. You think she's in on it?"

"Don't rightly know," Tyler said lazily. The bureau didn't have a firm number on how many smugglers were involved, but twin feelings of admiration and amusement flashed through him. If she was an accomplice, the woman was good, damn good.

"Guess he's planning to take flight 311 to Chicago."

"Looks that way."

"Should we stop him?"

"Nah. Better to see who meets him at the other end."

"I'll go make a call and set up surveillance in Chicago," Jake said. "You keep an eye on the cozy twosome while I'm gone."

"Roger that." *So what are you up to Red? You connected to this guy and the smuggling ring*? The woman was chatting up the men with some aim in mind. Or could she be a diversion especially for his and Jake's benefit? He'd always been a sucker for redheads.

Regina squirmed in her seat, not sure how long she'd been talking to the man, five or six minutes, perhaps. She couldn't even remember what they'd been discussing. How was she supposed to keep track with the compelling hunk behind her who was burning a hole clear through her head? He stood off to the side, all by himself now, and every time she glanced up, his gaze locked with hers like radar. Something told her the guy against the wall wanted to cut out the flirting and skip to the main event.

"So you're not taking this flight," the man next to her said.

Regina stared blankly at him. Had she told him that? "No, er, um, not exactly."

"You said you were here to meet your aunt."

"I did?" Mental gymnastics performed in her head. Apparently, she'd been so distracted, she'd developed a case of oral diarrhea. There was no telling what she'd said to this man. "Yes, my aunt." She glanced across the rows of seats. "Oh my gosh!"

"What is it?"

"My aunt."

"Why are you so surprised? You said you were here to meet her."

The lie had found her out and was about to come true. If she wasn't super careful, in a couple of minutes she'd not only be meeting Aunt Sophia but Uncle Guido, as well. *What were they doing here?* Of course! She patted her forehead with the heel of her palm. *The inbound flight was from Philadelphia. Their son Joey would be on it, returning home from Villanova.*

Regina cleared her throat, wishing she could clear the chaos in her mind, as well. "I have to go now. It's been nice chatting with you." She chewed at her bottom lip. Aunt Sophia possessed the eyes of a hawk. She'd see through the wig in a second and demand answers, and in a voice loud enough to attract the attention of everyone at the gate. Humiliation stood only feet away.

"Could you do me a favor?" The man's voice intruded her angst.

"A favor? Sure." For some reason she turned and looked at the man against the wall. Her gaze collided with his inquisitive, brown eyes again. The handsome devil stared at her from one direction while Aunt Sophia and Uncle Guido closed in from another—and this man wanted a favor. No problem, she psyched herself up.

"This present," he said taking a small package from his pocket. "I was supposed to go to the General Aviation Terminal, gate four, and give this to my brother-in-law for his son. It's a birthday present, but I didn't have time. Even though the flight's been delayed, I just got here, and the plane's taxiing up to the gate right now. My brother-in-law's a pilot. Could you deliver this to him? Otherwise, my nephew will have to wait until I can mail it to him."

"The General Aviation Terminal for private charters?" she asked with an inquiring tilt of her head.

"Yes, gate four," he said in an undertone. He leaned closer and looked around at the same time.

The private terminal was adjacent to the airport—away from here. And any place far away sounded good. The farther the better. She stared at the gift, festively wrapped in paper with clowns and balloons. "Gate four, you said," she repeated loud and firm.

"Yes. Ask for Bill Dawson. Here's my business card. Tell him I sent you. He'll be waiting."

She stared at the card. "Bill Dawson and you're Frank Foster." Regina took the package, dumped it into her portfolio, then stood. "I have to run." Before her aunt caught up with her and unearthed her disguise.

Aunt Sophia had a singular knack for dragging the truth out of everyone and a dramatic flare that served her well in the many amateur theater presentations in which she appeared. Two minutes with her aunt and every blessed person within a fifty-foot radius of the gate would know about Regina's flirting escapade.

She glanced furtively to her right. Aunt Sophia and Uncle Guido marched steadily toward her. She swung around only to face the handsome hunk, and sought refuge in his gaze, his thick, dark eyelashes capturing her attention. He watched her silently. Expectantly. Time was about to run out. Caught between the devil and the deep blue sea, otherwise known as Aunt Sophia and Uncle Guido, she had to do something.

She chose the devil.

"Hi, I'm Regina Citrano," she said breathlessly, walking right up to him. Aunt Sophia would never think to pair her with a man. Not this one, anyway.

"Hi." A playful grin curved his lips.

"I know this sounds silly, but I've been watching you."

"I noticed, and I've been watching you."

"I know." She stood so close to him now she could see the rich, brown irises in his eyes. "Something's come up. There's someone I don't want to see, and I was wondering if you could pretend you know me."

"I don't think I'll have to pretend." He cracked another crooked grin and gave her stare for stare.

"You don't?" She wanted to sound cool, appear self-possessed, but under his scrutiny she felt neither. Crossing her fingers, she turned her head. As her aunt stared at them, Regina linked arms with the man. The contact sent a jolt through her, but she did her best to ignore it. "M-Mind if we walk down the corridor?"

The man didn't move, and Regina tracked his gaze as he

zeroed in on her aunt and uncle. He must have seen her glance their way. Then catching sight of his buddy, he stood firm, waiting for his companion to stride toward them.

"Looks like she finally buzzed around to you," the man said coming abreast of them.

"Yeah. Say Jake, suppose you stay here at the gate. I'm going to go with the flow with Red here." Regina breathed a sigh of relief, then watched the handsome hunk whisper something in his buddy's ear. The man called Jake nodded, then grinned and walked away.

"Lead on, Red." The handsome hunk gestured with his arm.

"Red?"

"For your hair."

"Oh, yes, my hair. What did you say your name was?"

"I didn't. It's Tyler. Tyler Novak." His sexy voice sent tickles up and down her vocal chords. "Where you headed?"

"Over to the terminal for private planes."

He lifted a speculative eyebrow. "You don't say. The F.B.O."

"The F.B. what?"

"Fixed base operations. I'll accompany you."

"That won't be necessary." She just needed to get out of sight of Aunt Sophia without arousing her suspicion.

"But I'd like to."

"Oh." She couldn't hide the surprise in her voice.

"Know where it is?"

"No."

"Well, I do. Let's go, Red."

A low, deep, sexy rumble threaded through his laugh. Regina blushed at the provocative tone of his voice and the seductive gleam that surfaced in his eyes. She'd been right. Flirting had been the appetizer for him, and her intuition told her he was hungry for the entree.

She halted in her tracks, digging her heels into the concourse. "You think I'm coming on to you, don't you?"

"Whatever you say, Red."

"I'm not, and I appreciate your help, but it's really not necessary to take up any more of your time."

He cupped her elbow and gave her a forward nudge. "No bother. It's complicated getting over there. I have plenty of time and no way I'd rather spend it."

Tyler smiled at her mock indignation. *Lady, you're something else,* he thought to himself.

She even blushed an innocent shade of pink, guaranteed to make her look old-fashioned. He hadn't missed her earlier come-hither looks, but if that's the way she wanted it, he'd play along.

They hustled along the corridor in the direction of an escalator which would take them down a level. There they could catch a courtesy shuttle to the smaller terminal. He spent a great deal of time staring at her. From a professional standpoint, of course. And it proved a very pleasant pastime.

She wasn't knock 'em dead gorgeous, more like a pixie-playfulness to her face. Wide mouth, soft, full lips, and a great smile, especially the dimples low on either side of her cheeks. Mental images of this woman in action teased his imagination. Hard to guess her age, mid twenties, perhaps.

He let his gaze trail up and down her, taking note of her petite stature and small waist, always returning to her glorious mane of auburn hair. He wouldn't mind running his hands through it, but apart from his gentle grasp on her arm, he kept his hands to himself and wondered.

What the hell had been behind that exhibition she'd put on at the gate? To draw attention to herself? That didn't make sense.

At the crest of the escalator as the crowd increased, Red tried to wiggle free, but he handily reined her in. If she got too feisty, he'd produce his badge and put her under arrest, but he preferred not to tip his hand.

Shades of Sherlock Holmes! Tyler couldn't believe what had happened. He'd actually seen their quarry slip this dame a package. And it had to be the diamonds. They'd been covering the airports and every bus and train station in the area, waiting for him to show up. Once in the airport, the guy probably thought he was safe. But the Bureau had received a tip he might show up at flight 311.

Okay, so maybe Red and the package were decoys, but he'd left Jake back at the gate to tail the guy just in case the dude didn't board the plane, and if he did, agents would be waiting to follow him when he arrived in Chicago. One way or another they'd crack this case.

Tyler bet his bottom dollar that following the guy would lead to a dead end. He was ninety percent positive that the woman next to him carried the loot, and apparently Chicago wasn't its destination. Other people were in on it, and she'd lead him to them. He let his gaze slide over her and wondered again what kind of stunt she'd been pulling, playing up to nearly every Tom, Dick, and Harry sitting at the gate. If she was in on the heist, she had to be loco calling attention to herself that way.

Piece of luck for him, though. Batting those big, brown eyes of hers, she'd walked right into his web.

Or had he walked into hers?

As Tyler Novak guided her down the concourse, a bewildered Regina nearly tripped over her feet. At the torturous pace he'd set, people's faces whizzed by her. His fingers held her lightly by the elbow, his touch searing through her suit jacket to her skin, and she sensed perspiration had broken out on her forehead. Not exactly the image one wanted to project when one was flirting.

Something told her the flirting had ended.

He'd latched onto her like a lovesick lovebug, and she didn't know how to get rid of him. Wasn't sure she wanted to. Surely he didn't intend to harm her?

Impossible.

Regina looked uncertainly at him. She was letting the quirks of another of her crazy aunts' personality influence her. Overly suspicious and slightly whacky, Aunt Ruth, her father's sister, constantly invented conspiracies and spent hours wondering if the people she observed worked for the C.I.A. If Aunt Ruth were to see them this very minute, no doubt she'd dream up a scenario that Tyler Novak was an undercover agent.

Keeping up with Tyler's long-legged stride, Regina studied him again. *Face it,* her inner voice affirmed, *you did ask him to help you.* She desperately wished she could whisk out her magazine and check it for suggestions on disentangling oneself from an overly amorous admirer. But then again, he did know where the—what had he called it?—F.B.O. terminal was, and if there were any statistics available, she bet they'd make the trip in record-breaking time.

Regina froze, jolting to a halt. Heavens, maybe he wasn't leading her to the private plane terminal at all. All along she'd assumed he was infatuated with her. Maybe she should think more like Aunt Ruth and be less trusting. Tyler tugged at her arm, but Regina remained steadfast and wouldn't budge.

Regina Anne Catherine Mary Citrano, you might be in deep trouble.

Her gaze wandered from Tyler to scan the corridor. A ladies room. Where was a ladies room when a girl needed one? Maybe it wasn't vitally urgent at the moment, but it'd make a perfect excuse to ditch him. "Mr. Novak, please, where's the fire? Do you think we could slow down the pace?" Sprinting had never been her sport.

"Guess so."

Mercifully when they resumed walking, he slowed from their trot to a less taxing lope. "When we see a restroom, I need to stop." She'd forced a measure of authority into her voice, trying to establish control over the situation.

"That plane you need to catch might not wait," he swiftly countered.

Regina cocked her head. She didn't remember telling him she had to catch a plane, well actually a pilot. Had he been so smitten that he listened in on her conversation? "Look, Mr.—"

"Tyler's fine."

"Look, Tyler. If my bladder says we need to stop, it would be wise to pay attention to it." A malady common to the female contingency of the Citrano clan.

He nodded. "We're almost there."

"There?" Did the man possess prior knowledge of the location of restrooms throughout the entire airport complex?

"To gate four."

"Oh." She must have told him.

"Do you want to speed up so we can get to the gate faster and then find a ladies room, or do you want to keep this slower pace?"

She didn't know what she wanted. On one hand, she didn't want to push him out of her life, at least not until they reached gate four. After all, she'd never made a conquest like this, and she wanted to savor it a little longer.

Don't crawl back into your shy shell. Live a little.

Nodding agreement, she gave herself a mental shake. Her crazy idea that Tyler intended her harm was just that: crazy. Stopping, he whirled around in front of her, then placed his hands on her shoulders.

"Regina?" He paused a beat, obviously awaiting her answer.

"I... uh..." Blast, her meandering mind had scrambled her brain. She'd forgotten his question, but given a second or two, she was positive she'd remember.

"Take a deep breath," he quietly instructed.

She did.

"Feel better?"

She did.

Who wouldn't, when Prince Charming spoke in that low, soothing tone and his light brown eyes tenderly searched your own? Regina went limp. She blinked again, trying to sever contact with his captivating eyes, trying to crawl out from the spell they cast on her.

"Slow would be nice," she answered, finally, miraculously, remembering what he'd asked her. Who needed a ladies room? Certainly not her, although from the tingles stirring inside her, she might have need of one soon.

He clasped her hand. "Okay, we'll slow it down even more."

She gave a reluctant nod. The man oozed charm, and she had a sneaky suspicion he knew it. How did he do it? How did one look from him melt her down? This very moment his endearing, liquid gaze feathered up and down every inch of her spine. He was a natural at flirting, and she wondered if he'd read the article, then chuckled softly at the absurdity. She doubted he'd ever seen the inside of a woman's magazine, let alone read an article in one. As for her reaction to him, it had to be some aberration—a glitch in her system. One didn't ordinarily flip over strangers.

At least Regina Citrano didn't.

"Pretty name—Regina," he commented, breaking the silence and still holding her hand.

Regina swallowed at his uncanny remark. Could he read her mind like Aunt Della sometimes could? First, knowing the gate, and now this—only seconds after she'd mentally repeated her name. "My father chose it."

He raised a quizzical eyebrow. "Yeah? So what was your mother's choice?"

"Catherine. Her mother chose Anne, and Dad's mother chose Mary."

"Holy Toledo, how many names you got?"

"Four. Regina Anne Catherine Mary." She looked at him

through her lashes.

A ghost of a smile curved his mouth. "That's a mouthful."

"I'm Italian."

"Somehow I guessed that." His mouth quirked wider into a wry smile.

"How 'bout you?"

"Slovak and garden variety American."

"No, I meant how about your names." He'd steered her around the corner quickly, depriving her of the chance to get a good look for a restroom.

"Just Tyler Novak. Tyler was my mother's maiden name."

"Sisters and brothers?"

"A sister, and you?"

"Monica and Angela and Vincent, all older." He stopped walking for a second, his gaze snaring hers. Tension built between them, and she couldn't understand why.

"Where's home?" he asked.

"Here in Cincinnati. And yours?"

"Cincinnati for now."

For a man whose body language spoke volumes, when it came to conversations, he was exasperatingly quite. Her adventure would be over soon enough. Might as well enjoy his company while she could. "How much farther?" she asked as they exited the main terminal.

"Just have to grab this courtesy shuttle and we'll be there in a jiffy."

Chapter Two

Tyler smiled.

A jiffy. Not if Red had her way. She was doing her damnedest to brush him off.

No way, lady, no way.

Maybe those slender legs of hers could barely keep up with him, but he didn't dare turn her loose. He'd done his best to eavesdrop on her conversation with their target when he'd handed her the package, and heard the guy mention gate four. But it could be a ruse. If she managed to get away, he might catch up with her again at gate four, and then again he could be left holding the bag.

He didn't plan on letting Red out of his sight. As Tyler considered his options, he glimpsed at her sideways and grinned. Watching the pull of her eye-catching skirt over her derriere and the jostle of her hips as she'd struggled to keep up with him became the best entertainment he'd had in some time. The woman was the biggest turn-on he'd come across in months.

With her hand still securely tucked in his as they entered the private plane facility, Tyler checked his watch. Almost two, and the closer they came to their destination, the sooner he needed to improvise a plan. Dead sure she planned to turn the package over to someone at Gate Four and dead sure the diamonds were hidden in it, he was far from dead sure what to do. Would Red hand the package to someone and neither of them take a plane? He swore he'd heard the man who'd handed her the package mention the word pilot.

And pilot meant flying.

If Red didn't board the plane, should he tail her and phone in the particulars of the plane to headquarters? He could flash his badge and request the flight plan and destination from the tower easily enough. Or should he try and bluff his way onto the plane? Headquarters had deemed the surveillance relatively harmless, and ever mindful of unnecessary casualties and public relations, his superior had suggested he and Jake not carry guns. He doubted he could persuade the pilot to cooperate without one. Things could get dicey in a hurry. Sticking with Red sounded less confrontational and far more pleasant a duty.

But what if she boarded the plane? Should he let her go and have the plane tracked?

The hairs on the back of his neck sent him a warning. Jeeze, he was getting careless. He'd been so engrossed by Red, not to mention her provocative, offbeat conversation, he hadn't bothered to check and see if anyone had followed them. Instincts had saved his skin more than once. Trusting them now, he slowed their pace even more, taking the opportunity to glance over his shoulder. No one walked behind them. In fact, compared to the commercial terminal, the place was almost empty.

His gaze swept the area in front of them and then like a heat-seeking missile returned to the engaging woman beside him, belatedly noticing a large gold loop earring dangling from her ear. Her long auburn tresses had effectively hidden it from his view until now. As if sensing his stare, she slanted him a glance.

"Thanks for escorting me. I'm sure you have other things to do," she said. "You mustn't let me keep you from getting back to flight 311." She glanced at her watch, drawing Tyler's attention to her long lashes. "You weren't still planning on catching that flight, were you?"

"Nah. I was waiting for someone." *True enough. The surprise had been to discover it had turned out to be Red.*

"But the plane has probably arrived at the gate by now and the passengers deplaned."

"Jake will cover for me."

"What an interesting choice of words."

"How 'bout you, Red, not flying anywhere today?" *Except from man to man in the airport.*

"I'm not Red!"

"Your hair is." Her dazzling auburn hair, he'd still like to lose himself in it.

"But I'm n... "

She hesitated for a fraction of a second, causing Tyler to wonder what might be behind it. "You're what?"

"Still looking for that ladies room."

Tyler drew his lips into a thin line. If she really had to go, he was being an insensitive clod, but he wasn't going to be caught with his pants down. Sneaking in and out of restrooms was a standard ploy of criminals.

He'd been dying to ask her what she'd been up to at the gate, and it seemed the opportunity had arisen. "Were you meeting someone on flight 311?" They both knew she wasn't. Let her squirm out of that.

Regina hesitated. "Uh... it's complicated," she said with a shaky sigh.

Complicated, my eye! And there was that blush again staining her cheeks. "I'm not a brain surgeon, but I think I understand. You don't have to be embarrassed about it."

"I don't?"

Tyler wanted to groan. Big, wide eyes innocently looked up at him from beneath her fluttering lashes. "Nah. Lots of women do it." It was the oldest profession in the world.

"They do, don't they? And they're much better at it than

me."

Tyler gulped. He rather doubted that. Red was far too modest. Jeeze, she'd have to be ugly and fat, with a mustache to boot, to be lousy at it. "Don't be rough on yourself. That's a hard thing to measure. Different men like different women. You look like you'd be good." God, he couldn't believe it. Had he really said that?

"I do?" A troubled frown crossed her face. "Good at what?"

"Ya know, what you were embarrassed about."

"You were watching me the whole time, weren't you?"

He and every red-blooded man at the gate. "You noticed?" He cleared his throat.

"Yes, I noticed. I mean... well... since you saw me, was I too obvious?"

Tyler coughed. "The other men would have to answer that." Jeeze, he'd forgotten how women liked to over analyze the hell out of everything. His sister talked a subject to death. Apparently hookers did it, too.

"But if you noticed, then I was much too obvious."

"Guess you were." He shrugged. "Hell, actions speak louder than words, Red, and I saw you in action."

"Next time maybe I should try to be more discreet."

"Might be a good idea."

"Then again," she paused, confusion filling her eyes, "the object is to get your message across, and if I was too subtle, no one would respond."

Tyler shook his head in a double-take, attempting to digest what she'd said. Could she be a couple biscuits short of a dozen? Nah, the intelligence in her eyes belied that. "You're teasing me, right?"

"Oh, dear," she moaned. "I'm just so new at this. I don't normally do this sort of thing."

"You're a nice girl, right?"

"What an odd thing to say. Of course I am."

"Of course you are. You just need confidence in yourself."

Regina stopped walking and flashed a smile at him. "You're right. You understand, don't you?" She drew in a deep breath, her brown eyes brightening. "I just knew from the moment I saw you that you understood. I sensed a communication between us."

Damn right, Red. I was sending you signals left and right.

"Have you ever done it?"

Tyler fought to keep his face blank, and lost. He sputtered and coughed again. The little pixie could be brazen and unpredictable. He shook his head, trying to clear his ears, then turned away as he attempted to hold his laughter in check. "Done what?" he choked out his question. If she'd asked him what he thought she'd asked, he shouldn't be encouraging her.

"You know, what I was doing."

Facing her, he made a stab at recovery. "Can't say I have, Red. Can't say I have."

"You know it's funny but today was my first time—"

"First time!"

"Yes." She barely paused for a breath. "And you're right. Mind you, I don't mean to brag, but I did feel successful."

Holy crap! What the hell was going on? Why did he have the feeling she wasn't exactly keyed into their conversation? Was this woman part of the diamond ring, or a hooker, or both? Enterprising little thing, she probably worked both sides of the street, delivering the package and lining up future engagements with the men at the gate for when they returned to Cincinnati. The liquid pools of her eyes might be big enough to fit the whole state of Kentucky in, but he wasn't buying her first time act.

He wasn't buying, period.

"So," he said, "it's settled then. We both agree you were good." Mixed messages bombarded him. Tyler couldn't decipher whether the blush on her face was genuine or not. Was she so good she could blush on cue? And why couldn't he shake the gut feeling she was having a laugh at his expense? Granted, there was a freshness to her face, and she gushed when she talked. Hookers didn't gush, at least not the ones he'd run across.

"Do you believe in fate?" Regina asked.

Tyler groaned. With Red's screwball conversations, he wasn't sure what to answer. No telling where it would lead. "Sometimes," he muttered, lifting a cautionary eyebrow.

"My Aunt Della believes in fate. I think it had a hand in our meeting today."

More like the diamonds, he mentally mumbled under his breath. Let her dwell in her delusions. He'd never quite made a definitive conclusion about fate's influence on his life. Her eyes whirred away as if something momentous churned inside her. No doubt he'd find out what in a second or two.

"Maybe when I'm finished at gate four... well, since you know about me and all... " She broke eye contact with him. "Maybe I could try my technique out on you."

Tyler not only coughed, but he bent over, choking on air he'd swept too quickly into his lungs. *Priceless. Red was priceless.* How could a man resist an offer like that? But he damn well better. Red was a suspect, and regulations frowned at officers getting involved with suspects.

"Are you all right?" She leaned over, seeking his face.

"Fi-ne." He discharged a husky gasp.

"You probably swallowed air. Uncle Guido does that all the time." She stood behind him, then positioning her body over his, she wrapped her arms around his chest.

"What are you doing?" She'd linked her hands together beneath his diaphragm. Their position was provocative if not awkward, and her touch sent a thrill rushing down to his stomach.

"The Heimlich maneuver, I think."

"I'm fine." *More than fine.*

Joy to the world, his butt was tucked up against her firm stomach, and her hands continued to wander across his ribcage. Why spoil everything by telling her he wasn't choking? If the woman wanted to practice first aid on him, let her. She particularly seemed to enjoy practicing things. Problem was, she didn't know what she was doing. If he'd really been choking, he couldn't have answered her, but what the hell? He'd always been fond of playing doctor.

"Hold still, I'm trying to find the right spot," she fussed at him.

You've found it baby. You've found it. As far as he was concerned, anywhere would be the right spot. His body throbbed in places it hadn't throbbed for a long time. She turned him on faster than he'd ever been turned on in his life. If she kept it up much longer, the agony settled in his butt would work its way between his thighs. Bent over, with his head facing the floor, Tyler sensed they'd attracted a handful of onlookers. He knew he should put a stop to this nonsense, but he hated to break their intimate contact. In fact, he wished their positions were reversed.

Did the confounded woman have any idea what she was doing to him? Could this be part of her so-called technique? He was just about to straighten when she startled him by giving him a forward push, then rocked back on her heels, tugging at his diaphragm, and trying to carry him with her.

"What the hell was that?"

"Don't be so testy," she said, her breath warm on the back of his neck. "I know I'm not very strong. I was trying to get some extra leverage to push air up your windpipe."

"I don't suppose we could straighten up all the way now? I'm getting a crick in my shoulders." *Among other things.*

"Sure, if you're okay."

"Top of the world." He gritted his teeth.

She released her hold, and Tyler straightened, spun around on his heels, then looked down at her, his gaze fastening on her full, soft lips. He ached to learn the secrets of her delectable mouth, and her recent conversation indicated she was more than agreeable. He lowered his head an inch and swore she angled her chin a smidgen higher. The minx wanted the kiss every bit as much as he did. Spying an alcove, he guided her toward it and slipped behind a pillar.

Try out her technique, she'd said. He had a technique or two of his own he'd like to show her. To settle himself down, Tyler counted under his breath. She licked her lips, and he lost count. "Don't do that."

"What?"

Damn, if she didn't do it again. The tip of her tongue left a moist sheen on her bottom lip. It tantalized and beckoned him. If she was offering free try-outs, why not help himself to a sample?

Regina stood transfixed, her feet cemented to the floor. Somehow she knew there were a few people around, but she couldn't hear them or see them. Standing toe to toe with Tyler Novak, he filled her vision. Actually, the cleft in his chin did since he stood nearly a foot taller than she. She tilted her head. He, too, stood motionless, studying her, his eyes the color of her father's imported whisky.

His head lowered an inch, she could swear it.

This was turning out to be the most unpredictable day in her entire twenty-five years. A day that would go down in infamy in her diary. And all because of that silly magazine article. Imagine, meeting someone like Tyler. And even more extraordinary, discovering how empathetic he was. He'd seen her flirting and he seemed to approve—even seemed willing to let her experiment on him.

She kind of got a kick out of him calling her Red. She'd been all set to tell him she wasn't a redhead, but something had stopped her, and when he'd asked her if she was meeting someone on flight 311, how could she tell him the truth? It was too embarrassing to tell a man like him that she'd reached the age of twenty-five and only had a learning permit in flirting.

His head lowered another notch, and unconsciously she arched her neck. Breathing became difficult. If she wasn't mistaken, he was going to kiss her. But as she recalled, kissing hadn't been included in the article. Kissing went beyond flirting.

"Umm... er... Mr. Novak, I-I mean Tyler."

"Hmm?"

"I, umm, meant to wait until after—"

"After what?" Tyler interrupted.

Closer. His head dipped even closer in gradual descent, and his spicy cologne assaulted her senses. Regina paused to inhale its heady fragrance. "Till after we get to gate four, before—"

"Before what?"

"B-before we practiced," she stammered.

"But I don't want to wait," his muffled voice responded.

She wasn't sure she did either. He was so close now, his breath fanned her cheeks. "But you're a stranger."

"Easy to remedy."

"Uh, er—" Dithering, Regina closed her eyes. She had taken years and years of English, was good at it. Why couldn't she put a simple sentence together? Where had the subjects and predicates gone? As anticipation sparked to life, she tried to tell her feet to back away, but they, too, declared a mutiny.

Tyler settled his hands on her shoulders. "I just want to thank you for coming to my rescue. Hell, Red, we've prolonged this long enough. Let's see what you've got."

He brushed his lips over hers, setting off a chain reaction of shimmering flutters inside her. His mouth exerted more pressure, and Regina's eyes opened wide. It appeared she had a basic weakness for this man. Gentle, yet hot and powerful, Tyler laid claim to her lips.

As Tyler's lips teasingly plied her mouth, Regina tried to conjure up a dozen reasons why she should never have allowed this to happen, and a dozen more why she should stop it this very instant. But the rampaging flood of light-headed sensations sweeping through her fogged her thought processes.

Her arms fell helplessly to her sides, her fingers itching to touch him, yet somehow she managed to keep her response under control. She wasn't innocent. Men had kissed her before, but never a stranger. Never like this. It was rather like taking off in an airplane, and she, who preferred a train over a plane any day, sensed this would be a flight she'd never forget.

Regina congratulated herself on her reservoir of will power, when suddenly of their own volition, her arms reached out. The strap of her portfolio fell to the crook of her elbow, and her fingers curled around his belt buckle. With a moan of surrender, she snuggled closer.

It couldn't be happening! This roughshod man hanging out in the airport didn't fit the image of the man she'd pictured for herself. But the magazine article had been correct. Airports were a fertile hunting ground, and she'd bagged herself a prize catch. A catch, that if she had any sense, she'd throw back just as soon as she delivered the package.

The package! She needed to deliver the package. *Oh, but this kiss! His kiss.*

Overwhelmed by his devouring lips, she tightened her fingers around his belt for support. The kiss went on and on, and then, mercy of mercies, he released her. Wobbly and shaken, she struggled to find her sea legs. Her gaze meshed with Tyler's. Surprise flared in his eyes, and there was no mistaking the sly smile on his lips. Lips. She zeroed in on them, remembering the firepower they possessed.

Tyler stepped away and stared at the woman before him. The kiss had shocked him. God, she was trembling, or was that him? Looking hot and bothered, she stared mutely at him. *You're not the only one, Red.* He was hot and bothered himself. Seeking control, he balled his fist. "I'm sorry, I shouldn't have done that."

"No. You... We... It's—It's all right."

It was more than all right. The woman possessed magic. Why she scavenged the airport to drum up business beat the hell out of him. Nor did she need any practice. Dynamite. Their kiss had been dynamite. Less than an hour ago his world had been a gray routine, punctuated only by watching Red in action. And now that he'd tasted her lips, he wanted more.

More from a hooker?

More from a suspected member of the diamond ring?

Tyler groaned. He had the sinking feeling he had indeed been snagged into her web.

Red glanced down at the tile floor, breathed in a lungful of air, and looked him dead in the eye. "Mr. Novak—"

"Tyler, remember?"

"Tyler," she repeated. "As you can see we're at gate four, and I don't know how to thank you for escorting me here."

"I'm sure we could come up with a way, but what about your technique? You mentioned after—"

"I've changed my mind." Regina tossed her head. "I have a magazine to see about a package." She spun on her heel, then marched through the gate

Magazine to see a package? Not sure he'd heard right, Tyler shook his head. He just might have been right when he'd surmised not all her cylinders were functioning. He rocked back on his heels, crossed his arms over his chest, and spied her umbrella lying on the floor. It must have fallen from her satchel during their kiss. He picked it up and grinned.

That's what you think, Red. That's what you think. He'd give her a few seconds lead. After all, he had a great view as she sashayed out to the tarmac.

The warm June wind whipped at her wig, and Regina smoothed down her wayward curls. The sun shone brightly on the concrete, and she stopped for a moment, opening her portfolio and dipping her hand into her purse which was inside her briefcase. She fished out her sunglasses, put them on, then walked toward the man she saw standing in front of a small plane. He must be Bill Dawson.

A small tingle ran down her spine. She'd learned to tolerate flying in jets and larger propeller aircraft, but small planes still gave her the willies. Thank goodness, she wouldn't be flying in this one.

Another problem still loomed on the horizon. Her sixth sense told her Tyler Novak lingered at the gate, but she wasn't going to give him the satisfaction of knowing his whereabouts concerned her by turning and gawking at him. My, but she continued to have some day—one she wasn't likely to forget. Her encounter with him would furnish enough grist for a lifetime of stories.

Aunt Della, the one who believed in fate and Regina's only aunt who seemed to sympathize with her lack of interest in Johnny Barbato, would have described it as nature's way of calling out to her—that a chemistry brewed between her and Tyler Novak. Regina shook her head. What did she know? Shy and careful, she'd only succumbed passionately to love once in her life, and it had fizzled out by the time she and Paul had graduated from college.

When it came to flirting, Paul had been a master. He'd swept her off her feet with his dazzling style. Flirting might be her downfall, but sustaining a relationship had been his. She'd take her problem over his any day, a problem she was well on the way to overcoming—thanks to Tyler Novak.

As she approached the wiry man in front of her, Regina reached into the portfolio again and fingered the magazine. Had other women experienced these same dynamite results? She looked back on the afternoon and found it incredible. Here she approached a perfect stranger with a birthday gift foisted on her by another perfect stranger while a very sexy and even more perfect stranger loitered behind her.

With quick, short steps, she continued her journey across the tarmac. Perspiration beaded above her lips, and she knew its cause. A recurring terror of small planes. She credited her one and only flight years ago for her phobia.

Her Uncle Roman had recently obtained his pilot's license and insisted on taking all his relatives for a ride. When it had come to her family's turn, Regina had been given the seat of honor up front next to her uncle. Young as she'd been, she suspected she'd been delegated the seat not because of her youthful exuberance, but because the rest of her family had been too chicken—the only time the inherent Citrano confidence had failed to prevail.

She remembered the dive, the look of surprise only she could see on her uncle's face, the sweat on his brow, and the shake in his hands. She'd looked from the dive, to him, to the dive, then back to him, and was moments away from screaming her head off before he managed to level the plane. A second later she'd upchucked, and she'd never again set foot in a small plane. Even being near one challenged her composure.

The sooner she got away from here, the more comfortable she'd feel.

The man waiting by the plane looked impatient. He scanned the area and tapped his foot, checking his watch as she walked up to him. "Mr. Dawson?"

"Yeah?" His grim expression startled her. "What's it to ya, lady?"

Rude ruffian, she thought, definitely not good flirting material, not that she intended to flirt anymore... today. "A Mr. Frank Foster sent me. I have his card." She rummaged through her portfolio and purse. *Where had the darn thing gotten to*? The man's impatience grew, and she was just about to abandon her search and reach for the package when he spoke.

"Frank sent you?"

"Yes, and just so you'll believe me, let me show you his card." If she could just find it.

"And who's he? Frank send him, too?"

"Who?"

"The dude behind you."

Dude behind her? Frowning, Regina swung around. Tyler Novak, all six feet of him, strode towards them. Another man tagged after him, bringing up the rear. Squinting, she paused and focused on the second one, recognizing Frank Foster, the man who'd given her the package. What was he doing here? Why had he bothered to ask her to deliver it if he'd intended to show up here himself? Surely by now he'd missed his flight. And Tyler? He continued to walk toward them, totally unaware of the man behind him.

"Tyler," she said as he stopped in front of her, "I told you this wasn't necessary."

"Never know when it might rain." As he held out her umbrella, a devilish twinkle gleamed in his eyes. "You dropped it," he said, slipping it into her briefcase.

"Oh." Chastened, she bit back her plans to tell him to leave. "Thank you." She spun back to face Bill Dawson and shrugged.

"He bothering you, lady?" Bill Dawson asked.

In more ways than one. "'Umm-m-m not at the m-moment. I suppose now that Mr. Foster is here, you—"

A scuffling noise and guttural voices interrupted her. Before she could utter another word, a stray elbow jabbed at her back. She pivoted sideways, stunned to find Tyler and Frank Foster fighting. Whatever had prompted that? She sensed motion off to the side and saw Bill Dawson pull a hammer from the tool belt hanging around his waist. He slammed it against the back of Tyler's skull.

A resounding whack filled the air, and as if she'd been hit herself, Regina winced at the savage blow. "My stars, you've hit him! Leave him alone," she yelled. "He's really not bothering me."

No one listened to her. Tyler staggered to his knees then struggled to rise. He landed a fist in Dawson's stomach, and Regina cheered. It didn't take her long to pick sides. Her hand flew to her portfolio. Her umbrella—if she could just draw it out, she could even up this fight.

"Take care of the dame," Dawson barked to Frank Foster between punches. "Why's she here, anyway?"

"I had to wing it," Foster called out, stepping forward. "I was afraid I was being followed, and I didn't want to lead them here." Taking advantage of Tyler being knocked to the ground again, Foster walked up to Dawson and whispered under his breath. "She's got the package, and this guy's an agent. I figured he was one when I saw the dame walk right up to him. Gave me a few rough seconds, but I gave his buddy the slip and hightailed it over here. Guessed you might have some trouble."

"No shit," Bill Dawson cussed.

"Come on, Doll, ditch the dude and fly down to the Bahamas with us." Foster reached for her arm.

His vile touch and nauseating words made her cringe. "Please, leave me alone." Regina inched away.

She raised her eyes heavenward, noting the formation of thunderheads. Truly, she didn't know which was worse—this man's pawing, the talk of flying, or involving Tyler in this madcap fiasco.

So taken with the horror enfolding before her, Regina paid little attention to what the two men said. Her stomach lurched at the thought that all this had happened because she'd mentioned Tyler was following her. If you asked her, these men behaved a trifle overzealous in coming to her rescue.

When Frank Foster took a menacing step towards her and grabbed her hands, she got the sinking feeling that this fracas went beyond simply subduing Tyler. Pain shot up her arms from Foster's clamping grip as she watched Tyler block Dawson's attempt to hit him with the hammer again.

"Stop it, don't hurt him," Regina yelled as Bill Dawson succeeded. Blood ran down Tyler's face.

Incensed, she struggled with Frank Foster, flailing her fists at him, kicking and twisting, trying to get free as he manhandled her. Regina stomped her foot down on Foster's as hard as she could while at the same time slamming her elbow backwards into the pit of his stomach. He yelled out in pain. In retaliation he pushed her forward with enough force that her knees buckled and she fell to the ground.

Crawling around on her knees, she fetched her folded umbrella from her portfolio, then began to whack away at Foster's legs as Tyler and Dawson exchanged blows. It took a great deal of concentration to dodge out of the way and make sure she didn't hit Tyler's kneecap by mistake. Moments later, Dawson landed a powerful jab on Tyler's jaw. His body crumpled to the ground.

At the sight of his bloodied and helpless body something snapped inside Regina. Fear and self-preservation took over and she attacked with renewed frenzy.

"Get the bloody bitch off me!" Foster squealed to Dawson as he lifted his foot to kick her.

Still crouched on the tarmac, Regina grabbed Foster's raised foot and pushed him sideways. Teetering back, he lost his balance and landed firmly on his buttocks.

"Bully!" she cried out, thumping him soundly with her umbrella.

At first Foster backed away on his seat, raising his arms to shield himself. Then he reached out and grabbed the end of Regina's umbrella. He yanked her closer to him, his eyes bulging with anger while she hung onto the other end, not wanting to relinquish her weapon.

"Who the hell are you, lady?"

"Not who you think," Regina hissed under her breath, wrestling to regain her umbrella as their tug of war continued.

The man flung her backwards. She let loose a high-pitched scream. She sensed Dawson hovering behind her. A second later her head exploded into a rainbow of colors, and still clutching her umbrella with a death-like grip, she crumpled on top of Tyler.

Poor Tyler, she thought. *It had only been a harmless flirtation-n-nn....*

Then everything went black.

Chapter Three

A low hum penetrated her foggy mind. It droned, vibrated, rumbled, and gradually grew louder. Regina moaned. It seemed as if she were submerged in water, struggling to reach the surface. Everything felt heavy, especially her wrists. When she tried to move them, it was like moving cement blocks. Her head throbbed and itched. If only she could lift her hands to scratch under her wig.

More feelings inched their way to her brain. A coldness enveloped her, chilling her flesh, and the scent of plastic mingled with oil seeped through her nose. Then a sensation of swaying weightlessness followed. As she wondered how she could feel weightless and heavy at the same time, an engine whirred into her eardrums.

Engine?

Regina tasted fear, paralyzing fear. Her eyes flew open. Heaven help her, she was on an airplane—a *small* airplane. Panic churned in her stomach. It rose to her throat, forming a lump. Her eyes widened in terror, and when she tried to sit up and found her wrists bound, she screamed.

"Shut up," the dark-haired man in the pilot's seat yelled back at her.

"I can't. I have to get off this plane now. Now! Now!"

"I could push you out the hatch if you like."

Regina screamed again. Her deeply entrenched fear defied reasoning and threats. The man swore, did something with the instruments, and in a couple of strides walked back to where she lay. She panicked even more. No one was flying the plane. "Oooh..."

"Lady, I said shut up." He whipped a bandanna from his pocket, twirled it, and a second later secured it around her mouth.

The gag cut at the corners of her lips and tasted vile. Trying to loosen it, she lifted her tied hands to her mouth and tugged and tugged. No use. He'd tied it too tight. She wanted to upchuck, she wanted to scream, but most of all she wanted off this plane. *Wait a minute*! As he reclaimed his seat, Regina recognized him.

Bill Dawson. Why had he tied her up and thrown her on his plane? The ache in her head sharpened, reminding her someone had hit her. And someone had hit...

She blinked, pulling in the fuzzy memory.

Tyler.

Frank Foster and Bill Dawson had ganged up on him. All he'd done was escort her to the private plane terminal and return her umbrella. Why had they reacted so violently toward him? And why had Frank Foster asked her to deliver the present and then changed his mind?

The magazine article and her silly flirting escapade had roped Tyler into this mess. 'Course once roped, he certainly hadn't objected. This very minute he probably lay prostrate on the tarmac while this fiend, Bill Dawson, whisked her off to Lord knew where.

Unsure what Bill Dawson intended, Regina had news for him. By the time they landed—Lord willing that they did land—she'd be dead.

Dead from fear.

Hysteria returned, and despite the fact the gag muffled her voice, Regina screamed until her throat felt raw. If nothing else it helped to drown out the sound of the plane.

A high-pitched noise screeched in his ear, and Tyler drifted in and out of nether-nether land. His heavy lids refused to open, and he fell into a dreamlike trance during which Red slipped into his mind.

A unique woman if ever he saw one.

He'd never had a problem with women. Not that he considered himself a ladies' man, but on the whole he hadn't endured too many long spells without a girlfriend. He'd spent almost a year married, until his job started demanding more and more of his time. Lauren hadn't liked that, and each month of their marriage there seemed to be more and more she didn't like.

The marriage had been made in Heaven, but lived out in one long, agonizing battle after another. He'd have changed jobs in a minute if they'd had a child. But Lauren hadn't wanted children, something they failed to discuss before they'd married, and something that disappointed him. Too late, he'd discovered he'd like to be a full-time husband and father.

No, he'd never had a problem with women, but then they'd never dropped into his lap quite the way Red had.

Yet beneath her flirtatious actions and outrageous statements seemed to lurk a naiveté. He swore he'd caught glimpses of uncertainty and shyness in her, and they confused the hell out of him. As he fought his grogginess, twin streaks of pain spread from his head across his face, and that screeching noise in the distance didn't help, either. Sounded like a caged animal. A minute later it stopped, and he struggled to reconstruct what had happened. The airport, the surveillance, and Red.

Always Red.

He'd followed her out to the plane and then... whammy... nothing.

The memory of the unpleasant episode bounced around in his throbbing head as awareness swept over him. Noise and weightlessness. A plane. He was on a plane, and his wrists were tied.

Dammit, someone had bushwhacked him!

Had he been right? Had Red lured him into a web? Someway, somehow, he and Jake had been compromised. Sloppy on their parts. He slanted his gaze down to his arms, pulled tautly behind him. Silently cursing himself for being careless and gullible, Tyler clenched his jaw, heartened to find a bit of slack in the ropes.

As the sound of the engine rushed in on him, Tyler lay motionless on his back, computing his surroundings. From what little he knew about aircraft, he guessed the plane was a twin-engine customized Beechcraft, but he could only account for six seats. Four must have been removed for hauling extra cargo.

A man sat hunched over the controls. Tyler's sixth sense told him the man was alone, but that noise, that confounded noise. The incoherent, mumbling-moaning combination went on incessantly. Taking a deep breath, Tyler detected the delicate scent of a woman's perfume. Red?

Nah, more likely delusions from my throbbing head.

Damn, the moaning didn't stop, and it didn't help his splitting headache. He hitched himself up, then rolled over on his side, seeking the source of the non-stop sound.

What the hell? Red, bound and gagged and wailing like a magpie against the gag. Red, a fellow prisoner? Nah! They're playing games with me again.

To ward off her fear Regina had sung nearly every song she could remember. Keeping herself distracted from the roar of the engine seemed important, so she challenged herself to name all the states and their capitols, out loud of course, as best as she could with the gag. Systematically, she began with the East coast.

"Maine: Augusta," she strained against the gag.

"Vermont: Montpelier.

New Hampshire: Concord.

Massachusetts: Boston. Connecticut... uh... uh..." Regina hesitated.

"Connecticut: New Haven or Hart—"

She froze. Despite the hum of the plane and the sound of her voice, she sensed movement behind her, and her skin crawled. Someone had been watching her all this time. She shifted slightly, rolled to her side, and stared into a pair of angry brown eyes.

"Y-ler," she screamed.

Shocked, she shook her head so frantically her wig slipped off center. Those horrible men had tied him up and tossed him onto the plane, and the menacing look in his eyes told her he was angry with her. Guilt swirled inside her. He had every right to be angry, but didn't he realize she didn't know what was behind their abduction either? Of course if he'd heeded her instructions and left her alone, he wouldn't be in this predicament. Regina rationalized away a measure of her guilt by deciding he'd had every chance to leave. Was it her fault he'd stubbornly refused to take it?

Looking at his face, she regretted placing any blame on him. Dried blood dotted his forehead. Lord, she hoped his injury wasn't serious. For some strange reason they'd really beat him up. Her gaze dropped to his mouth, noticing he hadn't been gagged. Lucky him. But then neither had she until she'd started screaming.

"Oou okay?" she mumbled through her wet gag. Tyler just stared at her. She tried again. "Oou okay?" He gave her a perturbed look and shook his head. Okay, he couldn't understand her, but why didn't he just come out and say so. Maybe he didn't want to alert the pilot to the fact they were both awake now.

In need of reassurance and feeling isolated, she shivered. Singing would help. As she swung into the garbled lyrics to "On Top Of Old Smoky," she tried to come up with a reason for their abduction. Obviously, Foster and Dawson were criminals.

Drugs, perhaps?

She shuddered and hoped not. Drug dealers had a habit of killing anyone who stumbled onto their operation. And somehow she and Tyler had managed to do that, and she bet it had to do with that darn package.

My portfolio, where is it?

Regina craned her neck, searching for her briefcase. Spying it, she scooted back on her fanny. Thank goodness they'd tied her hands in front of her and not behind her back. It took several attempts, but she managed to fit her bound hands into her portfolio. They came in contact with the magazine, her purse and umbrella, but no package.

She turned, aware Tyler stared at her, a grim look lodged in his eyes. He'd probably watched her the whole time. She scooted back, glancing at the seat next to Dawson. The package sat on it. That had to be the answer. Delivering the package had brought this mess down on her.

Tyler watched her shuffle her body back to her portfolio and clumsily insert her bound hands. Turning his head caused a jab of pain to shoot down his neck. No doubt she hunted her precious package. Didn't surprise him when she came up empty.

Trouble in gangland? A double-cross?

Damn, but she had a mouth on her.

Throughout it all she kept up that mournful crooning. Didn't the woman ever run out of breath? She must possess the healthiest pair of lungs and nasal passages known to man. And no doubt there'd been a falling out among the thieves. Red appeared downright miffed to find the package missing from her briefcase.

Maybe he could turn the rift between the thieves to his favor and get Red to assist him. But he damn well couldn't concentrate with her perpetual howls splintering his eardrums.

There were compensations though. Each breath she took thrust her firm breasts against the peach blouse she wore beneath her jacket.

What now?

Red was on the prowl again. He watched her maneuver herself against the wall of the plane. She lifted her bound hands to the top of her head and scratched.

Got an itch, do you, Red?

He'd developed one or two of his own just watching her. In scooting her butt across the floor of the plane, her already short skirt had hitched up toward her upper thighs. And the most amazing thing of all was no matter what she did, her mouth never shut down. She was baying like a hound.

"Can it, lady," the pilot called out.

Tyler smiled. He wasn't the only one being driven over the edge by Red's infernal yowling. If it distracted the pilot, maybe he'd better rethink his intention to tell her to put a cork in it.

"...off...plane," Regina mumbled back, her eyes spitting fire in the direction of the pilot as she struggled to be understood.

Temper, temper, Tyler thought and grinned. He'd guessed right. No love lost between those two. The guy should've known better than to double-cross a woman, and a redhead at that. Tyler winced. Jeeze, Red's yowling was getting to him. If he wasn't mistaken she was singing, and even more incredible, he recognized the song. "Old MacDonald". The rhythm and the quacks brought it home to him.

Tyler narrowed his eyes. *Now what?*

Red rubbed the back of her head against the wall. As her hair fell across her forehead, his eyes nearly popped from their sockets. Holy Toledo! Her hair was sliding off her head. *Not her hair, dummy. Her wig*! Wisps of brown hair peeked out from under it. Red wasn't a redhead after all.

The minx had been in disguise. Yeah, the evidence was piling up. He'd walked right into her trap, all right. *Not too bright, Novak.* She stopped mumbling the song, and Tyler sent out a prayer of thanks. Apparently Red, no Regina, he corrected himself now that he'd discovered she wasn't a redhead, realized her wig hung on her head at an asymmetrical angle. Fit right in with her screwball personality. As he watched her roll those big brown eyes of hers, he couldn't keep a wry grin from forming at the comedic way she kept tilting her head in an effort to see what had happened.

Turbulence hit the plane, and Red's... dammit, he growled to himself. Red she'd been and Red she'd remain. Resuming his thought, he watched Red's eyes grow wider than the state of Kentucky again. Her moaning racket resumed, too, and this time he couldn't mistake the look in her eyes. It was unadulterated fear. Son of a gun, Red was scared to death, and if he hoped to enlist her aid, he'd have to squelch it in a hurry. Stealthily, he scooted over to where she sat.

"Psst, Red." She snapped her head around, terror in her liquid eyes, and eventually grew quiet after a final ee-ei-ee-ei-o. She mumbled something indecipherable, shook her head, and pointed to her slanting hairline.

"Yeah, I know you're not a redhead, but humor me. You've become Red to me. You okay?"

"Nooo..." She shook her head violently.

No mistaking that either. He inched closer, whispering in her ear. "Listen, if you'll sit directly in back of me and use your fingers, I think you can untie me. My ropes are loose. Once I'm free, we'll work together. How does that sound?" Tyler watched her chin quiver and her big brown eyes moisten.

Jeeze, he wasn't made of stone, even if he couldn't tell if she was glad or upset. Before turning his back to give her access to his wrists, he whispered a warning. "It might not be a bad idea to continue singing or whatever you were doing. If you're too quiet, the guy up front might get suspicious and come check on us." Muttering under his breath, he braced himself for the pathetic howls soon to come. He ought to have his head examined for suggesting it, but her howls would mask any other noises they made.

Having identified her as an enemy, he thought he'd be desensitized to her touch, but the feel of her soft fingers on his wrists ignited a need in him. Silent irony shafted through him. Allies though they might be at the moment, this woman was not a friend. He held himself rigid, grappling to resist her flowery fragrance and the nearness of her body. As she picked and pulled at his ropes, faint tremors in her fingers passed into his flesh.

"Come on Red, come on, you can do it," he softly encouraged, doubting she heard him over the roar of the motor and her inimitable rendition of "Old MacDonald." Her fingernail jabbed the raw skin where the rope had rubbed against his wrists. “Ouch,” he yelped.

“...orry,” she muttered, before she swung into another verse of the song.

One final tug did it, and his hands were free. As subterfuge, he kept them behind him. A second later she scooted in front of him and held her hands aloft in supplication. He stared thoughtfully for several seconds, desperately wanting to rub his chin. With her dirt-smudged face, gagged mouth, and tangled hair, he was hard put not to give in. Her dewy eyes especially chipped away at him, but he wasn’t ready to turn her loose.

And then when he didn’t respond, the most touching thing happened. She inched closer and as best she could with her hands bound together, she clutched his arm like it was a lifeline. Her pinching grip commanded his attention, and the wild, desperate look in her eyes tore at his guts.

As he’d noted before, Red was afraid. More than afraid. Scared spitless.

And if he didn’t distract her soon, she was going to cut off his circulation. “It’s gonna be okay,” he whispered, but he could see she didn’t believe him.

As thunder boomed and the plane lurched with the wind, he leaned his mouth next to her ear. “I’m gonna loosen your gag so we can whisper, but every now and then suppose you start that moaning you’ve been doing, just so the pilot won’t get nosy.”

Regina couldn’t believe it. The vile gag was loose, and a spasm of nausea threatened her. She drew several, deep breaths into her lungs, almost gagging on the air, and licked the sore corners of her mouth with her tongue. “Thanks,” she murmured, barely able to speak.

“You’re welcome.”

Steeling herself, she lifted her bound hands to his head and placed her fingers on the gash near his hairline over his right temple. When she’d been loosening his ropes, she’d noticed a nasty welt ballooning on the crown of his head. “Are you okay?”

Tyler nodded. “I’ll live. How about you?”

“I-I’m terrified of flying in small planes. T-this very minute, parachute or not, I’d jump out of it if I could.”

"Steady, Red. Look at me."

She did.

"Draw in three deep breaths."

She did.

"Feel better?"

She wished she did. With his soothing voice and hypnotic eyes, she knew she should, but nothing short of planting her feet on solid ground could override her fear. "A little," she lied.

"I need for you to stay calm. Can you do that?"

If she could zero in on his warm gaze and nothing else, she might pull it off. No guarantees of course. She was drawn to him, bonding with him, and trying to absorb the invisible static energy flowing from his body. And she hated looking like a fraidy-cat.

"Regina?" he quietly addressed her, waiting for her answer.

"Y-yes," she said, her gaze still locked with his.

"I'm not going to untie you. I want our buddy up front to see you're still tied, understand?"

She didn't, but she nodded, keeping her gaze riveted on his. The plane went into a downward spin, and she screamed, then suddenly fearful the pilot would realize her gag had slipped, she immediately closed her mouth.

Tyler sidled closer. "It's okay. We've run into a patch of bad weather and it's keeping him preoccupied. That's to our advantage. In a little bit I'm going to put your gag back on, and I want you to scream your head off, get up and start moving around, maybe you could do your bathroom bit, lure him back here. Then I'll grab this wrench and send our friend off to dreamland."

Regina digested what he said, her heart pounding fast and loud. The urge to start screaming this very minute gathered steam, and she fought it. "But...b-but—"

"But what, Red?" he prodded.

"Who's going to fly the plane?"

"Me."

"You know how?"

"Enough." Tyler let the lie slide easily from his lips. He'd only been up in a small plane twice with a friend, and the little amount of time his buddy had turned over the controls to him didn't qualify him to fly, especially with a storm brewing, but he had enough confidence to give it a try. No sense in alarming Red. He needed her as stable as possible. He smiled.

Considering what he'd observed during their short acquaintance, stable might be a bit too much to ask.

But there was another side to her. To have inquired after his welfare a few moments ago, despite being petrified, must have cost her. The woman had character. Compassion and character. "So you think you can do what I said?"

"Okay." She swallowed. "But first my hair. Could you fix my hair?"

Vanity, thy name is woman. He broke his vow to keep his hands behind his back and raised his arm.

"Could you scratch it, first?"

Tyler groaned. In that moment with her gaze trained on his, he was aware of nothing but her. A tightening coiled in his body, and he wished she could scratch an itch of his own. He obliged her, then straightened her wig. He considered pulling it off, but the pilot might wonder what happened. Tyler didn't want the guy suspicious of anything.

"Ready?" he asked, replacing her gag. Picking up the wrench, he linked his arms behind his back.

"...eady," she mumbled, raising her shoulders, sitting ramrod straight against the wall, her eyes glued to his.

With her knees visibly knocking from fear, he watched her draw in a deep breath and scream. She screamed and screamed and screamed, each one louder and longer than the last. He thought his head would burst. Why didn't the guy take the bait? Her shrieks clearly had irritated him earlier. Sooner or later she was going to run out of fire power.

"I said shut up, lady," the pilot yelled.

With her gaze still locked on his, Tyler gave her a grudging nod, and as if he controlled a string to her mouth, she took one more deep breath and let loose a magnificent howl. At last the pilot responded, slamming on the autopilot. He rose and walked back to face Red.

"Lady, I got my hands full and your yammering isn't helping. If you can't be quiet, I'll fix it so you are." He lifted his hand to slap her, and Regina cowered.

"Not a good idea, Buddy." Tyler jammed the wrench into the back of the man's ribs. "I've got a gun aimed at you."

The man froze. "A gun? You ain't got no gun. We checked, and there's none on this plane."

Tyler swore under his breath. He'd hoped to bluff this man and convince him to fly the plane to the nearest airport.

Regina watched in horror as Dawson lifted his hand to slap her. She tensed, expecting the blow, and a second later as Tyler spoke to him, Dawson's hand froze in mid-air. Grateful for the reprieve, she let out a sigh. She sent another prayer heavenward when she heard Dawson say there wasn't a gun on the plane. At least she and Tyler couldn't be shot. Totally ignorant when it came to planes, she wasn't too sure what effect a stray bullet hole might have on the plane's ability to stay aloft. She suspected it would be far from pleasant.

In the blink of an eye, a fight began. As Tyler raised his arm to get leverage to hit Dawson with the wrench, Dawson spun around, withdrawing his hammer from his tool belt with the speed of a skilled gunslinger. They fought hammer and wrench, each one drawing blood from the other.

Layer upon layer of panic washed over her. So many levels that Regina grew numb. Acutely aware of the empty cockpit, she'd feel so much better if someone were sitting in the pilot's seat. Autopilot aside, the friendly skies were overcrowded these days.

She wished she was tough like her Aunt Sophia. Her aunt wouldn't sit still for this.

Of course Aunt Ruth would be in her heyday, having stumbled onto a clandestine adventure.

And dear Aunt Della would distribute lace hankies and calmly explain as she stood over Regina's grave that it had all been predestined.

That thought did little to bolster her spirits.

For the first time she'd gotten up the gumption to step out and test the manhunt waters and what did she get? A plane ride with two crazy men trying to kill each other. Mercy! What if they knocked each other out? Regina drew in a shaky breath, hating how fear froze her wits. A pity the magazine hadn't the foresight to include an article on how to untie bound hands, subdue two fighting men, and safely eject from an airplane.

Huddled in her section of the plane, she peeked at Tyler from behind the seat. A blow to his jaw sent him reeling. "Oon't hit him!" Sympathy pains shot through her. How could the man do that to Tyler. *Inhuman thug*! "Y-ler don't bleed! Don't bleed!"

Do something, idiot. Help the man.

But the weightlessness and deafening drone of the motor continued to paralyze her. She'd sing, drown out the noise and then maybe she could overcome her fear.

"... inging in ain, ust inging in the ain...," she belted out through her gag.

Son of a gun!

Her umbrella. Moments ago when she'd checked her briefcase, it had been there. She scampered on her bottom, pitched her bound hands into the portfolio, and pulled out her weapon, never missing a note of her song. Having perfected her mode of transportation, she scooted within striking distance of the two men. She took careful aim. Bringing the umbrella back like a seasoned batter, she swung with all her might.

Wham!

Contact.

"Ow!" Tyler let out several vivid obscenities.

"Oops," Regina gasped. Well, what did he expect? She wrinkled her nose. Baseball had never been her forte, either. "...orry," she mumbled.

Besides, they'd hit a pocket of turbulence. How was she supposed to keep her aim on target with everyone bouncing around? Fear returned, if it had ever really left her, and she immediately swung into a rendition of "Raindrops are Falling on My Head." Seconds lapsed, and she struck again.

"Bitch!" Dawson swore.

Bingo! She'd improved. Blood poured from both men's faces. How much more punishment could they take? She lunged at Dawson's legs again and whacked and whacked. His howls matched her own. In the middle of another magnificent swing, turbulence flung her forward. Her umbrella smashed against the dials. If nothing else, it succeeded in getting Dawson's attention.

"Stupid bitch! Look what you've done!" He grazed her head with his hammer, and she slumped over. Dizziness surrounded her. Sensing that Tyler was about to pounce on Dawson, she gave one last feeble thrust at the man's legs. Her contribution must have helped, for a moment later, Dawson lay sprawled on the floor of the plane beside her.

Through her fuzzy vision, she saw Tyler tie Dawson's hand and gag him, even though the man was clearly unconscious. A steady trickle of blood ran down Tyler's cheek, and he whipped a handkerchief from his pocket and dabbed at it. She knelt on her knees and raised her hands.

He took a stumbling step toward her. "Thanks for your help, Red. Way to go! You swing a mean umbrella even if you did land one on my kneecap."

"Never... eave... ome without one."

"Smart move." He scratched his chin. "You okay?"

She shook her head, her eyelids fluttering.

"I'm with you. Don't feel too swift myself." Touching his hand to his head, he flinched.

"... ands," she persisted when he made no move to untie her.

"Oh, yeah, your hands." He dropped to his knees. "It's getting so I can understand you. That was Raindrops you were singing, wasn't it?"

She nodded. "... puleeze." She shoved her outstretched arms in his face. Surely after helping him, he'd untie her. But then to be perfectly honest, he probably was angry she'd gotten him into this mess and wasn't in a hurry to free her. But if he didn't do something soon, he'd regret it. Thirsty from the gag, faint from the airplane, and dizzy from the blow to her head, she was about to turn pea-green.

And pea-green meant...

Thank goodness. He'd untied the hateful rope. She flexed her hands, then pulled the horrid gag from her mouth. "Thanks," she said breathily and eyed her umbrella. One way or another she was getting off this plane even if she had to parachute to earth like Mary Poppins. *But first things first.* "You did say you could fly this plane, didn't you?"

"Uh huh."

His less than firm answer didn't exactly reassure her. "Uh... don't you think it'd be a good idea if you flew it now?"

"You mean before you start singing and screeching again?"

She nodded.

"You're probably right, but I've got a news bulletin for you, Red."

News bulletin? She blinked away her blurry vision and stared into his compelling eyes, anxiously awaiting for him to elaborate. An unsettling quiver triggered to life deep inside her.

"What's that?" she managed to ask.

"You're gonna have to help me fly this baby."

Chapter Four

Forget pea-green. The color of the moment was lily white. A bucket of ice-water had been thrown over her skin. Blood rushed from her head.

Every muscle in Regina's body quivered in a thousand directions, and every emotion she'd experienced during her uncle's unfortunate flight fourteen years ago crushed in on her. She hugged herself, almost cinching the breath from her lungs. Surely, that high-pitched shrill wasn't hers. It was physically impossible. Her voice was trapped by the lump in her throat.

"Settle down, Red."

Easy for him to say.

Tyler's strong hands gripped her shoulders. A hysterical giggle bubbled up through the barrier in her windpipe. "It's a joke. You're joking, aren't you?"

"I'm dead serious."

And I'm a dead duck. Him, too. "I-I... I..." Fear choked her voice. "I told you I'm petrified of airplanes. I can't—"

"You'll have to. My head's been used as a nail more times than I can count, and I'm fighting double vision. Dizzy, too."

So am I. Dear Lord, no. Don't let this be. No way could she do it. No way would she. Not by the hairs of her coppery-red wig.

He wrapped his arms around her, then leaned into her. Who was supporting whom? Who cared? Her own legs nearly buckling, she clung to him. "I think I'm going to faint."

"Dammit, Red, you can't. If we work together we won't—"

"Crash?"

He nodded, his glazed stare meshing with her panic-stricken one. Regina gulped. God bless America, his eyes echoed her confusion. 'Twas the blind leading the blind.

"Okay?" he prodded.

"Okay." But she didn't really mean it.

As he gathered her closer, tears pooled in her eyes. If she could choose a way to die, embraced in Tyler Novak's arms would be near the top of the list. She shivered, not sure whether it was terror-induced or Tyler-induced. Warmth from his fingers on the nape of her neck rippled through her and gave her the answer. Strangely, the closeness of his body had a soothing effect.

Imagine that! It was as if a measure of his strength had been transferred to her.

"Look at it this way." His voice was low, comforting. "If you hadn't picked me up, you'd be in this plane all alone, tied and gagged."

True. But with an experienced pilot, albeit, a dirty, rotten, crooked one. *Hold it! Picked him up? Of all the nerve! Totally the opposite.* For an instant he'd almost made her mad enough to forget her fear. Almost.

"You did say you've flown a plane before, right?" She touched his arm, her fingers closing over the hard muscle of his biceps.

"Correct. Once. In ideal conditions and not solo."

Terrific! Her stomach churned. Just her luck the man had to be so painfully honest. Couldn't he have sugar-coated his answer a wee bit?

She closed her eyes. He looped his arm around her waist, guided her to the pilot's seat, and buckled her in. Why did she feel as if she were being strapped into the electric chair? Opening an eyelid, she peeked out the windshield. Tall mountains hovered directly below. Very tall mountains. *Face your fears. Face your fears*, she railed at herself. Several deep breaths later, she slanted a glance at Tyler.

He plowed his hand through his wiry hair. "I promise when we land you can faint, scream, go into catatonic shock, whatever you want. Deal?"

"Deal." The tortured whisper escaped through her teeth. As she huddled deeper into the seat, he buckled himself into the one beside her. Darn, her head still itched. Taking a momentary break from her panicked state, she poked her fingers under the wig and scratched.

"Read the dials to me as I point to them."

"Dials?"

"On the instrument panel." He tapped at them, his voice hinting urgency.

Leaving her wig slightly askew, she blinked through her own foggy vision and complied.

"Try the radio."

"Where?"

"There." His fingers touched it. "Never mind. It must have been smashed during our fight."

"Sorry about that." Chagrined, she made a face. "I was aiming at the pilot's head. He ducked."

"Couldn't be helped. Better it than one of us. Wish I knew where we are."

"There're tons and tons of tall pines down there."

"Yeah. The flight plan must have taken him southeast. That's the heading you read on the compass. We could be over the Smokies. What's the fuel gauge say?" He pointed to it.

"The needle's flirting with E." Regina gulped. What color was her complexion now? Any dummy knew what E meant. But she winced more from her choice of words. If she survived, she'd never ever flirt again—or would she? Tyler creased his forehead. Immediately, she frowned. "What's the matter?"

"We must have sprung a leak. Either that or the guy planned to land somewhere nearby. Dammit, we need a strong tailwind and a decent place to land. See any flat areas?"

"What do you mean a p-place to l-land? Are we going to—"

"Yes. Do you see anything?"

"Just acres of Christmas trees." Enough to supply every household in the nation. "Dusk's setting in and for your information my own vision is none too clear."

"I know. Sorry about that blow he gave you." Tyler ran his fingertips across her forehead. They traced her cheekbone and lingered. Tingles feathered out from his touch. Lifting the off-center wig, akilter from her scratching session, he tossed it to the floor. "You certainly don't need this."

But she did. She felt naked without it. She braced her arm on the steering yoke and reached down to retrieve it. The plane banked to the right. Regina swayed into Tyler. "Oops."

"Steady. No sudden movements. Turn the yoke back to the left a bit."

She did. The plane skidded left, and despite his seat belt, so did Tyler's virile upper body.

"Not quite so far."

She compensated with a slow, long pull. The small plane shook, rattled, and rolled

"And not so jerky. Take smooth, easy movements, as if you were caressing the yoke."

No way could she manage caress, not with the death grip

she had on the controls.

"If we reduce air speed, we'll conserve fuel."

She liked the sound of that.

"Pull back on the throttle."

"This?" Her gaze darted from the instrument panel to him as she groped for what she prayed was the throttle.

"You got it." His large, bronzed hand covered hers and the plane slowed down. "You're doing fine."

Not true, and they both knew it. Decent of him to give her a pep talk though. She had to admire his coolness under fire. His life was at the mercy of someone who didn't know diddly-squat about flying a plane, someone who was scared spitless to boot, and yet he seemed remarkably composed. She focused on the landscape below, her palsied fingers gripping the yoke. Too bad he'd removed his hand. Tyler began to push some of the pedals with his feet.

"What are you doing?" she queried.

"Working the rudders."

"Oh." Sounded pretty good, whatever rudders were for. Seemed to her they had something to do with steering a boat. Maybe they steered airplanes, too. "Look! There's a grassy area." And not far beyond it, barren rock. Could be worse, she supposed. They could be about to crash into shark-infested waters.

"Tell me where on a clock's dial."

"About one-fifty-seven I'd say."

"One fifty-seven?" A trace of laughter echoed in his voice. "That's what I call being precise."

"I try to be." She blinked. "Anyway, there's a flat area in the vicinity of two o'clock if you prefer."

He squinted out the window. "If and when we aim for it, we're gonna have to come down fast, and we don't want to slide off the side of the mountain."

"D-down... f-fast, did you say?"

Where was her umbrella? No. She couldn't bail out. She'd pledged her help and a Citrano's word was sacrosanct. She bit her lip and strived for control.

Look on the bright side, she consoled herself. You always wanted to see the Smokies.

But she'd rather see the scenery than be a part of it. Years from now some bright-eyed geology student would find her skeleton plastered into the mountain's bedrock and wonder how she got there, mixed in with the remains of bears, bobcats, and raccoons.

Face your fears, she chanted again, trying to dispel the shivers dancing up and down her spine. If she survived this adventure, flying in a large airplane ought to be a piece of cake. Maybe her fear would be cured. And then again maybe she'd make a solemn vow never to come within a ten mile radius of an airport for the rest of her life. All her fault. If she hadn't taken the advice of the magazine and used the airport to test her flirting technique, none of this would have happened.

Regina risked taking her hand from the yoke and dutifully made the sign of the cross. *Dear Father in Heaven, forgive me all my sins.* A guardian angel would come in handy about now. One with very large wings.

"Push down on the yoke and ease back on the throttle," Tyler shouted.

She pushed it down as gently as she could, but with her fingers shaking like the tree limbs below, it was difficult to execute with any measure of precision. An instant later she felt the plane slow down some, but a sliver of panic crept back into her throat. Truth be told, despite her attempt to appear brave and calm, it had never left her.

"I don't think I can do this. Oh, God... " She heard the quiver in her voice. "I... I..." The speed combined with the nearness of the ground made her heart climb into her throat—right next to her stomach which had camped out in her windpipe ever since she'd regained consciousness.

"Hang in there, Red. When we approach, we want to come in at exactly the right angle."

"Angle?"

"Yeah, the earth and the belly of the plane have to meet like they were made for one another. You want to gently slide in on your belly. Remember what I said, caress the throttle. Make it respond to your slightest touch."

"Respond." She licked her dry lips. Tyler Novak had a way of making flying an erotic experience. The heat wave flooding the lower half of her body threatened to collide with the icy shards of fear feathering down her spine. She wasn't sure she wanted to be around when they met.

"Ease up on the control an inch. Feel the uplift."

"Hmm..." Uplifting wouldn't exactly be how she'd describe

it. From beneath her lashes she stole a glance at him. On a semi-conscious level she realized what he was doing—using sexy innuendoes to help her keep her fear under control. And it was working. Most of the time.

"Thatta baby. You've got the magic touch. We're almost drifting."

Speaking of magic, his gravelly vocal chords were downright seductive, sending her into her own private tailspin. He had her so flustered, she shoved the throttle forward, tightened her grip on the controls, and sent the plane into an upward spin.

"Holy sh—Gimme those controls." Tyler reached over and pushed her hands away. "Time for the first team."

Back to pea green and reciting the state capitols to override the guttural roar of the engine, she didn't dare look out. Because of her they were doomed. Her life passed before her eyes at the supersonic speed of a jet out of control. About the time she was ready to let out a healthy howl, Tyler righted the plane.

"Back to normal." He squinted, then blinked. "My vision's cleared up some. I'm taking over the yoke" Not wasting a second, he pulled the throttle all the way back.

The plane was losing altitude. Her stomach told her. They were going down like a free fall on a roller coaster. Amazed she wasn't screaming or singing, she extended a shaky hand. "Nice knowing you, Mr. Novak."

"Tyler." He squeezed her hand from the seat beside her. "My pleasure. Buck up, Red. I look forward to our next practice session."

Pract... Session? Confused, she batted her eyelashes, then dawning settled in. Incredible! Men and their hormones. Not even the threat of death put a damper on them. His mind dwelt on the heavenly art of snuggling while her stomach sought a more earthy rebellion. "We're not going to make it, are we?"

"Sure we are, and we owe a lot of it to you. Put your head down and link your hands behind your neck."

Bewildered, her breathing uneven, she somehow did as he demonstrated while tree tops whizzed by the windows.

"Brace yourself."

She had news for him. Despite hearing what sounded like landing gear being lowered, she didn't plan on being conscious for the impact. In fact, she was seconds away from oblivion. A teardrop oozed from her eyelid and scurried down her cheek. She couldn't bear for him to see what a coward she was and turned away. The belly of the plane hit the ground. Metallic crunches roared in her ears, then mercifully she slipped into a world of her own.

A world without airplanes.

Silence.

A dragonfly landed on his nose, and in his stupor, Tyler brushed it away. He groaned, opened his eyes, then slowly moved his arms. They worked. So did his legs. Alive and well, outside of a few aches and scratches here and there, thank God. All in all, damn lucky. A miracle, perhaps. Not many people walked away from a small plane crash. He swallowed and slowly rotated his head to his left.

Red! Unconscious?

His fingers quickly probed for a pulse, and he breathed a sigh on finding one. Damn crazy woman. She'd been scared to death, but he had to admire her grit. About to come unraveled at any moment, she'd hung on. She could have gone hysterical on him. Yeah. Maybe she didn't know it, but Red had guts. Man, what a day! In all his years with the agency he'd never had such a cockamamie experience. Fumbling with his seat belt, he shifted to look behind him, his ribs protesting the motion. The pilot was alive but still out cold.

Tyler checked the guy's pockets, searched his wallet, then stuffed it into his own hip pocket. William Dawson from Chicago. They had a warrant out for him. He thought the guy had looked familiar, but throughout the ordeal he hadn't been able to get a good look at him. Easing back into the pilot's seat, Tyler strained to see through the branches of a tree limb that lay across the windshield. He glanced out the window and whistled. They owed the tree a debt of thanks. Had the plane skidded any further, they would have dropped off a cliff four, maybe five, thousand feet.

The low hanging clouds and hazy blue cast to the mountain peaks confirmed their location. Definitely the Smokies. When he'd left his apartment this morning, he hadn't exactly planned on a hike in the mountains, and by the two inch heels on Red, she hadn't either. Tyler wrinkled his nose. Gas? There couldn't be much more fuel left, still he couldn't overlook an explosion. Damn! He'd have to work fast.

Twenty minutes later he sat safely away under a canopy of firs, two unconscious bodies, and an over-sized backpack containing blankets, first aid kit, two flashlights, batteries, a canteen of water, and some trail mix stowed at his feet. And even more important, Red's portfolio and the package.

A quick examination of her wallet verified who she was, that she was twenty-five. Her wig gone, she looked younger, more like a teenager. For a woman in her trade, she took good care of herself. He still couldn't get a read on the woman. Was she one of the smugglers and they pulled a double-cross on her? And why the hell had she latched on to him? Maybe he'd been careless, given himself away, and she'd been told to lead him into a trap. Yet she didn't kiss as if she were under orders.

He hoped he could trust her to remain on his side, that she wouldn't take the diamonds and run out on him. Damn, he wished he had a weapon. He fingered the hammer and wrench, then tossed them into the backpack. They'd have to do for now. Tearing the birthday paper from the package, he found a plastic jar of marbles.

Marbles, my ass!

The diamonds were mixed with them. The jar was too bulky for his jeans' pocket. He'd tuck it in the first aid kit. That done, he sat back on his haunches, his gaze straying to his number one problem.

Red.

Not a bad problem, nor bad on the eyes. His gaze slowly traveled from the sweep of her cheekbones and settled on her breasts. And what lungs! Enough volume for a diva in the opera. Then again with her propensity for singing off key no self-respecting opera company would dare let her near a stage. He poked a finger in his ear. It was a relief not to hear her screaming or singing, but her speaking voice was something else. Whisky-smooth and low, it conjured up candles and a hot tub.

A quirky dame. And a blasted riddle.

Maybe he should leave them both and make tracks. Naw! She had come to his rescue. She and her hot pink umbrella. He owed her that much. Probably a dumb move on his part returning a lethal weapon to her, but he'd done it anyway, slipped her umbrella back in her briefcase, right next to her magazine. Wandering around in these mountains could be dangerous, and it might come in handy. Besides, he argued with himself, abandoning Red meant no practice sessions. Spring nights in the Smokies bordered on chilly, and it'd be nice and cozy to have someone to cuddle up to.

Tyler ran his fingers through his shaggy hair and made another stab at bringing symmetry to the perplexing Miss Citrano. What the hell had she been doing at an airport if she was so petrified of flying? With her deep-seated phobia, her mission had to be damned important to lure her there.

Could be like he'd figured. She was there for the diamonds. Greed was known to be a powerful incentive, powerful enough to overcome most any phobia. Tyler leaned back against a fir and let his gaze roam slowly over her curves.

Uh, uh, Baby Doll.

We both know what you were doing at the gate besides some zany connection to the smugglers. Plying your trade. And what a technique! Pretending to be so innocent, so little-girl coy in need of instruction. That helpless ploy worked every time. Appealed to a guy's ego. Great gimmick, not that she needed one. Bet she had men lined up just itching to teach her a thing or two. Son of a gun, speaking of itch. Red's wig. Why the disguise? Only added to his suspicions.

Yessir.

Red was sticking with him. Not that he planned on going very far. Better to hang around the crash scene in case other planes came looking for them. If the plane did explode, the fire ought to attract attention.

He fingered the matches in his jean's pocket, the ones he'd heisted off Dawson after rifling though the guy's wallet. They'd come in handy, too. Licking his lips, he visualized the pack of cigarettes he'd found in Dawson's shirt pocket. Despite having kicked the habit six months ago, he'd been tempted to appropriate them. The shredded residue of tobacco lay at his feet, a testimony to the battle he'd somehow managed to win.

Less than ten minutes later, after hastily exploring the area, Tyler crawled over to Red and knelt by his cold-cocked, red-blooded hostage. He wouldn't treat her like one, but she'd be his captive all the same. If he played it right, he could let her think she was helping him. She seemed to like that concept. Yeah, he nodded, remembering how she'd tried the Heimlich Maneuver on him. Red liked helping people. Maybe he could even persuade her to testify against these guys.

"Oooh."

The Italian bombshell stirred.

Peace and quiet were about to end. She moaned, opened her eye, surveyed her surroundings, frowned, and closed them.

"Regina," he said, using her name for a change. He touched the back of his hand to her face.

"Hmmm..." Looking far from glamorous, yet seductively enticing, she cuddled into a fetal position and smiled.

He liked her reaction, but not now. Later, he promised. "Regina," he tried again.

"Ahh... " Her reply came out breathy and low. His mouth went dry at the images it evoked in his head.

"Hey, Co-pilot." He gently tugged her shoulder. "Wake up."

"Umm... bad dream."

With her eyes still closed, she sat up, slumped against him, and linked her arms around his neck. He cradled her head onto his shoulder and rested his chin on top of her crown. "Time to wake up, Red." Her flowery perfume assaulted his senses. She was completely uninhibited, burrowing closer and closer into his body, undermining his resistance. What the hey?

He placed a kiss on the nape of her neck and worked his way up her creamy skin to her earlobe.

"N-nice..." she murmured.

Damn right, and it'd be even better when she was fully awake. He combed his fingers through her tangled locks, straightening the brown snarls that spilled down to her shoulders. Tenderly, he tucked an errant wisp behind her ear. Her eyes remained closed, but that adorable, pouty mouth lay exposed and inviting. Hell, he was human. Why not play Prince Charming to her Sleeping Beauty?

He covered the smile on her lips with his mouth, feathering and teasing them.

"Oh," she purred, rocking back and forth in his arms.

Just as he'd thought. The woman didn't need lessons. He deepened the kiss, taking her breath into his mouth, relishing the shivers rippling through her and the yielding sway of her body.

She jolted awake. "My stars!" She jerked away. "Tyler?"

She looked at him, at Dawson, then the mountain crests and battered plane. Her eyes widened like balloons, and her mouth opened even wider. He recognized the look. A shriek was but a second away. No need to send every creature within a mile radius scampering for cover when the solution was simple. Before she could take another breath, he cupped her chin and smothered her scream with his mouth. He kissed her thoroughly, then placed his fingers over her lips and quietly spoke into her ear.

"Shhh. It's all right. Don't panic. We crashed and we survived." She trembled in his arms.

"Dawson? Is he... dead?" she mumbled into his hand.

"No." Tyler's heart sank. So, she knew the guy's name. He'd deal with that later. "Listen. It's getting dark. We need to get to a shelter, and it probably isn't a good idea to stay this close to the plane. It might—"

"Explode?" She stared at the wreck. "What about him?" She pointed at Dawson.

"I'll drag him further away and loosen his ropes. Apart from that he's on his own, understood?" She nodded. Tyler still wasn't sure of her relationship to Dawson, but he felt certain there was no love lost between them.

He released her and inched away. Their gazes met. Innocent, brown eyes looked at him. Questioning eyes. She didn't say a word. She didn't have to. Her eyes spoke volumes. Fear darted through them, followed by impassive acceptance.

"I hate planes," she whispered.

"Yeah, I know." He automatically touched his finger to his recovering eardrum. He stood and gave her a hand up, tugging her to her feet. "I did some scouting while you napped. A little further up this mountain there's an abandoned shack." His hand cupped her elbow, steadying her. "How's your vision?"

"Better, and yours?"

"Better." He loosened his grip, handed over her briefcase, and hefted the pack onto his back.

"My head still hurts though."

"Mine, too." *Hurt Like hell.* And it wasn't just from the blows he'd sustained. He glanced at his world champion screech owl. "Let's move out."

After pulling Dawson further away, he turned and started up the mountain, trudging several steps before he sensed no one followed. He swung around and in one swift, encompassing glance noticed Red standing over the guy's body. She worried her lip as she watched him. *Now what? Some kind of tie between them?*

"You coming?" He kicked his boot in the dirt.

"What about him?"

"What about him?" he challenged.

"You know, wild animals. Bears. Snakes. He's helpless, his hands tied and all."

Women! Go figure 'em! "I loosened his ropes. When he comes to he should be able to free himself." Damn with no weapon, he didn't particularly care to guard both Red and the man. Even though it appeared Red might be on his team, he still couldn't trust her. Better this way. Where could the guy go but wander around the mountains? Women. A pain in the—

"But—" Regina started to speak.

"But, what?" he growled, retracing his steps, his patience almost gone. "The man a friend of yours?"

"Certainly not. He's a..."

Chapter Five

"What?" One of Tyler's eyebrows shot up. He could have sworn she was about to admit something. Blast! Was she in cahoots with him after all? "What is he?"

"He's a barbarian, hitting you and me, hijacking us in that plane."

Tyler let out a long, slow breath. "Remember that. He's the one who forced you into one of your least favorite places. Stop fretting over him and let's vamoose. I'd just as soon be gone before he wakes up."

But Red wasn't ready to leave. To his utter amazement she stooped down beside the guy and loosened the top button of his knit shirt. Then after whipping a tissue out of her briefcase and blotting a drop of blood on Dawson's face, she looked up from the body and met Tyler's gaze, her brown eyes round and guileless.

"He looked uncomfortable," she explained.

Tyler shrugged at her upturned face. Her capacity to forgive was nothing short of incredible. No matter how miserably she'd been treated, Red definitely had a soft spot in her heart for people. He inclined his head. "A storm's coming. Rain might keep any spilled gasoline from exploding, so you won't have to worry about him." He flicked a glance in Dawson's direction. "I'm leaving. Unless you want to spend the night out here with this guy, you'd better hustle."

He turned and started up the mountain again. Five giant steps later, he stopped. His keen ears detected no footsteps. So she'd chosen to stay. What did that tell him? Dammit, he couldn't let her stay with the guy. She was *his* prisoner and it was about time she realized it.

"What now?" he demanded, throwing up his hands in frustration.

Regina gripped her portfolio strap. It wasn't as if she wasn't tense enough already, but his barked question intimidated her. During the past few minutes Tyler Novak had turned into a monster. With an attitude like that she wasn't all that sure she wanted to stay with him. But that hadn't been her problem. Little by little he covered the distance between them, towering over her, his eyes glinting.

"My shoes," she said softly. He lowered his gaze. "I don't think I can walk in them, and I can't go far in my hose."

"No problem." With lightning speed he fell to his knees, pulled off her shoes and snapped off the heels. "Solved." He handed them back to her, his gaze shooting into her like arrows. "Now get the lead out and let's move."

She slipped them on and struggled to keep up with him, righteous indignation flowing from every pore. "Those shoes cost me nearly a hundred dollars."

"Send me a bill. I'll buy you new ones," he hollered over his shoulder.

Why so gruff? Was he peeved at her for getting him stranded in these mountains? Guess she'd never understand the inner workings of a man. Maybe it was his way of dealing with the catastrophe they'd just survived.

Like a man made for the mountains, he set a rigorous pace, one she had difficulty keeping up with in her make-shift shoes, though she enjoyed the view immensely. His skin-tight jeans sheathed his superbly fit backside like the pants on a football player.

Trudging behind him, she ducked and hunched over, studiously trying to avoid the brambles and vines. Camping and hiking had never been high on her list. A low-hung branch snapped across her face and momentarily stunned her. Thorns in the rich, luxuriant undergrowth tore her hose and scratched her legs, but she refused to complain. She'd caused him enough grief, and she wanted to prove she could hold her own.

As she hobbled along, stumbling up the rugged incline, she thought about Tyler. Though his behavior resembled a bear, she was grateful for his company. She shuddered.

Bears.

The Smokies and bears went together.

The place had to be teeming with them, especially now that spring had blossomed. Bears had a nasty habit of coming out of hibernation. She cast a wary glance, slowly turning three hundred and sixty degrees, and quickened her pace to catch up with Tyler. No telling what kind of predicament she'd be in if it had been just she and Dawson. But then if Tyler hadn't showed up, maybe nothing would have happened. Maybe she would have handed over the package and Foster and Dawson would have let her go.

Foster.

Where had he gone? And the package? Dawson had set it on the seat next to him. Growing more clear-headed by the second, Regina stopped in her tracks. Good grief! The package. The key to it all. Aunt Ruth would be ashamed of her if she didn't get to the bottom of this mystery. Making up her mind to catch up with Tyler and tell him it was vital she return to the plane, she took a step, then froze.

A snake!

Directly in her path, his beady little eyes zeroed in on her. Not a good omen. She and snakes had never been on the best of terms. Gus Merwin had brought one to school in third grade. She'd thrown up. Wasn't the scare from the airplane enough? Too bad Aunt Della wasn't here with her tarot cards. It would be helpful to know what future catastrophes might lie in store.

Regina veered off to the left, but like Mary's Little Lamb, the snake followed. She dodged under a vine, lost her footing, and felt a bramble catch in her hair. Closer examination revealed a prickly blackberry bush. Tugging proved useless. She dropped her briefcase and pulled with all her might. As she lifted her hands to work herself free, the snake moved closer.

"Tyler," she yelled. His name ricocheted off the trees and carried through the coves and hollows.

Ever so carefully, she crouched to retrieve her briefcase only to feel another tendril snag on a vine. Stooped over as she was, she craned her head and peeked up through the stately pine trees. Tyler had been right. The sky was turning gray. Probably the same putrid shade that currently adorned her face. She swung her gaze back to the snake, daring him not to inch closer.

What was that silly poem about snakes? Something to do with red and yellow, red and black. Like the evasive capitol of Connecticut, she never could get it straight.

The deafening cannonade of her heartbeat pounded so loud as if the "1812 Overture" boomed in her head, making it difficult to think. Somehow, over the din, decoding the poem became immaterial. This snake had brownish-gray markings with large black dots on it, and since she hadn't the faintest idea whether it was poisonous, she'd treat it as an enemy.

"Scat, go. Shoo, snake, shoo," she urged the hissing snake to no avail.

It continued to stare back at her, its sliver of a tongue in perpetual motion. For an eternally long heartbeat, her brown eyes meshed with small beady ones. The snake went utterly still. Good grief, had she so mastered her flirting technique that she'd actually made a conquest and charmed this slimy creature?

"Tyler, help," she called out again with an ear piercing scream.

Where was her pilot-in-shining-armor when she needed him?

She eyed her portfolio and wondered if she could slip out her umbrella without antagonizing her admirer. If he slithered any closer, she might be able to scare him off with it. A twig snapped, and every nerve in her body froze.

"Tyler?" Her voice barely audible, she felt every hair on the back of her neck stand up. "Please tell me it's you."

"In person."

Startled as he pushed through the thicket in front of her, she jumped as far as the blackberry vine would allow. A glorious sight, he pushed through the tangled web of bushes, his muscular jean-clad legs standing before her. Unfortunately, trapped as she was, her gaze couldn't travel any higher than his belt, but the view had its compensations.

"Don't tell me. You're studying the flora and fauna," he

quipped, a trace of humor mingling with the impatience in his voice.

"Not exactly. Uh... I wouldn't move if I were you. There's a snake," she whispered, pointing a shaky finger at the creature.

"Why are we whispering?"

"Because I don't want to disturb him."

Tyler eased behind her and peered over her shoulder. "Lucky for us he's just a hog-nosed snake. I don't think we have to whisper," he answered in hushed tones. "He's harmless."

"Y-you sure?"

"Yes, ma'am. Scout's honor, unless you're a toad."

"But he's been following me."

"Snakes don't follow people."

"This one does."

"Yeah, well I have a piece of advice for him. If he's smart, he'll slither away as fast as he can. Teaming up with you could be hazardous to his health." Tyler stomped his foot on the twigs and leaves just inches from the snake. The snake hissed and puffed up in size. A second later Tyler touched it with a stick, and the slimy creature rolled onto its back.

"Will you look at that?" She stared, amazed. Exposing his underbelly, the snake lay as still as midnight—so lifeless she could have trailed her finger down his tummy had she desired.

"Yeah, he's just a pussy-cat, all hiss and no bite. If he can't huff and puff and scare you into believing his act, he rolls over and plays dead." Tyler placed his hands on her hips. "C'mon Red, let's make tracks for the shack I found."

"I can't."

"Whatta you mean you can't?"

"My hair's stuck and I can't move." After being crushed by the wig and caught on the bushes, she imagined it resembled a rat's nest.

"Why doesn't that surprise me?" A smoky-like chuckle sounded from his throat as he pulled on the vine. "It's not just your hair, your earring's snagged, too."

Bending even closer, Tyler pressed his chest and hips to curve over her back. As she visualized how he hovered over her, every nerve hummed.

"Looks like I'll have to break off this vine. It may pull your scalp."

"Whatever. I can't stay bent over like this the rest of my life."

"Not so sure I can either, though I wouldn't mind considering it."

Glory hallelujah! Neither would she. A virgin by choice, she'd fought many an inner battle to remain so, but no one had triggered her hormones like Tyler. Did the man have any earthly idea how he affected her?

"Ready to get free?"

She nodded and braced herself. It hurt for a second. A remnant of the vine snarled with her hair and fell across her forehead.

"Look at it this way, Red. The snake did us a favor. If not for him, we wouldn't have found these berries. We can gather them up and eat them later." He plucked a couple and popped one into his mouth. "Want one."

She tried to shake her head, but couldn't. "I'm still stuck."

"Your earring. Let me see if I can undo it."

He leaned closer, his breath fanning her ear. It tickled. She tried to suppress a giggle and failed.

"Gotta be still. I'm all thumbs with these contraptions."

Still? With him draped over her? Impossible. Each breath he exhaled tickled, and his nearness turned her to a quivering mass. Pure torture. She couldn't help twisting and squirming. Her movements brought her derriere in contact with his hardening groin. She tensed, discretion urging her to put some space between them. "You're tickling me."

"Can't compare to what you're doing to me."

"What?"

"Aw hell, I dropped your earring."

"That's okay." Who cared a twit about an earring at a time like this?

Tyler felt the unsteady rhythm of her breathing and released a shaky breath of his own. He leaned down and pressed his torso into her back, becoming increasingly aware of her body heat. He stretched his arms to the ground. "I can't feel it," he said, lowering his mouth to her hair. He tunneled his hand through the underbrush. "Ouch!"

"What?" She stiffened. "A spider? A scorpion? Another snake?"

"Damned prickly thorns."

"I told you the earring's not important."

"You sure?" He cocked an eyebrow and tried to straighten.

"Ouch." She flinched as he yanked her head upward. Wayward strands of hair flew wildly around her face. "Don't move," she implored, pulling him down so he no longer stood erect. "I think my hair's caught on your shirt button. Can you untangle it?"

"Don't know." Still bent over, he took a step back to assess the problem and heard her groan again. "Not good, huh?"

Upset that he'd unintentionally hurt her, he remained still, unprepared for the rush of concern that swamped him. It was hard to remain objective about Red. More like impossible. And dealing with her was difficult enough without her mishaps. By the time he got one solved, another tumbled along. But something had to be done. Knots of tension coiled in his stomach from prolonged contact with her—knots aching for release. Earlier when he'd leaned over her luscious backside, he thought he'd been about to turn blue.

Tyler considered his options. "I can't back away enough to get a good look, but I think you're right. Your hair's snagged. It's the top button. Can you move your head so I can see?"

"Can't."

"Nothing else to do but try and slip my fingers in and fiddle with it." He speared his fingers into her hair.

"Ouch."

She flinched at every move he made. "Sorry." He gave her upper arm a gentle squeeze. "It might help if we hobbled away from this blackberry patch. Want to see if we can move in sync?"

"Okay."

With his knees levered, he stepped backwards, weaving his way through the brambles. She had no choice but to follow him, the back of her head plastered to his chest as if it were an appendage of his body. Neither of them could stand upright.

"This is all my fault," she announced.

No argument there.

"It's the perm."

"Perm?"

"The perm I had just before my cousin's wedding. If I hadn't had it, my hair wouldn't be so frizzy and catch on everything."

Considering the source of this pearl of wisdom, it sounded ballpark reasonable to him.

"I'm getting a crick in my neck," she informed him.

Speaking of cricks, much like the one he'd experienced in the airport, he had a tightness of his own to deal with developing in a far lower region of his body. He curled his fingers into his palm. Ah hell, massages were his specialty. At least one of them might as well get some relief. Parting her curly strands, he gently caressed the back of her neck.

"Mmm..."

Their only points of contact were his fingers on her neck and her head pressed against his pounding chest, but her purring approval, combined with the creamy smoothness of her skin, did little for his control. He should never have started this. A man had his limits. Hell, how had they gotten into this mess anyway? Maybe Dawson had the right idea after all when he tied her up. He shuddered to think of the trouble she might have caused let loose on the plane.

Tyler noticed the darkening shadows. They needed to get to the cabin, and at the rate they'd gone the past few minutes, it'd be tomorrow before they got there. Was nothing ever simple with this provocative temptress? Good thing they were out in the middle of nowhere. Had anyone observed their combined contortions the past few minutes, they'd think them idiots. Bent over as he was, he dropped his gaze to her slender neck, and his lips twitched as he felt her tremble.

Tremble?

No! Giggling! At what? A fever blazed inside him while she was on a laughing jag. It stung his pride. "Red?"

"Mmm...?"

"You all right?" *Foolish question.*

"I think so." Her faint voice was tinged with uncertainty. "I was wondering if we'd have to spend the next few days stuck together like this, and then I began to see the humor. Don't you?"

"Yeah, I suppose." Yeah, she was right. Only a curmudgeon could stay angry with her. Quiet laughter rolled through him, and he joined her chuckles.

"Know what this reminds me of?"

He had no idea, but whatever it was, it had to be choice. "Can't say I do."

"A fairy tale my parents used to read me. The one where there was a goose or something and a boy touched it and was stuck to it. Then an old lady came along and touched the boy and she was stuck to him, then an old man became stuck to the lady and on and on until there was a whole chain of people glued together."

He could think of a couple of places he'd much rather be stuck to her than her hair. "Yeah, well, as amusing as that sounds, this isn't going to work. We can't stay hitched like this forever." Though there was something to be said for knowing exactly where she was at all times. He tried to slip his hand into his pocket, but unable to reach it, he straightened.

She screamed. "Don't do that. My scalp."

"Sorry," he mumbled again, buckling his knees to accommodate her. "Don't think I can get my penknife out of my pocket as long as I'm bent over like this. See if you can slip your hand into my right pocket and reach it."

In slow motion he watched Regina reach behind her and search for his pocket. Her first shaky stab brought her in contact with his butt. As her fingers continued to explore past the curve of his hip to his upper thigh, Tyler held his breath. Heat sluiced through his veins. Another few seconds and he'd be seeing stars. Blue ones.

She found the flap to his pocket and slid her hand in. "I think I've got it."

"You got it, Baby, and pinched me in the process."

"Couldn't help it, your jeans are tight."

"Yeah, well, they're even tighter now." His loin muscles were about to burst. "See if you can ease the penknife out."

She threaded her hand in further and tugged.

"Dig any deeper and you're gonna find more than my penknife."

"I... uh... think I did."

"I think you did, too."

"N-No, I-I... mean I found the knife."

Desire permeated his senses, and from her stammered words it was pretty clear he wasn't the only one aroused. "Take it out easy-like, hear?" he cautioned in a deep, raspy voice.

She nodded, the back of her head bobbing under his chin. "Oops."

"Oops, what?"

"It fell."

He swallowed thickly. Her hand no longer flirted with his manhood, but it took a second or two for the tension in his body to regroup. He willed his voice to sound normal. "Guess we're both butterfingers from the crash, and being taken hostage, and all."

He paused, his words triggering a theory he'd had only minutes ago about Red's hands being tied. The idea was beginning to have more and more appeal. Self-preservation and sanity, he supposed. "Tell me something. I can understand why they tied me up, or at least I think I can, but why do you suppose they tied you?"

As she shrugged her shoulders, they rubbed against his chest. "I've wondered about that myself, especially after doing them a favor."

"Favor?" *And just what kind of favor was that?* Speaking of favors, he'd better do himself one and soon, before he lost control. He settled his hands on her shoulders. "New strategy. Suppose we both get down on our knees, and maybe I can find the damn thing. Ready? On the count of three, we kneel. One, two, three, on your knees, Woman." Tyler grinned. He'd always fantasized about saying that.

Regina smiled, responding to the cajoling softness in Tyler's voice. In unison they fell to the ground. It looked to Regina as if they were praying. The family who prays together, stays together. How did that idea pop into her head? *Family and Tyler?* She pulled her scattered thoughts together. The emotional tension of the past few minutes had turned her into a basket case.

"I got it," Tyler shouted. "Hold your horses, and I'll have us untethered in a second." He slipped the knife between them. "Hold onto your hair at your scalp. I'm going to have to saw through the strands and it may hurt."

It did, but it was over in a second. Tyler whirled her around on her knees to face him. "Ever try out this technique in your practice sessions?" He skimmed his knuckles along her chin. "It's one of my favorites."

His breath grazed her cheeks. She tilted her head up to his. Barely three inches separated them. As they stared at each other, the gleam in his eyes revealed a rapidly improving disposition. "Thanks for rescuing me."

"My pleasure. I owed you."

Two inches apart now. Close enough to notice a tiny scar near his left eyebrow and the bruises on his face from his fight. Feeling responsible for his battered condition, she tentatively lifted her hand, but his sloe-eyed stare stopped her. His lips parted. A smile teased the corner of his mouth, the kind of smile that suggested slow music and dim lights.

Her gaze remained meshed with his—locked onto to him like radar. His gaze surrounded, suffocated, pulled her toward him.

"Are we practicing?" she managed to ask, her breath constricted.

"Think so."

Funny. This wasn't the kind of practice she'd had in mind. She thought flirting had more to do with foreplay from a distance and less to do with contact. Slowly, deliberately, his mouth angled over hers. Their lips had touched before and each time the touch sent her reeling. She opened her mouth and he seized the chance, the tip of his tongue probing into her mouth. The heat of his kiss traveled to every cell in her body. What was it about Tyler that so affected her? She'd only known him for a few hours, yet she felt more emotionally in tune with him than any man she'd been involved with. Shyness certainly didn't seem to be a problem where he was concerned.

Karma.

Aunt Della would call it karma.

His kisses were addictive—a habit she'd developed a taste for in a very short time. Losing her balance, she clutched at his shirt. Tyler gave a soft moan and lifted his head. Wrinkles creased the skin beside his surprise-filled eyes. His fingers played at her cheekbone. As they wended their way to her lips, they branded her skin. He brushed her mouth with the pads of his fingers, and a riot of tingles spiraled down her spine. He seemed so in control while she was melting.

Like Aunt Della's marmalade on a hot summer day.

"Better not linger," he said, his voice slightly hoarse as he cupped her chin. "We need to beat this storm, collect dry twigs for a fire, and I'd just as soon be far away before our pilot comes to. No sense in advertising to him which direction we headed."

She still couldn't speak. Wasn't sure she could move, either. He'd done it again—radiated iron control while she was swamped by a rush of sensations she was totally unprepared for. Holding out his hand, he pulled her to her feet. "Looks like your friend is gone."

"F-friend?" She tried to sound unaffected.

"Your snake."

"Oh." Something snapped in her mind. "Oh, I need to go back to the plane."

"Back where?"

"The plane. It's vital."

He blocked her path. "If it's a restroom you need, there's plenty of forest and I'll give you privacy."

"No." Though there was that. Mother Nature's subtle call had already made itself known. "I left something."

"That so?" His keen, brown eyes narrowed.

"A package," she explained. "A birthday present." And a lie. Even she was smart enough to know there was something fishy about that present.

He braced himself negligently against a tree trunk, his gaze raking over her. "Package, you say?"

"Yes, on the plane."

"Don't bother. I found it."

"You did!"

"Yeah. It's in the backpack." She detected a sharpness in his voice. "We'll talk about it at that cabin I found, okay?" He held out his hand.

Curiosity tugged and she hesitated. *Talk about it?* Something didn't compute. Why would Tyler have helped himself to a package wrapped in birthday paper? It had to mean he knew something was fishy about the package, too. Up till now she'd felt reasonably safe with him. Heck, she'd even regretted involving him in this mess. Now, she wasn't sure. Perhaps it was time to start thinking like Aunt Ruth.

Could be she was dealing with an altogether different kind of snake.

Regina brushed some thorns from her legs, picked up her briefcase, then slipped the strap over her shoulder. Since Tyler was so all fired up about practicing, she'd indulge him, her way, not his. She'd employ her flirting techniques. Maybe then she'd get some answers.

Then again, she could be flirting with danger.

Chapter Six

Tyler shifted the backpack.

Huffing and puffing in the thin alpine air, his star smuggler trudged behind. He could hear her. So could all the animals and birds. Everyone within three miles could hear her. Gladys Girl Scout, she wasn't. Ah well, she had other attributes, and at least she hadn't gone off on her own.

Jeeze, he felt like a grouch.

But she had the ability to put his emotions in turmoil. He'd been through the gamut since meeting up with her. He'd barely gotten over the nightmare of the crash when he'd had to deal with his suspicions about her. She knew Dawson's name, and she seemed so concerned for the guy's welfare. What was she, some namby-pamby hooker with a heart, not to mention a ying-yang with one or two loose screws?

And to top it off, she'd wanted to go back for the package. That had sealed his foul mood. She had to know about the diamonds.

She was something though, scared of airplanes and snakes, but not men. He'd never seen a woman so ready and willing to kiss. Once he got her softened up with some practice sessions, he should be able to ply information from her, but something inside him didn't want her to be involved.

Pipe dream though it might be, he wanted her innocent, the innocent dupe of these smugglers.

Trouble was he liked her too much. Liked her spunk and zany personality. Her contradictions fascinated him. She was so utterly different from any woman he'd known. And she'd come to his aid. He just couldn't figure out why. No more than he was able to take his gaze from her. He winced, a twinge of pain lingered above his right brow. Of course, he could easily chalk up his irrational thoughts to all the blows he'd taken to his head.

Several feet ahead, Tyler shuffled to a halt, and Regina expelled the longest sigh of her life. They'd finally made it to the cabin. She'd begun to wonder about its existence. Actually, it probably hadn't been all that far from the plane or Tyler would never have found it, but her feet felt like they'd trekked for miles. They were minutes from staging a rebellion. She was hungry, thirsty, footsore, plain tuckered out, and still coming to grips with her traumatic day.

Studying the dilapidated shack, she doubted it held many comforts of home, but it was shelter, and she thanked whatever guardian angel had led them here. Still, a bath, even a shower in an invigorating mountain waterfall, would be nice. Maybe Tyler knew if a stream was nearby.

"This is our motel for the night," he announced from behind her. "Not much, but it comes with a view."

Caught in her thoughts, she swung around and surveyed the valley, hundreds and hundreds of feet below. A hawk soared and dipped in the distance. As the clouds enveloped the mountain crests, she could almost see the mist roll in.

"Wow," she gushed. "It's beautiful."

"Takes your breath away. The Smokies are the crown jewels of the Appalachians. Always wanted to hike that trail from Georgia to Maine."

"Georgia to Maine. You realize that's triple A?"

"Say what?"

"Both their capitols start with an A, and the Appalachian Trail runs between them. Aunt Della would find that significant."

"Yeah, right." He rolled his eyes, making it clear he thought her crazy.

Well, it made perfect sense to her. Ever since she'd battled her terror in the plane by reciting the state capitols, she'd been frustrated by her failure to remember the capitol of Connecticut. Usually by now it popped back—

"I'll tell you what's significant," Tyler stated, breaking into her train of thought and stressing his last word, "the approaching rain and nightfall." He checked the low-hung clouds. "We need to shake a leg and gather as many twigs as we can for firewood."

Regina peered through the open door of the log cabin. A yeasty odor wafted from inside. "What is this place anyway?"

"With that stream nearby and from the looks of the cabin I'd say this served as a lookout for a still. I'm betting the stillhouse isn't far away."

"Stillhouse. You mean—"

"Yup. Someone used to brew moonshine here."

"Think that someone might pay this place a visit?"

"Not likely," he said, dashing her hopes. "Looks like it's been abandoned for years. What we have here is a one room shack where they watched for trespassers while they waited for the corn to ferment."

Tyler dumped his backpack on the floor of the cabin, then marched out the door, gathering small logs and carrying them back. Regina followed suit. She'd always liked to do her share, and watching his muscles ripple beneath his shirt as he grappled with the logs was a bonus. On her second foray she stooped to gather some twigs and froze. Her side vision caught movement.

Her snake was back.

At least he looked like the one she'd encountered earlier.

"Tyler, look, it's our snake."

"*Our* snake?"

"All right, my snake."

Tyler trudged over to where she stood and looked down at the verdant underbrush.

"You'll have to admit he looks the same," she said.

"He's a match but it's not likely he's the very same one."

Ignoring Tyler's disparaging remark, she stared at the creature. By George, she'd recognize those beady eyes anywhere. If he wasn't the same one, then Columbus wasn't the capitol of Ohio. Apparently, she'd made a conquest. "What did you call him?"

"Hog-nosed."

"Hoggy, that's what I'll name him. You did say he's harmless?"

"Yes, Ma'am."

"Good." Bonding with snakes wasn't exactly her thing, but the snake had chosen her, not she him. And she was banking on the fact that Tyler was right, that Hoggy was harmless. "Hi there, Hoggy," she crooned, bending down, yet keeping a respectful distance.

It hissed and puffed up.

"No one's going to hurt you, but get this straight, the cabin's off limits. You stay outside."

It was then that Regina noticed Tyler had wandered out of sight. Carrying another armload of kindling into the cabin and depositing it on the hearth, she decided to take advantage of his absence. She made a beeline for his backpack and fished through it, pushing aside food packets, batteries, camping gear, and the hammer and wrench. She continued her search, coming to the conclusion the only item in the sack that didn't make sense was a jar of marbles.

Marbles?

Could that have been the birthday present? Why had Tyler torn off the paper and stashed the jar in the backpack?

Because, Dummy, he didn't want Dawson to find it, if and when the man managed to free himself. Dawson had taken it from her briefcase, but then the package had been destined for him. Could Tyler have been following Dawson? She shook her head. No, if he'd been following anyone it had to have been Foster.

She wiggled her nose.

All that nonsense about accompanying her to the private plane terminal had been nothing but a farce. Tyler had latched onto her the moment she'd approached him, not out of any good deed, but because of the package.

She was dealing with a bunch of crooks.

The only problem was determining the good guys from the bad. Then again, they all might be scoundrels. She tended to give Tyler the nod towards being a good guy. Nothing in her system wanted to look on him as an enemy, especially her hormones. But then again, he could be bad. Could be a case of gang warfare, and she'd been caught in the middle.

You don't really believe that, an inner voice whispered.

"I..."

Without him you wouldn't be here in one piece.

"But..." She just didn't know.

She walked to the window and held the jar up to what little daylight remained. The setting sun appeared from below the bank of clouds, its rays glistening off the jar and sending fireflies dancing against the wall. Didn't look like anything but a bunch of marbles to her.

She flinched, positive she'd heard a sound. Tyler coming back no doubt. Before he could catch her red-handed, she dashed across the room and tucked the jar into her briefcase. Too obvious. She ran back to the canvas pack, flicked on the flashlight, and swung it around the dark room, catching spider webs in its rays.

Loverly, she grimaced.

Then spying a collection of empty whiskey bottles piled in the corner, she retrieved the jar and hid it among the bottles.

A flash of light caught Tyler's eye, and a niggling sensation in his shoulder told him Red was up to something. Taking care not to make a sound, he crept to the window. The sight did little to bolster his mood. Dammit, she'd lifted the jar from his backpack. As she swung the light around the room, it looked to him as if she sought a hiding place.

The corner, huh?

Dammit all.

She had to be guilty.

Knowing he was too emotionally involved, he kicked the door open with his boot.

"Tyler!"

"Yeah." He stalked into the room not at all happy with his train of thought. "This should be plenty of firewood," he announced, dumping his load onto the hearth.

"How long do you think we'll be here?"

"Just tonight I hope." Good recovery, Red, slipping into a diversionary conversation right away, but he'd heard the catch in her voice. After all, he'd been trained to detect nuances in people's voices, as well as nervous gestures that gave them away.

"I'm sure Dawson filed a flight plan, and people will be scrambling once they learn the plane is missing." Including the crooks, he supposed. He'd just have to hope Jake and the agency beat them to it. "Tomorrow morning we'll use some of these dry twigs to start a controlled fire near the plane, even though Dawson might still be there. It should attract attention. If nothing else, it might alert a ranger or someone who lives in the area."

As he moved to his pack, he saw Red tremble. Two could play this game. Taking his time, he made a big to-do out of digging through the canvas bag then dug out some beef jerky and a package of trail mix.

"How 'bout food? Do we have enough?" she asked.

"Enough for a couple of days if we're careful. We can pick more berries, and I might get lucky and trap a rabbit or a squirrel. If no one shows up after two days we'll hike down.

Bound to run across someone. It isn't as if the Smokies are as uninhabited as the mountains out west."

He rummaged in the sack for his matches. Tension shimmered in her eyes. She might be good at some things, but deception wasn't one of them. He knelt before the fireplace. "Tell you what. I'm gonna start a fire and chase out any critters that might be sharing this place with us." She flinched this time. Just when it looked like she was going to relax, he hunted through the backpack again and waited for her reaction. "Something wrong?"

"N-no. Not at all." Those big, wary eyes were a dead giveaway. Guilt shadowed her face. She knew damn well any second he was about to discover the jar was missing.

He pulled out the canteen. "Since there's no indoor plumbing, you'll probably need a little privacy in the woods. While you're there, you could make yourself useful by topping off this canteen with fresh water from the stream."

"By myself? O-out there?"

"I'll be right here in the doorway."

Her shaky voice almost did him in, not to mention the uncertainty that graced her eyes. He wasn't made of stone, but it wasn't as if he hadn't just checked the area either. The stream lay only a few feet from the cabin. Besides, he had business of his own to conduct while she was gone. Refusing to be swayed, he stood his ground. "Holler if you need me. Stream's over to your left. Best go now before it's pitch dark."

"Yes." She took the canteen, a hesitant smile on her lips.

Tyler tracked her with his eyes, admiring the sway of her pert, little bottom, then satisfied she was headed in the right direction, he swung into action. In two shakes he crossed the room, seized the jar, and looked for a suitable hiding place.

Her briefcase?

Risky, but probably the last place she'd think to look once she discovered her precious jar of marbles no longer lay hidden behind the whiskey bottles. By the time he got the fire started and posted himself back at the door, he saw her come into view. Damn, there was a hole in the pit of his stomach. He'd been hoping she wasn't involved.

Red met his searching gaze as she shoved the canteen into his hands and brushed past him. He admired her newfound composure and resiliency. Must have given herself a talking to while she'd been gone. He set the flashlight on the floor so it aimed on the backpack. She made a big pretense of walking around the room as if examining it, but he knew better. *Looking for the jar, aren't you, Red?*

"So far so good," he announced, squatting down on the floor and placing the canteen to his side. "You'll be pleased to know there're no critters in the cabin. Chow time."

She angled her legs beneath her and sat down across from him, tugging on her skirt as if its immodest length embarrassed her. Gawking at her legs clear up to her thighs, he found it hard to remember she was his adversary, harder yet to keep the anatomy below his belt from directing his thoughts. What harm would it do to let her think she had the upper hand.

He poured a measure of trail mix into her cupped hands. "All we have is beef Jerky and trail mix."

"There's a chocolate bar in my briefcase. We could share it for dessert."

Hells bells, he'd outsmarted himself. "Great," he muttered as rich invectives teased his tongue. She started to bounce to her knees. His hand lunged out and settled on her shoulder. "Suppose we wait till later. We're gonna have to ration our food." Accepting his premise, she sat back on the floor. Tyler poured some trail mix into his hand and lifted it to his mouth.

"Wait, no." Red snaked her fingers around his wrist. Trail mix flew from his hand and spilled onto the floor.

Irritation flashed through him. He shook off her grasp. "Dammit, the food's spilled. We can't afford to waste it."

"You're right. My mistake."

Biting back the urge to lay into a stream of curses, he scrambled to his knees and began scooping the food together. Dirt-covered or not, they might be grateful for these few fallen scraps.

"Let me do that," she said, carefully replacing her allotment of food back in the plastic bag.

"No need."

"I insist. It was my fault."

Tyler grunted. Before he could object, his over-zealous helpmate scooted onto her knees. A second later their heads collided.

"Ow!" Tyler fell onto his butt with a force that surprised him.

Her startled expression was the last thing he saw before

black and blue stars invaded his eyes. Jeeze, a five-foot-four inch female with a head like a cement truck had nearly zonked him unconscious. He shook his head, a trickle of laughter floating up from his throat.

"Oh my gosh, are you okay? I didn't mean—"

"Yeah, I know," he said with a touch of melodramatic sarcasm. "You never do." The black and blue stars faded to green. "Things just happen when you're around."

"Not usually. Most of the time things are routine, orderly, and predictable."

Not believing a word, he gave her the best wounded martyr look he could muster, flashed it at both her visages as he blinked away his double vision. He'd bet the entire state of Ohio that there'd never been a predictable moment in her life. He sat there and brought her into focus, breathing a sigh of relief there was only one of her. Two would be more than anyone should be required to handle.

She inched closer on her knees, and for a split second, out of sheer self-preservation, he seriously considered backing away, but discarded the idea when her fingers gently probed his forehead. His breath quickened. Brushing specks of soot from his shirtsleeves, he dared not connect with her gaze. Hunger crawled in his belly, but her touch reminded him of his desire.

Her gentle finger strokes stirred his frustration. A frustration that had been building since he'd laid eyes on her. No, as he imagined those dewy eyes of hers trained on his head, he dared not look. He couldn't be responsible for his actions if he did, not with her lush body so close and his libido overheating.

Not trusting her, he cursed. Then not trusting his own control, he swore again.

"You've a hard head," she said, combing her fingers through his hair and examining his skull.

"So I've been told. Hard-headed Novak." His mother had called him that often. His sister still did. "Did I hurt you?"

"No. I've got a tough skull, too. How 'bout you? You okay?"

"Tip-top," he answered, his voice a ragged mishmash of suppressed frustration.

He wondered if Red had a remote sense of how much he wanted her. Reprieve came when she lifted her hand from his burning skin and redirected her attention to gathering the scraps of food. And with the reprieve, his sharp edge of desire eased and a measure of control returned. He risked a glance, watching her graceful fingers collect the crumbs. Why had she'd grabbed his hand in the first place? Did she think the food was spoiled?

There probably was a very illogical reason for her actions and he probably was a fool to ask, but he'd bite the bullet and give it a try. "What the hell kind of stunt were you trying to pull? Why'd you snatch my hand? If you're concerned about the trail mix, it looks perfectly edible to me."

"It wasn't that," she said, meticulously gathering the last bit of food from the floor, its retrieval seeming to garner her full attention.

"Then what the hell was it?"

"It isn't as if I do this before every meal." Growing hungrier by the second, he watched in fascination as she tilted her head and looked askance. "I know I should, but I don't."

With Red, *don't* could mean anything. He waited to see where her conversation would lead this time.

"But after what we've been through today we should... that is if it wouldn't offend you, I'd like to say grace."

"The blessing?" *From a hooker?*

"Yes. I can do it silently if you prefer." She steepled her hands.

"By all means, bless away."

Gullible he wasn't. Sincerity spilled from her lips and oozed from her eyes. Zounds, he'd stumbled across a hooker who was a religious fanatic. How did she justify her profession?

Low shot, Novak.

His job had brought him in contact with a number of hookers, many whom he'd stack against pious zealots any day. As her eyelids fluttered shut, childhood memories invaded his thoughts. His parents had always given a blessing at their evening meal. Respectfully, he bowed his head and remained quiet while she gave thanks for their food, such as it was, their survival, a host of her relatives, and lastly much to his astonishment, himself.

At her conclusion he tentatively lifted another handful of trail mix to his mouth, then halted. He raised his head and an eyebrow as well. "Safe to eat now?" She nodded, her lips twisting into that pixie smile he'd come to associate with her. This was a day for the books. He shrugged, studying his companion. More to the point, Red was one for the books.

Chewing on a handful of trail mix, she remarked, "It's kinda bland and dry."

"Trick is to eat slow and drink lots of water. It'll fill you up. Then pretend you're eating something you like." He broke off a piece of jerky. "Like right now. I'm eating pepperoni off a pizza."

"I'll trade you."

"Whatta you got?"

"A spoonful of lasagna for your pepperoni."

"Sounds fair." He broke off another piece and handed it to her. She scooped some trail mix from her hand to his. "Good lasagna." He smacked his lips. "Spicy."

"My mother's recipe."

"No kidding. You cook?"

"A little. I'm still in the toss-up stage."

"Toss up?"

"It's fifty-fifty whether it comes out or not, and when it doesn't, it's for sure someone in my family is going to toss it up."

That he didn't doubt for a second.

She nibbled on more trail mix, then washed it down with a sip from the canteen. He watched a drop of water trickle across her lips and the tip of her tongue dart out to catch it. Every time she licked her lips, it drove him crazy, made him want to taste her mouth again. "More pepperoni?" he asked over the frog that had suddenly materialized in his throat.

She nodded. "I've been thinking if I succeed in what I'm doing now, it might come in handy to take cooking lessons."

"Handy?"

"You know. The way to a man's heart is through his stomach."

He'd make it a bit lower.

"It would certainly add to my skills and be a way to satisfy him," she added.

"Him? Him, who?"

"The man of my dreams."

He noticed her brown eyes sparkle with conviction. Damn, but she looked sincere. Sounded it, too. Maybe she hoped to latch onto a sugar daddy and settle in for a long relationship. He had to give her credit. At the least she was looking out for her future. And for the immediate future he'd have to come up with a damn good reason to reach into her briefcase before she went looking for that candy bar and discovered what a numskull he'd been.

"What's that?" she asked out of the blue.

"What's what?"

"That noise." A frown pulled at her brow. "Hear it?"

He tilted his head and concentrated. "You mean the honks? Probably a bear."

"I knew it. I knew they'd be here."

"Unless you mess with their cubs or they're hungry, they won't bother us."

"Hope you're right." She angled her head. "It's started to rain, too."

"You've damn good hearing." He stared at the ceiling and tuned into the lazy cadence of raindrops on the roof. "Guess I'd better make a trip outside before it starts to pour." He tugged the backpack to his side and began to fish through it, watching Red hold her breath again. "There's another flashlight in here."

"I'll find it for you," she offered, nearly knocking him off his keester as she crawled by him and stuffed her hand into the sack.

"Thanks." He couldn't stop the grin on his face. She was expending a lot of energy to keep him from discovering the jar wasn't in the backpack. He took the flashlight, then rose and walked across the room, his hand poised on the doorknob.

"Tyler, wait." He winced as her alarm-packed command filled the room with urgency. "It's already pouring buckets. Take my umbrella."

"Naw, I'm not an umbrella man." The thought of holding the flashlight in one hand and a hot pink umbrella in his other while... It wasn't an image he cared to cultivate.

"But you'll get soaked."

Like he'd noticed before, she had a penchant for mothering people. She scrambled to her feet and moved in the direction of her briefcase. Panic crept up his spine.

Ah hell, she'd outmaneuvered him again.

Suddenly developing a fetish for umbrellas, he spun on his heels, set down the flashlight, and in record time raced across the room. She had a head start, but his legs were more powerful. Simultaneously, their hands lay claim to the briefcase.

He yanked it from her. "On second thought it's a good idea." Her brown eyes narrowed as she watched him rummage through the case. "A great idea," he repeated. He turned his back on her, shielding her view as his fingers surrounded their target. "No need for you to fetch it. I'll get it myself."

She reached around his waist, and as much as he hated to, he fended her off with a delicate shove and lifted the umbrella high in the air like a prized trophy. A fierce rush of relief washed over him. He tossed the briefcase onto the moth-eaten mattress that lay on the floor across the room. Her arm still remained extended, and he twirled around, gallantly raising her hand to his lips. They'd dally later, he promised himself.

After they talked.

About the marbles.

"Thanks, Red, the umbrella's a capital idea." That ought to please her, seeing as she seemed preoccupied with capitols. "I won't be long and then we can—"

"Practice?"

"Yeah."

"Good," she said, a tinge of uncertainty coloring her voice.

And maybe not so good, she whispered to herself as Tyler strode out the cabin, a string of earthy epithets spilling from his mouth. She quickly walked to the corner of the room and flashed the light over the bottles.

The jar was gone!

Her hand shot to her heart at the implications. As sure as shootin' Hoggy wasn't responsible, and she didn't believe in ghosts, at least she thought she didn't. Ghosts were Aunt Della's department. Slowly, she prowled around the room, contemplating where Tyler might have hidden it. She eyed her briefcase. Suspiciously.

No, too obvious.

And yet.

Hadn't he almost had a cow when she'd started to search for the umbrella? Jutting out her chin, she marched to the mattress and fell to her knees. A triumphant grin curved her lips when her fingers grasped the cold, glass jar.

She could hide it again or—

Leave it, Regina.

Yes, that's what she'd do. She'd let him think it was still safely hidden. She balled her hand into a fist. And she'd hide her anger and disappointment, too.

Chapter Seven

The hot pink umbrella sat open in all its glory, close to the fire, drying. He was damn glad there'd been no one around to see him. He'd never live it down. Actually, Mother Regina had done him a favor. The blasted umbrella had kept him dry. The rain came down hard now, a veritable torrent slashing against the window and roof, and Little Miss Conniver sat by the hearth, looking like the cat who'd swallowed the canary. He didn't like the look, not at all. First chance he got, he'd check her briefcase. She'd had plenty of time to hunt through it and discover the marbles, plenty of time to stash them somewhere else while he'd been gone.

Too damn much time.

And it was past time to get her talking about something that made sense for a change. He slid his tired frame into the rickety chair, stretched his legs in front of him, and clasped his hands behind his neck. "Place has all the comforts of home," he idly commented.

"I guess." Regina managed an unenthusiastic nod.

"Look at it this way, it beats the hell out of sitting in front of the television and watching the Reds lose."

"You a Reds fan? Me, too."

"Figures." Smiling, he shook his head. Fitting that she should be a Reds fan. "Tell me something, why the wig?"

Regina patted her tangled curls. "You know."

"I do?"

"Yes, you said you understood."

Understood? His memory zoomed backwards. "Oh yeah, our conversation in the airport."

"I used it so no one would recognize me."

"I see." He wished the hell he did, but he'd go with the flow. "You wanted to be incognito."

"Exactly. I didn't want to run into anyone I knew."

"Naturally." Any self respecting hooker who was tangled up with diamond smugglers would want to avoid people who knew her, especially the law.

"And it gave me confidence."

"Excuse me?"

"The wig. It gave me confidence."

"Because it was your first time."

"Exactly."

"Exactly," he echoed. Lord help him, they were going around in circles.

"And now we're trapped in the forest."

"The Smokies."

"Yes." She crossed her arms over her chest.

Had he imagined it or did her voice betray an edginess?

"And as there's no one here but you, I guess there isn't any need for my wig."

"I volunteered to help you practice, remember?"

"I remember."

She trained those lush lashes and innocent eyes on him and smiled. He couldn't resist smiling back. She had a magical way of getting him to do that repeatedly.

"Next weekend," she said, pausing to sigh, "that is if we ever get out of here, I was going to try the mall."

Tyler did a double take. Now there was a picture. Red plying her trade at the mall. "You think that's a good idea?"

"Yes. Why? Don't you? You're frowning."

"It's just—"

"Just what?"

"There's families and kids to consider, and there's a lot of security at the mall. They might—"

"Send me on my way."

"Exactly." More like arrest her. No doubt about it, Red was two ticks from being loco.

"I hadn't thought of that." She glanced at the fire as if pondering his words, her eyes widening a second later. "I kinda liked the idea of having security around."

"You did?" He'd been wrong. One tick. He pondered an answer. "I suppose it's the challenge."

"Challenge?"

"Well, you know."

"I'm not sure I do. Personally, their presence reassures me."

Jeeze, Louise. He gestured, not sure what to say. "Well, there you go. Reassurance. Never leave home without it."

"You don't seem to have any trouble in that department."

He furrowed his brow, almost afraid to answer, having no earthly idea what she meant. "How's that?"

"Hooking up with a woman. I know you said you've never done it, but you seem so natural, so at ease doing it."

Far be it for him to admit he didn't. No red-blooded man would. Actually though, if he were honest, there had been times when he'd gone long spells without female companionship. Out of choice of course.

"Earth to Tyler. Did I lose you?"

Hours ago, Red. Hours ago. "Not at all," he lied. "And you're right. I ... uh ... as for getting along with women, I give it my best shot."

"It's reassurance, confidence, and the right technique."

"Especially technique." He was ready for her to stop this screwing around and get down to business. "And practice of course."

"You know what they say, use it or lose it."

Tyler nearly choked. "Like I said back in the airport, you looked like you had everything down pat."

"You think so? Maybe the basics."

Definitely, the basics. "So, next weekend it's the mall. I suppose your success depends on what time you go."

"Oh. You mean there'll be more men by themselves in the evening. I guess I'd be successful if we practiced—"

"What do you mean if? I thought it was a done deal."

"When we practice," she corrected herself. "You realize it'll be strictly platonic." A patch of heat colored her cheeks.

"Now there's an interesting word. Like professional, you mean?"

"I wouldn't want you to get the wrong idea, think I was leading you on."

Tyler coughed.

"You're not getting all choked up again, are you?" She gently tapped his shoulder blade.

"Just a little something wedged in my throat. You absolutely sure this is your first time?"

"Yes, and according to the magazine—"

"Magazine?" He coughed again.

"Yes, the magazine article has great instructions."

They actually had a magazine for hookers? Like *Hooker's Home Journal* or *Hooker's Illustrated.* This he had to see. "You're pullin' my leg, right?"

"Cross my heart, I'm not."

This was one very ditsy dame. "Let me get this straight. You're using a magazine article to try and improve your uh... technique."

"Right."

"So what's your problem?" Damn, he probably should never have asked. She had so many problems, she'd be all night listing them.

"I'm shy."

Another cough reared up in his throat. *Shy my eye!*

"And it's not good to do it with a man you know, a man you really like."

He was beyond trying to speak, but somehow managed. "So what's to worry? You don't know me."

"Not very well."

Silence. Seconds and seconds of it dragged by while he waited for her to speak. Any fool could see there was something significant churning behind that intense gaze of hers. At last she spoke. "It's the liking bit that's got me bothered. I may have to break that rule."

Rules? A hooker with rules! Holy Moses!

Ethics, he supposed. But what a zany rule, not doing it with someone you know. Considering the clientele and health problems in today's world, he assumed a hooker would prefer to deal with men she knew. Ah well, nothing about Red had made sense so far. Why should her rules? The liking bit left him every bit as bewildered. She'd as much as said she liked him, and that left a warm place in his heart. Lord help him, he liked her, too. So what was her problem? Maybe she looked on sex with someone she liked as unprofessional.

Standing, he stretched and worked a kink out of his back, then stepped in her direction. "Let me get this straight. Doing it with someone you like would be breaking a rule, but you decided to ignore it."

"Yes."

"I'm flattered. And honored. I like you, too." She was six, maybe seven feet away. He took a couple of steps toward her and watched color surge into her cheeks. "Any other rules I should know about?"

She shook her head and scrambled to her feet. "Don't think so. It's pretty wide open. It's not even supposed to matter if the man's married, but I could never do it with a married man, not knowingly."

"You mean you'd pass up turning a tri— You wouldn't do it if the man was married?"

"I couldn't."

He'd underestimated her. Red definitely wasn't mercenary, and she had class. Character, too. "Mighty noble of you. I admire a woman with ethics." He shuffled closer. "So you won't seduce someone's husband. Quaint."

"Seduce?" She blinked. "I suppose you could phrase it that way."

"Think I've heard tell that married men do it all the time. If they come looking for you, what do you do then?"

"I don't know 'cause this is my first—"

"—time." He'd heard that before. Another two steps brought him directly in front of her.

"You're so understanding. I sensed it from the beginning."

"The beginning?" Tyler rubbed his temple with his thumb. Smiles and beguiling looks aside, he definitely heard an undercurrent in her voice.

"Yes, back in the airport when I first saw you. It was there in your face." She dropped her gaze to his left hand, then slanted her head, and looked him dead in the eyes. "You're not married, are you?"

"M-married? Heck no."

"I'm glad." A flicker of a smile graced her lips.

"Me, too. I mean for right now. Married is nice, but married's for later." His one brief foray into matrimony hadn't completely soured him. "It isn't that I wouldn't ever want to be."

"That's why I'm doing this."

"Excuse me?" She was definitely driving him crazy.

"That's why I want to practice."

"To help you get married?" Could that possibly be what she'd meant?

"Yes." She took a step backwards.

"That's a novel approach." Good Lord, he'd guessed right. Frightening as it sounded, maybe he was beginning to understand her.

He quickly reclosed the gap between them. Her hair was a tangled mess, the tousled look a turn-on. A blackberry thorn snagged in a wayward strand jutted across her forehead. Whipping out his penknife, he cut the errant lock and let it flutter to the floor. “I suppose you want to be skilled enough to please your husband.”

“I hadn’t thought about it that way, but yes.”

A nub of anger rumbled in his stomach. “Ever consider your husband might be disappointed that you’ve left nothing for him to teach you?”

“Oh, I’m sure he could teach me lots. That’s the problem. I’m not a nineties woman. Actually, I lead a very sheltered life.

Tyler nearly choked on that one. Bunch of malarkey. Had to be. He fought a twitch at the corner of his lip, then coughed again while she continued to inch backwards.

“My upbringing, I suppose,” she said, not blinking an eyelash.

“Your large Italian family.”

“Exactly. My family’s very religious and my uncle’s a priest.”

More blarney. Enough to make an Irishman proud. “And your family doesn’t know about this side of you.”

“No, and I’d just die if they did. That’s why I wore the—”

“—wig.” Hot damn, they were back to the wig and out of space. Her cute little tush had hit the wall.

Check mate.

Practice hooking men to find a husband, she’d said. The scenario made his blood boil. Baser instincts invaded his system. He braced his palms on the wall and bracketed her head. “So let’s get down to it. Practice time.”

“But—”

“But nothing.”

He reached for her, pulling her into his arms, giving in to the tug of attraction that had plagued him all day. He’d show her practice. He set his mouth over hers, deliberately keeping the kiss hard, silencing her before she had a chance to say anything. Driven by anger and far from gentle, he pushed deeper into her mouth. She wasn’t participating. Not this time. She bucked and pushed and squirmed, but then as her lips softened so did her movements. For a split second her body pulsed against his.

Wonderful sensations assaulted him.

He was a goner.

The woman was a kisser.

He’d wanted to teach her a lesson, but desire raced through him, blunting his plan. He’d always enjoyed flirting and foreplay, but this woman burned him to the core before he even cranked up the furnace. His anger twisted back on himself. Why did the thought of this woman practicing on others rile him so? And why couldn't he take what she was offering? What stopped him? And why had she resisted him this time? While trying to sort things out in his mind, she wiggled free and shoved him away.

"This wasn't what I meant." Her agitated voice snapped.

Could have fooled him.

"This isn't right!" Her gaze tangled with his.

Fire glinted in her eyes. He figured there had to be another side to her funky, upbeat personality. Other than the time she'd hurled imaginary darts at Dawson on the plane, it was the first time he'd seen Red angry. And why? Because he'd been a little rough? Damned if he knew what she wanted. Could be something more. He'd sensed an attitude building in her since he'd returned to the cabin. Seeking control, he rested his clenched fists on his hips. "Says who?"

"Says me!"

Her chin shot up. Her saucy, pert, dimpled chin. She gave him a long-suffering stare as if she were fighting to subdue her temper, bent over, then took several deep breaths. He enjoyed every one of them.

"You've got this all wrong," she said, taking a step back. "Way off base from the magazine."

Her voice still held a trace of tartness, but he sensed from the look in her eyes she couldn't stay mad at him any more than he could with her. "Then clue me in."

"Let's start over. You're much too close."

"Too close?" Not by his standards. "Close is not good?"

"Well, maybe later."

Later. That's what he was waiting for.

All business, she tapped her fingertip on his chest. "We need to start at a distance as if we didn't know each other."

He'd have sworn the opposite was true, but he'd let her call the shots. Four large strides took him several feet away. "This far enough?"

"Perfect. Now pretend you're back at the airport, casually looking at the people at the gate."

Tyler did as instructed. He let his gaze drift over the room. "This casual enough for you?" At her nod, he continued. "Better yet, we could pretend we're at a reception and the

Governor is giving a cocktail party."

"The Governor! Of which state?"

"This state."

"What state is this?"

The state of confusion where Red was concerned. "I'm not sure. Why should it matter? We're just setting the scene here. You know, ambiance."

"Oh. I was just wondering which state we were in. Maybe I'd know the capitol."

"Say North Carolina."

"That's... uh... Raleigh, I think. Just as long as it's not Connecticut."

"This definitely isn't Connecticut."

"Good, 'cause I don't know its capitol."

"It's New London." Though why the hell she was so hung up on the state of Connecticut beat the hell out of him.

"You sure?"

He shrugged. "Who cares. Set the scene. We're at the Governor's cocktail party. Chandeliers. Lush carpets. Waiters with trays of champagne. There's a bar over there."

"Where?" She took a few steps and peeked over his shoulder.

"There, along that wall." He pointed to his left. "Over there's a string quartet." He pivoted and pointed to his right. "And behind us a fire roars in the fireplace, and dozens of people are milling about the room."

"Sounds nice." She closed her eyes as if savoring the scene, getting with the program. "You have a good imagination."

"Thanks," he replied as she opened her eyes and walked back to where she'd been standing. "Just wanted to get into the spirit." It wasn't as if he was beyond romance.

"Ooh, look." An impish glimmer lit her eyes. "There's the Governor."

"Where?"

"By the door."

"Fashionably late isn't he?"

"She." Her voice matter of fact, Red didn't blink.

"Beg pardon?"

"The Governor's a she."

"How could I have missed that? But then, I only have eyes for you," he smoothly replied without missing a beat.

The whimsical light in her gaze told him he'd scored a point, that his remark pleased her. And in that instant he realized he'd spoken the truth. Even his anger moments ago pointed toward it. Had this rustic shack been jammed with people, without Red, it would have been empty. Irresistibly, she'd weaved her way into his system.

Brushing his perplexing discovery aside, Tyler cleared his throat. "Forget the Governor. What's next?"

"First and most important, we have to notice each other."

No problem there. He made a big pretense of looking around the room, then focused his eyes on her, letting them drift up and down in exaggerated appraisal until they rested on her face. Even though they were playing a game, his gaze ached to reunite with hers. Darned if mischievous sparkles didn't dance in her light brown eyes. The woman was dynamite. He couldn't believe she didn't know it.

Rubbing his hands up and down the side of his jeans, he sought control. Red's unique personality was downright contagious. She was going over the edge to who knows where and damned if she wasn't taking him with her. "So," his voice wavered ever so slightly, "what's the second thing we do?"

"Eye contact. The longer the better. That telegraphs your interest in me and mine in you. Five seconds is supposed to be good. I usually count it out to myself. One tela-goose, two tela-goose, three tela-goose—"

"What's with the tela gooses?"

"It lets me know a second has gone by."

He'd heard about *Women Were From Venus and Men Were From Mars*, but what planet was Red from? "Where'd you make up such nonsense?"

"It's not nonsense. It's Carmen Miranda."

"Come again?"

"Carman Miranda."

"Miranda? Like in reading someone their rights, miranderizing them?"

Her brows furrowed, and her cute, little face looked at him as if he were the screwball. Maybe she was right. "What an odd conclusion," she quietly remarked.

Not half as odd as her gibberish. Could Carmen be the name of one of the smugglers? "Who's Carmen?"

"An old movie star. My Aunt Sophia features herself to be an actress. She stars in a lot of local musicals, and she has this fabulous collection of tapes of old Broadway and Hollywood musicals. Carmen Miranda's one of her favorites. Surely you've heard of her."

"Who, your Aunt Sophia?"

"No silly, Carmen Miranda. She was that Latin singer with a fruit basket on her head."

How fitting! Only Red could come up with something like that. The temptation to comment on their whacky comparison was almost too much to resist. Naw, he'd better let it pass. "You still haven't explained the tela goosa bit."

"She'd dance around like this." Red swung her hips and moved her hands in a motion similar to a hula, but to a Latin beat. And then she sang, "One tela-goose, tela-goose, tela-goosa," flapping her elbows.

His eyes nearly bugged out of their sockets as her skirt pulled across her hips.

Her short skirt.

Her tight skirt.

Her very short, very tight skirt.

Great legs, too, as he noticed before. A pity they were scratched. Tyler's mouth watered, not to mention the increased pressure in the region of his fly. Red's demonstration was a sight that would remain engraved in his brain until the day he died.

She stopped swaying and continued her explanation. "It's just something that flicked into my mind—a way to mark off how many seconds I'd stared at a man instead of using something mundane like counting one thousand and one."

Perish mundane. "What's next according to the magazine?"

"After several five second stares we exchange smiles, maybe even nod at each other."

Tyler complied. How could he resist her heart-wrenching smile?

"That's good." She nodded approval.

"All this is what the magazine instructed?"

"Yes. It says you have to send a message that you're approachable—see how many men you can magnetize in an hour."

"Magnetize in an hour?" Damn fancy way of saying book appointments for later if you asked him.

"Now comes the hard part, at least for me. If they don't take the hint, you have to find a reason to approach the person and talk. It's important to get the man talking about what interests him—to ask him questions and find things to compliment him on. Body language comes into play, too."

"I bet it does." He moved to within inches of her. "So, now we're closer, and we talk."

"Yes. Do you realize we haven't had a single meaningful conversation. I don't even know what you do. What do you do?"

"Uh... I'm connected to a government agency for the uh... for F.A.A. Airplane regulations and such." He didn't like lying, but it came with the job. Too damn dangerous to come right out and admit he was F.B.I. Far more likely to get more from her if he kept her in the dark.

"So that's why you were in the airport. You work in the control tower?"

"That's it. I'm an air flight controller."

"But what were you doing at the gate?"

"I wasn't working today."

"Waiting for someone?"

"Yeah."

"They must be worried."

"How's that?"

"Well you went off with me and I told you it wasn't necessary to escort me all the way but you insisted and then you got caught up in this mess and here you are stranded in the Smokies." After her very long sentence, she stopped to inhale. "The person expecting to see you at the gate must be worried sick about you. She's probably frantic."

"She?"

"Naturally, I assumed it was a she."

"Naturally. Well, it wasn't."

Red brightened. "Then who?"

Tyler arched his brow. Holy Toledo! He slapped the palm of his right hand to his forehead. The mysterious hostility he'd detected earlier was long gone. Now with the tenacity of a mule yet the delicacy of a spider web, he was being interrogated—and by Red of all people. Sly little thing. "Hold the fort. We're drifting off track here."

"No, we're not. I'm trying to have a significant conversation with you while maintaining eye contact, smiling, and keeping my body stance open."

"That last part sounds good."

Regina hesitated. Despite her earlier misgivings about

Tyler, she was enjoying herself. When she'd discovered he'd hid the marbles, anger had mingled with her suspicions. And then when he'd pulled him into his arms and roughly kissed her, she'd been furious.

Enough to ream him out. Enough to kick and scream.

And she would have, except that his kiss tingled her lips, warmed her funny bone, and sent her pulse thundering through her ears. Nor could she forget the disturbed look in his eyes when she'd shoved him away. He'd regretted his behavior. She was certain of it. And he'd felt the pull between them every bit as much as she had. Uncanny, how each time the man touched her, she responded. Even now as he stood inches away, she felt his uncomfortable gaze studying her. The warm hand clamping her stomach told her just how uncomfortable.

Utterly ridiculous, being attracted to a criminal. Tyler, a criminal? Her instincts refuted it. Nothing about him hinted of being a hardened criminal, and on the off chance he was involved in something a teensy-weensy shady, she believed he wasn't beyond redemption.

But this wasn't working out exactly as she'd envisioned. Par for the day. Nothing had worked out as planned. She still hadn't learned anything important about him. And if she was going to save him from a life of crime and herself from this situation, she'd best get to work.

"Your folks, are they still living?" she asked, trying to ignore his protests and the sizzling effect he had on her metabolism. Like sausages spit sparks off the griddle.

"My folks are fine," he answered cryptically.

"They live in Cincinnati?"

"Cleveland."

"Cleveland's nice." She could see by the twitch in his jaw he wasn't eager to discuss himself. What was he hiding? "Did you go to college there?"

"Ohio State."

"You said you flew a plane once. Did you enjoy it?"

"Yeah, I did."

"You did a pretty fair job of flying it today, saved our lives. I'll never be able to thank you enough."

"You helped too, Red. Look—"

"You don't like talking about yourself, do you? It bothers you."

"I just think we're wasting time here."

"Talking about yourself, your feelings, your hopes and dreams is never a waste of time."

Tyler's mouth drew into a thin line. He grew quiet. Had she finally cracked his barrier? As his lips curved into a roguish grin, she caught a gleam in his eyes. "Touché," he said several seconds later. "You mean that, don't you? You're not just making idle patter." His voice dropped in pitch and volume. "There's a lot more to you than I realized."

"I beg your pardon?"

"Look Red, I appreciate your interest. I really do, but—"

"You're stubborn. You'd rather keep your mysterious image."

"I'd rather get back to what we were doing. Skip to the next step."

That was the problem.

She wasn't sure what the next step was, but she had a fairly good idea where Tyler wanted things to head. She knew because the gnawing ache inside her craved the same thing. To keep from reaching out for a man she had no business touching until she got to the bottom of his connection to the package, Regina took a deep breath and hugged her arms around her waist. Impulsiveness had gotten her in this mess.

Time to discard Aunt Sophia's '*Go for it*' policy. She needed clear-headed thinking and the farther away she kept Tyler, the clearer her head. Seeking space, she walked over to the fireplace and turned her back to him.

For the past five hours her emotions had been taxed beyond their limit. She was exhausted, but she dared not give in to sleep. Her instincts told her that survival depended on her remaining alert. She so wanted to trust Tyler. On one level she did. At least her body did. His imaginative touch about the Governor's reception had pleased and impressed her. There was a lot to be said for the guy.

Maybe she was letting Aunt Ruth's overly suspicious nature influence her. But no, dammit! Tyler and those idiot marbles were connected.

Marbles. What was so all-fired important about marbles that two men had beaten up Tyler and kidnapped him? Her, too? She had a sneaking hunch she knew the answer.

When she thought about it, she knew something else. Tyler had been right. In her own fumble-bumble way she had fought through her fear and helped him with the plane. And she'd survived her encounter with the snake. Surely, she could accomplish something as simple as getting this man to level with her. Her gaze wandered to her briefcase. If she could only sneak a peak at the magazine. Maybe then, she'd know what to do next.

Suffering Sandusky!

She remembered. The article had recommended that once you gained confidence in your flirting technique, it was time to direct all your skills on *"the guy."*

The man who most sexually attracted you. The man you wanted to get to know.

And then you were to select locales where you expected to find men who shared qualities and interests similar to your own. Which in her case would be ice skating rinks and fabric stores. Neither sounded promising.

'Don't worry, Bambina. Whatever is meant to be will be. It's in the stars.' Aunt Della's voice, depositing her two cents in Regina's head.

Ah well, when it came to dealing with Tyler, she guessed she'd have to improvise and skip to the next step as he suggested.

The wind blew and the door creaked. The fire flickered, too, drawing her attention to it. A perfect setting for the Adams Family. Morticia, Gomez, and Lurch would love it here. Movement caused her to turn. She watched Tyler put his hand to the small of his back. He'd taken brutal punishment today. How could she have entertained the idea he was involved with Foster and Dawson? But he definitely wanted that package.

Her gaze collided with his. She had the sensation he'd been watching her the whole time she'd turned her back to him. Devilishly handsome, oozing quiet strength and a primitive magnetism, the man sent her a knowing smile as if he'd telepathically channeled every thought she'd had these past few minutes. Nothing left to do but show him she wasn't putty in his hands.

"Your back's bothering you, isn't it?" He'd been fretting with it constantly.

"Among other things," he quipped.

"Sit down over here by me, and I'll rub it for you." She patted the spot in front of her with the sole of her broken shoe. After the wonderful massage he'd performed on her, it was only fair she returned the favor. And there was a method to her madness. Once he was settled facing the fire, she knelt behind him.

Tentatively at first, then firmly applying pressure, she worked her hands into his neck, occasionally guiding her fingers higher to caress his scalp and behind his ears.

"Mmm," he murmured.

She slid her hands down the nape of his neck and kneaded his shoulders. Sparks shot out from her fingertips wherever she touched him. Moving her hands over the corded muscles of his back, she was grateful Tyler couldn't see her face. No doubt it'd be a dead giveaway to what currently crossed her mind. Namely, kissing the back of his neck.

"Feels good." His reply came out in a throaty whisper. Exactly the response she'd hoped for.

"You have twenty minutes to stop it," he said, leaning back into her hands.

In twenty minutes her fingers would be burned to a crisp and her arms aching. Other places, too. He dropped his head forward, and she trailed the heels of her palms back to the nape of his neck, then buried her fingers in his hair. She was trying to soften him up, but it was backfiring. Badly.

"Let me tell you, Red, being stranded with you has its compensations."

Ditto, she thought, her defenses on the brink of collapse. "So, Tyler," she paused to clear her dry throat, and striving for as much single-mindedness as she could muster, renewed her interrogation, "where would you be right now if you hadn't taken this unexpected detour to the Smokies?"

"Where? At the airport I guess."

"With your friend?" She remembered he'd had a buddy with him. "That other man."

"Oh, Jake. Yeah, Jake."

"I suppose that's why you're not concerned about missing the person arriving on the flight because Jake was there to cover for you." Actually, now that she thought about it, it kinda made sense. In fact, if her memory served her right, Tyler had said those exact words in the airport. "Will he be looking for you?"

"Who?"

"Jake."

"He damn well better be."

Chapter Eight

"Speak up, I can't hear you," Jake Tobias growled into the phone.

It wasn't any wonder. Pandemonium ricocheted from every corner of the room. The Airport Security Office was packed with people. Too many. And all of them talking a mile a minute.

Where had they come from, for cripes sake?

"What's that?" he hollered into the mouth piece. "Look, suppose I do the talking since you can hear me and I can't hear you—bring you up to speed and then later," he cast a jaundiced gaze around the room, "when we clear these jokers out of here, I'll call you back."

Jake paused. For a moment he thought a security officer and one of the ladies, who bore a slight resemblance to Rosanne, were about to come to blows. Having been known to wager now and then, Jake would have bet good money on the hefty woman.

Irritated, Jake gripped the phone. "You still there? We've determined Tyler accompanied the suspect to the F.B.O."

Nearly six hours ago. Night approached.

"You know the place," he continued, "it's next to the Cincinnati Airport. Took some time to pin it down. Not five minutes after Tyler left, I was tailing another suspect in that same direction when the guy gave me the slip. We have witnesses here at the F.B.O. who say they saw a couple resembling Tyler and the female. A mechanic reported a scuffle out on the tarmac. That's the good news. We have reason to believe Tyler is on a plane that took off from here about six hours ago, and we have its flight plan. They headed to Atlanta. The bad news is..."

Jake choked up and balled his free hand into a fist. "The bad news is the plane never made it. We think it crashed. The security officer here is calculating where it might have gone down. The flight plan could have been bogus or it could have secretly landed somewhere else, given the smugglers were probably on board."

The noise level in the room increased, and Jake stared at his white-knuckled hand still clenched into a fist. This was personal. Tyler was more than his partner. They were friends. "Hold on a minute."

He cupped the mouthpiece and faced the crowd. Champion whistler that he was, he lifted a finger to his mouth and let out a whopper. No matter what their position, everyone froze, and even better, their mouths snapped shut. Blissful, blessed silence. Wide-eyed, they faced him. "Could you keep it down? On second thought, take it outside."

He nodded none too politely in the direction of the door, then motioned to the Airport Manager who stood a few feet away. "Help me get them out of here."

"I've tried, but they won't leave."

"What's the cop doing here?"

"He's with them. Says his sister is missing."

"Sister, you say?" Jake knitted his brow. "Get their names. Don't let them leave."

"But you said—"

"Forget what I said. Just keep 'em quiet as long as you can." Jake lifted the receiver to his ear. "Sorry for the interruption, Chief. Yeah, yeah, Tyler's the best. He has good instincts. We won't lose him. Like I was saying, a report has come in from the North Carolina State Police. Someone out in the boonies thinks they saw a plane flying erratically."

A middle-aged lady with an emerald green hat distracted Jake. She was bouncing her pointed finger off the chest of the harried Airport Manager. Maybe she and the Rosanne clone were a wrestling tag-team.

Jake regained his train of thought. "Look Chief, I think we need to contact our personnel in Knoxville, Johnson City, and Asheville. And I'd like two choppers available here at the F.B.O. A.S.A.P. Yeah, right." He glanced at his watch. "Gotta go. Got a fire to put out here." *More like an explosion.* "Call you within the hour, sooner if there's anything important. You can reach me here at the F.B.O."

Not a soul saw him put the receiver down.

Not a soul looked in his direction.

Not a soul cared an iota about him.

His whistle had lasted only so long. They were back to it again, everyone arguing with everyone else. They were a demonstrative crowd, waving their hands to make their points. He started counting, ticking them off on his fingers. The Cincinnati Airport Manager, two security personnel, the F.B.O. manager, a mechanic, four middle-aged women, two middle-aged men, and a policeman. Twelve agitated people plus himself in an office that would be crowded with eight.

These were not happy campers. Concern, even a touch of fear showed on their faces and resounded in their voices. They were volatile, desperate, impatient. And they were in his way.

Hmmm. Or were they?

The cop's sister was missing.

Naw, it couldn't be.

Too neat a coincidence. Too easy.

No way the redhead could have a cop for a brother. Her actions had clearly broadcast hooker, and there wasn't a doubt in Jake's mind that she was connected to the smugglers. The redhead's image lingered in Jake's mind. Attractive and very sexy. Best set of legs he'd seen in many a day. For a short time after Tyler's disappearance, Jake hadn't worried. He figured Tyler had gotten lucky. But as the hours passed, he discarded that idea. It wasn't Tyler's style to be silent for so long. He'd have reported in.

Noise intruded Jake's thoughts again. He grimaced, then patted his breast pocket. There was one sure way to clear the room. Removing a cigar, Jake held it under his noise and savored its rich aroma.

Damn smoking laws.

Though he understood and obeyed them, he'd give the world to light up a cigar this very moment and take a deep, relaxing drag. How the hell had Tyler managed to quit smoking, anyway? As he reluctantly replaced his cigar, the large framed woman glared at him. She pushed her way through the crowd, dragging a diminutive gray-haired man by the sleeve.

"Guido, you tell this man we found Regina's car in the airport parking lot." Jake watched the woman shift her gaze toward him and he swallowed. She was big, with a voice loud enough to be heard in a stadium. Without a microphone. "Tell him she's here, Guido."

"You already have, Sophia." Guido rolled his eyes.

Jake cracked a smile. For a small guy, Guido had cunning and courage.

"She's here, or she's been here," the lady with the hat said, her tone softly caressing in contrast to the woman called Sophia. "I know it. I feel it in my bones."

Her emerald hat clashed badly with the pea green walls of the office. Though why he noticed such a ridiculous observation in the midst of all this mayhem beat the heck out of him.

"It's a plot," the woman with bright, red-rimmed glasses announced. "Someone has abducted my niece."

"Pshaw, Ruth, that's nonsense," the big woman with the bigger voice refuted. Sophia, Jake remembered. The red-rimmed glasses was Ruth.

"Maybe not," the hat woman intervened. He didn't have a name for that one yet. "I have a very bad feeling about this," she went on. "Ruth could be right. There might be a conspiracy."

Jake was growing dizzy trying to keep up with the fast paced conversations and who everybody was. He turned his attention to the fourth woman, the one he'd labeled as the quiet one. She fingered a crucifix around her neck and started to cry. One of the men offered her a handkerchief and draped his arm around her shoulder. Jake decided they must be the parents of this missing young woman. Jake was just about to holler over the din when a priest burst into the room.

A priest?

"Where is she?" the priest asked, nearly out of breath. "What happened? I got here as soon as I could." He strode across the room and hugged the woman with tears on her face.

Jake shook his head. All they needed now was a doctor, a nurse, and the kitchen sink. He sidled up to the cop. "Jake Tobias, F.B.I." He extended his hand.

"Lieutenant Vincent Citrano." The guy's grip was firm—a match to his muscular body. Jake reckoned few who tangled with the lieutenant ever came out winners. He looked like bench-pressing four hundred pounds would be no trouble at all.

"What say you and I step outside so we can hear one another?" Jake led the way through the sea of bodies toward the door. He didn't get very far. The eyeglass woman grabbed him by the arm. "Did you say F.B.I.?" Suddenly the room quieted, all eyes on Jake.

"Yes Ma'am."

"I knew it." She removed her glasses and waved them triumphantly to the others. "This is serious. F.B.I. Regina's been kidnapped."

"Regina?" Jake knitted his brow.

"My sister, Regina Citrano," the policeman supplied.

The nameless hat lady stepped forward. "Regina Anne Catherine Mary Citrano, if you please."

Jake raised his hands. "Whoa, folks, I wouldn't get carried away. I think we have two different cases here. You're looking for this Regina while I'm looking for my partner and some smugglers, one of whom happens to be a female."

"Smugglers?" The excitement in the voice of the woman with the crimson spectacles was palpable. Jake swore he saw laser beams dance in her eyes.

"You'll have to excuse my family, Sir," Vincent Citrano apologized to Jake.

Jake's gaze swept the room. "They're all your family?"

"Well, not everyone!" Sophia shoved the hat lady aside. "Not the managers, the mechanic or the security agents." She pointed to each one as she spoke. "And of course not you."

"But everyone else is?" Jake turned to the sane voice of the cop. "Even the priest?"

"Yes, Sir. Father Costello is my uncle."

"And this sister of yours is—"

"Gone. Missing. I know it probably sounds off the wall."

Jake readily nodded as the policeman tried to shush his relatives. That was one battle Jake bet the guy rarely won, regardless of his imposing size.

"You see, my aunt Della claims to have the gift."

"Gift?" Jake cocked his head.

"Yes, E.S.P. And more often than not she's been right. A few hours ago she woke from a nap screaming."

Probably par for the course with this clan, Jake started to say but bit back his remark. No matter, at least the emerald hat lady had been christened—Della. Emerald hat—Della. Red-rimmed glasses—Ruth. Yes, that was it, and who could mistake Sophia?

Vincent continued. "She swore she saw a plane crash and Regina was on it when it went down."

A muscle in Jake's jaw twitched. A missing woman and a plane crash? Had the woman overhead him on the phone? Impossible. He couldn't even hear himself on the phone. He studied her for a second then shifted his gaze back to the policeman. "Did she now?"

"Yes, Sir. Of course when Aunt Della called my aunt Ruth, Ruth didn't believe her. Anyone who knows Regina knows she wouldn't be caught dead..." The cop hesitated. "My sister's afraid of airplanes, especially small ones."

"That a fact," Jake interjected.

"Yes, Sir, but Aunt Ruth can be excitable—"

"You can say that again," Jake remarked. There was still a buzz in the room, but as Vincent related his story, the Citrano clan seemed to have gathered around, poking each other and nodding their approval.

"Aunt Ruth has a suspicious nature, and she agreed that if Regina was on that plane, then it had to be due to bodily force. Then Aunt Della and Aunt Ruth drove to my parents' house," Vincent said nodding to the woman who clutched a handkerchief and the man who stood beside her. "While they were there, Aunt Sophia and Uncle Guido arrived. Aunt Sophia claimed she'd seen Regina at the airport. Then after no one could find my sister, they descended on me at the precinct. It was then Aunt Della suddenly had another vision and insisted we search the airport parking lot. I rounded up some help, and I have to admit we located Regina's car. According to the ticket, she's been here since noon."

Sophia lifted her chin with a dramatic tilt. "I knew I saw her, but—"

"Excuse me Ma'am," Jake interrupted, then cleared his throat. "Just exactly where in the airport did you think you saw her?"

"At the gate where flight 311 was arriving, but let me tell you—"

"Flight 311?" Jake stiffened. "About what time, Ma'am?"

"I'd say around 12:33, wouldn't you Guido?"

"That's very precise, Ma'am. Twelve-thirty-three on the dot?"

"My wife is like that," Guido explained, "precise about time. We were there to meet our son."

Since the flight had been delayed, Jake suspected that at 12:34 the airline had heard about it from one bombastic-voiced Sophia. Amusing as that scenario might be, Jake grew uneasy. The coincidences were piling up. "Any of you happen to have a photo of this Regina?"

Instantly, four women and two men fumbled through purses and pockets.

Della produced one first. "Here. Isn't she a beautiful bambino?"

"Yes, Ma'am, she is that, but I need something a little more recent than a baby picture."

"Here! Here!" Sophia waved a wallet sized photo at Jake. "Here's a picture of her in her prom dress."

Jake squinted at the full length photo of a slim, attractive dark-haired girl who stood next to a gawky young man. The faces were too small. "Sorry, but this won't do either."

"How about this one," Regina's mother offered. "She had it taken this year at one of those glamour places."

"Thank you Ma'am." Jake respectfully took the photo from her. Before he glanced at it, his gaze locked with the quiet woman's. The pain in her eyes got to him. A lump formed in his throat. "I'm sorry your daughter is missing."

He examined the photo. A real beauty stared back at him. Unfortunately, a dark-haired beauty. There was a passing resemblance, but she wasn't a redhead. "Very nice." He handed the picture back. "But the woman I'm looking for has red hair."

"You're looking for Regina. I know it." Della barged her way into his space. "In my vision Regina had red hair."

Sophia spoke up. "Della's right. I'm positive I saw Regina at that gate, and I've been trying to break in and tell you that. The face was Regina's but she had red hair. Before I could catch up with her, she'd disappeared."

With her hat akimbo, Della looked at Jake, her eyes pleading for confirmation. "Since you've been in the airport, maybe you've seen her, too. She's about five-foot-four—"

"Three," Sophia interrupted. "Five-foot-three on the nose."

Jake fought a smile. Apparently, Sophia was precise about everything.

"Five-foot-three, then," Della conceded, adjusting her hat, "and real nice-looking."

"More than nice-looking." Ruth clapped her hands. "Regina's ravishing!"

Jake grew impatient. Reason told him these women were barking up the wrong tree. "The woman I saw was a dish."

"Dish?" Della repeated. "Are you calling our niece a plate?"

"No, Della," Sophia said. "He's complimenting her.

As the three middle-aged women crowded in on him, Jake took a step away. "Red hair or not, this woman couldn't be your niece, or your daughter. I appreciate your interest, but if all of you would just clear out of here and let us do our job."

"Ooh." Mrs. Citrano moaned, clutching her hand over her heart. "Della, you think Regina is on that plane, don't you, the plane that's missing?"

"Look this can't be pleasant for you folks," Jake cut in. "You're jumping to conclusions. I'm looking for a female felon along with another crook, and—"

Jake never finished his sentence. Another F.B.I. agent rushed into the room, plunging into what little space was left. "Jake," he shouted, searching through the crowd, "they think they've found Tyler. A plane crashed—"

"In the Smokies," Della, the hat lady blurted out.

The agent's mouth dropped open. "We just learned that ourselves. How the hell did you know that?"

"I don't know. I-it j-just c-came to me, like it always does." Nervously, she straightened her hat which had begun to slide down her forehead again.

When the agent swung his questioning gaze to Jake, Jake helplessly hunched his shoulders and shrugged. Maybe the woman did have the gift! This family was screwy enough for at least one of them to be wired into the nether-nether world.

If Regina Citrano was the woman with Tyler, what did he care?

So what if it wasn't by the book?

So what if a bossy drill sergeant, a female Sherlock Holmes, and kooky soothsayer in a crooked emerald hat solved the case?

He'd use anything at his disposal and then some if it would lead to Tyler.

"Sophia," Ruth hissed through her teeth. Her voice was barely above a whisper, but Jake heard it anyway. "Sophia, you shouldn't have said that about Regina being a redhead."

"Why?"

"Because he's looking for a redheaded jailbird, that's why. You've thrown suspicion on her."

"Della was the one who went on and on about her redheaded vision," Sofia defended herself.

"Then you're both at fault." Ruth slid her glasses back on the bridge of her nose. "Poor Grace, we've upset her."

Jake watched the three women compassionately stare at Grace Citrano. Barely five seconds later those same three sets of eyes swung in his direction. Decidedly less than compassionate, their gazes sent chill bumps down his spine.

Knowing his moments were numbered, Jake eyed the door. If he hustled, he might avoid their ambush, but no, he was already too late. Seconds later, cursing under his breath and surrounded by three boisterous women, Jake popped an antacid pill into his mouth. As they prepared to brain wash him, yet another man came barreling into the room.

"Grace, Joe, I heard Regina's missing," he yelled, nudging Jake further into the room and the clutches of his three over-eager musketeers. "My plane is here if you need me to fly you anywhere," the man announced.

"Roman, Roman," a chorus of voices sang out.

Jake groaned. Instead of a doctor, nurse, or the kitchen sink, a pilot had joined the menagerie, and it was a sure bet he was yet another relative. Probably the whole damn city was related to this bunch.

The night promised to be a long one.

Something told him it had just gotten even longer.

And something told him that before it was over, he was going to wish he could trade places with Tyler—wherever he was.

Tyler, good buddy, he sent out a silent plea. Where the hell are you?

Chapter Nine

Dammit, she was nesting, cocooning herself into the blanket he'd dug out of the backpack.

Tyler forced his gaze away and stirred the fire with the poker. Ever since trying to turn the tables and wheedle information out of him, she'd been quiet. Too quiet. But it gave him time to think about Jake. Surely his partner had initiated a full-court search by now. And surely Jake and the agency had linked the missing plane to his own disappearance.

Jeeze, what if they hadn't? What if they never checked the

F.B.O.? What if they didn't even know the plane was missing?

No sweat.

He and Red would trek down these mountains tomorrow. Shouldn't be too long before they ran across someone. Meanwhile, he needed to redirect his energies into learning more about his vivacious companion. And it wouldn't hurt to sample some of her wares during the process, get back in that practice groove. After all, despite the fact that she might be a criminal—

Might be?

How could there be any doubt?

Okay, so there was doubt. Probably due to the fact that she activated his hormones as they'd never been activated before. But attraction or not, he was positive he could keep his emotions under control. Whatever she was hiding with her come-hither looks and zany antics, he'd uncover. And maybe that wouldn't be all he uncovered.

Tick.

Tock.

The clock was ticking. Or would be if there was one in this cabin. Meanwhile his digital watch digited away. He'd endured the silence as long as he could. He should have enjoyed it, but silence and Red were unnatural, almost scary. Threatening. The inevitable had been delayed long enough. Time to get back to work, and if he got lucky, to some side benefits, as well.

Firelight shimmered in her lustrous hair, and sensing his stare, she met his gaze. Dammit, she had a way of looking at him that would melt the resistance of an Eskimo. How the hell was he supposed to stay clinically detached? He blinked, trying to visualize her as fat, butt ugly, and cross-eyed.

It didn't work.

"What?" she asked.

She'd caught him off guard. He'd been primed to start the conversation, not answer more of her questions. "What what?" he fired back.

"You were staring."

"You're easy to stare at."

She blushed. "I thought you were about to say something."

"I was."

"But?"

He shrugged. "I got sidetracked."

"I knew it!"

"You knew it?" Had his eyes given away his lusty thoughts? "What did you know?"

"Actually, I didn't know what you know. I just knew it."

Tyler took a moment to digest that one. He was reconsidering the wisdom of initiating any conversation with her. Talking with her was like eating jello with chopsticks. "There's a difference?"

"Yes. I didn't know what sidetracked you, but I definitely got the feeling you were flummoxed."

"Come again?"

"I got the feeling you were flummoxed."

Not an everyday vocabulary word, at least not in his dictionary. "Sounds like something a plumber would do. What kind of a word is *flummoxed*?"

Her lips quirked into a mischievous smile. "That's an old fashioned word my Aunt Della uses."

Back to her aunts again, and the word *old-fashioned* that conjured up others like *sweet* and *modest*. Tyler refused to let her fluster him, but it wasn't easy with those big, trusting eyes of hers that dripped with innocence.

Yeah, right, Novak. Just remember she's probably been scored on dozens of times, and no doubt she's performing a world class snow job on you this very minute. "So what does this old-fashioned word of your aunt's mean?"

"It means baffled, stumped, unsettled."

"Yeah, all of those." *Flummoxed* was the perfect word to describe what she did to him, but he wouldn't let it distract any further. "Say, Red, just now you were sulking, weren't you, because I realized you were pumping me for information?"

"I wouldn't call it pumping." Her eyes took on a pleased-as-punch look. "I'd call it being successful at my techniques."

"If interrogation is part of your technique."

"That's not what the magazine says. They call it getting to know the guy. It's step five."

"Step five! For crying out loud." Tyler swallowed, to gulp some air, to smother the cough, to cover the laugh that threatened to erupt from the bottom of his throat. "That magazine is all wet. Guys don't like being put through the fifth degree."

"I'd like to ask you about that."

Her gaze locked dead on with his, her long lashes fringing her impish, brown eyes. After spending the last few hours in her company, and almost being glued together a time or two, he knew that look. Only problem was he hadn't a clue what the disturbing expression lurking in the depths of those eyes meant. It could be snakes, or fate, or saying the blessing, or fear. Even flirting.

She was a natural at flirting.

She oozed with it.

"Shoot your question. I'm ready." He crossed his fingers.

"You remember when I said it was important to get the guy talking about himself, about things he's interested in?"

"Yeah."

"Well, if they don't like being interrogated, do they usually like any kind of talking while doing it?"

"Doing it? Oh yeah. Not especially. I mean I can only speak for myself."

"That's why you were irritated, wasn't it?"

Falling into her trap had irritated him more. She had a way of loosening his tongue. "Like I said, talking's low priority when you're with a woman."

"That's too bad. Men would really impress women if they talked more—exposed more of themselves."

Tyler did a double-take and shook his head as if clearing his ears. Clever how she'd snuck in that play on words. He'd just as soon cut out the jawing and get down to his version of exposure.

"Men need to work on their techniques too, you know." She saucily tilted her chin.

He let a nod suffice.

"I always thought men were flattered when you tried to center the conversation around them. So how do you know?"

"Excuse me?" Tyler felt as if he'd been tossed into the spin and dry cycle and left there. For days.

"If a guy won't talk, then how do you know what subjects they like? Just what do guys like?"

The question was choice!

Unbelievable.

She'd served him up a soft ball. He could see himself smacking it out of Riverfront Stadium, clear across the Ohio River into Kentucky, whose capitol was ...

Freaking Frankfort! Red's disease had rubbed off on him.

Disgusted, Tyler brushed aside the disconnected nonsense. He had a more important mission facing him.

How many men over how many centuries had waited for a woman to ask them what they liked? On behalf of the male segment of the human race, he had an obligation not to let them down. Taking her question as an invitation to re-open the practice sessions between them, Tyler sauntered over to the mattress where she lay curled up in the blanket.

As Tyler approached, Regina hitched the blanket over her shoulder. She wondered if he knew what a sexy, swaggering gait he had. Reaching the mattress, he stood, his dark eyes drifting over her with deliberate slowness. Despite the barrier of the blanket, heat radiated from each spot where his gaze lingered. She had a sudden urge to pull the blanket tighter. An urge she resisted.

His irritation and reluctance to talk about himself deflated her. How was she going to learn the truth about whether she could trust him? 'Course that wouldn't be difficult. She liked him. Each time their gazes locked, like right now, she intuitively knew Tyler Novak was a decent man. All she wanted was something concrete to verify her instincts.

That was the route she should follow, gain his confidence, butter him up for her own self-preservation until she was positive he wasn't involved with Foster and Dawson. While she was at it, she might pick up some valuable pointers for her flirting techniques.

Strangely, she had this innate sense that she had nothing to fear from him. And this same sense allowed her to hold her ground as his unwavering gaze zeroed in on her. He dropped to his knees, his gaze never leaving hers, then sat so close she could have touched him. He laid a hand on her back. Warm, bubbly sensations tingled up her spine.

"You're warm," he said.

"Mmmm." Was she ever! Fire branded her back wherever his fingers rested.

"That's something guys like. A warm woman."

As she waited for him to continue, the blanket slipped from one of her hands, and she pressed her palm to her pounding heart.

"I like a woman who smiles a lot."

Hadn't she done that? "I've been trying to, but with the plane and all, it's been difficult. It was especially hard because

I hate small planes."

He raised his eyebrows. "Yeah, you told me."

"Oh right." Of course she had. He had her so discombobulated she'd forgotten. Then too, anyone with half a brain would have surmised from her frenetic behavior on the plane that she was less than thrilled about it. An explanation seemed in order. "I had a bad experience in small plane when I was little, and I've never been on one since."

"Figured it had to be something like that. Speaking of small planes," he paused, "why do you suppose those guys tied you up and tossed you into the plane?"

Regina lifted a cautionary brow of her own. She remembered him asking that before. His question hinted of more than idle curiosity.

"It's a mystery to me." She shrugged. "I've never seen those men before today."

He regarded her with that skeptical, trademark expression of his. "That so?"

"Guess the next time a woman asks you to help her out, you'll think twice."

"In an airport I will."

"If you hadn't insisted on accompanying me all the way—"

He jumped on her words. "Then you'd be hog-tied on that plane all by yourself."

"I'm not so sure. It wasn't until you arrived that the trouble started."

"They ambushed me." Annoyance laced his voice.

"I know. Why?"

"Why what?"

"Why did they gang up on you?"

"Beats the hell out of me? I thought you might know."

"Me? I haven't a clue." She chewed on her lip. Except for the package, he seemed innocent. "But you're right."

"I'm right?" Tyler looked as if he had trouble understanding.

Though she found him intelligent and well informed, several times before she'd sensed he had difficulty following a simple conversation. "What I mean is, even though I don't know why it all happened, I'm glad you were with me." Closing her eyes, she replayed the harrowing flight. "I owe you my life."

"And I owe mine to you."

At his humble admission, a quiver of compassion feathered

through her. Though she still had a hunch none of this would have happened if Tyler hadn't followed her out to the plane, she couldn't look at him without visualizing him as her knight in shining armor. And what a swash-buckling knight he'd have made! She could see him rescuing damsels in distress, defanging dragons the likes of Foster and Dawson, and defying death.

Death.

She and Tyler had shared the fear of death on that plane. Aunt Della believed people who survived something together formed a mystical link. And now Regina knew it was true. No matter who Tyler turned out to be, the bond between them would live forever.

She stared into his eyes.

He stared back.

Quietness surrounded them. Slowly, he eased his fingers beneath her blouse. His warm, callused hand wandered across her back, leaving another trail of fire in its path.

"Guys like touching." His whisper tickled her ear.

"G-guys." She heard the stammer in her voice. Had he?

"I like touching." His voice was husky. "It's much better than talking. Call it one of my steps."

"Steps?" He had steps, too? Her fingers trembled and the remaining end of the blanket slipped away and pooled around her.

He sat beside her, half cradling her back into his chest, while his fingers explored her shoulders. They traveled in lazy circles along a circuitous route to the nape of her neck. As she leaned back into his hands, her tension was kneaded away by his sensuous touch.

"Mmm." She probably shouldn't encourage him. This wasn't anything like the magazine had suggested. They had gone far beyond flirting.

"Men like their women to touch them. I like it," he added his voice lower, smoother.

"Touch you?" Her fingertips itched with the temptation.

"I like my woman to touch me."

His woman. His soft, persuasive tone made her wonder what it would be like to be his woman. She shifted and raised her hand to his bristly chin. Tracing his cleft, she drew her fingers along his cheekbone and the rough contours of his face. Though merely a touch, it felt like a shattering religious experience. And Tyler liked it, too. His erratic breathing gave him away. It was then she noticed his bruises. Discoloration had set in and heightened them. She lifted the pad of her finger to the purplish blotch near his temple.

"Oh, Tyler," she murmured, then winced, remembering the blows he'd taken.

"Shush. Kissing's next."

"Yes." Her disjointed breaths made it difficult to answer.

"Do it, Red."

"Do it?" She swallowed.

"Kiss me."

At his whisper-soft voice she became intimately aware of him, of his closeness, his musky scent. He slid his hand behind her neck, and her mouth tingled. Electricity surged clear down to her little toe. Bells clanged. Ever so gently she tilted her lips to meet his. He trembled. So did she.

She brushed her mouth across his from side to side, then stopped, magnetically connected to him. She pressed her lips firmly against his, stroking the sides of his mouth with her fingers. His mouth opened and without a moment's hesitation, Regina slid her tongue past his lips.

Need exploded in her.

It crescendoed like a drug. She'd heard about it, read about it, had come close to experiencing it once. Even more mind-boggling was Tyler's response. From the warmth of his skin and the throb of his heart, she knew he traveled the same skyrocketing route as she. He came alive, his thumb caressing her jaw. Then pushing her tongue from his mouth, he thrust his into hers.

He'd said he liked to be touched. She obliged by fervently stroking his back, his neck, shoulders and arms. Then she ran her fingers through his hair, wanting to explore every inch of him. The staccato thump of her heartbeat slipped from a sprightly two-step to a fast-paced polka.

He responded by cupping her buttocks with his hands then tracing the curve of her hips. Slow torture took over as his fingers traveled to her breast. Her nipples strained against her blouse, aching for release.

"Oh, Tyler." She released a quivery moan against his open mouth.

"Warm, hot," he mumbled, "like I thought you'd be."

He lowered her to the blanket and unbuttoned her blouse.

At the touch of his finger to her nipple, she groaned deep in her throat. He eased back and looked down at her. Desire that mirrored her own threaded from his gaze to hers.

"You don't need lessons," he whispered as his tongue nuzzled her ear.

At this moment she agreed. What she needed was equilibrium.

"You're fabulous, Red, fabulous."

Reaching around her back, he unfastened her bra, then lowered his head, and nudged her blouse open with his mouth. His lips toyed with her nipple and she writhed. The sensation drove her to such an edge that she couldn't remain still. He sucked and swirled his mouth over her breast. Then one of his hands crept up her thigh, and Regina crashed back to reality.

Regina Citrano, what are you doing? You don't know this man. You have to stop now, while you can.

"I can't," she whispered weakly.

"Can't?" Tyler pulled away, his troubled brown eyes seeking hers.

"No!" She tugged at his shirt and pulled him back, tightening the embrace. He'd misunderstood.

"No?"

"Yes, no." But her conscience refused to let her alone. *Your family will be mortified. Your father will put him through the wringer. Your aunts and uncles, too.*

"Yes," she breathily answered, all too aware of how her family would react.

In another era they'd have hunted him down with shotguns. And what about protection? *If this goes any further, have you thought about that?*

She ignored the voice until two seconds later as Tyler slipped his finger into her panties. Where was her control, her common sense? She'd always marched to a moral code that dared anyone to ridicule her choice to remain a virgin.

"No." She pushed Tyler away, torn between her need and the voice that hounded her.

"No? You said yes." Stifling an oath, Tyler inched away.

Didn't she know she couldn't heat him up and back away? A man could take only so much. His loins were about to burst. How could she cut off her emotions like that?

He glanced down at her, and Tyler had his answer.

She couldn't.

He cupped her chin, forcing her gaze to remain linked with his. Dark and smoky, her hooded eyes reeked of emotion. His pulse throbbed at the discovery.

She'd been every bit as hot as he'd been. And still was. His gaze traveled from her eyes to her neck, then lingered on her bare breasts. He could still feel their creamy softness. Sensing his stare, she pulled her blouse together. He wanted to reach out and stop her.

A crazy kind of connection arched through him, a connection every bit as emotional as physical. Lifting his hand to his face, he traced his bruised temple, remembering how gently she'd touched it.

After tomorrow he'd probably never see her again. And though it might be a boost to his sanity, he found the thought depressed him.

Admit it, Novak, she's unique. One-of-a-kind!

Yeah right! The kind who needs a keeper.

Bad idea.

He couldn't seem to get a fix on what was happening to him. He couldn't be—

No, not possible. With Red? With Regina?

No way. Naw.

His gaze roamed over her delectable body.

Well, maybe sort of. Could be lust. But love?

No!

Aw, Jeeze... Was it possible he was falling for her?

He'd known her less than twenty-four hours. He wasn't an over-sexed adolescent. But why couldn't it happen? Did love operate on a time table? Was there some set formula that decreed you must know someone 15.4 days before falling in love? As far as he was concerned, a whole lifetime had been squeezed into these past hours.

He knew what he wanted in a woman. She had to be generous, a good sport, have a good sense of humor, be dependable.

Red was all those and more.

No debating her zany sense of humor, and she hung in when the going got rough. He liked that in a woman. There were just a couple of stumbling blocks, her connection to the smugglers and the possibility that she was a hooker. Course knowing Red, there might be a perfectly illogical explanation for both. But even if there wasn't, he couldn't deny his feelings.

Something told him this wasn't lust.

"It's my fault," she announced, sitting up and edging away.

"Imagine that!" He had no earthly idea what she referred to, but she probably was right. The way he had it figured, every dad-blasted thing could be laid at her doorstep, including the spell she'd cast on him.

"I apologize."

She took a deep breath and tried to look down, but Tyler wouldn't let her. He ran his thumb over her moist lips, swollen from their kisses. "You apologized earlier."

"That was for getting you involved. I meant now. I didn't mean to lead you on like that."

"Was that what you were doing?"

"No." The color in her cheeks deepened. "It just happened. I wasn't teasing."

"I didn't think you were." Yet something was out of whack. And why should that surprise him? Their bodies communicated so magnificently. Why couldn't their minds?

"It's just too fast."

He seconded that. Passion ignited between them so fast it had been scary. This very moment his arousal still strained against his jeans. "Fast but good." *Damn good.*

"No one has ever made me feel so out of control."

He could relate to that, too. "Ditto for me, but you can't do that to a man, Red. You can't respond the way you did."

"I know," she paused, her gaze sliding downward for a second, then meeting his. "That's why I had to stop."

Her voice trembled and he reached for her hand. He wanted to hold her but saw the determined set of her jaw. Why he cared so much about this woman still confounded him.

"I couldn't let things go any further. I need to know more about you. You're very good, by the way."

"Thanks. Coming from you, I take that as a supreme compliment."

"You do?"

"Yeah, considering all the other men you've known."

"But I haven't known that many. This is my f—"

"Getting to be a broken record, Red."

"But it's true." Holding both his hands, she scooted up onto her knees and knelt before him. "Tyler, we have to talk. I know in my heart I couldn't respond like this unless I cared about you, and I couldn't care about you unless you were a good decent person. And you are. Maybe something's led you temporarily astray."

A redhead who turned out not be a redhead had led him astray.

"That's probably my fault, too," she said, her hands still clinging to his.

His eyebrows shot up. "Your fault?" Experience told him her explanation would come within seconds. After all, reason streaked through her mind at the speed of light, while daffy incoherency seemed to have taken up permanent residence.

"Yes, I'm responsible for leading you astray, putting temptation in your way."

Bingo! "But such a nice temptation."

"No, Tyler. You need to resist it, resist breaking the law."

"Practicing with you would be breaking the law?" He gritted his teeth. Sounded like he'd been right about her being a hooker.

"No, silly."

As her eyes sparked to life, his gaze dropped to her lips, and he couldn't help himself. He wanted to taste her. "You'd be worth the risk."

"Me?"

He brushed his lips across hers. "You."

"Tyler." She inched away and released his hands.

He scooted closer. "What?"

She shook her head. "This is serious."

"Yeah." Dead right again. He'd finally admitted things were serious between them and he seriously wanted more.

"Tyler, I meant it. Nothing is worth compromising your good name. I don't want you arrested."

He kissed her earlobe. "I appreciate your concern, but I don't plan on being arrested." Nothing illegal about free samples.

"You shouldn't be so cocky. There must be programs available like Crooks Anonymous."

"Crooks Anonymous?"

"Aunt Ruth might know one. A few years back she had a slight problem with Bloody Marys and attended some meetings. I could go with you, vouch for you, be your sponsor. Keep you on the straight and narrow and rehabilitate you."

Tyler's mind went blank. She was doing it to him again, leaving him in limbo. He told himself not to pursue an answer, but his tongue glibly refused. "What the hell are you talking about?"

"Look, I know all about it."

"Know about what?" he asked, touching his lips to her cheek. A little more distraction and he'd have her back to where they'd been earlier.

"The marbles. I know there's something fishy and you've been hiding them."

"What?" Tyler bolted onto his knees, his mind scrambling in a dozen directions.

"Whatever you think they might be, you have to turn them over to the authorities."

"Damn right I will!"

"You will?" Silence stretched between them while she computed what he'd said. "You're not a criminal?"

"Criminal?" He clenched his jaw, then frisked through his pocket and pulled out his identification. "I'm F.B.I. I arrest criminals." He shoved it in front of her face. "Tell me, what do you know about the marbles?"

"F.B.I.!" Regina's mind spun, her breath faltered. Never in her wildest dreams would she have pegged him for an agent. "You're F.B.I.?" She grabbed his wallet and examined his badge. Glory be, her instincts had been right. He wasn't a criminal! All this time she'd fought her suspicions and so hoped he wasn't, yet there'd always been a nagging doubt. Now relief and elation swirled through her. She was just about to hug him when a trace of anger welled up. "You lied. You said—"

"I know. I let you think I worked at the airport. A technicality. I *was* working there."

Not satisfied, she eyed him suspiciously. "Why?"

"Why? Because we had a stake-out going on."

"No. Why did you lie to me?" She slammed his wallet back into his ribcage.

"Part of my job when we're undercover. You walked into the web and—"

"Web? Where?" Her gaze tangled with his.

"Flight 311."

"And you thought I—?" Taking a deep breath, she replenished the air in her lungs. "You do, don't you? You think I'm some kind of criminal."

"I couldn't be sure." He stuffed his wallet back in his hip

pocket and grimaced. "I kept wondering if it was a set-up, wondering of all the men at the gate, why you asked me to accompany you."

"Aunt Sophia was closing in on me, and I had to make a spur-of-the-moment decision. I'd noticed you, noticed your smile. I couldn't help it. Maybe it was fate. Maybe it was... " Regina bit her lip. She wouldn't lie. Not to him, or to herself. "The truth is—"

"The truth is," he interrupted, "I couldn't see how you could be a criminal, but you were with them."

"Them?"

"Foster and Dawson. Cripes you were sitting next to Foster. They're smugglers."

"Smugglers?" Regina asked. "And the marbles?"

"Have diamonds mixed in with them."

"Oh, my gosh! Oh, dear! Oh, no!"

"I thought you knew."

"I-I didn't. I suspected. You had last hidden them in—"

"Your briefcase. Yeah."

"I'm not a smuggler," she defended herself, unsure whether she was hurt or angry. "In my whole life I've never stolen anything except my sister's bike, and I returned it the same day. How could you think I—"

"Listen, Red. I didn't want to think it. But after I was shanghaied, I wondered."

"But they tied me up, too."

"I thought you might have had a falling out with them."

"That's what I suspected about you when I sensed you were so interested in the birthday package, and when I caught you hiding the marbles."

"You thought I was with them?" He shot her a disgruntled look.

"Yes. And I hated it 'cause I thought I was falling in—" She stopped.

"Finish it, Red."

Her mouth went dry. She was reluctant to tell him what she'd only just realized herself, yet his velvety command seduced her. "F-falling for a criminal, and I knew I could never... "

"Never what?"

"Never care that way about someone on the shady side of the law."

"I had the same problem. I flipped over a redhead who turned out to be wearing a wig and had just about decided you were on the level, when you started playing hide-and-seek with the marbles."

"Oh, Tyler." She dipped her head.

A lone finger skimmed along her cheek, then tilted her chin, forcing her head upward to meet his dusky gaze. "I know," he said. "I feel the same. It's like we had no choice. It's good to know you're an honest citizen, Miss Citrano."

"You, too."

Slowly, he moved his hand away then raked it through his hair as if struggling for control. "So much for stumbling block number one."

"I beg your pardon?"

"Nothing." He stared at the fire, his face taking on a reflective expression before his gaze drifted back to hers. "How'd you get messed up with them? I saw Foster slip you the package at the gate."

"You mean you didn't accompany me just 'cause I asked you?" She suddenly felt vulnerable, less assured, embarrassed.

"No. I played a hunch he'd slipped you the diamonds and wondered about your involvement."

"Then I wasn't responsible." She let out a long sigh. "All day long I've been beating up on myself thinking I involved an innocent by-stander, at least until after the crash when I began to wonder if you were connected to those thugs."

"Shh." His fingertips shushed her lips. "I involved myself. It was a job, but if I hadn't been on assignment, I'd have accompanied you most anywhere," he said in a deep compassionate voice, then leveled his intense gaze at her. "Why did you take the package?"

Encouraged by his words, Regina brightened. "All I could think about was getting away from my aunt before she discovered what I was up to. It seemed so innocent, so harmless. He said he had to catch the flight that was about to leave and asked me to do him a favor—to take the present to the General Aviation Airport."

"He was trying to throw us off, probably sensed he was under surveillance and hoped we wouldn't see him slip you the package. Regina." His voice was barely audible. "I never wanted you to be part of them. Even when I thought you were,

I couldn't believe it."

"And what's been happening between us wasn't—"

"—wasn't an act if that's what you're thinking. I can't explain it either." He opened his arms. "Come here." She crept forward on her knees and moved into the protective circle. "Now tell me how you happened to be at the gate and what you were doing with all those men."

He was obsessed with her and men. "Men?"

"Yeah, men. The bald man, the soldier, the businessman, and the guy in the baseball cap."

"That's right, you watched me."

"And went quietly insane."

Chapter Ten

Quietly insane.

Interesting. Informative.

Delicious. Delightful.

Regina smiled. No man uttered such words unless he was jealous. It definitely sounded as if he cared, as if he was interested in her.

Good.

'Cause she was interested in him.

She'd set off on this exercise to hone her skills to find the man of her dreams. And on her very first try the fickle finger of fate had intervened and Tyler had fallen into her lap. Of course they barely knew each other, but that could be remedied. Now that she'd learned he wasn't a criminal, something her instincts had told her all along, she just knew he was the man for her. They could take it slow and easy over the next few weeks. That was the sensible approach, but she was feeling far from sensible. She felt like a woman in...

Love?

Odd that she felt so comfortable with a man she'd known only a few hours. Odder still that she was so intensely drawn to him. What else, but love could make her feel safe as a bug in a rug in this abandoned shack with Tyler after the harrowing day she'd had? Most people would be scared out of their wits.

Yes!

She was falling in love with him and the very best part was he seemed to feel the same way. While the crackling fire distracted him, she admired his angular cheekbones. He was handsome, and yet he wasn't. Pretty-boy-looks had never appealed to her. But it wasn't his looks alone that turned her on. It was something inside him.

He reminded her of her brother. Vincent tried to appear hard and tough, but like Tyler, it was all a sham. Earlier when Tyler had appeared irritated and snapped off the heels of her shoes, she'd thought him a wretched grump, but it hadn't lasted. Soon after that he'd come to her rescue, and he'd been genuinely concerned.

She liked that in a man.

In her men.

When it came to showing their feelings, her father and brother never missed a chance to be openly demonstrative.

Still reveling over Tyler's comment, Regina let the heady sensations sweep through her. "Quietly insane, huh?" she asked as he swung his gaze back, trying to stare her down.

"Yeah."

She saw right through him into the marshmallow softness that lay beneath his questioning glare. "Those men in the airport meant nothing. I was just passing time with them."

"I bet!" His lips curved contrarily, almost little boy-like. "You sure have a friendly way of doing it."

She'd been right. He was jealous. "You needn't worry. There's no particular man in my life."

"That's what worries me."

She frowned at his curious remark. "You did say you weren't involved with anyone, didn't you?"

"No, I didn't."

"Oh." She crossed her fingers. "Well, are you?"

He reached for her fingers and uncrossed them. "There's no one special, except—"

Her heart sank. "Except?"

"Till today." He winked.

Warm, fuzzy tingles raced through her. He rubbed his thumb over the back of her hand, and she swallowed, then closed her eyes at his tantalizing touch.

"You still haven't explained about the men."

"The men?" Her eyes flew open and a flush tinged her cheeks. A flush that had nothing to do with the fire blazing in the hearth. "I thought I explained. I was just trying out the magazine article on them."

"That's what I thought. Like I said, you can chuck it. You don't need lessons."

His finger crept to the crick of her elbow, and she took a deep focusing breath, inhaling the fragrant smell of pine from the burning wood. "That's because you bring out the best in me."

"I try."

Understatement of the century. This very moment his every touch was about to send her into orbit. She shifted her gaze from his dark, predatory eyes to the flickering fire and patterns of light it cast on the wall. A short time ago he'd dragged the mattress closer to the hearth and there was warmth from the fire and even more from his heated glance.

Self conscious, she searched for something to say. Anything that might divert his obsession from the men and the magazine article. "It's hard to believe that a little more than twenty-four hours ago I was standing in a teller's cage. So much has happened."

"Teller's cage!" Tyler dropped her hand. The cage fit, but a freaking bank? "You work in a bank."

"Yes. Why?"

"Nothing. I forgot you're not hooked up with the smugglers. If you were, putting you in a bank would have been tantamount to letting a rooster loose in the hen house." The rueful look in her eyes told him he'd mis-spoke. "I'm sorry. My mind is fried. I didn't mean to offend you. I just never pictured you as a teller in the bank, considering—"

"I understand."

He wished he could understand her half as well. It just didn't equate. A sedate teller moonlighting as a hooker? Next thing she'd be telling him her father was a policeman.

"Debits and credits, that's how I spend my days. Speaking of which, I'll never be able to repay you for saving my life," she commented, her words slicing into his thoughts. "I'd have never survived on my own."

Somehow he doubted that. If she'd charmed that snake, she could manage anything.

"Spending time in the woods just isn't my thing."

He imagined not. Not many Johns lurking in the forests these days. "More call for your line of work in the cities, I suppose."

She wrinkled her nose, tilted her head, and remained quiet for a few seconds. "Tyler."

Her voice was too faint, too wispy. He recognized the signs.

"I have a question."

He steeled himself for it.

"Do you think love at first sight is possible?"

"Not before today. I imagine you're going to tell me that one of your aunts does."

"All three of them do."

"Good for them. That makes four of us."

"Five." She looked at him with that perky smile of hers.

He cleared his throat. "About our relationship."

"Relationship?"

"You and me hanging out together. It drives me crazy thinking about you being with other men." No time like the present to address the problem. He was all for encouraging a woman in her career, but he drew the line at prostitution.

"Now that I've met you, any others I've known are forgotten, just like that." She snapped her fingers.

He appreciated the sentiment. In fact, it stroked his ego. "It's the future I'm thinking about. You're going to have to give up your sideline."

"Sideline?"

"Yeah, you know."

"But I don't." Regina arched a brow and studied the man who sat beside her. Sometimes Tyler could really be out to lunch. Like right now. Noticing the downward curve of his mouth, she ran a finger along his chin. "What sideline?"

A muscle tightened in his jaw. "What you were doing today at the gate in the airport."

"Doing?"

"Hustling those men."

Back to the men again. Why was he so hung up on them? Didn't he know he was the only one she cared about? This very moment she had the urge to run her hands across his chest. Instead, she tried to concentrate on what he'd said. Her thoughts zigged, then zagged. *Of course.* "You mean my practicing?"

"Yeah, your *practicing,*" he said, emphasizing his last word.

"But how am I supposed to get better at it?" She snuggled closer, inhaling his masculine scent, her fingers resting on his collar.

"You can do all your practicing on me."

"But if I don't see you again—"

"You'll see me. Count on that."

"I do," she said, loving the sexy undertones of his low and gravelly voice. "I count on you. I've counted on you all day, and I plan to count on you in the future, but I don't understand why you want me to stop flirting with others."

She'd hardly begun. Suited her fine, she supposed. She'd always been nervous and shy about it. "That's kinda drastic, isn't it?" she asked him. "Even after years of marriage my parents flirt with other people now and then." But then again she didn't think she'd could stand to watch Tyler flirt with a bunch of women. "Course, you may have a point—"

Tyler's whistle shattered her eardrums. "Whoa, back up the truck! Where did flirting come from?"

"What do you mean?" She swayed against him, bracing her hand against his chest to balance herself. He gazed down at her, his eyes flickering. Maybe he was right. Maybe she didn't need the magazine.

"Flirting came from the magazine," she said, falling deeper under the spell of his gaze. "Even you said you understood what I was doing."

"Flirting?"

"Yes."

"Didn't look like it."

"I told you I'm not very experienced."

"Flirting's kind of a fancy name for it."

"What else would you call it?"

"Hooking," he said under his breath.

"I beg your pardon? H-hooking? Hook—" Regina's breath stalled. "Did you s-say—"

"It's the nicest term I can think of right now."

"You did say it. You're joking, right?"

He shook his head.

Astonishment drained the color from her face. Indignation brought it back. "Hooking? You think—"

"I care about you."

The man was incredible. It was impossible to remain peeved at him. She'd been all set to ream him out. Any trace of anger melted away.

"And I don't fancy sharing you. I want you all to myself. No more being a hooker."

Her mind raced backwards, resurrecting the day, minute by minute. Then seeing it through Tyler's perspective, she smiled. Understanding stuck like a thunderbolt.

An involuntary giggle wiggled its way up her throat.

Her giggle cascaded to chuckles.

The chuckles exploded into full-blown laughter.

"What's so funny?" He lifted his brows.

"I ought to be furious," she managed to answer over her giggles.

"That so?" Gently touching his fingers to her lips, he stilled her laughter.

"To think you thought I was a hooker."

"Thinking had nothing to do with it. I saw you in action." He paused as though contemplating something, then plowed his fingers through his hair. "Maybe your aunt knows of a group you can attend."

"Like Hookers Anonymous," she supplied, still laughing.

"Yeah. I'd go with you. Better yet, I'd volunteer to keep you so booked up and occupied you wouldn't need a support group."

"You'd do that for me."

"My pleasure."

And hers as well, she suspected. She looked at him for a long moment. "You've a soft heart, Tyler, and I appreciate how you feel, but I'm not a hooker."

"Denial's common."

"Tyler." She lowered her voice to a whisper.

"Yeah."

"Look at me," she implored. Their gazes locked, his eyes meshing with hers. "I've never been a hooker and never plan to be."

"But I saw you."

"What you saw was me practicing my flirting techniques." Loathe to break the spell that had sprung between them, she crawled across the lumpy mattress and pulled the magazine from her briefcase. Conscious that his eyes had tracked her every move, she scooted back more gracefully, then sat down beside him and flipped to the article. "See, ' FIVE STEPS TO FLIRTING.' The article caught my eye a few days ago."

Less than a minute after he started reading, a tide of red crept up his neck. “You mean you’re not—”

“Cross my heart, I’m not.”

“Man was I off base.” He read some more. “This is fascinating. I’m sorry. It just looked like—”

“I imagine it did. Looking at it from your angle, it’s kinda funny.”

“Damned embarrassing. But I could have sworn you were hooking.”

She slid her finger to his lip. “I know. I can see where it would look that way, and if it wasn’t so funny, I think I’d be mad, insulted.”

Slowly, Tyler drew her fingertip into his mouth. The delicious sensation shimmered down her arm and wended its way to her breastbone. “I’m sorry,” he mumbled, “won’t do to have you mad, but it doesn’t change how I feel. Even when I thought you might be a hooker or connected to the smugglers, I liked everything about you. And who was I to judge? There are circumstances to consider and you seemed to have ethics. I kept thinking maybe I could—”

“Reform me?”

“Yeah.”

His easy smile endeared him to her. “That’s what I thought, too. That I could reform you.”

“Flirting, huh?” He shook his head, then kissed the tip of her nose.

“Mmmm.”

“Son of a gun, just flirting.”

“Just flirting,” she repeated, lifting her face until his lips touched hers. They feathered across her mouth and a small sound snuck from the back of her throat. “Plain and simple flirting, that’s all.”

Plain and simple! No way!

Tyler groaned.

Not plain. Not by a long shot. One look at Red’s vivacious smile, stunning looks, and supple body, and plain flew out the window.

And simple?

His life had grown even more complicated. His whole world exploded around him.

He wanted her.

Every fiber in his body wanted her with a need so great he burned. With a need so biting he could taste it. A need that had been building all day. A need he dared not give in to. Insight told him he'd blow his future with her to smithereens if he did.

Regina Anne Catherine Mary.

Adorable.

Admirable.

And if his instincts served him right, virginal. He didn't doubt for a minute she had struggled to maintain that status. Guys had probably lined up to hit on her, and from her red-blooded responses, Tyler sensed she'd struggled against her own inner desires to succumb. Just about everything she'd done today had jump-started his libido, and it was up to him to put a lid on it.

But she wasn't making it easy.

A few moments of silence slipped by as he absorbed the shock of his discovery. For his own protection, he shifted away, determined to keep her at arm's length. He had his own moral yardstick and set of ethics. "So," he slurred with a rising inflection, "why?"

"Why?"

Her brow crinkled. Good. It was her turn to be flummoxed. "Why the magazine? Why the experiment?"

"An act of desperation, I guess. I'm shy and... it's not that I don't like men."

"I know." He smothered a grin. "You aren't shy around me."

"With you it's been different. Kinda like—"

"—magic," he finished.

A blush hovered on her cheeks. "Until today I had a problem attracting men."

"Bull s... baloney!"

"No. It's true." She snagged a dust bunny off the blanket. "I'd get all flustered and sit back and wait until a man approaches me rather than try to get his attention, and—"

"And?"

"That doesn't happen too often. When it does, it's always Mr. Wrong. To my family's lament I'm the only Citrano female in recent history who hasn't been married by her twenty-fifth birthday. My aunts took over arranging one blind date after another. It got so embarrassing I decided to outflank them."

"And today was your first attempt."

"Yes."

Tyler rubbed his beard-stubbled chin. It would be her last if he had anything to say about it.

"I'd only intended taking baby steps today, but wham-bam, there I was in the middle of Cincinnati Airport taking big time giant steps. It was kind of overwhelming. But then again if I hadn't found that magazine, I wouldn't have seen the article, and if I hadn't seen the article, I wouldn't have come to the airport, and if I hadn't come to the—"

"Regina," he whispered.

"Mmm?"

"You know I care about you."

"And me, you."

Too many promises shone in her eyes. He clenched both his fists, wanting to kiss her, yet refusing to weaken. He knew if he did, there'd be little resistance from her. Nearly at the end of his tether, he jumped to his feet, grabbed the backpack, and strode across the room.

"What are you doing?"

"Preserving my sanity. I can't guarantee what'll happen if I touch you, and don't tell me you feel the same way because I damn well know you do. Remember when you said it was too fast, too soon?"

She nodded.

"You were right." He fought the desire to recross the room and pull her into his arms. "It's like we've been hit by a tidal wave." He glanced at the flickering flames before daring to look at her again. "We both want more out of what's started up between us than a quick roll in the hay. Agreed?"

"Agreed." Her voice said yes, but the same thoughts that threatened to undo him gleamed in her eyes.

"I have a sneaking suspicion those aunts of yours would be none too pleased if I took advantage of their niece."

"You wouldn't be taking advantage."

"Regina!"

"Tyler?"

Dammit! Despite the shadows he could still see the sultry tilt of her chin. A sensual current flowed clear across the room. "Don't push it unless you want me to spend the night cooling off outside in the rain."

Red gathered the blanket around her. "I don't think I'll sleep. I'm too keyed up."

Join the club. "Try counting sheep like I plan to do."

But she had a better idea. Not sheep, but capitols.

Maine: Augusta

New Hampshire: Concord

Massachusetts: Boston

Connecticut: uh ...

With the backpack serving as his pillow, Tyler lay on the rough, wooden floor and started his own vigil.

One tela-sheep

Two tela-sheep

Three tela-sheep

Dammit.

He'd been Carmen Mirandized!

Sunlight streamed through the window and took dead aim on Regina's brow. She gripped the blanket, cracked open an eyelid, then quickly closed it. This wasn't her peach and white bedroom, nor her mother's patchwork quilt. Inhaling a most peculiar bouquet of ashes, yeast, and pine, she wrinkled her nose. Certainly didn't smell like the elusive capitol of Connecticut, either. Half a heartbeat later, she bolted upright and opened her eyes. After a lifetime of awakening in the comfort of her bedroom, the reality of the cabin sunk into her fuzzy brain.

The cabin.

The Smokies.

She smiled.

Yesterday hadn't been an illusion after all. Yesterday had been a banner day. A Tyler Novak Day. And there he lay.

She brushed the sleep from her eyes and with a vague sense of awe focused her gaze on him as he slept across the room from the fireplace. He didn't stir. No wonder! Neither of them had gotten much sleep, and as she'd had the benefit of the mattress, she couldn't blame her restlessness on the hard, cabin floor. Tension had been the culprit. Enough to fuel a rocket ship.

They'd talked way into the night. He'd told her about his childhood, his family, and his brief marriage. He'd told her how his family often went to the Reds' games, and he'd snared a foul ball once. She told him how her family went to the ballpark, and she'd snagged her skirt trying to get Pete Rose's autograph. He told her how he enjoyed being a Boy Scout and had learned to tie knots. She told him of the time she'd fallen out of a tree and got a knot on her head while practicing the part of Juliette for Aunt Sophia.

She'd gone on and on about her large complex family until he was thoroughly confused. She smiled, remembering something he'd said after she'd told him they were a close knit family and her mom was her best friend, the kind of person she could share almost anything with.

"Does your mother know about this?" He'd rolled onto his back, his hands propped behind his head.

"This?"

"This flirting adventure of yours."

"No. Only you know."

"Then maybe I'm your best friend, too."

"I think you're right." His words, his intimate tone had struck a chord deep inside her. "You're my new best friend." Utterly weary yet wide awake, she knew only sheer will power kept her from crossing the room to join him. Tyler's grunts had told her he fought the same battle.

Eventually, they'd fallen asleep. But throughout the night she'd wakened periodically and listened for sounds of him, heard him toss and turn. Each time she'd toyed with calling out to him, until her eyes drifted close and sleep made the decision for her. Tyler had passed the night as fitfully as she, and she reckoned, sunlight creeping across the cabin floor or not, it'd be some time before he wakened.

And she couldn't think of a better way to put that time to use than to prop her elbow on her knees and watch him as he lay sprawled on the floor, one arm tucked under his cheek, the other flung out by his side. How lucky she'd been that the magazine article had sent her to the airport. First time out of the gate and she'd bagged the prize. And all because she'd been in the right place at the wrong time. Or something like that.

Her gaze slid over Tyler, drinking in his tousled hair, his white cotton T-shirt molding his muscular back, and his chiseled face. A quivering stirred low in her belly, and unconsciously she rubbed her hand down the back of her neck, imagining what it would be like to curl up beside him.

But he'd warned her. He'd as much as said he'd reached his limit and any move on her part would be an open invitation for sex. A tantalizing thought, but a risky venture. Though her emotional nature welcomed the idea, good sense weighed against it. Anyone with an ounce of logic knew making passionate love to someone you'd known less than twenty-four hours was foolhardy. Sex had consequences and shouldn't be treated casually, at least not in her book.

Knowing their private interlude might end today and wishing she could listen to her heart, Regina sighed and balled her hands into fists. It would be hard, but she'd adhere to the Citrano creed, accept the mission thrust upon her. Despite her unquenched desire, she'd remain strong, resist temptation.

She licked her lips.

By heavens, she was thirsty. And nature called, too.

Scrambling to her feet, she dragged the blanket and soundlessly crossed the room. As she looked down at Tyler's sleeping form, a flood of tenderness squeezed her heartstrings. What harm could one teency-weency little touch do? Since the Smoky Mountain sunrise had not yet warmed the chilled cabin, surely, he could use her blanket. She fell to her knees, then shook the rumpled blanket and draped it over his body. A cloud of dust floated over them.

Tyler coughed, mumbled, then twitched his nose.

Doing her best to prevent dust from landing on his face, Regina waved her arms in the air and nearly landed flat squat on top of him. She braced her hands on either side of his body, seconds away from impaling his chest with her elbow. Sleeping men looked like such innocent little boys, she thought, regaining her balance and concentrating on Tyler's long, dark lashes as a particle of dust nearly landed on them. She huffed and puffed and blew it away.

Even in his sleep, a roguish grin creased his face. Longing shimmered through her, and she surrendered to her impulse—to the itty bitty touch. Barely daring to breathe, she held her trembling hand aloft and debated which spot on his body was least likely disturb her sleeping tiger.

As if engaged in a mystical ritual, she slowly lifted her finger to her mouth, moistened it, then came within a hair's breath of dropping a fingertip kiss on his lips. Instead, she stroked his forehead. He responded with an almost imperceptible shiver as if the transfer of her emotions had penetrated his layers of sleep. Warm, wistful memories of their day together spun in her head as she inched backwards. A deeper intimacy would have to wait.

"Sleep well." She exhaled a shuddery sigh and rose to her feet.

After the beating he'd taken yesterday, he deserved all the rest he could get. And although he'd sloughed it off, she felt responsible for his injuries. Perhaps she could make it up to him, do something useful. Like prepare breakfast. She glanced over her shoulder at the window. Forests were full of nuts and berries, weren't they?

Grabbing Tyler's backpack, she tiptoed to the door and cast a cursory glance around the cabin. In the blink of an eye the Governor's reception Tyler had painted for her materialized. By the time Tyler awoke, she'd have laid out a feast fit for a king. She could see it now. Tapestries, coats of arms, goblets, and a circular oaken table. They could pretend they were breaking fast in King Arthur's court.

Minus the Connecticut Yankee, naturally.

Unless, of course, he chose to reveal its capitol.

Chapter Eleven

Morning mist clung to the mountain peaks.

In contrast to the quiet, Regina stumbled through the underbrush, thrashing at it with a twig, announcing her presence to any creatures who might lurk in her path. Earlier, before embarking on her expedition, she'd filled the canteen from the rock-studded creek, then freshened up. Recalling the bracing coolness of the water, she hunched her shoulders and shivered.

Now as she searched out the blackberries, she took extra care not to become snagged on the thorny briars. And she'd been diligent about marking a trail with torn remnants of her short petticoat so she could find her way back. Hunger gnawed in her stomach, and unable to find anything else to eat, she gave in to temptation. She sampled some of the juicy berries, then paused to collect a bouquet of wild flowers, honeysuckle blossoms, and shiny leaves.

They'd make a great arrangement, add a romantic touch to their meager meal.

As she emerged from the dappled shadows, childlike wonder washed over her. Captivated by the view of unscalable ridges and the emerald gorge below, she halted to admire it more fully. Sunlight winked through the leaves and a breeze quickened the limbs. The same breeze blew a strand of hair across her face while a crow cawed sharp and shrill. For the first time in her life she experienced a genuine appreciation of the wilderness.

Tyler's doing, no doubt.

He seemed to have heightened her senses. About everything. She squeezed her eyes shut. Too bad he wasn't here to share it. There was something primitive here, something elemental, like their relationship. Man, woman, wilderness. She crossed her fingers, hoping what she and Tyler had found would survive in the real world.

Inhaling the fertile, humid air from last night's rainfall, she opened her eyes and then she saw it. A low built loghouse hidden in the mossy undergrowth and tucked against an incline. It must be the stillhouse Tyler had mentioned. A yeasty sour odor greeted her at the weather-beaten doorway. The one room shack wasn't made for comfort, the ceiling so low she could barely stand. Satisfied the place was deserted, she caught sight of an amber colored bottle.

Moonshine, she bet.

She shook the bottle, surprised to discover it wasn't empty, then stowed it in the backpack for good measure. According to Aunt Ruth, good whiskey came in handy for medicinal purposes, if nothing else.

Several minutes later as she retraced her steps, a rustle sounded from the bushes. She clutched at the straps of the backpack and halted. "That you, Hoggy?"

She spun about. No sign of her pet snake anywhere.

The thrashing persisted. Uneasy, Regina scanned the area and tensed. Sensing a presence, she turned and swore she saw a shadowy figure. Suddenly, the forest came alive. Insects buzzed, birds sang, leaves whispered and something whumped.

A bear? Did bears whump-whump? Sounded more machine-like than animal.

It didn't quite compute, but she didn't care to stick around and satisfy her curiosity. Setting her legs in motion, she jogged back to the cabin, not stopping till she neared the stretch of pines that surrounded it.

The cabin door lay open. She frowned. She'd closed it, hadn't she? Perhaps Tyler had gone to the stream and left the door ajar. This very minute he could be searching for her. All set to call out to him, she opened her mouth, then hesitated. Tingling sensations down the back of her neck warned her not to speak.

Grunts and groans, followed by a series of crashes came from the direction of the cabin. Fear twisted in her heart, surrounding it like ivy choked the tree trunks.

Sweet Lord, Tyler.

She ducked behind the cover of a pine tree, her heart pumping in quick, hard jerks. Had a bear invaded the shack? Her legs threatening to buckle, she fell to her knees and shakily crept to the window. She held her breath and peered into the cabin.

Dawson!

Never having been a bloodthirsty person, in one sense she was grateful the man had survived the night, but in another she was outraged. Apparently, he'd surprised Tyler while he slept. Guilt reared up. She'd been the bleeding heart who'd persuaded Tyler to loosen Dawson's bonds. Her good intentions had placed Tyler smack-dab in the soup again. Dawson, the no-good ingrate, was tying Tyler's hands and legs, and she could just imagine the foul thoughts rumbling around in Tyler's head.

A shudder rippled through her, followed by an inner call to arms. Tyler needed her help and this time was different. This time the stakes were higher. This time it involved the man she loved. Her first impulse was to rush to his aid.

Better sense prevailed. She lifted her fists to her temple and grimaced. What she needed was a plan. She glimpsed over her shoulder at the backpack, then shimmied out of it. The wrench, the hammer, and the whiskey bottle were stashed in it. But how could she hope to use them against a strapping man like Dawson? He could easily overpower her.

She needed a secret weapon.

A way to outthink him.

She snapped her fingers. Flirting! It just might catch him off guard.

She could do it. Repugnant as it sounded, she had to—had to charm the pants off him. Well, maybe not quite that far.

Rising to her feet, she squared her shoulders and crossed herself. She reckoned it wouldn't hurt to call on a higher authority for a bit of extra help. As it was, she'd have to draw on every skill she'd just learned. She dragged the backpack by a solitary strap, then slowly walked toward the open door.

A second before she entered, she spared a glance to her right and let out a sigh of relief. Hoggy lay coiled up in a patch of warm sunshine. "Stick around," she whispered. "I may need you."

Yesterday's sessions with Tyler had given her confidence, and Hoggy's presence fortified her even more. She paused at the threshold and primped at her hair, remembering to paste a provocative come-hither smile on her face. A subtle sway to her hips wouldn't hurt either. She hoped to turn in a performance worthy of Aunt Sophia, skilled actress that she was.

And...

Fool that he was, Dawson would soon learn it was unwise to make an enemy of a Citrano.

Three small steps and she was inside. "So there you are!" Regina gushed, sweeping into the cabin, emulating a stage entrance her Aunt Sophia would die for.

Dawson swung around, his flinty eyes meeting hers, his mouth opening to speak.

She didn't give him a chance. "I went back to the plane looking for you and gracious sakes here you are."

"Lookin' for me?" His eyebrows slanted together.

Yuck! He was tougher looking than she remembered. "Why, yes." She fluttered her eyelashes. "I was worried about you."

"Worried?"

"Why I even had Ty—uh, I had Mr. Novak loosen your ropes so you could get your hands free and take care of yourself."

"You did?" His gaze speared her like a memo nailed to a corkboard. At least she'd gotten his attention. It was important to make him think they were a team. And confuse him, too, though she wasn't sure that was one of her strong points. Come to think of it, Tyler had seemed perpetually confused. Maybe she possessed the knack and didn't know it.

"You did notice they were loosened, didn't you?" She took a sultry step forward, hoping Dawson didn't notice her tremors. "Let me see those poor little ole wrists of yours. They didn't get all red and chafed, did they?"

He took a step backwards. Good. It was working. She had him off balance, but lawdy, she sounded like a dime store imitation of Scarlett O'Hara. Where had the southern accent come from? Listening to Aunt Sophia rehearse, she supposed. Regina blinked again, still not daring to glance Tyler's way. Poor guy. Was he hurt? Was he conscious, and if he was, what was he thinking?"

"You're not wet," she remarked, letting her eyes roam up and down Dawson's body in such an exaggerated fashion that even an idiot would get her message. "Where did you spend the night?"

"In the airplane after I got free."

"Clever you." He puffed up, her sarcasm sailing by him like a fast ball over homeplate. "Good thing the plane is intact and hasn't exploded. Do you think it's airworthy?"

"Ain't you with him?"

"That's not correct."

"Come again?"

"Ain't is an improper word form." She blinked, wondering if her eyelids would drop off from overuse. "You probably meant to ask—aren't you with him?"

"Naw, I'm not with him."

Neanderthal, she thought.

He shuffled his feet. "How about you? You with him?"

"Him?" She stared blankly at Dawson, then let a pouty smile cross her lips. "Him who?"

"The dude. Him there." He pointed to Tyler.

The moment of truth had arrived. No choice but to acknowledge Tyler's presence. "Oh, you mean Mr. Novak," she answered in her best poor-little-ole-me voice.

Dead silence followed except for a muffled grunt from Tyler's direction. Slowly, reluctantly, dreading what she'd see,

Regina swung her head eighty degrees and gave Tyler a sidelong glance. He didn't look too comfortable. She winced.

Please, please, she silently intoned, *trust me Tyler. Trust me.*

It wasn't good. She'd lost his regard. She could see it slipping away in his confused and disillusioned eyes. How could he doubt her after saying he cared for her? A man thing, she supposed. They just didn't appreciate the fine points of playacting and deception.

"Wh-what makes you think I'm with him?" she asked, her back to Dawson, her gaze still locked on Tyler's. Trust me, she mouthed. Tyler narrowed his eyes to slits.

"You took his side at the tarmac by the plane," Dawson answered.

She turned. "That was your mistake." Time to take another hip-swiveling step forward. Dragging the backpack across the floor, she mimicked a rumba, or was it a samba? "I tried to tell you Frank sent me. Then suddenly there you were ganging up on Mr. Novak after he'd been so kind to escort me to your terminal. I felt sorry for him. I thought you were beating up on him because you thought he was bothering me." Regina shivered. Tyler was bothering her now, but in a different way.

"How come you know his name?"

"A girl doesn't survive a plane wreck and spend a night in the woods with a man without getting to know a little something about him." For extra insurance she winked at him.

She dropped the backpack strap and planted both her hands on her hips. She had to. Otherwise Dawson would notice her trembling hands. They wobbled almost as badly as the ceiling fan on aunt Ruth's back porch. Singing had helped subdue her fear on the plane, but belting out "Old MacDonald" might not convey the aura she wanted to exude just now. A good steamy torch song would—if she could think of one.

Perspiration broke out on her skin, and her voice threatened to quaver. Now wasn't the time to get cold feet. To cover her unease, she drew in a fortifying breath. "So how come you know his name?" she threw back at him.

"Frank went through his wallet before we stashed him on the plane."

And to think this world-class genius managed to remember it all this time. Amazing, she thought.

"He's a Fed."

"I beg your pardon?" She knew darn well what Dawson meant but wanted to keep him talking. So far he hadn't pegged her as the enemy.

"You mean you don't know it?" He spoke in a whisper, tilting his head in her direction as if he was about to share a secret.

She used the opportunity to sashay one step closer. "What should I know?" she whispered back.

"He has a badge. F.B.I."

"My stars!" With theatrical pomp, she held her hand to her mouth, ignoring Tyler's angry hisses.

"Laying it on a little thick, aren't you, Red?" Tyler's voice boomed out into the room.

His entry into the conversation made her jump. She was just about to tell Tyler to hush when Dawson looked at her, swung his face to Tyler, then shifted his gaze back to her.

"Thought your name was Reagen?" Uncertainty colored Dawson's voice as he spoke.

"He was one of our presidents."

"Huh?"

"Reagen. He used to be president."

"And who are you?"

"Well, I'm certainly not the president, though I was president of my dorm one year."

Tyler groaned sardonically, the sound clearly unrelated to physical pain. She ignored him. Cautiously, she extended her hand to Dawson. "I'm Regina. Regina Citrano." He shook it, and she wanted to retch.

From the peanut gallery came the comment, "You're forgetting the Catherine Mary's."

Dawson released her hand and scratched his head. "But he called you Red?"

"Shows what he knows. Does this hair look red?" She tossed her head while waving her hand in a scolding motion behind her back. She might have known. Here she was trying to rescue Tyler, and he was undermining her efforts.

"But you were..." Dawson squinted.

"Were what?" Regina could almost see his two cylinder brain clicking away.

"A redhead."

"It was a wig," Tyler inserted.

"Wig?" Dawson frowned.

"The wig was Frank's idea," Regina quickly improvised. "Don't let him rattle you, Mr.—"

"Bill. Call me Bill."

"Bill," she repeated with enough sugary sweetness to make her barf. Mild oaths floated from the sidelines. She heard them all, every colorful one, then whipped her head around and shot Tyler her most ferocious evil-eyed look.

"Uh, I don't suppose," Dawson mumbled.

Once again she spun her head around, beginning to think she was at a tennis match. If they kept this up much longer she'd get whiplash, not to mention cross her signals and sweet-talk Tyler while she sent Dawson nasty looks.

"Nah." Dawson shook his head as if answering a silent question. "I don't understand."

A baritone voice piped up from behind her, "Join the club," followed by a series of chuckles, and though she wasn't looking Tyler's way, she could visualize the smirk on his face.

Regina continued to ignore him, took a deep breath, and forced her best toothpaste-ad smile at Dawson. Quivering stomach aside, if her memory served her right, according to the steps in the magazine, it was time to give him the smile treatment. Fortunately or unfortunately, she wasn't sure which, Dawson returned a broad, toothy grin.

"What don't you understand?" She tried to make her voice sound soft and compassionate.

"Why you helped him overpower me on the plane."

"Can you blame me? You tied me up. I thought you'd double-crossed Frank and me. Let's not quibble."

While Dawson furrowed his brow, several more choked coughs came from Tyler's direction. Regina shoved the water canteen into Dawson's stomach. She rolled her eyes, pivoted around, and took several steps toward Tyler. "Puh-leeze. This is a private conversation."

"Did I say anything?" Tyler asked, as she walked over to him.

"You coughed."

"There's a law against coughing?"

"It's the way you did it. You were snickering."

"I wasn't. I was coughing."

"You were snickering." She checked to see that Dawson was occupied with unscrewing the canteen and lowered her voice. "And you don't trust me."

"You read all that into my coughs?"

"If Aunt Della can do it, so can I." *Stretching the truth a wee bit, aren't you Regina*? "Too bad you can't read me."

"Now there's a challenge. Lord knows I'm trying. Can't say I've liked what I've heard."

"Think about tela-goose."

"Counting? What has blasted counting got to do with buttering up Einstein and sounding like you're in this up to your ears?"

"Then think of the number five. As in steps."

"Holy Toledo! You're practicing on him! Now wait a damn min—"

"Have faith. You said I was good."

"There's good and there's good. He's gonna want to take it further than five measly steps."

"Got any other suggestions?"

"At the moment, no." He tried to jerk his wrists free.

She leaned down and whispered in hushed tones so Dawson couldn't hear. "Then help me, Tyler. I need your support. It's my fault you're here. You rescued me, now it's my turn to save you. I know I can do it."

She swallowed and made an inarticulate sound. At closer quarters she noticed one side of his jaw was puffy. He looked queasy. Definitely queasy. Daring not show sympathy for Tyler's bruises, she chewed on her lip. He hadn't stood a chance against Dawson's surprise attack, although from the welts she'd seen on Dawson's face, Tyler had put up a decent fight. As she stared at Tyler, his back propped against the wall, his face grew thoughtful, tender, the intensity of his gaze so powerful, it felt as if he'd reached out and squeezed her hand.

His brown eyes slowly crinkled. A crooked grin crept across his mouth. "I know you can do it, too," he whispered in a husky voice, and then his smile faded. "Be careful, Red, you hear?"

She basked in his encouraging words until an ear-shattering whistle blasted through the cabin. Feeling hot breath on the nape of her neck, Regina jumped. So absorbed with Tyler, she'd momentarily forgotten about Dawson.

"What's all the yammering about?" Dawson peered over her shoulder.

"He was just smarting off, that's all."

"Want me to gag him?"

"No!" Her heart hammered, and she pivoted on her heels, nearly bumping into Dawson's chest. "I can handle him." And now she knew she could handle Dawson, too. Tyler's rallying words had erased her doubts. As she led Dawson away from Tyler, she flashed another enchanting smile while cringing inwardly.

"Yeah, well, I'm only interested in one thing."

Thank the Lord for small miracles. Dawson looked like the type who could only handle one thought at a time, and suspecting it was the package, she cut him off. "Food. You're interested in food. There's no telling when you last ate. A big man like you. Why your stomach must be 'a rumbling and 'a grumbling. Now if you'll just sit right—"

"Yeah, I'm hungry," he rudely interrupted, "but what I want to know is where the package is."

"Don't worry about the diamonds."

"You know?"

"Of course I know," she said with conviction, tossing her head for extra emphasis. "I told you I was with Frank. They're perfectly safe, but first things first. Let's get you something to eat."

And drink. Lots and lots of that well-aged shine.

Tyler groaned, tugged at his ropes, then swore.

Blast!

Save him, would she?

His head throbbed, his bones ached, and they were up to their armpits in trouble again. No surprise there. Trouble and Red were synonymous. For the second time in twenty-four hours Dawson had sucker punched him. His head felt like a baseball in batting practice. Since meeting up with Red, life sure hadn't been humdrum. Maybe she'd share the wealth and bring a bit of bad luck to Dawson as well. Tyler upbraided himself. He'd been a lucky son-of-a-gun to find her but ... there was another side to Red, a side that called for hazardous duty pay.

Look where a routine surveillance and a simple walk in the airport had led him.

He really shouldn't worry about her, though she'd had him on the ropes for a minute or two, listening to her cozy up to

Dawson. Wackiness aside, she was one helluva vamp, and novice or not, she was a whiz at flirting. Sooner or later, she'd have Dawson sweating. And if that didn't work, her attempts at conversation should befuddle the life out of him. There were telltale signs already when Dawson's eyes glazed over, and the creep looked like he didn't have a clue what she was talking about.

Tyler shook his buzzing head. He could almost sympathize with the guy. Almost.

The woman thrived on confusion, he thought as he watched her crook her finger and lead Dawson away. Despite the pain behind his eyes, Tyler saw something else. Something he'd missed when he'd noticed her in the airport. Red was nervous. She'd told him she was skittish about flirting, but she'd so dazzled and bewildered him, he hadn't noticed it. Now her hands trembled, her voice quivered, and she had difficulty looking Dawson in the eye. Considering the stakes and the lowlife she was dealing with, it was understandable.

Strange that she lacked confidence in flirting when she possessed such an instinctive flair for chitchat, disjointed chitchat. Nevertheless, his gutsy, Italian bombshell wasn't going to let her fear deter her from her mission.

Filing his thoughts away, he gritted his teeth and wiggled his ankles and wrists, desperate to free himself while Red chatted up Dawson like a pro. Moments ago her dewy eyes had begged him to cooperate, and he hadn't the heart to undermine her efforts. Her vow to save him touched him, and he truly believed she was capable of doing it.

The problem was Dawson.

Not only was he a red-blooded male but a first-rate slime bucket without a shred of decency. Given Red's wild, untamed hair, pie-eyed seductive gazes, and shimmying hips, it wouldn't be long before Dawson hit sensual overload.

A soft whistle slid through Tyler's teeth. Hell, he was half way there himself just watching her.

As he struggled with renewed vigor against the ropes, a twinge unrelated to desire pulsed through him. His career with the agency had placed him in dicey situations a time or two, but never with someone he cared about. The threat to Red brought home just how much he cared. He hadn't felt this way in years, always protecting himself behind a mask of indifference.

He sure as hell wasn't indifferent now.

Knocking chinks left and right with her innocence, refreshing spirit, and zany sense of humor, Red had broken through his barriers. Anxiety for her safety raged through him, along with lethal urges toward Dawson if he dared harm her. Though her talent for confusion might rule the day, he couldn't count on it. For Red's sake, he'd damn well better get free before Dawson took advantage of her.

Holy Toledo! Tyler's eyes nearly bugged out of their sockets. *What was she up to now?*

So far, so good.

Regina warily eyed Dawson as he squatted before her. She sank to her knees, crept closer to the backpack, and pulled out the whiskey bottle.

"Ta-da!" Lifting the bottle aloft with nary a tremble, she spoke with gusto, then paused for effect, growing into her flirtatious role minute by minute. "A surprise."

Dawson's gaze zapped onto the bottle like a laser beam. The hairs on the back of her neck told her Tyler was watching, too. "That's for me?" Dawson asked, his gaze flashing to hers.

"Just for you." *Every last drop.* "Pretend it's your birthday."

"Ain't my birthday."

"But pretending is fun." She shifted her legs beneath her.

"This is June. My birthday's in September."

"No kidding. September's a great month for birthdays. My Aunt Sophia's birthday is in September and my cousin, Melva's, too," she said, warming to the subject, glad to have something to talk to him about. After all, that was one of the steps in the magazine. "Come to think of it, my father's mother was born in September. So what day?"

"How should I know?" He scrunched up his shoulders.

"Beg pardon?"

"How should I know what day your mother's father—"

"Father's mother," she corrected, reaching out and straightening his crooked shirt. "You're flummoxed, aren't you?"

"Flummoxed?" He cocked his head, licked his lips, and looked at her as if he was in the twilight zone. "You callin' me something nasty? That a dirty word?"

"Certainly not. Aunt Della uses it all the time. I should have said what date?"

"Date? You want a date? Suits me, Sugar Baby. If you and Frank aren't an item, then sure, we can date."

"Never mind." She heaved a sigh. Finding the date of his birthday was immaterial—an excuse to keep him talking. And apparently a lost cause. She'd succeeded in confusing him, but in the process nearly confused herself, as well. "Have some of this." She thrust the bottle into his eager hands, remembering to flutter her eyelashes.

Dawson struggled with the ancient cap, then chugged down a healthy swig. A third of the bottle by her calculations. She'd been right. He was a rude ruffian with no manners.

"Wow!" His eyes spun, he smacked his lips, then placed his hand to his throat. "Stuff has a kick. Burns clear down my gullet."

With luck it'd burn a hole in his stomach. A hole to match the one in his head.

"Good, huh?" she asked with cheerleader enthusiasm.

He answered her with a curt nod, then tilted the neck of the bottle to his lips. Just as she'd thought. He was dehydrated, and his thirst had taken his mind off the diamonds.

"Where'd you find this?" His searching gaze scanned the cabin.

"In a shack nearby. A stillhouse, I think."

"Still?" Excitement filled his voice. "Were there other bottles?"

"Not that I noticed. After we eat, we could go back and explore." Regina crossed her fingers that he'd be knocked to kingdom come long before that. "Why?"

"Why?" A frown crossed his ugly face as he took another swallow. "Why what?"

"Why more?"

Dawson shook his head. "Lady, you're gonna have to finish out your sentinels."

Sentinels? This time he had her. Utterly lost, she screwed her brows together and watched him guzzle more whiskey. "Oh," she brightened, belatedly deciphering his gibberish. Obviously, he hadn't been a grammatical scholar. "You mean finish my sentences."

"Amen to that!" Tyler's husky whisper floated across the

room.

She tensed, then cast a quick glance at Dawson, but he'd been too busy sipping his whiskey to hear Tyler's comment. All set to turn around and remind Tyler he'd promised to be quiet, she pressed her lips together. He'd had a bad day.

A very bad day.

She let out a frustrated sigh and waited for Dawson to look at her. "I meant to say why did you want more bottles. Isn't this one enough for you?" Just her misfortune the man had a hollow leg.

He wiped his mouth on his sleeve. "This'll do me, though I wouldn't mind having a steady supply. Durn good shine. I'd like to meet up with the guy who brews it and cut a deal. Smuggle it out of the country for him."

"Think Frank would like that?"

"Fart on Frank!"

"E-Excuse me."

"He don't have to be in on every deal I make."

"Of course not. Far— Uh, phooey on Frank. Here, have some berries and trail mix." As he set the bottle down beside him, she gently poured trail mix into his hands. The dry mix should add to his thirst. "Pretend it's pizza."

"Don't like pizza."

Spoilsport. "What do you like?"

"MacDonalds."

She snapped her fingers. "A Big Mac. The berries can be fries." Though the gesture repelled her, she coquettishly lifted a berry to his mouth. "Wash it down with your whiskey." The bottle was more than half empty now. Considering his empty stomach and the potency of the brew, something should begin to happen. He wolfed down the food, and despite being hungry herself, his disgusting eating habits killed her appetite.

He chugged down more whiskey, then held out the bottle between them. "Want some, Sugar Baby?"

"Thank you, no," she answered, proud that she'd neither gagged on his endearment nor trembled under his repulsive leer. *Sugar Baby* must mean her flirting campaign was succeeding. "Be my guest." She waved her hand towards the bottle.

"Think I will." He swallowed some more, then hiccuped. "Shay," he slurred, "what about the diamonds?"

"After we eat."

"No, now."

"Now?" She held her breath.

"Now," he insisted.

Now was good. Why antagonize him when the liquor seemed to be doing its job. "They're in my briefcase. I'll get them." She crawled to her briefcase.

"No, I'll get them." Dawson huffed and puffed, scooting past, the fumes from his whiskey breath nearly overpowering her.

She slid her hand into her portfolio, meeting Dawson's. A tug of war began. The lid loosened, and marbles, mixed with diamonds spilled across the floor, skittering in all directions.

"Ooops," she muttered.

"Look what you did."

"You did it, too."

"Have to pick up the diamonds." He bent over, examining the stones and marbles.

She'd never get a better chance than this. Regina scurried on her knees to the backpack, wrapped her fingers around the wrench, and crawled to within inches of Dawson. He was so absorbed in culling out the diamonds, he didn't hear her creep up behind him. Rising to her knees, she lifted the wrench, a second away from delivering a blow to the back of Dawson's head.

He turned.

She panicked.

Before he could see what she held in her hand, she abandoned Plan A, flicked her wrist, and tossed the wrench.

Backwards.

She visualized its trajectory as it flew through the air towards the opposite wall. More precisely, the corner.

A dull thunk sounded.

Tyler howled. Or was it a scream?

Regina blanched. "Oh, no!"

A body slumped to the floor, followed by, "Aw crap!"

She covered her mouth with her hands. The wrench had landed.

And she knew where.

"What was that?" Dawson demanded, bleary-eyed.

She sagged back on her fanny. "Ty— Uh, Novak, I think." Silence hung in the air. Not a moan, not a shuffle, not even a swear word. Sheepishly, she craned her neck around. Tyler lay sprawled on the floor.

"What's his problem?" Dawson demanded.

"I think something hit him." She took a deep labored breath. "Maybe I'd better go check."

"Not a chance, Sugar Baby." His grimy hand closed around her wrist. "You and me got our work cut out here."

Torn between wanting to rush to Tyler's side and wanting to keep Dawson happy, she chose the latter. Perhaps Dawson was right. Reviving Tyler might not be a good idea just now. Better to concentrate on her main objective—to knock Dawson senseless, and to do it soon, while he was still under the influence of the moonshine.

She flashed him another supersonic smile, then set to work sifting through the marbles, depositing the diamonds in a stack near her briefcase, but her heart wasn't in it. Twinges coursed through her, unsettling her stomach. Tyler needed her. She was supposed to save him, not fell him with a wrench.

Picking up a diamond, she tensed, squeezing her hand around the cold object. From the blazing heat gathered at the nape of her neck, she swore this very moment Tyler sent lethal looks her way, but each time she snuck a glance, he lay motionless on the floor. He'd be furious when he regained consciousness—turn the air blue with curses—probably want to strangle her barehanded.

If he ever got free.

Five minutes into her chore, Hoggy slithered to the rescue. Regina saw him slip through the open doorway. It wouldn't be long before Dawson discovered him.

Chapter Twelve

Less than a minute later Dawson let loose a howl that by Regina's calculations echoed clear across the mountaintops to the state of Tennessee, its capitol being Nashville, of course.

"A snake, a snake," he yelled.

"Where," she asked, playing dumb. "Oh, my!" She clamped one hand on Dawson's shoulder. "Shoo him away. Don't let him come near us."

"Shoo him away? With what? He might be poisonous." Dawson knelt rooted to the floor, then raked his hand through his hair. "Well, I'll be a rat's ass."

How fittingly true. She tapped a finger against her lips as her tongue danced with the delicious temptation to verbally agree with him.

"Dang snake swallowed a diamond," Dawson grumbled.

Good for Hoggy. "Maybe he's a she."

"Huh?

"A she. Diamonds are a gal's best friend, you know."

"Yeah, well, we're not going to let her slither away with thousands of dollars jiggling around in her belly."

"What do you plan to do?" She cringed. Surely, Dawson wouldn't operate on Hoggy.

"Kill her and slit her open. Sure wish I had a knife or a gun."

"No reason to get greedy. We've plenty of diamonds. Let her go in peace. Just keep her distracted, and I'll look for something to shoo her out the door with."

While Hoggy swung into her infamous, ferocious, snake act, Regina edged away. Her hands literally shook as they dipped into the backpack. Thanks to Hoggy she had a second chance and this was Do-Or-Die-Time. Same plan—different weapon. She rummaged around the canvas bag until her fingers gripped the hammer. Crawling stealthily, she positioned herself behind Dawson.

This time she wouldn't be denied, but first— "Tell me, Bill," she asked in soft dulcet tones while Dawson's gaze remained riveted on Hoggy.

"Yeah, what?" he snarled over his shoulder.

"You haven't by chance ever spent some time in Connecticut, have you?"

"Connecticut?"

"Yes." Her breath quickened. Perhaps she'd finally solve the nagging mystery.

"Naw, I don't think so."

"Then you wouldn't know its capitol?"

"You crazy?"

Ah well, it'd been worth a try. "Too bad. I wanted to make sure before..." She paused, her fingers tightening on the hammer.

"Before what?"

"This."

Regina offered up a prayer, then with all the strength she could muster, slammed the weapon down on the back of his head. Already on his knees, Dawson collapsed to the floor, his head coming to rest inches from Hoggy. For extra measure, she whacked Dawson again, dropped the hammer, and gazed in horror at what she'd done. No sense agonizing over it. Her violent act had been necessary.

She whirled on her knees, all set to spring to her feet and rush to Tyler when footsteps pounded outside the doorway.

Everything happened at once.

The room filled with men, four of them, their guns pointed at her, their shirts identifying them as F.B.I. After checking out the fallen bodies, one man knelt by Tyler's side while the other three surrounded her. They didn't look friendly.

"Thank goodness you've come." She rose to her feet and tried to sidestep one of them.

The man she recognized from the airport as Jake blocked her way. "You think so?" His foot skidded. "What's this mess on the floor?"

"Marbles and diamonds," she blurted out. "They're mixed together."

"Clever, weren't you?"

"Not me, him." She pointed to Dawson.

"Sure, that's what they all say. Cuff her and book her," he ground out his orders.

"You're arresting me? But I'm not a crook," she protested as one of the agents snapped handcuffs around her wrists.

"It won't wash, Lady." Disbelief tinged Jake's eyes.

"But it's the truth." She tugged against another agent's restraining arms, her gaze seeking Tyler. Unconscious, he couldn't vouch for her. Pent-up anxiety poured through her. If only she could touch him, reassure herself he was all right.

Jake's bushy brows furrowed. "Your name Regina Citrano?"

"Yes, how did—"

"Figured it was. I recognize you from the airport."

"Hey, Jake," a gaunt looking agent called out, "Watch it. Two o'clock—a snake headed your way."

Everyone's gaze zeroed in on Hoggy as he went into his act just inches from Jake. It looked to Regina as if Hoggy was trying defend her.

"Get that thing away from me," Jake ordered in a no-nonsense voice.

One of the men grabbed her pink umbrella that lay open by the fireplace and closed it, all set to clobber Hoggy as the snake pretended to launch an assault.

"No, don't." Her shout ripped through the cabin. "Don't hurt him." Hands cuffed in front of her, she wrenched free and stood between the man with the umbrella and Hoggy. "Put my umbrella down. I can take care of this." As Hoggy puffed up and hissed, she knelt down almost eye level with the snake.

"Hoggy, it's okay. Shoo now, shoo. Go back out in the woods and play," she cooed, picking up her umbrella.

Like her Beagle dog, Dixie, Hoggy cocked his head to the side, acting for all the world as if he wasn't sure he should leave. "I'll be okay, Hoggy." She touched him with the tip of her closed umbrella. "Roll over and play dead."

The snake obeyed.

"Look at that," the gaunt agent beside her remarked. "If that don't beat all."

Gasps of amazement spilled from the men's' lips. They all watched in awe as seconds later Hoggy crept toward the door. The snake paused at the threshold and turned its little head back, as if seeking confirmation one more time that it was okay for him to leave. Regina honestly believed if Hoggy possessed a tail, he would have wagged it. Her gaze strayed to the umbrella she clutched in her cuffed hands, and she wondered if she could use it to her advantage. Jake must have read her mind. He snatched the potential weapon from her.

"You some kind of snake charmer or something?" Jake looked at her as if he wasn't the least fazed by what had happened.

"No. Just a special bond that cropped up between this particular snake and me."

"A gift like your Aunt has. The one with powers of insight."

"You've met my aunt Della?"

"That's one way of putting it." Jake kicked at the marbles with his foot. "These all the diamonds?"

"I believe so. Except for—" They'd have to slit Hoggy open to retrieve the diamond the snake had swallowed. Hero that it was, Hoggy deserved to walk away with a piece of the booty.

"You were saying," Jake prodded.

"Nothing." She gave him a measured look. If they weren't

going to believe her, why should she cooperate? They'd learn the truth when Tyler regained consciousness. *Tyler,* she silently moaned. Instead of trying to play super sleuth, she should have rushed to his side the minute the wrench hit him.

Jake pulled his mouth into a grim line. He shifted his gaze to Tyler as another man loosened Tyler's bonds and tried to revive him. Regina saw Jake's fist tighten to a ball. "Who punched out my Buddy?" He swung back to face her, his eyes boring into hers.

"Uh..." Sensing her answer wasn't going to help her case, she lowered her head and stared at her feet. "I guess I did."

"Guess?"

"It was an accident."

Jake held up his hand. "Say no more." His face twitched with rage. "Take her down to one of the choppers. We'll put Tyler and this scum bag in the other one and rush them to the hospital."

"E-Excuse me, did you say helicopter?"

"Yeah."

"As in airplane? A small one?" She shot him a withering glance as she felt color drain from her face.

"Yeah."

So that's what the whump-whumps had been. Helicopters, not bears. Nausea welled up in her. "I won't go." She jutted out her chin, her Citrano temper coming into play. She'd walk down every inch of the blasted mountains barefoot if she had to, but under no circumstances would she set foot in another small airplane, unless Tyler was there to help her through it.

"Get this straight. You're going even if we have to hog-tie and carry you on to the copter."

"That's probably what you'll have to do." She could understand the testiness in Jake's voice, the anger in his movements. Tyler was a fellow agent, a friend, and Jake believed her responsible for Tyler's injuries.

And Lord help her, she was.

Heartsick, she stared at Tyler's lifeless body, aching to check his condition. She took another step in his direction, but the agent beside her seized her arms. She'd managed to break free and come to Hoggy's defense. But they were far more vigilant in keeping her from Tyler.

"He's going to be all right, isn't he?" she beseeched Jake.

"For your sake, I hope so."

"C-could I see him?"

"Lady, I'm not letting you within ten feet of him."

"But it's not what you think. I mean Tyler didn't know what he was getting into. Neither did I. We got to the plane and then Frank showed up and..." Her voice trailed off. Jake's stone face indicated he cared less about her explanations. She straightened her shoulders. "I'm not part of the smuggling ring."

"You don't say! You seem to know a lot about it." He turned to one of the agents. "Get her out of my sight, and be sure and read her her rights. Looks like she might sing."

Sing. He could be certain of that. She'd sing her head off until they reached the copter. And then she'd faint.

As two men tugged, dragged, pushed, pulled, then finally carried her through the doorway, Regina broke into a song.

Shuffling across the room, Jake knelt beside Tyler and touched his hand to his buddy's forehead. He shook his head once, twice. Son-of-a-gun, he swore he heard the refrain...

Ee-ei-ee-ei—o.

No mistaking it, the quacky woman belonged to the Citrano Clan. And he belonged on vacation. Those ding-a-ling aunts of hers, so ultra positive of her innocence, were in for one heck of a surprise. Their precious niece was involved with these smugglers up to her armpits.

He cocked his head and listened again. Yep, that's what he heard all right.

Ee-ei-ee-ei—o.

Days had passed and she was restless. As restless as a June-bug impatient for the month of May to end.

From the comfort of her parent's den, Regina gazed out the picture window at the crystalline blue sky. Great day for flying a plane. If flying was your thing.

"Regina!" Aunt Sophia shouted. "You missed a prompt. You're drifting away on me. How will I win the lead in *Hello Dolly* if I don't learn these lines for the try-outs."

"Go easy on her, Sophia," Della chided from the card table where she sat dealing out her tarot cards. "She's got more important things on her mind than you winning the lead in the play, don't you, dear?" She shot Regina a motherly look. "How long has it been since you've seen that Tyler Novak fellow?"

Regina suspected Aunt Della knew the answer every bit as well as she did. “Three days.”

Seventy-five hours and fourteen minutes to be precise. Far longer than the action-packed twenty hours she and Tyler had shared. Though short and sweet, every second was etched on her brain. She picked up the magazine with the flirting article and stared at it, hoping in some mystical way it might connect her to Tyler.

“I went there again this morning,” Ruth announced.

“Where?” Sophia slapped her rehearsal booklet against her palm. “Really, Ruth, we've been telling you for years to finish your sentences.”

Regina angled her head. Where had she heard that before?

“Regina knows where I went.” Ruth raised an eyebrow, then glanced at Della. “And I suspect Della knows where, too.”

“I should have known, the F.B.I. office.” Sophia shook her head. “You've darkened their door every day.”

“And every day I've had a run-in with that agent Jake Whatever-his-name-is. I demanded he tell us where Tyler Novak was and the status of his condition.”

“Did he?” As she moved to the edge of her chair, Regina's heart hammered in her ribcage.

“No such luck”

Still antsy, Regina crossed and uncrossed her legs while her aunts argued. Bless them, since coming home, they'd hardly allowed her any time alone, determined not to let her mope. Her whole family had been there at the airport when the helicopter landed. She'd passed out during the flight and remembered how their raucous voices had wakened her. Despite her family's efforts, and they'd been vociferous and many, the authorities had held her in custody.

A few hours later the agents apologized and released her. She figured Tyler must have regained consciousness and cleared her involvement with the smugglers. After that the agency debriefed her, but the real interrogation began at home—a minute by minute, detailed account to her family. Once the aunties heard about Tyler and her flirting campaign, they rallied round and made his whereabouts their number one priority. They were back in their matchmaking element again, only this time Regina didn't mind their interference. Ruth had organized them into calling every Novak in the Greater Cincinnati phone book. Probably the whole state as well. Unfortunately, they'd turned up empty.

Regina let out a long, slow sigh.

Tyler, where are you?

Each day that passed increased her concern. Had she seriously injured him?

"He'll show up, Dear." Della's soft voice broke into her thoughts. After straightening her scarlet beret, she turned and cast an I-told-you-so look at Sophia. "I know he will. I feel it in my bones."

Regina hugged the magazine to her chest. Trust Della to read her mind. She only wished her aunt could give them a clue about what had happened to Tyler.

"They probably needed to keep him in the hospital for observation," Ruth supplied.

"But we've called all the hospitals." Regina sagged back into the chair and brushed a strand of hair from her brow.

"Maybe they registered him under an assumed name. And remember the debriefing procedure for an agent could be long and involved." Ruth spoke as if she was intimately familiar with the inner workings of the F.B. I."

Regina crossed her fingers. She hadn't been wrong about Tyler, had she? She couldn't have been! Tyler's words floated through her mind.

It drives me crazy thinking about you being with other men. You can count on seeing me again. We both want more out of what's started up between us.

She remembered his sexy brown eyes, his bone-melting smile, and the undisguised emotion in his voice when he'd admitted he believed in love at first sight.

At the sound of the doorbell, Regina jumped.

All three aunts went still.

"Go, go." Sophia gestured toward the living room. "It might be him."

"I know it is." Della scooped up her cards.

"We'll stay here. In the den." Ruth winked.

Her pulse throbbing, Regina tossed the magazine to the floor, popped out of her chair like a jack-in-the-box, and raced to the door. She flung it open.

"Hi." Tyler's voice was husky and low and a jaunty smile played across his face.

"Tyler!" She greedily soaked up every inch of him. "You came."

"You bet."

"I was worried about you." Mist filled her eyes.

"They kept me in the hospital twenty-four hours for observation."

"My fault. I hurt you. I'm sorry." It was impossible to stand there and not brush her fingers along his scalp—proof that other than the scars inflicted by Dawson, she hadn't injured him.

He leaned against the door frame and captured her hand in his. "It was just a concussion, and I should have known."

"Known?"

"Things sometimes screw up when we're together. I should have realized giving you a weapon might backfire." Mischief twinkled in his eyes. "Speaking of which, here's your umbrella." Releasing her hand, he pulled the umbrella from a brown, paper sack and handed it to her. "How about you? You okay?"

"F-fine now." Except for the dry itch lodged in the back of her throat.

"You had me going for a while. You did such a bang-up job of flirting with Dawson, I was afraid he might attack you. From what I hear, you knocked him out cold. My turn to thank you for coming to my rescue. It took a lot of courage to lead him on like you did. Sorry I missed the finale."

"Ahem." Three unseen voices called out from the adjacent room. "Ask him in," they urged.

Tyler's brow wrinkled.

"My aunts. They're hiding in the other room." Visions of them peeping around the archway danced in Regina's head as she stepped aside and gestured for Tyler to enter.

Dropping the paper sack, he kicked the door closed with his foot and opened his arms. "I've had just about all the separation I can stand."

"Me, too." The umbrella slipped through her fingers as she threw herself into his sheltering embrace.

"I missed you, Red."

"Missed you, too. I've been trying to get in touch with you."

"The Agency told me. Said they've become well acquainted with several members of your family. I'm sorry about the delay. After they released me, I had another full day of debriefing and paper work."

"But you didn't call." She burrowed closer against his

chest.

"Dumb, I know. I was planning to, then Jake got to me. He thought he had to protect me, talk some sense into me."

"Protect you?"

Tyler waited a beat. "Yeah, from myself." Actually, Jake had phrased it a bit more graphically. Something along the lines of Tyler having his head examined and thinking twice before becoming entangled with her family. "Jake knows I don't do marriage well, and that I barely know you. He wanted me to think it over for twenty-four hours. Worst twenty-four hours of my life. You were a fever inside me I didn't want to shake." He paused. "No second thoughts, yourself?"

"Well, kinda— Uh, actually, no, none. That's not to say my parents and my brother don't, but as for me and my aunts—"

"Kismet, huh?" He interrupted her stammering and rested his chin on the crown of her head.

"Exactly."

He cracked a smile. Things were back to normal. He'd actually missed her disjointed conversations over the past three days. "This morning I asked Jake to be my best man."

"You're getting married?"

"Let's say I have high hopes."

"Oh?" Her lashes fluttered.

Tyler regarded her expressive face. Question marks flickered across it. "That's if a certain redhead who isn't a redhead will take a chance on me." He eased his head back and waited till her upturned gaze meshed with his. "I'm nuts about you, Red. Whadda you say to spending the rest of your life with me?"

"Ahem!" Voices from the other room spilled out in loud condemnation, followed by much clearing of throats. No mistaking their unified displeasure.

"Sorry, " he called out, his gaze never having left Regina's. He slid his hands up her back to her shoulders. "Let me rephrase that. Marry me, Red. Brighten up my life."

"Oh, yes, Tyler, yes. I love you, too."

"I realize we need to get to know each other, not rush into this," he hesitated, clearing the gravel from his throat, "make sure we have what it takes for the long haul."

"I've been waiting a long time for you to come into my life."

"You're going to have to learn to adjust to my career."

"And you're going to have to learn to deal with my family."

"You've got a point. Jake's mentioned them several times." Along with several choice adjectives. Tyler nuzzled the side of her neck. "Probably be best to meet a few of them at a time."

"Mmm. I think that can be arranged. There's a lot you don't know about me."

That he didn't doubt for a second. Life should prove interesting. Considering the number of mishaps he'd encountered in Red's presence, he made a mental note to increase his insurance policies.

As she tilted her head and fluttered her thick, dark lashes, he chuckled. "You by chance practicing on me?"

"I certainly hope so."

"Keep that up and you're gonna learn a lot about me in a hurry."

"Ahem." The vocal chorus came from the archway.

"Your aunts, again?" At Regina's nod, Tyler scanned the room. Jake had specifically warned him about thc aunts. "Something stuck in their throats?"

"Something called curiosity."

"Sophia, Della, and Ruth, right?" he asked, verifying their names. "How 'bout it, Aunties? Do I have your approval to kiss her?"

Their enthusiastic yes resounded through the room.

Wasting no time, he slid his fingers into her hair and tilted her head back. Regina closed her eyes and lifted her mouth to meet his. He brushed his lips back and forth across hers slow and easy. Urgency and hunger pushed him to savor and explore. He kissed her long and hard and deep. As a groan of desire rumbled from his throat, he heard her sigh, then felt her hands sliding up his chest. Twining them behind his neck, she answered his kiss with a fervor of her own. The dynamite between them was back.

He shuddered. Or was it her? Or both of them? He pulled her closer, crushing her against his body. At the sound of clapping, Tyler ended the kiss. His breathing ragged, he swept her off her feet, twirled around as he held her fast, then slowly slid her down the length of his body until her feet touched the floor.

"They must have peeked," he commented on their applause. "Guess we did good."

"Mmm." Entranced, she stepped aside and stumbled over her umbrella. Her gaze drifted to the floor. "You dropped your paper sack."

"Oh, yeah. I bought a magazine."

"Magazine?"

A mischievous grin spread across his face. "And not just any magazine. See." Stooping, he pulled it from the sack and pointed to the cover. " 'Five Surefire Ways To Propose To The Woman You Love.' We can practice on each other. You still have your magazine, don't you?"

As Regina opened her mouth to answer, Della swooped into the room, thrust the magazine into Regina's hands, then raced away.

Tyler blinked his eyes. "What was that red blur?"

"Aunt Della and her hat. She always wears one."

"Nice hat, Della," Tyler yelled toward the other room.

"Thank you," Della's ladylike voice filtered back.

Tyler cupped a hand around his mouth. "So, ladies, do I have your blessing to practice my proposals on your niece?"

"On two conditions," another voice floated back. "One that your intentions are honorable."

"They're honorable, Ma'am. And in case you can't see, I'm crossing my heart."

Regina's heartstrings tugged as she watched Tyler cross and recross his heart.

"What's the second one?" He winked at her as they awaited the answer.

"A private tour of the F.B.I."

Tyler flicked his gaze to her and arched a brow. "That has to be Ruth, right?"

"Right. You're getting good."

"It's a deal, Ruth. You have my solemn promise."

Regina stood on tiptoe and touched her lips to his cheek.

"What's that for?"

"For being so sweet to my aunts."

Curving an arm around her shoulder, Tyler reached for the doorknob, then halted. "So, Ladies." He turned so they could hear. "If we're all square here, Red and I are off to practice."

"Who's he calling, Red?" Sophia's voice indignantly boomed from the adjoining room.

"Regina, dear," Della answered. "While she was missing, I communed with my telepathic friend in Connecticut—"

"Connecticut!" Regina and Tyler shouted in unison.

A gleam danced in Tyler's eyes. She answered it with a smile. "You first," she offered.

"No, you." He touched a fingertip to the tiny hollow in her throat.

"Together, then," she said.

"The capitol of Connecticut is Hartford!" They yelled together, trying to outdo each other.

"Now that we've settled that, you game to try the airport?" He opened the front door and motioned to her.

"And after that the mall." She slipped her hand in his and stepped over the threshold. "So how did you find out?"

Not missing a beat, he answered, "My atlas, and you?"

"Encyclopedia on my computer. It's been bugging me for days."

"Me, too. Whadda you think about going there for our honeymoon?"

"Connecticut?" Not exactly in her top ten locales for a honcymoon.

Yet, warming to the idea, she could see it now. A multi-gabled New England Inn, nestled on a rolling hill, surrounded by a grove of maple trees, glistening in the sunshine with brilliant crimson and orange leaves, a fieldstone hearth with a roaring fire, mulched cider brewing—

"Hey, Red." A wicked grin on his face, Tyler leaned forward. "Got an even better idea. We could go back to the Smokies."

"To the cabin and Hoggy! Oh, Tyler, that's perfect, but-but not in an airplane."

"Deal."

With a magazine clutched firmly in each of their hands, they melted into each others arms, and Tyler pressed a gentle kiss on her mouth.

The aunties applauded.

SUNDAY SCHOOL AND THE SECRET AGENT

Chapter One

Susan Stewart fingered the engraved invitation then set it down on the table. “Haven't you ever done anything impulsive?” She raised an eyebrow, challenging her two friends who shared the booth with her.

Pam picked up the invitation to Susan's class reunion. “Impulsive yes, but nothing as crazy as this.”

Robin, always the more direct of the two, leaned closer. Taking the invitation from Pam, she faced Susan. “You're serious about this, aren't you?”

“It's either find a man or kill myself.” Susan bit her lip and looked away. *Or better yet, commit a mythical murder since the man in question doesn't exist..*

Glancing across the smoky combination restaurant, bar, and pool hall, she noticed one of the men tending bar. He was good-looking in a rugged sort of way, and the smile lines etched in his deeply bronzed face radiated a congenial warmth. Made her feel comfortable about being here, considering the questionable reputation of the place. Judd's Western Palace wasn't exactly Mrs. Smith's Tea Room, but a girl had to have a little spice and variety in her life now and then, and as she and her two friends enjoyed country and western music, Judd's was as good a place as any in Las Cruces for their monthly Friday night outing.

Suddenly, as if he sensed her stare, the man's eyes flickered and caught hers. For the briefest moment an intense awareness arced between them. Then with a slight lift of his eyebrow, he severed contact and flashed a crooked smile at the woman sitting on a barstool directly in front of him. Susan gave her shoulders a tiny shrug and dropped her gaze to the invitation.

“According to this invitation, your high school reunion's barely two months from now, in early July,” Pam commented. “And you say you told your friend, Mary Sue—”

"Mary Ellen Hathaway," Susan corrected, shifting her attention back to her friends.

Disbelief filled Robin's eyes. "You actually told your friend you were engaged to a policeman?"

"An undercover agent." Susan slumped down in her chair. "Me and my big mouth."

Pam took a sip of her beer. "Just don't go."

"Not so easy." Susan shook her head disparagingly, then let her gaze wander back to the bartender again, the one with the dark hair, five o'clock shadow, guarded gray eyes, and a look that would intimidate a lion. The lazy, predatory gleam emanating from his eyes ought to be labeled "dangerous to one's health". Wondering why she kept staring at the man, Susan promptly refocused on her friends.

"What's not so easy?" Pam set her glass down and looked at Susan.

"My parents' fortieth wedding anniversary is a few days after the reunion, and my sister and brother are planning a big bash, so I have to go. Actually, I want to go to their party. At least I thought I did." Susan twiddled a spoon in her fingers. "It's just that Mary Ellen told my folks about my fiancé."

"And now they're expecting to meet him, too," Robin supplied.

"Exactly." Susan sighed. "Mom's so excited she's called twice this week asking why I hadn't mentioned anything about Shane to her."

"Shane?" Robin frowned.

"Shane Orr," Susan supplied. "I invented a name and a whole persona. It was kind of fun, and in a way I got attached to him." Robin and Pam exchanged glances, and Susan could just imagine what they were thinking.

"It's easy to see you've been too long without the companionship of a red-blooded male." Robin smiled, leaning closer to Susan. "What does this Shane look like?"

"I'm not sure. His face is always fuzzy in my dreams, but he has a body to die for."

Susan's gaze drifted across the dimly lit room to the bar. He was looking at her again. She didn't know what motivated his stare, but she sure knew what drew hers. Strength—the wiry strength and energy evident in his hands and arms when he served up drinks to the customers or loaded the trays of the waiters and waitresses.

For some reason, which she simply chalked up to hormones on her part, they seemed to be sizing up each other.

A burst of cheers from the room to her right diverted her attention. All she could see was a sea of cowboy hats, faded jeans, and checkered shirts crowded around one of the pool tables. Smoke wafted up in spirals toward the overhead light. Apparently most of the customers who frequented Judd's had yet to get the word that smoking was hazardous to your health.

"Susan, why don't you just announce that you broke the engagement, or kill the guy off?" Pam asked, true to her more practical nature.

"I may have to, but Mom is going to be disappointed. My younger brother and sister each married right after college, and then there's me, thirty-two, single, and about to attend my fifteenth high school reunion. Mom keeps hoping. Last time she phoned she was talking about putting an engagement announcement in the local paper. It was on the tip of my tongue to confess what I'd done, but I just couldn't." Susan took a deep breath and sighed. "If only I hadn't let Mary Ellen get my goat, hadn't bragged to her how I was engaged to this undercover agent."

"You could always say he was away on an overseas assignment," Pam suggested.

Robin took a bite of her enchilada and spoke while chewing. "I'm for killing him off."

Susan gazed at her friends for a moment and broke into a chuckle. "I'm seriously considering it." She drew an index finger across her throat. "It's the guillotine for Shane."

This time instead of looking in the direction of the bar, she glanced around the room. It was Friday evening, and through the archway to the left she could see that the place was filling up. Soon the band would replace the country music twang from the jukebox. Only this past Saturday her handyman, Mr. Garcia, knowing her fondness for country music had recommended Judd's because his nephew played in the band.

"Ever been to a reunion before?" Robin asked.

Susan broke off her thoughts and shook her head. "No. Like everyone else, I guess I looked on them as a drag. How could I have been so—"

"Stupid?" Robin supplied.

"Exactly. I shouldn't have let Mary Ellen get to me, but

when she called about the reunion and started in on her lawyer husband, her Junior League activities, and her 2.3 children—along with how well some of our classmates were doing—I could hear her quietly wondering what had become of poor, little ole Susan Stewart."

Susan pushed a wayward strand of hair from her face. "Unfortunately, I learned about the reunion before my sister informed me of their plans for the anniversary party. It was a spur of the moment thing—something came over me, and I concocted my story to Mary Ellen, thinking it would be fun to just let my imagination run wild. I thought, what the heck, I wouldn't be attending, and no one would ever be the wiser. If nothing else, it would give them something to think about other than boring Susan Stewart."

Robin snapped her fingers. "So why not go with your original idea and get someone to play the part of your fiancé?"

Pam picked up the invitation from the table and waved it at Susan. "It's a super idea. Might even be fun. I bet we could find someone to do it."

"We?"

"You, of course. I got carried away."

"Even if I did, the guy would be sure to think I'm a nut case," Susan replied.

Pam winked. "Well, that's entirely possible."

"Forget it," Susan tossed the invitation down on the table. "Just imagine how you'd react if a total stranger moseyed up to you this very minute and asked you to pose as his fiancé."

"Then ask someone you know," Robin said, enthusiasm growing in her voice.

"That's the problem. I don't know anyone—at least someone I'd want to pass off as my fiancé or who could get away with posing as an undercover agent."

Susan retreated into her thoughts while her two friends started running through a list of men they knew. She'd moved here two years ago to live with her great aunt Kitty, and between teaching school and caring for her frail aunt, she hadn't had much of a chance to meet unattached men. Her aunt had died months ago, and until now she hadn't had a whole lot of time to date anyone. The only man she'd been out with recently was a man who attended her church. He was almost old enough to be her father and most assuredly not secret agent material.

"Susan, you've got to ask someone. Think how much it would please your mother, not to mention how it would put Mary Ellen in her place. Can't you see her drooling?" Robin leaned forward, her dark eyes aglow with an impish gleam.

"Can I ever," Susan said, enjoying the vision.

She could easily visualize Mary Ellen decked out in a designer dress, jewels sparkling on her ears and neck, and not a hair out of place in her tightly coiffured hairdo. There'd be just the proper amount of background music in the banquet room, and classmates would be gathered around Mary Ellen as she held court, just like she'd always done in high school.

Suddenly, a hush would ripple through the crowd when she and Shane Orr entered. All eyes, especially those belonging to the female contingent, would be trained on Shane. He'd be strikingly handsome with a renegade smile and a slightly arrogant swagger. The room would buzz with whispers, but best of all, Mary Ellen's eyes would bulge out of their sockets. Mary Ellen always had wonderful taste in men, and Shane wouldn't disappoint her.

Susan nibbled her lips. What she wouldn't give to see that scene unfold.

"Come on, Susan, I agree with Robin. You can do it. You have to," Pam encouraged her.

"In fact, if you find someone to pose as your fiancé, we'll put up the money for his air fare." Robin's eyes twinkled with mischief, as if she wanted to become more involved in the bizarre scheme. "I'll even go one more step. We'll turn it into a bet. If you pull it off, I'll clean your house for a month, and if you don't, then you can clean mine."

"You two are corrupting me."

"You're the one who invented this nutty dream, Susan. Live it," Pam urged.

"And just where in Las Cruces am I going to find such a man?" Susan demanded. As she spoke, she noticed that the musicians were approaching the platform.

Pam lifted her arm in a waving gesture. "He could be right here in this room."

"Sure he could," Susan facetiously countered, her gaze sliding over a couple of tough-looking men as they exited the dance area and walked by the booth on their way to the pool tables.

"And if you're picking one, I'm all for picking one who's

good-looking, one who fits the part, one like that hunk over there." Robin pointed to the bartender. "He could play James Bond for me anytime."

Susan swung her gaze in the direction of Robin's finger, her mind registering what Robin had said. Prickles danced up and down the back of Susan's neck.

It was, she thought, on looking at the man again, *possibly worth a try.*

Twelve days later Ric wiped the glass mug dry and set it in the top tray of the small refrigerator tucked under the bar as he did every afternoon just moments before Judd's opened its doors for business. For a Wednesday he was in a good mood. Wednesdays were almost as dull as Tuesdays.

"Hey, Ric," a large, burly man called, setting down a carton of Carta Blanca beer. "That's the last trip I'm making to the stockroom. Want anything else, get it yourself."

"I like to be organized, and you forgot the lemons and limes," Ric answered, opening the carton.

Al groaned and wandered off while Ric began emptying the carton and neatly placing the bottles in a cooler under the bar. It was early yet, only a little after four-thirty. Too early for the Wednesday night regulars. The place wouldn't start jumping for another hour when the happy hour crowd drifted in. Then there'd be the supper crowd. The small band cranked up at seven, along with instructions on country line dancing, and since it was a week night, the place would be deserted by midnight.

Four to midnight—good hours, and overtime on Fridays and Saturdays when Judd's stayed open until two a.m..

Ric shoved the empty carton under the counter and out of his path. He'd been here at Judd's for three weeks now and was beginning to get the hang of his new job. Tending bar could be fun, and he discovered he had a knack for it. He might have to consider a serious alternative to being a lawyer if he didn't pass his upcoming bar exams. Bartending wasn't bad, nor the hours, and he enjoyed being able to ride his motorcycle out into the desert during the day.

"Hey, good buddy," a man said, slipping onto a bar stool, "how about a draft?"

"Sure." Ric shoved a frosty mug under the tap, filled it,

and set it on the counter with a thud. Scooping up the man's money, he deposited it in the brass cash register, and then he froze.

There she was again—sitting over in the same booth all by herself.

The soft lights in the lounge area reflected off her mahogany brown hair. His eyes narrowed slightly as she gave him the briefest of sidelong glances and immediately cast her head down as if embarrassed that he'd caught her looking at him. Her smooth, chin-length hair was shaped so when she tilted her head, the hair on the left side of her face swung down and covered her features.

He'd caught glimpses of her before. She had a Sunday School softness to her, and this was the fourth time in a dozen days that she'd been at Judd's. The first night she'd been with two other women, but a few afternoons ago she'd come alone, as she was now. And obviously out of place.

The last time she couldn't have stayed more than twenty minutes. After she'd left, Angela, her waitress, had teased him about having a secret admirer—said the woman had been asking about him. But Ric wondered about her motives.

Had his hints that he'd lost a lot of money gambling on the Mississippi Gulf Coast finally paid off? Maybe she was here to check him out.

He hadn't expected a woman. And she certainly stood out like a sore thumb. Drug dealers usually preferred using someone who didn't call attention to themselves, but then again they might be clever enough to do the unexpected.

Uh-oh.

Brown Eyes was at it again. She was peering at him through a strand of her hair. What was it with the woman? If she just wanted a harmless flirtation, why didn't she sit on the barstool and speak up? Ric grinned. He got a kick out of her interest. She wasn't beautiful, but then he wasn't exactly beautiful girl material himself. But she was damned good-looking in a cute, perky kind of way.

A scrubbed, clean, going-to-church kind of way.

Maybe she was one of those women who sat on the sidelines and stalked you—like that woman who'd hounded David Letterman. He shook his head. The few times their gazes had met during her visits, she had an alert, intelligent look in her eyes. She did dress kind of prim and proper though. Most of the women who came to Judd's wore jeans. Not Miss Sunday School. Three visits and three very nicely tailored skirts. Being a leg man himself, he didn't mind the skirts, but they'd been a bit long to suit him. So what was she pussy-footing around for?

Was she trying to establish contact? If she was, her fastidious appearance was one thing in her favor. No one would ever remotely suspect her of being involved with drugs.

What a cover—if it was one.

His superiors had ordered him to move to Las Cruces, get this job, and keep a low profile. All he had to do was wait for someone to approach him. They said it might take weeks before he met the right people and was able to infiltrate their organization. Right now he was establishing his cover while keeping his ears and eyes open.

And his eyes were open now.

So far Miss Sunday School was the only person who'd expressed an interest in him, apart from some of the women who worked here. He'd managed to keep them at arm's length. After all, he was here on assignment, and he had to be careful, very careful. There was no edict against getting friendly with some of the female population, just against getting too closely involved with any of them, unless he suspected they were part of the drug operation.

Anyway, Sunday School wasn't his type. She seemed uptight, and she wasn't a blonde. Blondes with great legs—that's what he liked.

Of course, he was pretty uptight himself, on edge, always observant, always alert for a critical contact, but that was part of his job description.

Two women sat down at the far end of the bar. Ric walked down to take their orders. A minute later, after chatting with them, he glanced back at the booth.

Sunday School was gone.

Susan walked briskly across Judd's parking lot, climbed into her station wagon, and let out one of the deepest sighs of her life.

A chicken, that's what you are.

Before her inner voice worked up a head of steam and began making cluck-cluck noises in her brain, she picked up a notebook from the adjacent seat and fanned herself.

Something about sitting at Judd's and watching Ricardo Ramsey sent her temperature rising. She wasn't a coward, she thought defensively, just a normally cautious person, observing her subject before deciding how to approach him.

After all, she couldn't very well speak to him at the bar in front of everyone, could she? Nor could she keep going into Judd's and staring at him.

Of course, there was no denying he was fascinating to stare at. He had a fabulous smile—wide full lips and white, white teeth against that coppery bronze skin of his. She'd seen him flash that smile at nearly every woman who had sat at the bar. He'd even smiled at her once. His hair was dark brown, and she envied the gentle waves. He wore it collar length in the back and tapered around his bronzed face. It and his name hinted at Indian and Hispanic ancestry, and the combination was devastating.

Ricardo Ramsey.

Name had a nice ring to it, too. After her second visit curiosity got the best of her and she'd asked the waitress for his name. And since he hadn't been listed in the phone book, Judd's appeared to be the only place she could contact him.

Susan rested her forehead against the steering wheel. She was probably completely out of her mind to ask him to go to the reunion with her. He could be married or involved. He could be crazy. He could be any number of things, and she'd already wasted nearly two weeks dilly-dallying over whether she was going to ask him or not. It wasn't as if she hadn't searched for alternatives wherever she went—single men at church, men in the grocery and drug stores, the cleaners, the gas stations, the library, the university.

She'd come up empty.

Almost as empty as her lovelife had been. She hadn't had a decent date in months. Not one that set her insides to quaking. Some women had to beat men off with a stick, but she'd reached the grand age of thirty-two without that happening. And she suspected from the fantastic sales of the bestseller book on husband-hunting that her experience was more often the case than not.

Looked like it was going to be Ricardo Ramsey or nothing.

She'd just about decided if he didn't pan out, the mythical Shane Orr was going to be called out of the country in early July. She'd send him to the Middle East. If ever there was a locale that constantly threatened to bubble over with intrigue that was the place. She could even conveniently have him die there.

Dreaming up how he courageously gave up his life for his country might prove interesting.

Ridiculous.

Susan tossed her notebook back on the seat and slid her key into the ignition. Inventing a fiancé who was a secret agent had seemed colorful yet safe. Colorful, because of the dangerous life agents led, and safe because they were never home. Utterly confused, she shook her head. If her aunt were alive, Susan was certain the elderly woman would be having a conniption over her great niece's behavior.

Losing touch with reality—that's what she was doing. She'd been acting more like a teenager than a mature young woman the past several days, not at all like her normal self. Ordinarily, she'd never think of dashing to Judd's the minute the school day was over. Her life was systematic, orderly, and boring.

Very boring.

And here a whacky adventure sat staring her in the face, and she lacked the gumption to cross the threshold. How could she when it seemed so frivolous, so nonsensical compared to all the serious problems and tragedies that faced people today? But she was the new Susan, and the new Susan would do this.

Do it, Susan. Robin's voice replayed in her head. *It isn't as if you have to commit yourself. You can back out anytime.*

Think of it as interviewing him for a part, Pam had chipped in, adding, *come to think of it, the idea's such a neat gimmick, I wouldn't mind trying it out myself.*

A knock on her window startled her. A-not-too-savory-looking man stared back at her. He was saying something and pointing to the back of her station wagon. She cautiously rolled the window down an inch.

"Lady, your left rear tire is flatter than a pancake."

Susan raised an eyebrow. She hadn't noticed that. Was it a ruse to get her out of the wagon? He could be a carjacker, a mugger, or worse. The old Susan was surfacing. Seconds ticked by, then bolstering her courage, she rolled the window down further and looked out. Goodness, the man was right. "Thanks."

"You're welcome," the man answered, staggering away.

Obviously drunk, she thought. What now?

Although she'd never done it, she thought she knew how to change a tire. She surveyed the parking lot, chock full of dust-covered pickups, Jeeps, and Broncos. There were hours of daylight left, but she wasn't exactly sure she wanted to change the tire in this neighborhood. Bending over and using a jack would put her in a precarious position, a most tempting position that might invite trouble, and besides, she didn't want to get her clothes dirty. Pulling her keys from the ignition, she quickly came to the decision to call the auto club and let them handle it.

Ric couldn't believe his eyes. Sunday School was back. He stole a look at the wall clock while he finished mixing a margarita for a customer. Five minutes. She couldn't have been gone more than five minutes tops, and this very second she was headed his way. He grinned, then let out a low whistle. One way or another he was finally going to get some action.

Thoroughly enjoying the subtle sway of her hips as she strode toward him, Ric placed his hands on the bar and flexed his elbows. She was a five foot five bundle of energy, and he got a good long look at those dark, dancing eyes of hers when she wedged herself between two barstools and leveled her gaze at him.

"Could you tell me where I could find a phone?"

The old where is the phone ploy, he thought, smiling to himself. "Sure." She looked agitated. "Back by the restrooms," he said, watching her set her purse down on the bar and frantically search through her wallet. "Something wrong?"

"My station wagon, it's got a flat."

Sure it does, Sunday School, sure it does. He shrugged, momentarily struck by the melodious warmth of her voice. *Maybe the tire was flat. Maybe that was her gimmick. Yessir, things were looking up.* He'd go with whatever she said. "Hey, Max, cover for me," he called out to a waiter. He ducked under the bar and faced her. "I'd be happy to fix it for you."

"You would?" Susan let out a sigh of relief, a dozen thoughts milling around in her head. Why not let him? It would be an opportunity to get to know him. "That's not necessary," she said, looking into his steel gray eyes and discovering a faint green cast to them. "I was going to call my car service—"

"It'd take them half an hour just to get here," he interrupted.

"It would?" She flicked her wrist, noting the time. "It probably would." And she was supposed to be back at the house by five-thirty to meet with the handyman. "But you're working."

"No problem. Always time to help out a lady."

His smile melted her resistance and a whole lot more. "I'd appreciate that."

He looked her squarely in the eyes. "No problem, Miss—" He paused, obviously waiting for her to fill in the blanks.

"Stewart. Susan Stewart."

"Ric Ramsey." He held out his hand.

She stared at the large tanned hand he extended and froze. *Shake it, Dummy. It's a meaningless, commonplace gesture. It's not as if you were signing your life away.*

"I—" Whatever it was that she wanted to say stuck in her throat. Susan blew out a long steadying breath and placed her hand in his. His touch produced an unexpected kick in her stomach. "Nice to meet you, Mr. Ramsey."

"Ric."

"Ric," she breathily repeated.

Maybe the bet was about to begin, after all.

Chapter Two

Susan was so taken with the coup she'd just achieved that if someone had asked her, she couldn't have told them how she made it from the darkened building out to her wagon. Her feet had taken her there she supposed, but it felt more like floating over a layer of hot New Mexico air. The whole time, she'd been overly conscious of Ric Ramsey close behind her. Not only had she sensed his presence, she'd felt his eyes drilling into the back of her head.

Well, perhaps not her head.

From the warm spot currently settled in her hips, she

suspected his gaze was aimed a bit lower. And though she may have appeared calm, inside she was a quaking mass of jelly. Here she was stretching her wings, opening herself to adventure, yet she feared her solo flight.

Nonsense.

She'd go with her instincts. There was something trustworthy in his eyes. Overcoming her uneasiness, Susan dropped the tailgate and began to move some of the items out of the way.

"I'll do that," he offered, gently nudging her to the side.

She noted his charming, sexy smile, wondering how many women had fallen victim to it, then handed him the jack and stepped away. "Have you been here very long?"

"No." He slipped the jack under the car.

"I mean at Judd's."

"No," he repeated, hunkering down and loosening the nuts on the wheel.

She leaned against the fender of the car parked next to hers and studied the back of his head. Warm golden highlights glistened in his deep brown hair. He had broad shoulders and a wide, muscled back, and he worked quickly and competently. If she didn't speak up soon, he'd be done before she could get a conversation going.

"Are you new to Las Cruces, too?" she asked. He tilted his head up and gave her the oddest stare from under his thick black lashes. Perhaps she was being a bit nosy, but a girl couldn't afford not to be thorough when interviewing someone for her prospective fiancé.

"I've been here a little over a month. And you, Ma'am?"

His speech was a pleasant mixture of western and southern, and his husky voice brought goose bumps to her arms. "Me?"

Yeah, you Sunday School. He rose and walked to the tailgate, pulling the spare tire from its bracket. "Are you a native?"

"Goodness, no."

He hadn't thought so. There was a Yankee twang to her voice. "Thought I heard a northern accent."

"Probably Pittsburgh."

"Pittsburgh, huh? Steelers, Pirates, and—"

"The Penguins," she finished as he slipped the spare tire in place.

"Quite a sports town. How long you been here?"

"Almost two years." She dragged her gaze away from him.

Ric nodded, absorbing her information. From what she'd said she could be part of a drug ring, but then her information could be false. It wouldn't be the first time that a female fed him a bunch of crap. "So, you're sort of a newcomer, too. You here by yourself?"

"I beg your pardon."

He glanced at her slim, hose-covered ankles, thinking it a shame that he couldn't see more of her legs. Then he looked up, fastening his gaze on hers. "What I'm asking, Susan, is did you move here with anyone? Are you living with anyone now?" *Is there someone I have to deal with to get to know you—a man perhaps?*

"Now—" Her voice died a sudden death. "—I live alone." She hesitated for a second. "I came here to care for my great aunt, but she passed away six months ago."

"Sorry," he mumbled. Her story sounded contrived. Great aunt, and now she was all alone. He'd already memorized her license plate. Once he called the DMV and learned her address, he could check out her story. "So, you stayed on after she died."

"Yes. It was the beginning of the school year, and I couldn't just walk out on my students."

Ric coughed and gave the nuts on the wheel another twist. "You're a teacher?" He watched her nod. Of course the university would be a prime location to deal drugs. "You work at the university?"

"No. I teach fourth grade."

He winced. How low did this gang stoop? They wouldn't use a fourth grade teacher as a cover, would they? Then again, maybe she was the genuine article and not involved in smuggling drugs at all. She looked innocent enough, but looks, as everyone damn well knew, could be deceiving. Such as now. For all the gaga eyes she'd been making at him these past few days, he'd been expecting her to make a hit on him, and unless the flat tire was deliberate, she hadn't made a move.

"Thinking of staying in Las Cruces?" he asked.

"I don't know. Are you?"

Smooth answer, Sunday School. Smooth answer. "For a while."

"Through the summer?" she inquired.

Now why the hell did she want to know that? What was so all important about the summer? The department had hinted that they hoped to know something solid by then. "Depends." He shrugged. Let her chew on that. He levered the jack down and removed it. "I like it here, might even stay longer than that. It's a hospitable place," he said, rising.

"It is, isn't it?" The breeze blew a strand of her hair across her face. "Speaking of hospitality, let me repay the favor you've done me."

Ric arched a brow. Finally, she was done dancing around. Well, he was open to whatever she suggested.

By the wicked gleam gracing his eyes, Susan could just imagine what he was thinking. She wasn't born yesterday. "What I mean is, uh, I'd like for you to come to my house for dinner." *There, she'd done it. She'd crossed the threshold. Dinner together would be good.*

"I work nights except for Sunday and Monday."

"Oh, of course," she murmured, momentarily deflated. She snapped her fingers. Sunday lunch would be even better. There'd be more time to get to know one another. "Are you off the whole day on Sunday?"

"Yes Ma'am."

"Would Sunday noon work for you?"

Ric smiled, fascinated by the wide array of emotions he'd seen play on her face the past few seconds. So, Sunday noon for Miss Sunday School. He should have figured. He'd much rather go riding on his bike, but her invitation was too good an offer to pass up. "Sounds good to me. How about a compromise—a picnic?"

"Picnic? Okay."

At least on a picnic he might get a glimpse of her legs. He pointed at the tire he'd just put on her station wagon. "You realize that's only temporary. If I were you I'd head right to a gas station or tire place." He glanced at his watch. "Some stay open 'til nine."

"Thanks, I'll do that, just as soon as I finish meeting with my yardman." She started to turn away, then spun back on her heels. "You're not married, are you?"

"No. That a problem?"

"No problem at all. In fact, it's perfect."

Yeah, perfect. What did she have up her sleeve? "How 'bout you, Susan. You married?"

"Me? No. Not yet, anyway."

"That mean you're engaged or something?

"Engaged?" Color drained from her face. "H-how did... w-what... " She cleared her throat and cast him a wary look. "What made you say that?"

"Just curious." Ric watched her wrap her purse strap around her fingers until her knuckles nearly turned white. Jeeze, you'd think he'd asked her if she was an ax murderer or something. In less than a second she'd gone from calm and cool to a frenzy of agitation. "So are you?"

"How's that?" Alarm riddled her eyes.

"Are you engaged?"

"Uh, not exactly."

Ric arched a brow. *Not exactly? What kind of a half-baked answer was that*? "You feeling okay?"

"F-fine."

Susan steadied her nerves, wondering why he'd asked about her being engaged. He couldn't possibly know her plans, could he? No. No way. Definitely flustered, she inhaled a deep deliberate breath. Ric placed the tire in the wagon, and she walked over next to him and leaned in to look for a rag. She found one, then scrounged in her shoulder bag for a towelette. His body was inches from her.

"Here," she said, "for the grease on your hands." She tore it open and handed it to him. He didn't move, and neither did she, her gaze trained on his hands as he wiped off the grease.

She watched him rub his hands together. A pang rushed through her mid-section. Growing warmer by the second, she ever so slowly raised her head. His gaze was there waiting for her, and though he didn't touch her, she felt the sensuality flowing between them. When he exchanged the towelette for the rag, their fingers barely touched. Still blatantly holding her gaze, he leaned slightly forward, and Susan drew in a quick breath.

He's going to kiss me.

But he tossed the rag into the back of the wagon and set one hand on her shoulder while he slammed the tailgate shut with the other. Vibrantly aware of his hand resting on her shoulder, she stood motionless, a feeling of claustrophobia washing over her.

"You're staring," she whispered.

"And so are you."

"So I am." She took a tentative step back. They continued to look at each other as the sun slowly sank in the crystal blue sky.

"Staring seems to be a habit with us," he drawled.

His face split into a friendly grin while she was still dealing with disappointment. On one hand she was glad he'd been a gentleman and hadn't kissed her, but on the other she felt cheated. And she had the weirdest feeling that he could read her thoughts—that he felt the arc of electricity between them.

"I have to go," he said. He turned to walk away, then stopped. "Where do you live?"

Great, Susan, great. Invite the most incredibly sexy man you've ever met to your house and don't tell him where you live. "El Camino Drive, 705 El Camino Drive. I can give you directions." She reached into her purse for a piece of paper.

"Don't bother. I'll find it." And just what else would he find there, he wondered. The woman was an enigma or a con artist he thought as she drove away.

He shook his head—a damned station wagon!

As Susan drove down the street of the old historic district and pulled into her driveway, she noticed her yardman sitting on the front stoop. She dashed out of the wagon, and he rose as she walked over to meet him.

"Sorry I'm late, Mr. Garcia."

"No problem, no problem. I came for my money and wanted to make sure you needed me for Saturday."

"Saturday's fine."

For nearly two years, ever since her aunt had become ill, Juan Garcia had served as their combination yard and handyman, and knowing that he had six children, she hadn't had the heart to terminate him after Aunt Kitty had passed away.

"Did you walk here?" she asked. Usually a friend dropped him off on Saturday mornings, and he called them to come get him when he was done.

"My friend drove me, but he couldn't wait."

"I'm sorry. I had a bit of car trouble."

"You did, Senorita? I didn't notice anything wrong last Saturday."

"Just a flat tire. I'd like you to clean the pool next

Saturday." Since Juan Garcia had no phone, communicating with him was often a problem. She got in the habit of letting him come, even when she didn't need him, or had plans to be gone all day. Last Saturday he'd left before she returned and could pay him.

"Come on in," she said, unlocking the door. "I'll write out your check." She filled it out and handed it to him. "You live on the east side of town, don't you?" At his nod, she continued. "I'm on my way to the tire store in that direction. I'll give you a lift."

"A lift will be good, Senorita. I'll walk home from the store. And Senorita?"

"Yes."

"You haven't forgotten about our trip to Juarez a week from this coming Sunday?"

"I haven't forgotten. My calendar is clear."

"Bueno."

Susan smiled, grateful she could be of some help to him. About a year ago Juan Garcia had asked her if she'd be so kind as to drive him, his wife, and a friend to Juarez every other month to visit their parents who still lived there. She suspected the thrifty family was taking money to their elderly parents, and they always returned laden down with parcels of home baked Mexican food.

As she didn't know the language, driving alone to Juarez was something she'd never attempted. But she was taking a class in Spanish two evenings a week at the university now to help her understand some of her students' parents, and once she became proficient in the language, she could add driving to Juarez by herself to her adventures.

Mr. Garcia always insisted she park at a popular shopping plaza rather than drive into a section he didn't think would be safe for her, and he always arranged for some of his cousins to keep her company while he, his wife, and friend borrowed her wagon and drove to visit their relatives. It was for her own protection, he insisted, and she appreciated his thoughtfulness. With their assistance she always managed to pick up some good buys.

Maybe the next time they went, she'd get something for her parents' anniversary. A silver tray perhaps. Or then again, a basket.

★★★

He'd jogged, he'd showered, and he'd dressed. Ric peeked out through the dust-laden blinds at the late Sunday morning sun, then ducked into the cramped bathroom of his rented trailer to comb his hair. The place was nothing to write home about—rusty sink, holes in the upholstery, dingy curtains. It was a crummy neighborhood, and an even crummier trailer, but it was cheap and mercifully temporary, he hoped.

After four years of ROTC in college, plus four years in the Marines, followed by four years with the Agency, he'd had enough of a rootless lifestyle, of living in hovels and assuming fake identities. He thought he'd left it all behind him when he quit to go to law school. But two months ago, right after graduating, they'd called and asked him to come back.

It was something he thought he'd never do, and he wouldn't have gone back except for Johnny Montoya. Johnny had been a powerful incentive. He'd met Johnny in the Marines, and they'd both joined the Agency and worked together several times. Friends like him were few and far between. A little over two months ago Johnny had been found in Las Cruces, not far from Judd's, with a knife in his back.

Ric scowled and clenched his hands into fists then caught himself and forced them to relax. It would serve no purpose to put another dent in this dump by pounding his fist into the wall. Johnny was dead, and he was here to help find his killer. More precisely, he was waiting until the Agency could transfer an agent to Las Cruces to replace Johnny. Drew Matthews, their superior, had explained that the Agency was stretched thin, and Drew had asked him as a special favor if he'd temporarily hold down the fort while the trail was still warm.

Four months tops, Drew had said.

Four months out of his life wasn't much to ask in order to find Johnny's killer. As far as Ric was concerned, he'd be available for as long as they needed him. There was plenty of time to select a location to practice law and to tackle the bar exams after that.

Shortly before his death Johnny had sent word that he had some leads that might uncover the kingpin, and the Agency was hoping Ric could unearth them. Ric wasn't under any delusions about the fact he was slipping back into a dangerous world. Johnny had been employed at Judd's when he'd been killed, and Ric figured that as a stranger he was already under observation. After dropping hints that he was looking to make some quick money, he was almost certain that the gang responsible would feel him out, try to discover if they had another snoop on their hands. In the process he intended to check them out, too.

So far, he'd befriended some of the men and women who worked at Judd's, and the only one outside of his place of employment who had showed any interest in him had been Sunday School.

Susan Elizabeth Stewart.

Ric drew a comb through his hair and grinned into the mirror. He'd had the Agency check her out and now had a complete dossier on her. Thirty-two, she had a younger sister and brother, both married, and one niece and one nephew. All of them, including her parents, lived in Pittsburgh. Her father was a retired electrician; her mother, a retired teacher.

Like mother, like daughter.

And then there had been Aunt Kitty. Katherine Elizabeth Norman. The elderly woman had been comfortably well off, leaving her sister and her sister's children small bequests. Susan had inherited the house and a small trust fund for its upkeep as her portion. On the face of it, everything Ric had learned about Susan Stewart seemed to be on the up and up. She'd never been married, lived a quiet, unobtrusive life, always paid her bills and taxes, and never had a brush with the law—not even a traffic ticket.

Ric walked back into the bedroom, waded through the pile of clothes on the floor, and pulled on his boots. Personally, he couldn't believe she'd never been married. It had to be her choice, because there had been one vital fact missing from her file—she was an attractive and vivacious woman. While the Agency had been delving into her past, he'd wasted no time checking into her life here in Las Cruces. Five days a week she taught school, two evenings a week she took Spanish at the university, and one evening a week she devoted to choir practice. On Sundays she attended Mountainside Methodist Church.

There hadn't been time to ferret out her friends and associates or to discover if she was dating anyone. That was next on his agenda. Hell, the woman was a paragon of virtue. *She was Sunday School, and she was too damn good to be true.*

Why would a supposedly upstanding young woman, whose life seemed completely predictable, go out of her way to flirt with a bartender she knew nothing about? And why pick Judd's, a bar with a less than stellar reputation in a seamy neighborhood? Except for the clientele attracted by the country line dancing, most of the customers bordered on thugs and bums.

There had to be a catch. It could be possible that before inheriting her aunt's house, she'd let herself be enticed into doing something illegal. Maybe she had a boyfriend in the group who had persuaded her to become involved.

Ric slipped on a light windbreaker and sighed. It sure as hell would make things easier if she were involved. It would help him keep his perspective about her, because there was something about her that attracted him, some niggling awareness that this woman could be special.

Sunday School had started this, and the pull in his loins told him how he'd like to finish it.

For the fifth time Susan checked the food and supplies for the picnic lunch. And for the fourth time she walked back to the full length mirror riveted to the back of her bedroom door and checked her attire. Jeans, pink and white gingham blouse knotted at the waist and matching pink sneakers. She loved coordinating canvas deck shoes with her outfits and spent hours on end scouring the discount stores in search of them. Screwing up her nose, she made a face at her image reflected in the mirror.

Then, on a whim, she rummaged through her over-sized schoolteacher's purse—which could easily pass for a small suitcase—and lifted out a festive, hot pink umbrella. She opened it, striking poses like the fashion model she'd never be. Shaking her head, she dismissed her foolish primping as just another crazy impulse, much like her creation of Shane Orr and the acquisition of this umbrella. More suited to the gray, misty weather of Pittsburgh, umbrellas were impractical out here, though she had used it to shield the sun on her shopping excursions to Juarez.

She'd never been quite clear as to whether she'd claimed the umbrella or it had attached itself to her.

It had been lying under her seat in the Pittsburgh Airport

when she'd stumbled across it on her visit home last Christmas. And to her amazement there'd been no one sitting nearby. She'd considered leaving it there, lest the owner return. But seconds away from setting it back on the floor, she'd felt a strange, inexplicable thrill dance up her arm. As if magically endowed, the umbrella begged to be kept, its cosmic force so powerful that against her better judgment, she'd carried it back to arid New Mexico.

Susan closed what she'd come to look at as her enchanted umbrella, then tucked it into her purse. Not one to put stock in mystical fantasies, she wondered if this inanimate object had cast a spell and contributed to the birth of the new Susan. Ever since its appearance in her life, her behavior had turned unpredictable. Such as today and her spur-of-the-moment luncheon invitation to a perfect stranger.

She ran a hand over her hair.

Nervous? Of course not.

Yes, she was nervous. She didn't know Ric Ramsey from Adam. Thirty minutes from now she could be knocked out cold and everything of value stripped from the house, she thought, eyeing her aunt's silver tea service through the door that led to the dining room.

Stop fretting and go for it, Susan, an inner voice urged.

Break out of your worn out rut.

And she would. Today would simply be a harmless picnic in the backyard. New Mexico, at least this part of it, wasn't exactly suited for sitting in a meadow and picnicking like back home. And in mid May the weather was borderline hot already. At least in the back yard there was shade and a pool, which, considering the small amount of rainfall in the area, was a luxury few people could afford. Her aunt and uncle had lived in the same house for over forty years and the pool had been their only concession to extravagance.

As if her aunt were alive, Susan could see her standing across the kitchen table, shaking her bony finger and lecturing her for being so reckless as to invite a total stranger to the house.

In comparison to others, she supposed she'd led a sheltered life. By thirty-two most women were married or had had an affair or two. When it came to men, she'd had two heartbreaking romances, after which she'd simply directed her energies into her career, and although she wouldn't mind marriage and a family, there just hadn't been anyone she really cared for, anyone who had set off an undeniable zing in her.

Until Ric Ramsey.

Plain old chemistry could be behind her fascination with this man, or it could be a subconscious awareness of her biological clock ticking away. That might explain her impulsive reaction to Mary Ellen's remarks about how many of their classmates had children. And it would also help explain her crazy stunt of inventing a fiancé, and her goofy scheme to ask Ric Ramsey to play the part.

Susan walked over to the counter, opened a cabinet door, and pulled out a tray. In less than two weeks it would be June. If Ric Ramsey actually showed up today and he didn't turn out to be a jerk, then mid-June would be her deadline. That's when she'd decide whether to ask him to pose as Shane Orr. Like Robin had said—no harm in screening him to make sure he fit the part to the hilt. And no harm in having a little adventure on the side for a change. Shy and ordinary might best describe her, but she'd always felt a streak of recklessness buried deep inside. Way past time to dust it off and put it to use.

The doorbell rang and Susan froze.

If she had an ounce of sense, she'd cancel this date the moment she opened the door.

The new Susan wouldn't hear of it.

Chapter Three

Susan opened the front door, and it was like being turned loose in an old fashioned candy store and allowed to choose whatever her heart desired. Ric Ramsey was mouthwatering in a bright blue T-shirt, form fitting stone washed jeans, a wide leather belt, boots, and a navy blue windbreaker. But most devastating of all was his sexy smile.

"Hi," she murmured, angling her head in both directions beyond him. "You walked?" She didn't see a car.

"Rode my bike."

"Oh." She liked the sound of his answer. Bicyclists usually

were responsible, health-minded people, and Ric Ramsey, if nothing else, looked the picture of health. “Come in” she invited, pleased that he was on time. Another good sign.

“Brought this for you.” He held out a paper bag.

“Thanks.” Susan took it and lifted out a bottle of Chablis.

He shrugged. “I wasn’t sure what you liked, and it seemed a pretty safe choice.”

“It was, and it’s Beaujolais.”

“Come again?” Ric frowned.

Seemed like a perfectly straight answer to her. “Your choice was safe. I like most wines, including Chablis, but my favorite one is Beaujolais. How about you?”

“Beer, cola, whatever you’ve got.”

She’d figured right. Just yesterday she’d purchased a six pack just in case. “Lunch is ready,” she said, leading him back into the kitchen. Opening the refrigerator, she placed the Chablis inside. “I’ll let this chill for another time. There’s soda and beer in the cooler. Hope you like baked chicken. I would have cooked Tex-Mex, but I’m haven’t quite mastered it yet.”

As Ric followed her, she was exceedingly conscious that he stood very close behind her. She turned to see him slip out of his jacket and drape it on a kitchen chair. As it was fairly warm outside, she thought it odd he’d chosen to wear one.

“Chicken’s fine,” he replied. “Home cooking is always appreciated.” She felt his gaze cling to her hips as he’d followed her further into the kitchen. “I eat a lot of Mexican food. You can get in a rut.”

True enough, but she was about to turn over a new leaf. Just thinking where it might lead brought a blush to her face. She handed him the cooler and picked up the picnic basket. “I thought we’d eat out by the pool.” She saw his deep-set eyes widen. “I know, a pool is an extravagance out here, considering what they charge for water, but Aunt Kitty grew up in Pittsburgh—ice, snow, long winters. When she married and moved here, it was her dream to have a pool.”

“Everyone should have a dream. It’s nice when they come true.”

Dreams. She knew what hers were. What were his?

He smiled at her, exposing a dimple, and she felt her lips curve upward in response. And that wasn’t all she felt. Suddenly, the air in the room closed in on her. To her relief, he turned away and opened the door that led to the patio, gesturing for her to step by him. As she eased in front of him, Susan let out a long, slow breath and stepped onto the sun-drenched patio, bordered on one side by rose bushes already in bloom.

She set the picnic basket on the poolside table that had a striped umbrella poking through its center. His manners surprised her, and she chalked them up as another point in his favor. As she emptied the basket, she tilted her head and snuck a glance at him through the strands of hair that fell across her left eye.

"How about you, Ric?" she said, testing the sound of his name on her lips. "Have any special dreams?" Her question apparently brought him up short. He halted his search of the cooler and quirked his brow, his smoky gaze narrowing suspiciously. She filled a plate and handed it to him.

"Dreams?" Ric frowned. The crazy direction of their conversation confused him. *Strange way of pumping him for information—if that's what she was doing.* And if so, what should he tell her about himself?

At the moment he wasn't in deep cover, wasn't even using a fictitious name. All the Agency wanted him to do was observe what was going on, be prepared if someone approached him. And if someone did check up on him, they wouldn't find anything. Three years ago when he'd quit, the Agency had conveniently hidden his employment with them. Anyone snooping into his background would discover that after being discharged from the Marines and before starting law school, he'd been employed by an import-export firm.

Ric studied Susan as she filled her plate. There was something so guileless and naive about her, including the blush that had reddened her cheeks moments ago. But a more vigilant part of him warned that she could be a clever actress, and that her intelligent eyes would see through any duplicity on his part. From past experience he knew the closer you stuck to the truth, the easier it was to avoid mistakes—to gain another's trust. He'd level with Sunday School. And if anything he told her got passed on, he'd have his answer.

"My dreams?" he repeated, then looked her dead in the eye. "Being a lawyer."

"A lawyer?" Susan dropped her fork.

Ric picked it up and handed it to her. Her face was a dead giveaway. "You're surprised."

"Uh, no, I—"

"You were." A bristling edge crept into his voice. "You're surprised a bartender would want to be a lawyer."

"No. Er..." She dropped her fork again, and again he handed it to her. Susan winced. She hadn't meant to sound disapproving. Her gaze rested on his well worn jeans. His appearance, a far cry from the preppy law students she'd known back East, had thrown her off. "Lots of people take jobs to put themselves through school, like tending bar. I waited on tables, myself. It's just that you're uh—I thought—"

"I know what you thought. You thought I was a drifter with no ambition."

Susan pushed her salad around her plate. "You said that, not me." She raised her chin a fraction. "For the record, I don't look down on anyone. Like you said, you took me by surprise. Wanting to be a lawyer is a wonderful dream. Why don't you go after it?"

"I did." He handed her a can of cola from the cooler and flipped one open for himself.

"You did?" Rattled by the man sitting opposite her and feeling a warmth creep through her, Susan held the cold can to the side of her neck.

"Graduated a few months ago." His boyish grin tugged at her.

She took a sip. "Are you saying you're already a lawyer?"

"Fresh out of law school, but I haven't taken the bar or hitched up with a firm yet."

"I see, kind of treating yourself to a sabbatical."

"You could say that." His chin took on a determined cast.

"Well, congratulations." She studied her would-be fiancé. "What school did you go to?"

"University of Texas, undergraduate and graduate, and before you say anything else, I know I took a long time doing it."

"I wasn't going to say anything." His defensive remark led her to believe that his resentments had been forged long ago, long before whatever remarks she'd made, and that the anger bubbling inside of him hadn't necessarily been directed at her. "It's the doing, the seeing a dream through the daily grind and not the when and how long that's important."

Ric frowned, annoyed with himself. Her compliment took the wind out of his sails, Something about Susan Stewart got to him. "Guess I'm sensitive about folks wondering why it took so long for me to decide what I wanted to do with my life."

He slid further back in the webbed chair and wondered if there was a purpose to this cozy lunch, or whether they were simply going to exchange small talk and case histories. His impatience to cut to the chase was another sign that he'd made the right decision in quitting the cloak and dagger business. Ric took a bite of his chicken and watched her nibble on her own. Would she remain prim and proper as her dossier had implied, or would she eventually come on to him?

He'd play along, asking questions to which he already knew the answers and see where they ended up. "Where'd you go to school?"

"Pitt—undergrad and masters." She paused. "I envy you, living your dream."

"Not quite, but I'm almost there, and how about you, what's your dream?"

"Mine?" She certainly wasn't going to blab about her goofy scheme of a make-believe fiancé. Susan gathered her thoughts while blankly staring at the baskets of bougainvillea and impatiens hanging from crisscrossed beams over the patio. "I guess I'd like to be the best teacher I can be, affect as many children as I can for the good—make a difference in their lives."

"I bet you're already living that dream."

"Maybe. Pecking away at it anyway." She pulled a grape from the bunch and popped it into her mouth. "You know, sometimes I wonder about people who wait and wait, and dream and dream, and work hard for what they think they want, and then when they finally attain it, it turns into a nightmare. I wonder if wanting something so desperately might not turn you into a different person?"

Ric cocked his head. That had happened to him. He'd dreamed of the adventure and excitement of being an agent, and he'd gotten it in spades. Johnny Montoya had gotten it in the back. "Hey, Suse," he said, looking at her over the top of his soda can as he brought it to his lips. "I've had those same thoughts, too."

Charmed by the nickname he'd called her, Susan jumped at the sound of the phone. There'd been an intimacy, a sensuality in his eyes, and the mesmerizing effect undeniably disturbed her. She grabbed the cordless off the table and held it to her ear. “Hello?”

“Susan, everything Jake there?” A woman’s voice quietly spoke into her ear.

“Beg your pardon?”

“Jake, Susan, Jake. You know. Jake’s undercover lingo for, are you all right?”

She let out a breath. It was Robin. “Everything’s Jake.”

“Just checking in. Drove by and saw he was there.”

“Yes,” she answered. Robin must have seen his bike.

“So, how’s it going?” From the sound of her voice, Robin was enjoying this adventure.

“Can’t talk now.” She darted a guilty look at Ric. “Details later. Bye.”

The daunting expression on his chiseled face as she hung up clearly spelled curious. Had he guessed they were talking about him?

Growing more uncomfortable by the moment, Susan looked longingly at the pool and immediately swung her gaze away. Visions of the two of them in the pool sent her temperature rising. Self-conscious, she laced and unlaced her fingers, then reached for the platter of chicken. “Care for another piece of chicken?”

Ric pushed his suspicions aside and nodded. “Don’t mind if I do. It’s delicious. I’ll have some more potato salad, too, and then suppose you tell me more about Susan Stewart.”

Ten minutes later she’d pretty much told him what he already knew, but this time he’d gotten a different slant on things. Unable to be deceptive about anything, she’d given him a window to her emotions, and from the lackluster in her eyes he surmised she looked on her life as dull and routine. The only animation he’d seen was when she’d talked about her teaching.

“So, teaching turns you on,” he commented.

Susan fanned herself with an extra paper plate. “Not until I moved to Las Cruces. Before I came, I was seriously considering a career change, but something touched me here. The Hispanic kids, I guess. I guess that’s why I’ve signed up for another year. My family keeps asking when I’m going to put the house up for sale and come home, but—”

“Are you?”

“Not yet.” She leaned forward on her elbows, her lips moist and slightly parted in a smile. “I’ll let you in on a secret.”

Ric nearly dropped his can of cola. She looked so alluring, so desirable, leaning towards him with that twinkle in her eyes. Was she making a move, or was she sweetly devoid of any knowledge of how seductive she looked? And what secret did she plan to tell him?

"Secret?" he asked, his head tilted toward her.

"I may never go back to Pittsburgh. Things are going so good here I can hardly believe it."

What things, Ric wondered.

"I can see why my aunt never wanted to leave."

Ric slid back in his chair. "Like you said, you didn't feel as if you'd been living your dream till you came here." He paused, choosing his words. "Maybe you've hit the jackpot here."

"Could be." *Jackpot.* She liked the sound of that. Smiling whimsically at him, she said, "Know what, I just may have hit it."

He winked, and heat flooded her cheeks. The twitch at the side of his mouth widened into a broad grin. "Yeah, right. I just bet you have." He reached across the table, tousling her hair. "Hey, we're both much too serious for a gorgeous spring day."

"Feels more like summer." She fanned herself again.

He slanted his gaze at her. "You were here last summer, weren't you?"

She nodded.

"Then you know very well that compared to what's ahead, this is nothing."

She nodded again, flipping her hair off her neck. It might be spring, but her body had no earthly idea what season it was. Goosebumps feathered down her neck and spine when he touched her. In a matter of seconds her metabolism went from hot to cold to hot again.

Ric withdrew his hand. "You said you're definitely staying in Las Cruces another year?"

"Yes, I signed a contract a few weeks ago, and I've registered for another Spanish course at the university this summer."

"Learning the language, huh?"

"It's a necessity around here. I hope to tutor some of my students this summer, and speaking and understanding even a small amount of Spanish is essential, but it's coming so slowly."

"Maybe I could help you."

Susan thought she'd died and gone to heaven. Not only did she want to pump a fist into the air and shout 'yes', but she felt as if she could climb her aunt's apricot tree and jump to the ground in one fell swoop. Ric Ramsey was more than she could hope for. A bicycling, health-minded, well-mannered, about-to-be lawyer, who not only carried on a decent conversation, but who also had depth to him, had just asked if he could help her.

Could he ever!

If ever there was a man ideally suited to play the part of Shane Orr, Ric Ramsey was it. And Glory Hallelujah, meeting regularly to improve her Spanish would be a perfect excuse to get to know him better.

"I'd like that." She could barely keep the eagerness out of her voice. "I kind of wondered whether you knew the language."

"Intimately, Senorita, intimately."

His soft, husky tone sent more tingles up her arm. "Where are you from?"

"West Texas."

West Texas was good. Suited his appearance, and it was far away from Pittsburgh. The further the better, and the less likelihood of anyone knowing him. "So I guess you grew up hearing the language. I know I can use all the help I can get."

Ric studied her eager face. Her desire to learn the language seemed straightforward and harmless and yet... *What's behind this, Sunday School?* His mind flew back to her phone call, a short and cryptic conversation if ever he'd heard one. Had his presence deterred someone else from showing up? Harmless or not, the Spanish lessons would give him a convenient reason to keep an eye on her. In fact, it was one of his better ideas.

"How about Sundays for our Spanish sessions?" he asked. "It seems to be the best time to mesh our schedules. We could start next week."

"Great." Susan snapped her fingers. "Oh, no, I forgot. Next Sunday is out. I have to go to Juarez."

"Oh?"

"It's something I can't cancel."

So, she couldn't cancel it, Ric thought. And what was the lure of Juarez? "You go there often?" he asked, keeping his tone casual and indifferent. She seemed preoccupied as she began to clear the table. He rose to help.

"About once a month." She didn't look at him as she answered.

Once a month? Crap. It didn't sound good. With her snow-white past and innocent demeanor, he'd begun to think she was in the clear when she'd suddenly muddied the water. Now he'd have to arrange surveillance for this trip to Juarez.

"How about a week from tomorrow?" she suggested. "That's a Monday. You said you're off on Mondays, and it's the only other evening I have free that you're off, too."

"A week from Monday it is." He carried the cooler as he followed her back into the house.

"Come for supper if you like."

"How 'bout I bring a pizza?" He placed the unused beer and cola in her refrigerator.

"Sure. That'll be great." She mentally pasted another star by his name for thoughtfulness. The list was growing, along with her inclination to ask him to pose as Shane Orr.

Ric glanced at the kitchen clock. "It's only a little after one. How 'bout we go for a ride on my bike?"

His bike? Surely they both couldn't fit—though the vision of them trying was most provocative. "That's a great idea, but I have my own bike. It's in the garage."

"I doubt you'll be able to keep up with me."

"That so?" She saucily challenged, staring at his infuriating grin.

"Yeah." He clamped his hand around hers and led her through the house and out the front door. "My bike," he said waiting for her full attention and pointing to his shiny black Honda.

With her feet glued to the ground, Susan looked at the bike, darted a glance at Ric, and looked uncomprehendingly at the bike again. "But that's a motorcycle."

He nodded. "I have a spare helmet. Got any boots?" He glanced down at her shocking pink sneakers.

She shook her head, her throat growing dry.

"How about a light-weight windbreaker. I know it's warm, but a jacket will keep the wind and sunburn down."

"Wind burn?" Her throat grew dryer.

She just stood there and stared at him, and Ric loved every minute of it. He wished he had a camera to capture the expression on her face. She was trying so hard to act blasé, but the quiver in her voice and the shock in those stunning eyes of hers gave her away. He was tempted to pull her to him and kiss the crown of her head. “A pair of sunglasses would probably be good, too. Lock up, and I’ll take you for a spin.”

“Spin?” She was already spinning.

Susan stared at the slightly bemused expression on his finely sculpted face. Standing there in a wide-legged stance, his arms crisscrossed over his chest, she could tell he expected her to decline. A rebellious urge to prove him wrong rippled through her. She’d never been on a motorcycle, never desired to since her brother’s best friend had been killed on one.

The phone rang. “Don’t go away,” she called as she dashed to the front door. “I’ll be right back.”

She ran into the kitchen and picked up the receiver. “Hello.”

“Susan, you okay?”

“Pam.” She took a breath and let her rapidly beating heart slow down. The phone call didn’t surprise her. Both friends had hinted their interest in her adventure. “I’m fine. Where are you?” Was Pam prowling the streets, too?

“At my place. Robin just got here. So what’s happening?”

“What’s happening is I’m going for a motorcycle ride with Ric Ramsey.”

“Did you say *motorcycle*?”

“Yes.”

“Where?”

“Around Las Cruces, I guess.” Susan wound the telephone cord around her finger.

“We wouldn’t miss it for the world.”

“But—”

“Remember, Robin and I are in on this too. Stall him. We’ll be there in ten minutes.”

Susan hung up the receiver and looked toward the ceiling. Stall him, Pam had said. Ten minutes of contemplating a ride on his bike and the old Susan was likely to faint.

Chapter Four

Straddling his motorcycle, Ric leaned back on the seat and watched with amazement as Susan Stewart stepped through the front door, pulled it shut, and locked it. The navy windbreaker she wore, the sunglasses she carried in her hand, and the sheer look of panic on her face as she approached confirmed that she intended to ride his motorcycle.

Son of a gun, for a prim and proper young woman, Sunday School's got spunk.

His grin of anticipation for the excuses he'd expected to spill from her mouth rapidly faded. "So, you're going to join me."

"Just for a short ride if you don't mind. I've never ridden on one of these things."

"Kind of figured this was your maiden voyage." He chuckled. "A short ride it is."

He handed her a helmet. When she struggled with the chin strap, he motioned for her to step toward him. He adjusted it and ran his forefinger over her chin for good measure. It was then he discovered she was trembling.

"Hey, it's going to be okay, Suse. I won't let anything happen to you—to either of us. I've been riding these babies since I was eighteen."

"And that was years ago."

"Years and years." There was something so sweet and fragile about her that he had a sudden impulse to pull her into his arms and reassure her. "Swing your leg over behind me," he said instead, patting the long saddle seat. She braced her arm on his shoulder, and he watched as with grim determination she lifted her leg and settled onto the bike. "You're going to have to scoot up closer and hold on tight."

"Like this?"

"Yeah, like that." The minute her arms encircled his waist and her legs came in contact with his thighs, Ric knew he was going to remember this ride. For a good long time. "Look, we won't be able to talk with all the noise. I'll turn my head and holler at you when I think I need to tell you anything, but the wind is going to carry your voice away from me. Suppose if you get feeling panicky or want to stop, you tug on my right arm three times. Got it?"

"I've got it. Three times."

He kicked-started the engine and gunned the motor, letting it idle for a few seconds. "Put your feet up, Suse. Here we go."

As the wind streamed by her face, Susan closed her eyes and hung onto him for dear life. The combined noise of the wind and engine bellowed in her ears, giving the illusion they were traveling over one hundred miles an hour. No matter what the speed, she'd just as soon not be on it at all. She clenched her hands even tighter around his waist. So what if she cut off his air. Maybe then he'd have to stop.

She took several deep breaths and began to think that she was ready to open her eyes. Big mistake. Everything blurred, making her dizzy. She thought about tugging on his arm, but right now not even a crowbar could jar her arm from his waist. When Ric turned a corner without slowing down and she saw how close her right knee tilted toward the pavement, she automatically compensated by leaning her body to the left. The bike wobbled and her heart nearly flip-flopped onto the pavement.

"Don't do that," he yelled back at her.

She scrunched closer to him and yelled back. "What?"

"Don't pull away on the turns. Lean into them."

Lean into them, the man said when any idiot knew the natural inclination was to lean away. Self preservation dictated it. Ah, well, what choice did she have. If she pulled away, the motorcycle might tip over and the two of them would end up as splats on the road. Better follow his instructions than flirt with death. "I'll try."

"Atta girl," he said, turning back to face the road after executing another right turn.

Susan sent several prayers toward the heavens, among them one solemnly promising she'd never climb onto a motorcycle again if only the good Lord would deliver her home safe and sound. Irrational though it was, she suddenly wished she'd brought her hot pink umbrella along. She'd come to look at it as possessing secret powers or at the very least capable of instilling an extra dose of confidence in her. Goodness knows at the speed they were traveling if she opened it, the wind might carry her aloft and deposit her on the side of the road.

Tug his arm three times, he'd said..

That's all she had to do, and she could end it right now. Easy for him to say. She couldn't unglue her arm if she wanted to, and even if she could, she wasn't going to give him the satisfaction of discovering how scared she was. For some reason she didn't understand she didn't want this man to find her lacking. She'd ride this confounded contraption even if it killed her. And she wasn't at all sure it wouldn't.

When, she wondered, *was all this nonsense going to end?*

Ever since telling Mary Ellen Hathaway that her fiancé was an undercover agent, nothing about her life had been normal. And what would her parents think when they learned she'd been killed while riding a motorcycle? She could see them now, gathered around her casket, their gazes incredulous, shaking their heads in a quandary as people passed by to express their condolences.

Stop it, she chattered to herself as vibrations from the danged machine rattled both her bones and teeth. It was going to be all right. Hadn't Ric said it would be? Ric. Concentrate on Ric. Not a hard thing to do with her pelvis tucked against his buttocks, their thighs touching, and her breasts flattened against his back. They couldn't be any closer if they were in bed, their bodies covering each other like a warm blanket.

The thought sent hot flushes rippling through her, and despite the cooling wind that whipped by her head in what surely had to be fifty mile gusts, beads of perspiration dotted the back of her neck.

With her head hugging his strong sinewy back and their bodies pressed together like fiberboard, Susan felt her nerves begin to send out a different sort of jangle. Not to mention the vibrations climbing up her legs. Hard to tell if they were due to the motorcycle or the man riding it. Ric Ramsey was like no other man she'd ever met, and her body seemed to take on a different personality whenever she was near him, a personality she'd better control if she wanted to keep their relationship strictly business.

The wind filled their jackets, puffing them out and flapping them, and Susan turned her attention back to the road. Ric slowed the motorcycle. Finding that she could adapt to the slower speed, she saw that they were riding through the University. Gradually, she relaxed so by the time Ric turned onto the interstate and picked up speed, she was able to handle it. She wondered where they were going.

Some short ride.

With her fingers laced together at his stomach, she also wondered if Pam and Robin were following them. Moments before she'd climbed on the motorcycle, she'd thought she'd seen Pam's car parked down the street.

He turned off the highway, twisting and climbing on a two lane mountain road. The angle threw Ric's body back and even closer into hers—if that was possible. He slowed the bike and turned onto a dirt road. Minutes later he pulled off onto a scenic overview, cut the engine, and kicked down the parking stand. Reluctantly, she released her grip on him. He swung his leg over and a second later lifted her off the bike.

"You did great." He backed away and unsnapped his chin strap. Hanging his helmet on the chrome bar, he fastened his gaze on hers.

She handed him her helmet and took a wobbly step on her rubbery legs. "Thanks." Taking a deep breath and hoping it would find a home in her air-starved lungs, she looked over the city, an array of tans, coppers and terra cottas spread before her. "Wow, what a view," she said, trying to sound as in control as possible.

"You've lived here two years and never been up here before?" His dark eyes captured hers, and her stomach did a flip-flop under his piercing gaze.

"No."

"I drove up here the first week I moved here. Couldn't resist it. Farther on up there're streams and ponds."

The sun beat down on them, and she moved into the little shade cast by a mesquite tree. *Say something*, she whispered to herself as she struggled for composure. Getting her bearings, Susan glanced at the University far below. "I think this is the same mountain where the Indians hold their pilgrimage in December."

"Pilgrimage?"

"Something to do with Our Lady of Guadeloupe. I saw them last year as they were preparing to walk up the mountain dressed in costumes, carrying torches and lanterns." Seeing he'd removed his sunglasses, she took hers off and pushed them into her pocket.

"It must have been a ceremony or a feast day," Ric commented, still standing next to her.

Ever so conscious of how close he was, Susan shut her

eyes, and remembering his taut body, she took a step away and shrugged her shoulders. "I'm not sure."

His comment reminded her of the faint hint of Indian she saw in his face. Something to do with his cheekbones and the set of his jaw she supposed. Ill at ease, she shifted her gaze to his motorcycle, only to look back and glimpse him staring at her. He looked dangerous and enticing, and if she never saw him again, he'd be a man she'd never forget. She wrinkled her nose and pointed to his bike. "The ride was quite an experience. Just how fast were we going?"

He laughed. "Never broke fifty. But with the wind beating at you, you get the sensation you're going faster. Figured you wouldn't want to go any faster your first time."

First time? Apart from their return trip home, did the man think there'd be another?

She had news for him. Still, it gave her pause to think. It implied that he intended to ask her to ride again. Her gaze swung back to the bike with a vengeance. Yes, there was a measure of comfort in his statement, if you could call the thought of climbing back on that machine comforting.

He placed his hands on her shoulders. "From your grip around my waist I expected a scream or two."

"You mean you didn't hear them?" She pivoted to face him, the heat of his stare drawing her attention, and she gave him a tentative smile.

"Didn't hear a thing, but I did feel you tremble a time or two.

"I've had this phobia about motorcycles ever since someone I knew was killed on one. Guess I couldn't hide it."

"Then this was a big step for you. A couple of more rides and you'll feel better. It grows on you." He winked. "I promise I'll get us both back in one piece. Don't worry."

"Then I won't." The heat must have affected her brain. The idea of riding on the bike with him was beginning to have some appeal. Then again everything about him was appealing, including the faint scar by his right temple.

Ric watched her thick, lush lashes slowly rise to meet his gaze. Her big-eyed stare of trust hit him like a two-ton truck, and he couldn't help feeling a grudging respect for her. Trust. She gave it so easily. Could he trust his instincts about her? She'd been scared, possibly still was, and yet she sloughed it off and placed her faith in him. And that scared him.

He slid his hand around hers. “Know what I think?”

“Uh uh.”

“I think we should sit down, relax, enjoy the view, and get you psyched up for the ride home.”

Maybe by filling her in on some of his life, she’d open up and talk more about herself. He took off his jacket and motioned for her to remove hers. Placing them on the ground, he sat down and propped his back against a mesquite tree. He stretched out his arm, inviting her to join him, fighting the impulse to take her into his arms.

Snuggled beside him, he took her hand again. “The countryside here reminds me of where I grew up.”

“Where was that?”

“On a ranch outside of San Angelo. My father was the foreman.”

“Any brothers or sisters?”

“One brother. Tommy was four years older than me.” Ric tensed. Normally, he didn’t like talking about his family, but this was a ready-made opportunity to study her reaction. “We were into football and riding horses. Especially my brother. Tommy wasn’t too fond of the books.”

“But you were.”

“Nah. I wasn’t much for studying either. Just lucky enough to get by better than he was.” He crossed one of his legs over the other. “Took some knocking around for me to wise up and appreciate an education. Tommy wasn’t so lucky. He fell into some rough company. By the time my folks realized what had happened, he’d tried so many different drugs that his mind was scrambled before he turned twenty.”

“That’s terrible.”

“Yeah, it nearly killed my mother. Drugs will do that to people,” he said, taking his measure of her. “You’ve probably never been exposed to any…” he hesitated.

“Illegal drugs?”

He gave her credit. Her eyes held the proper amount of outrage and indignation. “Yeah, illegal.”

“Not personally, thank goodness. Never wanted to. I tried smoking a cigarette once and coughed for nearly a week. There was a boy in my high school class who got messed up pretty much the way you said your brother did. I heard rumors that it was easy to buy drugs at school, especially marijuana. Some people smoked it in college, but none…”she swallowed air, “no one but... the only..."

Her voice trailed off and her eyes took on a faraway cast. She might be looking down the mountain, but he sensed her eyes were focused on something within herself. "What is it, Suse?" He took her hand and squeezed it.

"An unpleasant memory," she said, still avoiding his gaze.

Promising, he thought. He'd like to pursue it, but sensed it would be wise to wait. "Life's peppered with them. I have an album full myself."

"An album?"

"Just a figure of speech. I was in Saudi with the Marines, and it was mostly good, but there were some unpleasant memories." He gritted his teeth at the lie. Most of them, if not all, had come later during his hitch with the Agency.

"You were a Marine?"

She tossed her shiny brown hair, and Ric stared at the corona formed by the sun shining behind her head. Somehow the fact that she wasn't a blonde seemed to matter less and less. "That's how I got through college—R.O.T.C. Then I had to pay back Uncle Sam."

"I guess you do have some bad memories, far worse than any I have."

He couldn't imagine her having any bad memories. In fact, he was having a damned hard time getting a fix on her. There was nothing in her past that suggested misery, hardship—nothing to trigger unpleasant memories—nothing that hinted someone might be blackmailing her to work for them. During the past hour he'd mulled over what he knew about her and zeroed in on blackmail as the strongest possibility. Susan Stewart was either on the level or one of the coolest actresses he'd ever come across.

And he didn't think she was acting.

She might have been born and raised in Pittsburgh, but it was as if she was straight off of one of those Pennsylvania Dutch Farms he'd read about. Refreshing and open, she'd shown genuine remorse when he mentioned his brother. But there was something in her past that the investigation must have missed. And his gut told him it had to do with the word 'engagement.' Why the hell should she nearly panic when he'd asked her if she was engaged? It had been the only crack in her cool facade.

How else to explain why a pillar-of-the-community-type

woman had hung out at Judd's and flirted with him? It was totally out of character. There had to be some pressing reason behind it. Even now, he was convinced that her flat tire had been purposely contrived as a way to meet him.

Engagement and blackmail. He'd lay odds they were connected.

It was only natural to suspect whoever killed his ex-partner would want to sniff out his replacement. He'd shown up in Johnny's job barely two weeks after his death. And he didn't dare underestimate the gang's creativity. Sending a woman like Sunday School would be a stroke of genius. Who would suspect her? Who wouldn't open up to her? Even he was having trouble on both scores. There was something disarming about the woman that caused his tongue to loosen.

And there was more. Much more.

The whole time they'd been riding, he wondered if she had any idea of the provocative thoughts that had passed through his mind. It had been damned disconcerting to feel her abdomen pressed to his butt, their legs clinging together, and the pressure of her cheek against his upper back now and then. And those arms and hands of hers wrapped around him and digging into him as if he were a life preserver, not to mention how her hands were laced together over his lower stomach, resting dangerously near his groin.

It had taken a monumental effort to concentrate on his driving. Everything about her pushed his system to overload. When he should have had his eyes on the traffic, he'd been visualizing what it would be like to touch her legs and thighs, to bury his head between her breasts. And it irritated the hell out of him because he didn't know what to think about her—how far he could trust her, and most of all, why he had such strong protective urges about her.

Ah, well, life had been getting dull.

"What else?"

Her question jolted him. "How's that?"

"Football, horseback riding, Marines, law school. What else is there about Ric Ramsey?"

"That's about it." He leaned back against the tree silently watching her. He'd thought they were off the subject of him, but her eyes held questions. "Just an ordinary guy."

"Not ordinary," she swiftly contradicted. "Compared to me, you have an exciting life."

"Is that what you're looking for, Suse, excitement?" He watched her cock her head as if giving his question deep consideration.

"I honestly don't know. A couple of months ago I thought I knew myself, but now I just don't know."

Ric studied her. Maybe she was just kicking up her heels. Maybe her excursions into Judd's and approaching him had all been a lark. But he didn't like coincidences. She'd arrived in Las Cruses a year and a half ago and that's when the traffic had picked up. And she'd started haunting Judd's shortly after he'd arrived. "If excitement's what you're looking for, Judd's is the place. Go there often?"

"Actually, I've only been there a couple of times since I moved here."

"Four times in the past twelve days." As he grazed his fingers over the inside of her wrist, her pulse fluttered.

"You were counting?"

Damn straight. If she'd timed her visits any later in the day so would have everyone else. "So what's the big attraction?"

"Attraction?" Her lips trembled. "The food. I love their enchiladas. And the band. My yardman recommended them."

Yeah, sure. "Most folks come for the line dancing. You might enjoy it. No telling where it could lead you." Certainly not down the blind alleys she'd been leading him. "Why, just the other night one of the couples got engaged," he said, testing his theory, waiting for her to react.

Right on cue, her palm moistened. Son of a gun if her lips weren't trembling, too. Telltale signs that something connected to engagements freaked her out. Worth having the Agency investigate.

"Oh look!" She pointed at the sky. "The balloons. Aren't they gorgeous? Funny they're up now. Usually it's early in the morning when I see them."

"Has to do with the wind." He drew his lips into a thin line at her swift change of subject. "It's light this afternoon, good conditions for them."

"I've always wondered what it would be like to fly in one. I guess it takes an adventurous soul to try."

Susan stared at their linked hands. His grip was strong and possessive, and his callused palm branded her with fire. She lifted her gaze, meeting his hypnotic gray eyes. He trailed the back of his finger across the curve of her cheekbone, and

Susan stared at the taut muscles in his arm. His hand moved around to her neck, massaging her nape.

It was heavenly, and she closed her eyes for a moment. "I'm not—"

"Not what?"

"A reckless person."

"Could have fooled me." He lifted the hand that held hers captive and placed a kiss on the inside of her wrist.

He leaned closer, his gaze lingering on her lips. "Sometimes being reckless can be fun."

Laughter crinkled at the corners of his eyes. His fingers crept across her cheek to gently caress her ear, and Susan felt her breath catch in her throat. This time she knew he was going to kiss her. He brushed his mouth over hers and rational thought fled. Never in all her life had she been so aware of a man's sexual magnetism.

"Like this," he said, cupping his hands on her face and covering her mouth.

Susan trembled as a host of sensations assailed her. Years had passed since she'd felt such pleasure. His mouth continued to press down demandingly on hers, setting it on fire. It was their first kiss, and it was like she'd been waiting all her life for it to happen. She was tired, so tired of being alone.

He lifted his head. "If you don't want this, tell me now, Suse, tell me now."

Mutely, she stared at him, her tongue tied, a lump stuck in her throat. She couldn't answer. She couldn't say yes, and she couldn't say no, but she knew what she wanted. She wanted Ric to kiss her. With gentleness, he nibbled on her lips and plied them apart. He traced the inside of her mouth with his tongue, and Susan melted into him. A quivery feeling spread from the pit of her stomach to just below her breastbone, and she wondered if he felt her tremors. As his tongue continued to probe the recesses of her mouth, she swore she could hear their hearts beating in unison.

And then far, far away, she thought she heard the sound of a car's engine. Perhaps it was the thunderous beating of her heart. She wasn't sure, but she opened an eyelid and took a peek over his shoulder. It was definitely a car. Both her eyes fluttered open. Pam's old brown Chevy.

Oh, Lord, she'd die of embarrassment if they saw her, or if he saw them. Had Ric heard the car?

Impulsively, she clasped one arm around Ric's neck and held him to her, while trying to wave with her free arm for her friends to back up and turn around. Deciding the best way to keep him occupied was to respond with all her might, she placed her free hand behind his neck, linked her fingers together, and pulled his body more tightly to hers. Hearing his throaty moans, she pushed his tongue out of the way and deepened the kiss.

What started out as a ploy to prevent him from turning around and discovering the car kicked out of control. A passion she didn't know she possessed surfaced. She couldn't get enough of him. Feverish and trembling, she closed her eyes and instinctively combed her fingers through his hair. Hot yearnings flew through her like tidal waves, and she clung to him, her breath coming in short gasps.

Seconds later he pulled her onto his lap. She buried her face in the crook of his neck and with the tip of her tongue tasted his sun-warmed skin. His body tensed beneath her, and Susan struggled again with her breathing. Angling her head over his shoulder once again, she saw the car was just about out of sight, and though her body was ready to explode, though she didn't want to end their embrace, she forced herself to push away from him.

Ric felt her nudge him and reluctantly released her. Or maybe she released him. Sunday School had surprised him. Her savage response had nearly knocked the wind from his throat. She'd met him kiss for kiss, touch for touch, practically writhing in his arms. As for himself, the pain in his groin told him he was far from satisfied. He watched her pull away, staring at the glaze of desire coloring in her eyes.

So, there was another side to Sunday School after all, and she hadn't learned it in church.

With his heart beating rapidly, Ric chanced to look up at the road and saw the fender of a brown sedan disappear around the bend. It brought him up short. When they'd been driving on the motorcycle, he'd noticed a beat-up brown car following them, but it had faded from sight when they started up the mountain. He looked back at Susan. Those brown eyes of hers were staring up at him with all the innocence of a puppy dog—almost too quick a change from the desire that had been there moments ago. Leveling a piercing gaze at her, he grimaced.

Was there a connection?

Had the car been following them?

Did she know about it?

Like a cold shower, it took the edge off his passion.

Susan scrambled out of his lap and picked her jacket from the ground. "I-I— " She stared at the sky, then at her feet, her senses still on overload. "That got a little out of hand," she murmured.

Not a sound. Not a word from Ric. As she stood to shake her jacket, she glimpsed his rigid jaw and brooding glaze seconds before he masked his eyes with a smile.

Something was wrong.

"You're right, it sure was something, wasn't it?" he remarked.

Was it? She didn't know. All she knew was her intuition told her something was deeply wrong. Surprised by the fire that had blazed between them and confused, she stared at him.

Ric stared beyond her, his brow creasing in a frown, a grimace tightening his lips. *It was something, Sunday School.* Something like he'd never known. But was it real or all a sham?

Chapter Five

"Okay, tell us about yesterday," Robin urged as she watched Susan dish out the take-out Chinese onto three platters.

Susan poured their iced tea and looked at her friends. Pam was climbing out of the pool and drying herself off.

"What's our dreamboat like?" Pam inquired, walking over to the table.

Susan pulled up a green and white webbed chair. "Quite nice, actually." For picking a man at random, Ric Ramsey had proved to be better than she could hope for. Memories pressed in on her. The bottle of wine he'd brought, the way he'd assured her that he'd take care of her when they'd been on his motorcycle, and how he'd offered to help with her Spanish. "He just graduated from law school."

"No way! Our bartender? Law school?" Robin cut into her words.

"Yes, and he's intelligent, easy to talk to." He was lots of things, and she could barely go to sleep last night thinking about them. His reaction to their kisses had especially perturbed her.

Pam raised her glass to her lips and looked at Susan over the rim. "Do you believe him?"

Susan sat still. "Yes. Yes, I do." The memory of the defensive tone of his voice and the sincere look in his eyes when he'd told her about himself reinforced her. She nodded for extra measure. Heaven help her, she believed him.

"Hey guys, this cashew chicken is delicious." Robin helped herself to some more. "So what school did he go to?" she asked.

"University of Texas, undergrad and law school."

"At Austin?" Pam cocked her head.

"I think so."

"You don't know what year he graduated, do you?" Robin followed up her earlier question while spooning the chicken onto the other two plates.

"No, why?" Growing suspicious, Susan sent a threatening glare in the direction of her friends. "What are you up to?"

"Well, there's no need for you to hog all the excitement in this adventure. Pam and I could play detective and check him out for you."

"I don't know ..."

"Hey, Susan, he could be a con artist or something. Wouldn't it be comforting to learn that he'd been telling you the truth?"

Susan bit her bottom lip. Pam was only looking after her welfare, and she was right. It was better to be safe than sorry. "Still—I can't put my finger on it, but I believe him."

"You believe everybody, and I'd believe him too, if I was wrapped in his arms," Robin interrupted. "By the way, Pam and I tailed him home one night after Judd's closed up."

"You what?" Susan blurted.

"He lives in a trailer park. On the surface there's nothing wrong with being a bartender in a cruddy hangout, riding a motorcycle, and living in a trailer, but you've got to admit it doesn't sound like a lawyer. Certainly not any lawyer I know."

"And you've got to admit something else," Pam interjected,

"the mystery does make him a neat model for an undercover cop or something. Sounds to me as if he's feeding you a line."

Robin ignored Pam's remark. "It just so happens I have to fly to Austin next week to do an audit for a client, and since I have some comp time coming from tax season, why not put it to good use?" She turned to Pam. "How about you? Can you get off next week?"

Pam nodded. "No problem. If we both go, we could drive." Pam switched her gaze to Susan. "How do you spell his name?"

While Susan spelled it out for Pam, Robin distributed more food from the other cartons onto their plates. "So, what do you think? Is he going to be Shane Orr?"

"He's available isn't he? And single?" Pam quirked an eyebrow and waited for Susan to nod. "Did he say where he's from?"

"San Angelo."

"Great." Robin snapped her fingers. "After we've found out what we need to in Austin we can drive to San Angelo."

Susan shook her head. Pam and Robin had turned into a couple of first-class snoops. "You two sound like a nineties version of Charlie's Angels, and isn't this going to be expensive for you?"

"Since we said we'd pay for Shane Orr's air fare to Pittsburgh, suppose if you really get this guy to go, you repay us for our trip to Austin," Pam suggested.

"Maybe we'd all be better off financially if I just dropped this nutty scheme."

"Come on, Susan, you have to admit that our lives have been pretty dull lately," Robin commented. "Pam and I are hoping you get this Ric to agree. I almost wish we could go with you just to see this Mary Jane—"

"Mary Ellen," Susan corrected.

"Just to see Mary Ellen's face." Mischief lit up Robin's eyes. "Are you going to see him again?"

"Next Monday evening," Susan said tentatively. He hadn't mentioned it when he'd brought her home, and considering how aloof he'd been, she wasn't certain that when Monday came, he would show up. "He's going to help me with my Spanish lessons."

"He speaks Spanish?" When Susan nodded, Pam said, "Smooth, Susan, smooth. Neat way to get him to come by regularly."

Her friends were right. There was a lot she didn't know about Ric Ramsey, and his mood after their kisses left her no peace. He'd tried to hide it, but she'd caught that strange look in his eyes.

"So, when do you plan to ask him to pose as your fiancé?" Robin poured herself more iced tea.

"I thought I'd wait two or three weeks."

"Good." Pam wrinkled her nose. "By then we should have the scoop on him, and you'll know if he's on the up and up."

"Look guys, I hate you wasting your time and money on this trip. I might not ask him."

"Susan Stewart, don't you dare not ask him," Robin insisted, "that is, if we give you the green light."

"He might not show up again."

"If what we saw up on the mountain is any indication, he'll show up, and if he doesn't, we'll figure out something to make him," Pam said.

But they hadn't seen what she'd seen. "And if I ask him, he might refuse."

"He wouldn't dare," Robin countered. "And don't you worry about us. Our fingers and toes are just itching to get involved."

Pam and Robin raised their glasses. "To the success of Operation Shane Orr," they said in unison.

Avoiding her friends' eyes, Susan curled her fingers around her glass and slowly lifted it. "To Shane Orr," she repeated, her voice whisper-soft in comparison. As the dusk deepened, activating the solar cells lights surrounding the pool, she kept thinking they'd left something very basic out of their calculations.

Ric drove his motorcycle up to the fast food window, paid his bill, and set his bag of food in a leather saddlebag, then he gunned the motor and parked in one of the slots around in back. The fast food restaurant overlooked Interstate 10 leading into El Paso from the West. Swinging his leg over the bike, he grabbed his burger and sauntered over to a black car.

God, he was dead on his feet. He'd worked late Friday, searched around Las Cruces for a car to rent on Saturday, worked late again that night, and risen at dawn on Sunday. An hour later he'd been parked a block away from Susan Stewart's house in his rented car and tailed her into Juarez. She and her companions had returned to Las Cruces by four in the afternoon, but Ric hadn't followed her home.

Instead, he'd parked across the street from where she'd left her passengers. Minutes later they were picked up by a blue Taurus, and he'd followed them to what he assumed was their house. This morning, wishing he could sack in, he'd returned the rental car, and here he was on the outskirts of El Paso.

Ric opened the car door, slid into the seat next to the driver, then slammed the door shut. He extended his hand. The man sitting behind the wheel was slight, dark skinned, and wore glasses.

"José Vella," the man said, shaking his hand. "We've talked on the phone."

"Ric Ramsey."

"So, how was your trip to Juarez?"

"Dull as dust. I followed Senorita Stewart from her house to a couple of intersections past Old Mesilla where she picked up two men and a woman, all Hispanic. They drove to a mall in Juarez near the bull ring, arriving around ten in the morning. She got out, was met by another couple, and then her passengers drove off in her station wagon."

Ric rubbed his jaw. He always did when he was tired. "I sure wish you could have spared someone to help me. I had to make a decision, and I'm afraid I made the wrong one. I stuck with Senorita Stewart. Hell, I couldn't miss her. The whole state of Texas could see her—stood out like a neon sign, carrying that hot pink umbrella of hers."

"Umbrella?"

"Yeah, and no, it wasn't raining. She used it for sunshade. And, yes, it seems damn stupid calling attention to herself like that. Then again, it could be cunning."

"You think it was a signal?"

"I kept wondering if someone slipped a shipment of drugs in with her purchases." Ric chuckled. "Ever spend a day shopping with a woman?" Even though he hadn't been physically by her side, Ric felt as if he'd been intimately involved in every purchase she'd made. He slanted a look at José who nodded and joined his laughter. "Then you know how tedious and dull it can be. I knew there was a reason I'd quit the Agency. She and her companions took a bus to a couple of other locations. She bought baskets, scarves, a silver tray, and more baskets."

Ric paused and shook his head. "Have you any idea how many basket shops there are in Juarez?" He'd watched every single move she'd made. The only time she'd been out of his sight had been her trips to the ladies room.

Thinking about her excursion to Juarez, he grinned. Another motive behind her Spanish lessons could be that she wanted to become proficient in the language in order to negotiate her shopping expeditions on her own. That was probably the reason she owned a station wagon. The vehicle seemed incongruous with a woman her age, though as a teacher he could see where she might have use for one. But now he knew better. She needed a station wagon to haul all her loot home from Juarez.

"After lunch she went through an Art Museum," Ric said, resuming his report. "Her Juarez companions waited outside for her, and I could have used back up there, too."

"Sorry about that, buddy," José said.

"Yeah, well, at approximately three o'clock, give or take a few minutes, they met back by the bull ring and the original group headed back to Las Cruces." Exasperated at how fruitless the day had been, Ric glanced out the car window and scowled. He'd forgotten the boring side of his old job, the hours on end cramped in a car or doing your damnedest to shadow someone on foot and not be detected.

"At customs," he continued, "she showed what she'd purchased, and all her passengers carried with them was what looked like home-baked food. They'd carried bags of groceries over with them when they left in the morning. I definitely hitched my wagon to the wrong star. Nothing suspicious happened the whole time I had her under surveillance."

José had been eating and nodding the whole time Ric had been speaking. "Eat your cheeseburger and fries before they get cold," José urged him.

Ric took a bite, chewed, and swallowed. "Did you get a fix on the address and license plate of the Taurus I phoned in to you last night?"

"The address belongs to Juan and Angelina Garcia. The Agency will check on them. Nothing back yet on the car, and of course until we see what you've got, we won't know who the other man with them was, nor the people who shopped with her in Mexico."

"I took pictures of everything and everyone, the

passengers—the people who met them in Juarez and every bloody store and transaction Susan Stewart made." He fished out the film and handed it to José. "I think I'm chasing up a blind alley." At least he hoped he was concerning Sunday School.

"But it's the only alley you've got so far, right?"

"Right." Ric paused and frowned. "But something's fishy. I paid a visit to Senorita Stewart a week ago Sunday. Everything went fine except for a very suspicious phone call, and I could swear someone tailed us when we went for a ride on my motorcycle. I couldn't get a good look at the car, but it was definitely brown and old."

"Play it out and see. If another stronger lead develops, you can drop the Stewart woman. Any leads at Judd's yet?" José rolled down his window and lit a cigarette.

"I think one of the men playing in the band is a prime candidate. He visits the parking lot to take a smoke every now and then, and once I observed him having a conversation with someone who stayed in the shadows." He took a sip of his cola and leveled his gaze on José. "Any word on my replacement?"

José shook his head. "Not for at least six weeks. The Agency really appreciates what you're doing."

"Anything for Johnny."

"Right. Here's some more cash." José handed Ric an envelope. "Oh, and if I were you, I wouldn't be too quick to cross Senorita Stewart off your list. The investigative team just turned up something they'd missed—not much, but it's definitely a stain on her lily white record."

"That so?" Ric didn't know if he was happy or disappointed. Part of him wanted Sunday School to be a law abiding citizen. But another part, the part that was attracted to her too damned much for his own good, wanted her to be guilty so he could put the brakes on his emotions and remain objective about her. "What did they find?"

"Back when she was in college, her senior year, she had a boyfriend, serious relationship they believe."

"Were they engaged?" Ric interrupted.

"Not sure. Could have been. No matter, the guy was busted for selling cocaine." José flicked his ashes out the window.

Ric remained silent for a moment and pressed his lips together. "Did she know he was dealing?"

"Apparently not. According to the trial transcript, she was

called as a character witness for his defense, but when cross examined she swore she hadn't known anything about it. She wasn't charged."

"You said they were tight?" Ric narrowed his eyes, uneasy with his thoughts.

"That's what one of his fraternity brothers remembers."

"Then she had to know." He muttered a curse and closed his eyes. *What's going on, Sunday School? Are you or aren't you what you seem to be*? A chill swept over him. "What's the guy's name?"

"Jerry Westphal. He's out now. That was eleven years ago."

"Whereabouts?" Ric finished his cheeseburger and crumpled up the paper.

"He's employed at an auto plant in Dallas."

"Dallas! Cripes sake, what's a guy from Pittsburgh doing in Dallas?" Ric didn't like where his thoughts were leaping.

"Makes you wonder, doesn't it? Dallas isn't exactly next door, but it sure is in the area."

"You going to put surveillance on him?"

"Spotty. As you know, we're stretched thin, and we don't have any firm reason for an around-the-clock unless you turn up something on this end that connects him."

Preparing to leave, Ric closed his fingers around the door handle. "I'm seeing Susan Stewart this evening. If I turn up anything, I'll let you know."

"Yeah, we'll keep in touch." José took another drag on his cigarette. "Watch your back."

"You bet."

The voices of Rosalita and Roberto Cisneros hummed in the background as Susan sat at the patio table, watching them sit on the side of the pool and kick their legs in the water at the shallow. She'd just finished tutoring the two children, and although they were dressed in their school clothes, she'd given in to their pleas to let them take off their shoes and socks and dangle their feet in the pool.

Exams were only a week away, and Roberto, having already repeated the fourth grade, was still struggling to pass this year. It was embarrassing enough to be in the same class with his sister who was a year younger, and it would be even more traumatic for him if his sister passed and he didn't. But then,

Rosalita was having problems, too. That's why Susan had taken them under her wing. Naturally concerned, she'd offered to tutor them after school on Mondays and Fridays, the only days in her busy schedule that she didn't have an evening commitment.

So, Susan, you want to make a bet with yourself whether he'll show up or not?

Her wristwatch read ten to six, only a few more minutes until the time she expected him. She shook her head. What was that quaint British expression she'd heard? In for a penny, in for a pound. And she was in for every gloriously well-proportioned pound of one Ric Ramsey. She raised a hand to her lips, remembering how his kisses had shaken her to the core.

She found Ric too pleasant, too attractive for her own good, and she secretly hoped that Robin and Pam would return with a favorable report. Yet it somehow seemed unsavory, unethical to be checking up on him. But that was ridiculous, considering the nuts loose today and how little she knew about him. It would be foolish not to.

Watch it, Susan. You're back to being practical, sensible. Dull.

Emotions bounced back and forth in her, and that brief unsettling look she'd seen in his eyes confounded her. It had haunted her all week, even on her excursion to Juarez yesterday. She cocked her head. Odd how every now and then when she'd been shopping, chill bumps had crept up her arm. She'd had the eeriest sensation that she was being watched, even followed. Shrugging it off, she stood and walked closer to the pool, the memory of Ric's wary look staying with her.

Everything had gone so well that day, and he'd seemed genuinely interested in her. He was the one who'd invited her to ride his motorcycle, and he'd been the one to initiate their kiss. An errant thought ticked in her head, and Susan felt her cheeks stain with color as she remembered how wantonly she'd acted after seeing Pam's car. She'd practically attacked him, pulling him harder and harder against her body.

Never had she acted so wild—and never had she so enjoyed the taste of a man.

Had her behavior turned him off? Impossible. Though Ric Ramsey appeared to be a gentleman, everything about him from the tip of his toes to the rakish sparkle in his gray eyes spoke of a man who thoroughly enjoyed women, a man who wasn't a stranger to their advances. That had to be it. Ric Ramsey was used to being the hunter, and for a few minutes she had turned the tables on him. She drew in a deep breath and expelled it.

You know darn well what it means, Susan Stewart. It means that if he comes to dinner, pizza might not be all he devours.

Chapter Six

The rumble of a motorcycle broke Susan's trance. Ric was here.

"Rosalita, Roberto," she called to them. "Sit at the table until I come back." She waited until they obeyed her. "Please stay away from the pool. I'll just be a minute." Entering the house, she was only steps away from the door when the bell rang.

When Susan opened the door, Ric nearly dropped the pizza and brown paper bag he carried. *Sunday School was wearing shorts.* His eyes zeroed in on her lime green shorts and matching tennis shoes. As his gaze lingered on her long shapely stems, his fingers itched to touch them. *Damn, but Sunday School was a well packaged female.*

"Evening," he said, nodding. It was a sin to shift his gaze from her gorgeous legs, but he sensed it was time to acknowledge the rest of her. "Here's the—"

"Miss Stewart, Miss Stewart, *ayuda me, ven rapido! Pronto, pronto, Senorita Stewart,*" a little girl screamed, racing towards them at break-neck speed.

Ric and Susan spun around at the shriek. Sheer terror showed on the young girl's face as she broke into a rapid spate of Spanish.

"*Cálmate. ¿Qué pasa ¿Qué dijiste, niñita*" Ric softly asked the young girl.

"*Roberto se esta ahogando en la charca,*" Rosalita answered.

As Ric spoke rapidly to Rosalita in Spanish, the words jumbled together, but Susan knew something had happened to Roberto. She swung around to face Ric. "What is it? What's she saying?"

"I think she's trying to tell us that Roberto's drowning in the pool. Here."

He shoved the box of pizza and the paper bag into her arms, and with Rosalita on his heels, dashed through the house. Ric shed his windbreaker on the way and stopped only to pull off his boots. Bringing up the rear her heart ticking erratically, Susan scampered behind them as fast as her feet could carry her not stopping as she tossed her packages on the kitchen table and raced out to the patio. Ric was already in the pool, clothes and all.

Seconds later he hauled Roberto out and lay him on his stomach, pumping on the back of his ribs.

"Is he breathing? I know C.P.R.," she offered. With each competent push and with each intense frown on Ric's face, Susan's admiration for him grew.

"So do I, but I don't I think it'll be necessary," he said as the boy sat up coughing and sputtering. Ric checked the boy's face and lightly tapped on his back. "Fortunately, all he seems to have gotten is a good scare."

Rosalita sidled up to her, and Susan wrapped her arm around the girl. "I should have never left them alone," she chastised herself. "I told them to stay at the table, that it would only be a minute."

Poor Rosalita. She was sobbing as she tried to speak. "Will my brother be all right, Senorita?"

"Don't worry, he'll be fine," Ric intervened. He gently patted Rosalita on her head. "And don't beat up on yourself, Suse. This young man looks old enough to know that if he couldn't swim, he shouldn't have been in the pool."

"He's eleven," Susan supplied, then glanced at Ric. He was tall, strong, and fully in charge. Had been from the moment Rosalita screamed. And the tender concern in his voice gave her pause. "I knew they didn't swim. I should have made them come to the door with me." If anything had happened to the boy, she could never forgive herself. "I'll get some towels." Barely a minute later she returned with two oversized beach towels. They wrapped one around Roberto.

"Sorry, Senorita." The boy slouched as they seated him in a chair.

"It's okay, Roberto, but don't go in that pool ever again without me, *comprendo*?" She forced a threatening tone into her voice.

"*Si.*"

"We'll have to see about teaching you to swim this summer. Maybe we can keep up your school lessons at the same time so you'll get a head start on the fifth grade." She stepped away and crossed her fingers, hoping both he and his sister would both pass the fourth grade.

"*Muchas gracias, Senorita.* We'd like that."

Five minutes later Mr. Cisneros arrived to pick up his children. His alarm over his son's accident was most understandable. Susan was grateful that Ric was there to help her explain what had happened. Ric conversed with him in Spanish, and after Mr. Cisneros calmed down, she apologized. Several times. He graciously accepted all of them while mildly chastening his son to obey her rules. She waved good bye, shut the front door, and leaned her back against it, releasing a long, shaky sigh.

"Thank goodness you were here." She reached for one of Ric's hands and cupped it between both of hers. "You were wonderful, so calm under fire. You saved his life." Trembling, she released his hand and turned away, quietly trying to absorb the shock of almost losing Roberto.

Ric placed his thumb under her chin and slowly forced her head around. He towered above her, his intense gray eyes insisting she meet his gaze.

"It's okay, Suse." He trailed his thumb across her jaw line then dropped his hand. "You would have handled it if I hadn't been here. Then again it probably wouldn't have happened in the first place if I hadn't come. You would have never been called to the door."

Ric received a jolt when he'd touched her. He hadn't intended to initiate anything with her tonight, but a yearning to do so had cropped up in his loins. *Who are you kidding, Ramsey? You know damn well that if she takes up where she left off two Sundays ago, you aren't going to back off. Not by a longshot.*

He let his eyes roam over her once more all the way down to her bright lime tennis shoes and back to her eyes still brimming with concern. Sunday School had been beautiful during the crisis, offering to help, holding the fear that was evident in her voice under control, and comforting Rosalita. When she'd hugged the boy to her breast, Ric had wanted to trade places with the kid. This very minute he wanted to pull her into his arms, but a thread of reason held him back.

Susan tried not to look at him, but the potent sensuality simmering between them ensnared her. They stood face to face, inches apart, gazing at one another. Silent and still, neither one of them moved. He presented a powerful attraction as he stared hungrily at her, and she struggled against its pull. She'd been right about his appetite. From the gaze in his eye, dinner wasn't the only thing on his mind.

"You're soaking wet," she whispered in an attempt to break the spell.

He grinned. It was such a lovable, boyish grin that Susan sucked in her breath. His thick, dark hair was molded to his scalp, and her gaze remained riveted on him like a magnet, noting how his wet clothing clung to every muscle and ridge of his finely toned body. Then turning abruptly, he walked through the house and out to the patio. Unable to do anything else, she trailed behind like a puppy following it's master.

"That water felt good. Mind if I take some laps?"

"Laps?" Susan stopped dead in her tracks, almost sure of his answer. "In your clothes?"

"No."

That's what she'd thought he'd say. God save America, did he plan to swim in her pool buck naked? Palpitations hit her full force.

He chuckled and began unbuttoning his short sleeve shirt. "You can put my shirt, jeans, and socks in the dryer, if you would please."

"You mean—"

"Yup, I'll swim in my skivvies. They're about the same as wearing a bathing suit." He tauntingly arched an eyebrow at her. "Join me?"

"Uh... " *In his skivvies or in the water*? Both thoughts were tempting.

As her metabolism overheated, her palms grew moist. His whole upper torso was bare now, and there were hints of hair across his diaphragm. A line of fuzz swirled down to his navel where his jeans— Lord, she gasped, his jeans were off now, and there he stood, all six feet of him with a soaking wet pair of kelly green bikini briefs molded around his tight buttocks and outlined his maleness. Her gaze dropped to his thickly corded thighs.

He was magnificent, a physique teeming with power poured into those skimpy briefs. The sheer sexuality of the man landed a direct hit to her lower stomach. The same mental pictures of them splashing in the pool that she'd envisioned two Sundays ago came rushing back. Right before her eyes she saw a clone of herself mysteriously leave her body and spread her hands over his chest.

"I'll, uh..." She braced herself against a patio chair. "You take your laps, and I'll put your clothes in the dryer and warm up the pizza." From the devilish twinkle in his eyes she knew she must be blushing.

"Okay, Suse. We'll have our lesson later."

"Lesson?"

"Spanish, what else?" He winked.

"Oh, yes, of course." Saints preserve her, no doubt every inch of her skin was lit up like a pink neon sign. She picked up his sodden clothing, her body almost as wet as his from perspiration. "There's a towel on the chair."

"And, Suse, there's Beaujolais in the paper bag."

He'd remembered. She fought to keep her gaze from lingering on his nearly naked body. She started to say something else, but he'd turned and jumped into the pool. It was then that she saw the scar, nasty and jagged on his lower left back, beneath his ribs and almost level with his waist. Probably an accident from his motorcycle. She winced, then shrugged and made a beeline for the house.

Ric sliced silently through the water, burning off his adrenaline. Things were certainly unpredictable where Sunday School was concerned. With that kissable mouth and those sexy legs, her hair could be purple for all he cared. Blondes had totally lost their appeal for him. He might never go for one again.

And he liked her. He turned underwater and pushed off the wall to begin another lap. Not just the way she was packaged outside, but he liked her inner self, too. The dedication he'd glimpsed in her eyes when she'd talked about teaching had been recreated right before his eyes tonight. She was so damned concerned for those two kids that she was tutoring them free of charge. There was no faking how much she cared for them.

Nor how much he cared for her.

His groin had given him away, and she hadn't missed it either. Sunday School had been all blushes and stuttering words once she'd spied his condition. Could a woman of thirty-two be as innocent as she seemed? It was a question he'd dearly like answered. He couldn't seem to get a handle on her. At times her personality was confident and seductive, at others, vulnerable and shy. But whichever she was, there was always a wholesomeness about her.

A Sunday School manner.

He'd been dreading facing her tonight, torn apart over what to believe about her. And minutes ago when they'd stood by the front door, he'd wanted to hold her, soothe her, but he'd held himself in check.

And now he was more confused than ever. He was having one hell of a time remaining professional about her.

Susan re-entered the kitchen after tossing Ric's clothes in the dryer. Things sure had gotten out of hand in a hurry. Within twenty minutes of arriving, Ric Ramsey was swimming nearly stark naked in her pool. She lifted a plastic place mat off the table and fanned herself. It did no good. She set it back down and flew into action, placing the pizza in the oven to warm, gathering the contents for a salad from the refrigerator, the only problem being that she kept wandering to the window to watch him swim.

Susan Stewart if you don't keep your wits about you, sometime tonight you're going to end up in that blasted pool with him.

The doorbell rang and Susan frowned. The Cisneros? Had the kids forgotten something? She scanned the kitchen. Was something more seriously wrong with Roberto? Wiping her hands on a dish towel, she scurried across her aunt's Oriental rug in the living room to the front door and peeked through the small side window.

She tensed. Virgil Tate, her minister.

What was he doing here? Her gaze flew back in the direction of the kitchen. Beyond it lay the patio and the pool, and one very nearly naked man. Though none of Virgil's concern, she grew uncomfortable. Naked men and the old Susan did not go hand in hand. If Ric would just stay in the pool, she'd get rid of Virgil as quickly as possible. Offering up a prayer, Susan opened the door part way.

"Virgil, what a surprise."

"I imagine it is. Hope you don't mind the intrusion, but I was in the neighborhood. I meant to call first."

Having ceded control to the old Susan, she bit back the admonishment for him to have done so. "That's okay."

He pushed the door open a tad and stepped into the room. "Do you have company?"

"Oh, the motorcycle. Yes. It's in," she hesitated, catching her ridiculous error. Ric wasn't an *it* by any yardstick. She was so tongue-tied she wasn't sure what she'd been trying to say. Finding her voice, she took a calming breath. "My guest's out by the pool."

"Great night for a swim. As for why I'm here, Susan, I was preparing my sermon for Sunday and realized that I needed a special reference book that I'd lent your aunt months and months ago. I wonder if you might know where it is?"

"Where?" She hadn't the faintest idea, but there was one bedroom that had been converted into her aunt's study. "It's probably in her study."

"I know you have company, but could I just look through the books? There's no need to stop what you're doing."

There was every reason to. The bedroom faced the back, more precisely, it overlooked the pool. "Uh... " She was just about to say that she'd accompany him when she saw Virgil staring over her shoulder, his eyes wider than saucers.

She closed her eyes, immediately fluttering them open. She didn't have to guess the reason for Virgil's wide-eyed stare. Nothing in the past few weeks seemed to go smoothly. Why should she expect it would tonight?

In slow motion she edged her head a few inches to the side. Out of the corner of her eyes she saw him, and her stomach sank to her ankles. Bigger than life, draped in her peach and blue beach towel, Ric Ramsey stood regally behind her like an Indian warrior clad in a war blanket. Thank goodness the towel was extra large and covered most of him, though it did her little good. The memory of his near naked body still flashed through her mind. Wishing she could vanish, sink through a crack in the floor, Susan twisted her fingers together and stared directly at her minister.

"Uh," she muttered, twisting her fingers some more.

"And this young man must belong to the motorcycle."

"Yes." She choked on her answer. "Ric Ramsey, Reverend Virgil Tate. Virgil, Ric Ramsey."

"Good looking machine you have," Virgil remarked.

"Thanks," Ric answered.

Susan glanced briefly back at Ric and privately agreed with Virgil. Seconds later, she blushed six shades of crimson. Virgil had been referring to the motorcycle while she'd—

Quickly she faced Virgil. "He's a friend," she stammered.

"I can see that," Virgil replied.

"A good friend," Ric amended from behind her.

With her back to Ric, Susan rolled her eyes.

"Naturally," Virgil said to Ric. "I came for a reference book. Don't let me disturb your swim."

"Oh, I was done. I came in to see if my—"

"—if his supper's ready," Susan interrupted with lightning speed. She whirled around just in time to spy the teasing glimmer in Ric's eyes.

"Yes, well, Susan, if you'll just show me to Kitty's study, I'll look for that book," Virgil suggested.

"Sure. Ric, you can get dressed while we're looking." She emphasized the word 'dressed' out of all proportion. "You know where it is Virgil, I'll follow you."

"Nice meeting you, Ric."

"You, too, Reverend," he replied.

The minute Virgil turned, Susan swiveled around and made a face at Ric, and indicated for him to vamoose by waving her arms.

"Smells good, Susan," Virgil called out over his shoulder as he walked through the living room. "What's for dinner?"

"Go," she whispered hoarsely at Ric as he continued to stand pat, a disarming grin on his face.

"What did you say, Susan?" Virgil asked.

"Crow. We're definitely having baked crow for dinner."

"That a fact," Virgil stated dryly. "And I imagine you intend to serve a goodly portion to that young man of yours. You know, Susan, sometimes you have a sense of humor just like your aunt."

Ric rescued the pizza from the oven, finished chopping the salad, uncorked the wine bottle, and sat down at the kitchen table. His keen ears heard the front door shut, and he silently began to count. One thousand and one, one thousand and two... He was up to one thousand and eight when Susan bustled into the room.

"I have a bone to pick with you," she said nearly out of breath, determination ablaze in her eyes.

"I figured you did. Sit." He motioned to the chair across the table from him.

"Sit?"

"Now." Clearly on the warpath, she sat down and opened her mouth. "Uh-uh," he said, winking at her, "no talking while I eat crow."

Susan relented. How could you be angry with a man who had a rascal-like gleam in his eyes when he winked at you. "It's just that if— " If Virgil had ever gotten a look of Ric in his briefs, she didn't know what he'd think. It shouldn't matter, but it did. All her life, her reputation had mattered.

Breaking her train of thought, she stopped as Ric stood up. For the briefest of seconds she considered closing her eyes, but the memory of him in his jockey's compelled her to look. Anticipation turned to shock. "You're dressed." She'd been so flustered that she'd failed to notice he'd been wearing his shirt. "Where are—"

"In the dryer."

"Oh." She thanked the stars, but the thought of his jeans covering that bare, tight tush of his was almost as erotic as the sight of him in his briefs had been.

Ric chuckled. Sunday School was Sunday School. No getting around it. If she got this uptight over a scantily clad man being found in her house, how in the world could she be involved with unsavory drug runners? Especially when she was so concerned about children. He couldn't imagine her having anything to do with drugs that might eventually fall into young people's hands.

"I knew you were teasing earlier." She paused, then dipped her chin. "But if you'd have said—"

"I wouldn't have said anything to embarrass you." And the lady was definitely embarrassed. He'd heard the car when he'd stood in the pool to take a break between laps, and not wanting to miss anyone who might be stopping by her door, he'd wandered back in the house. The minute he saw the elderly man, he'd recognized him as her minister. The past week he'd driven around Las Cruces checking up on her, her friends, her co-workers. Her church connections had been among them. He'd observed the man leaving the church one day and verified who he was.

The buzzer went off. "Pizza's ready." He rose and retrieved it from the oven, then poured them both a glass of wine.

Susan stared at him in amazement. Not only had he warmed the pizza, but he'd finished chopping the salad, fished the dressing out of the refrigerator and opened the wine bottle. She was impressed by his willingness to pitch in, take charge. He was especially apt in taking charge.

Ric sat down across from her and asked, "Did your minister find the book he was looking for?"

"Yes. I can't imagine why he didn't call first." She picked up her napkin and fanned herself.

Ric smiled. He noticed she did that a lot.

"I thought it might be Mr. Cisneros— " She took a swipe at a wayward strand of hair. "—that something might be wrong with Roberto."

That had occurred to Ric, too. "Do you have homeowner's insurance?"

She caught the odd expression that had flickered in his eyes. "You're not suggesting that if Roberto is injured they'd sue me?"

"No, but they might want to put a claim out on your policy. As your unofficial legal advisor, let me know if they do. They may have a legitimate claim if he's hurt, but from my cursory examination he seemed fine."

"I can't believe they'd manufacture an injury. If there is one, naturally I'll assume responsibility." She washed a piece of pizza down with a sip of wine.

"You're very trusting."

"Not always. There are lots of times when I'm suspicious and leery of people." Like she'd been of Ric, although after what had happened with Roberto, she no longer felt that way. "Once I get to know someone, I guess I do trust them. Sometimes even though I might not know them well, my intuition tells me they're all right."

Ric arched a brow. Was that behind her approach to him? Maybe she was so innocent that she hadn't even realized she'd been flirting with him that first night he'd seen her. And the flat tire could have been on the up and up, and she'd simply trusted his offer of help—trusted him enough to invite him to her house for a picnic.

But there was another Susan, too. A Susan who was a ticking bomb of emotions just waiting to explode, as she'd been up on the mountain. A Susan who, though she didn't seem to know it, could be as provocative as hell just fanning herself. A Susan who had cars follow her, took strange trips to Juarez, and may or may not have had a drug encounter in her past. Two vastly different Susans.

Threads of a snicker intruded on his subconscious, and he snapped out of his trance. Susan was chuckling. Her eyes glistened like dark gemstones, and her face was split with a pixie-like smile. She giggled harder, those alluring strands of her hair covering part of her left eye.

Speak about provocative. She was a picture of it.

"What?" he coaxed, feeling the contagion of her laughter. He broke out into a half smile.

"It was... " She burst into laughter and looked up at him. "It was kind of funny."

"What was funny?" Her impish smile charmed him, and he curved his mouth wider.

"Virgil, so prim and proper, and you—" She broke into full blown gusts of laughter. "And you standing there, dripping wet, looking for all the world like some Indian chief with a peach and—" Again laughter choked off her words.

Rick joined in, throwing his head back and chuckling heartily. "Indian chief, huh?"

"Can you imagine what Virgil was thinking?" She stared into his eyes, and together they laughed until his laughter ceased, and hers did, too.

As her gaze meshed with his, Ric found himself spellbound by her dark glittering eyes. He watched her face grow serious. They continued to stare, captives of each other's gaze. Tense. Silent. The tension he could slice with his pocket knife, and the silence crashed around him like a desert sandstorm. She blinked, and he blinked, seeing her lips part and hearing the sharp intake of her breath. The intimate moment cried out for more, but Ric simply brushed the hair from her face. Then breaking contact with her gaze, he poured them both some more wine, letting the moment pass.

Later, Sunday School, he told himself, *later.* There were still some things he needed to learn.

Chapter Seven

"*Repita,*" Ric said.

"*Tu eres un caballo amable,*" Susan repeated what she'd said seconds ago.

"Not on your life, Senorita."

She laughed at how wounded he sounded, his eyes feigning outrage. "You're not? What did I say?"

"You said I was a nice horse."

"A horse? I said that?" Susan eyed him doubtfully.

"*Si, senorita. Un cabello* is a horse."

She shrugged. Perhaps she had erred by calling him a horse, but there was something to be said about calling him a stallion. Many of the same adjectives could describe them both.

"*Tu eres loca,*" Ric whimsically added.

"No Senor, I'm not crazy." She angled her head, his steady glance wreaking havoc with her concentration. "I meant to say you are a nice gentleman."

"*Caballero,* not *caballo.*"

"Oh."

"And it's been a long time since I've been called a gentleman." A tinge of cynicism crept into his voice. "Whatta you say we call it a night? *Repita* after me," Ric instructed. "*Besa la maestra.*"

"*Besa la maestra.*"

He leaned over and placed a kiss on her cheek. Surprised, Susan looked up at him. His answering smile was incredibly sexy, a threat to her composure.

"Only obeying your command, teach."

"My command?"

"You just said kiss the lady teacher."

"*Besa la maestra* is kiss the teacher?"

"Yup, if the teacher's female, and you definitely are." He leaned over and placed a light peck on her other cheek. "My reward for teaching you."

Unable to ignore the devilish curve to his lips, she smiled. He was incorrigible, and despite being charged up about seeing him, she could feel herself growing weary. It had been an eventful evening. Susan glanced at the kitchen clock. Nine. Time had flown since Virgil had left, and the wine bottle was nearly empty. Mostly due to her consumption. During their entire session she'd swallowed against a dry throat and kept sipping more Beaujolais, but the wine only made her more thirsty, and, she suspected, had contributed to her drowsiness, as well.

Ric had stopped after one glass, citing he indulged lightly when he was driving. Grudgingly admiring the man, she mentally pasted another star by his name for responsibility. The constellation was multiplying. Susan stretched and yawned.

"Tired?"

"Yes, and I'm going to have to kick you out in a while. I like to be in bed by ten thirty on school nights, and I still have some papers to grade." But she was reluctant to see him go, and if she could have her way, the evening would never end.

"I can leave now, if you like." He pushed his chair back from the table, scraping its legs against the vinyl.

"No, stay a bit. I'll make some instant coffee. It'll wake me up." And keep her awake most of the night, too. "How about cappuccino?" she asked as she walked over to the oven and flicked on the burner beneath a copper kettle.

"Cappuccino's fine. You ever listen to the radio?"

"All the time." Did he want music? She had tapes that were far better. All brawn and then some, he lounged lazily against the back of his chair, his legs stretched out in front of him and crossed at the ankles. He looked relaxed. Music would be good. She was just about to suggest a tape when he spoke again.

"They advertise some tapes on the radio for learning Spanish."

"I've heard about them."

"I think between your class at the university and those tapes, not to mention all the opportunity you have to use your Spanish around here, you'll pick up the language in no time."

"You think so?" She spooned cappuccino mix into two mugs.

"I know so."

"Let's not overlook my own private tutor." You'd have to be blind to overlook Ric Ramsey. She sensed his stare, lifted her head from filling the mugs, and met his gaze. Shivers fluttered in her stomach, and she knew it wasn't a reaction to the wine.

"You might want to order a tape," he suggested.

"I just might. You're very fluent. Did you speak Spanish at home?"

"Very little. My father was Anglo and only used a smattering of it with some of the men who worked for him. My mother's father was Mexican, but she didn't speak that much Spanish either. Only when she was angry at Tommy or me."

"Which I imagine gave her plenty of opportunity to use the language."

Ric smiled wryly. "There was a time or two."

"I bet your mother spoke more Spanish when you were young than she did in her entire life."

"Are you implying I gave her a hard time?"

"Wouldn't doubt it for a minute," she said, entranced by the roguish gleam in his eyes. Gray-green eyes surrounded by thick black lashes. Eyes that could make a woman melt under their power. Unconsciously, she reached for a napkin and fanned herself. Perhaps she should turn the air conditioning lower. "Didn't you say you had Indian blood in you, too?"

"My maternal grandmother was an Apache."

"Apache? Geronimo's tribe?"

"Geronimo and Chochise."

"Fierce warriors, weren't they?" She poured the hot water into their mugs and stirred them. That wasn't all she'd stirred up. Images of Ric donning a war bonnet, war paint on his face, and brandishing a hatchet while garbed only in his tiny green briefs as he sat astride a horse sent her temperature climbing.

"The fiercest," Ric replied. "The Comanche pushed them South, and before the Apaches turned their wrath on the white man, they made life miserable for the Navajos."

While he'd been speaking, Susan's mind had been working overtime, continuing to imagine Ric as an Apache warrior, and she wasn't sure whether the provocative images or the steaming kettle had sent her temperature upward. "Can you speak Apache?" she asked, fanning herself again.

"Not a whisker. Don't understand it, either." He paused. "You all right?" With his thumbs hooked in his belt loops, his gaze roved her face.

Intelligent words momentarily fled. “I’m f-fine.”

Ric grinned. *Temptation, thine name is Sunday School.* And this very minute he suspected she was close to overheating. They both were.

It had been dark for some time, and an overhead Tiffany lamp shone down on them, reflecting on Susan’s dark, shiny hair. He clenched his fist against the impulse to run his fingers through it and wondered yet again how a demure brunette could charm him away from his fascination for blondes. Of course, her legs were a big factor.

He let his gaze circle the kitchen where they’d spent the past two hours. An array of baskets on the ledges above the kitchen cabinets caught his eye, and he smiled. So that was where all the baskets from Juarez had ended up. Apart from the baskets, most of the room, and what he’d seen of the rest of the house, too, had a decided Victorian look to it.

“Your aunt must have liked antiques,” he remarked.

“I know it looks totally out of context, all this Victorian furniture in a typical Southwestern stucco house, but these were my aunt’s treasures. Every nook and cranny of the house is cluttered with china cups and saucers, porcelain figurines, and crocheted lace doilies. I haven’t had the heart or the money to redecorate.”

Ric’s brow wrinkled. There she went again, saying she didn’t have the money and her bank statements verified that. Was she planning to augment the small bequest from her aunt by getting information on him? Her persistent questions certainly suggested that. She’d been getting more and more inquisitive as the evening wore on. Suited him fine. First opportunity, he planned to grill her on her relationship with Jerry Westphal, her college boyfriend.

Ric took a sip of his cappuccino. “This tastes good.”

“My favorite.”

“That and Beaujolais,” he drawled, drawing a bead on her shapely legs. What a shame she kept them covered so much of the time. He was grateful she hadn’t tonight.

“I meant to thank you for bringing it. Roberto’s accident sidetracked me.” She stared at the wine bottle. “Looks like I finished the bottle.”

“I helped a little.” When he’d seen her gulp down the first glass, he’d wondered if the wildly passionate Susan Stewart would make an appearance, but from the tone of the evening so far, Sunday School had held sway.

Silence fell between them, and Susan self-consciously pushed her glass away. “You said you rode horses.”

He nodded. “Yeah, I rode.” Her meandering conversation challenged him. Could be they both were fishing for information from one another. Right now she seemed to be very adept at turning the conversation away from herself. “Even tried my hand at rodeo for a while.”

“Rodeo? What event?”

“Roping dogies. I was pretty lousy at it. If Tommy hadn’t gotten himself so messed up with drugs, he’d have been the star of the family.”

“I’ve always had this hankering to see a rodeo, in person, I mean. I’ve seen bits and pieces of them in the movies or on television.”

“Well, you’ve come to the right place. There must be a rodeo in every direction you travel from here and nearly every week of the year. I’ll check it out.”

“Something else I plan to do while I’m here is go up in a hot air balloon. Have you seen them?”

“Only that time up on the mountaintop with you. Given my job, I’m afraid I don’t rise early enough to see them. I guess because of the wind, most of them are back down on the ground by noon time. I’ll tell you a secret,” he said, remembering how she’d disarmed him with the same phrase over a week ago.

“What?” Susan leaned across the table, drawn by the seductive look in his eyes.

“I’ve always wanted to go up in a balloon, too.”

“How about next Sunday?”

“Beg your pardon?”

Down, Susan down. He’ll think you’re chasing him.

In a way she was and for a specific purpose, but he might interpret it in another light.

And why shouldn’t he what with the way you light up like a Christmas tree every time you see him, and how you jump to manufacture opportunities to see him again, like this balloon ride.

Strictly business, she insisted.

Tell me another, her conscience immediately countered.

Susan pushed away her disturbing thoughts and managed a bright smile. “There’s a man in my church who owns a balloon. He said to let him know any time I'd like a ride. It would have to be real early though. Want me to ask?"

"Sure, and I'll ask around if there's a rodeo going on that afternoon. I think I saw a poster about one in El Paso." He paused. "What do you want to do about your Spanish lesson?"

She sat back in her chair. Next Monday wouldn't be good. Roberto and Rosalita would be here, at least she hoped they would, and Pam and Robin would be flying back late next Sunday, and she knew that they'd be itching to come by and see her that following evening. And she'd be every bit as eager to learn what they'd discovered. Maybe then their niggling doubts about Ric would be put to rest.

"Next Sunday evening sound good to you?" she asked. "School isn't out for another ten days, so I'll probably have Roberto and Rosalita over the next couple of Monday evenings. Once school is out, I can meet with them earlier in the day."

Every time she looked up at him, she caught him watching her, his gaze hawk like. There'd been no repeat of the grim expression she'd witnessed on the mountain, but occasionally there'd been an unsettling look that she didn't understand.

But there were other looks, as well. Looks that made no attempt to hide his blatant interest. Looks that sent sizzling undercurrents in the air whenever he was around.

"Next Sunday sounds fine," Ric agreed. Sunday School seemed to have a monopoly on his Sundays.

Restless, he rose from the table and carried their empty cups to the sink. He walked back to the table, snaked his hand in a chair slat and turned it around, straddling it as he sat down. Time for him to go to work— if only he could think of a way to change the subject. "It'll be good to see a rodeo again," he said, hoping to steer the conversation in the direction he wanted.

"You mentioned your brother, Tommy, a couple of times— that he rodeoed. You also said that his mind was scrambled by drugs."

"Yeah." Ric drew his mouth into a tight line. Sunday School was cooperating, but talking about Tommy always made him see red.

"Was he on drugs when he was riding?"

"Not on the youth and junior circuit. If he'd hadn't been hooked, he'd probably have made a name for himself in the big time rodeo. He was so bombed out of his mind, he had to give it up by the time he was eighteen."

"I'm sorry." Compassion laced her voice. "Must have been rough."

"Yeah."

Ric grimaced. Visiting his brother at the state institution wasn't his favorite thing to do. He didn't know how his mother faced it every week. Each time he paid Tommy a visit, the sight of so many lost souls, especially his brother's, turned his stomach.

He'd watched his brother practically kill himself and in the process shatter his parents' hearts. And all because of drugs. Not that Tommy wasn't accountable, but he'd been a kid when he'd started—a sixteen year old kid. Ric had joined the D.E.A. as a personal crusade to seek vengeance on the drug dealers, and the thought that Susan Stewart might be involved twisted his gut.

Susan glanced at him and caught his narrowed eyes assessing her. She didn't know quite what to say. "What's your brother doing now?"

"Living like a zombie in an institution."

Ric's words came out in a grinding growl, and his gray eyes glinted, leaving no doubt in Susan's mind how unpleasant the subject was for him. She identified with the grief in his voice, and with practically no warning, a shared anger shot through her.

"I'm sorry," she said again in an uneasy whisper.

Don't be, Sunday School. Grim though the subject might be, he'd learned over the years to deal with it, and at least she'd given him an opportunity to pry into Jerry Westphal. "Thanks," he muttered. "Mind if I ask you something?" He crossed his arms on the top of the chair, hoping his question sounded casual.

"Not at all."

"Last Sunday when we were up in the mountain, I had the feeling you were going to say something about drugs, yet you didn't. Did someone in your family have to battle drugs, too?"

"No." She shifted in her seat and cast her eyes downward.

He wanted to ask her straight out about her former boy friend, but bit back the urge. "My mistake."

"You weren't mistaken."

That piqued his interest, and he decided to press the issue. "What was it, Suse?" He reached for her hand. "What happened that still upsets you? Was it someone else close to you?"

In his job, lies had flowed easily from his lips, lies that had insured his survival, but this one didn't sit well with him. *Remember Johnny Montoya,* he cautioned himself. His brain told him that if Susan was involved with a drug ring, his life could be at stake, but his emotions were telling him something else.

"Yes..." Susan hesitated. "A classmate, a good friend. It was a long time ago."

Ric noted the wan expression on her face. What the hell was going on? Was she still involved with Westphal? Did she still care for him? "Sounds like I'm intruding, sorry," he mumbled. "It's just that—" If she was on the wrong side of the law, he could be in big trouble, but he decided to go out on a limb with her. "It's just that I'd like to see the scum that sell drugs to people, especially kids, locked away for good."

"I couldn't agree more." She glanced down at the floor, her lashes hiding her eyes. "When you start practicing law, I hope you get to do that."

"I do, too."

"That's why you became one, isn't it?" Slowly, she raised her head and met his gaze, her eyes luminous and moist.

Ric stared back, an uncanny connection to her punching through him.

"It's your way of fighting the drug runners."

He squeezed her hand. She was dead on target, and it made him wonder if she could read other things on his mind, as well. "I'm hoping to join a district attorney's staff. I don't want other parents having to go through what mine did."

"I was such a fool," Susan murmured.

"You, a fool?" He followed her gaze as she lowered it and focused their joined hands.

"It's a part of my life I've kept closed off. Only my family and a couple of close friends back home know about it."

Aw hell, Ric swore under his breath, having second thoughts. Sometimes his job could be a pain in the backside. He wanted to tell her that she didn't have to tell him—that it was okay, but he couldn't. For professional and personal reasons she had to cough up her secrets, so he said nothing. As he held her hand, he could feel her tension slacken. *Come on, Sunday School, tell me about Westphal.*

"I was a senior in college and in love, at least I thought I was in love. It's a period of my life I'm not proud of."

His gaze homed in on her, and suddenly he was afraid she was going to tell him that she'd experimented with drugs. He'd never thought of that angle. No, he protested. It was impossible.

She licked her lips and drew in a deep breath. "But I couldn't have been in love," she said in a rambling tone. "I never really knew him. I must have been in love with love. We were planning to get engaged, and then shortly before we were both set to graduate, he was arrested for selling cocaine. I didn't know—never even suspected."

"You were young."

"And stupid. How could I not have suspected?"

"Because you were in love. If there was something to suspect, you couldn't see it." Jeeze, he couldn't remain impersonal, he thought, studying her face. She had such expressive eyes. Right now they looked sad, and melancholy, and ashamed. Sunday School was ashamed that she'd been duped.

"You'd think I'd at least have had the brains to sense something was strange. He always had wads of money, drove a convertible, belonged to a fraternity, took me to expensive restaurants. I just thought he was wealthy."

"You said he sold drugs. Did he ever use them himself?"

She shook her head. "I'd have known that. He'd have acted high or moody or unusual. No. He wasn't a user, and I never saw a transaction or heard a strange conversation that might have been about a sale. He was so smooth." Her lips curved lightly, and she laughed sarcastically. "For awhile I don't think the police believed me."

"The police?" he prompted. His instincts convinced him she was telling the truth, but he wanted to hear everything she had to say.

"He was arrested. There was a trial. I was questioned several times. So were a lot of his friends. None of us knew, but even I can see where the police were coming from. For nearly six months Jerry and I had dated steadily, and the last few weeks before his arrest we'd talked about getting engaged and married. We were inseparable."

How inseparable? And why the hell should I care? His mind grasped at the word *engaged*. It couldn't possibly be the root of her panic after all these years, could it?

"Sounds incredible that I wouldn't have known." She remarked.

Susan fell silent, her blank gaze focused on the table. What was even more incredible was how warm and comfortable and safe she felt with this man who sat across the table from her. This man whom she barely knew. Barely knew? Several times these past few minutes she'd sensed they'd been in tune with one another's' minds, as if words hadn't been necessary for them to communicate. There'd been a bleak look on his face when they'd talked about his brother, but now his dark brows knit together and he looked sympathetic.

Her gaze strayed back to his large bronzed hand, the one that still held hers in a warm clasp. She wanted to dismiss the tingles spiraling up her arm from his touch as an aberration, but she remembered how fiery hot her hand had been when he'd held it a week ago.

Thoroughly confused, she sighed. "I guess I wasn't the only one on campus who was duped. He sold to people at school and the teenagers who lived near the university. That's what made me so sick. Made my skin crawl. To think that I loved a man who could do such a horrible thing. If I'd only known, I'd have turned him in myself."

Ric snapped his head up. Raw sincerity resonated in her voice, and he knew without a moment's hesitation she meant every word. No way Sunday School could still be involved with drugs or Jerry Westphal. Relief swept through him, and so did a familiar itch down in his loins. He wanted to shout hooray to the rafters.

He wanted to explain to her what had brought him to Las Cruces.

He wanted to stay up all night and talk with her.

He wanted to hold her in his arms and kiss her.

He wanted her.

He wanted soft, sweet Sunday School, a woman with a hidden spark inside her that could consume a man.

"Jerry was the wrong man," she uttered after a long silence. "If I'd been in love with him, I'd have stood by him. I would never have condoned what he did, but I'd have stood by him. I have a habit of falling for the wrong man."

Ric let her vent her self reproachment. She really was down on herself. And what did she mean, she had a habit of falling for the wrong man? He'd always assumed that an attractive woman like Sunday School had to have a history. How many men had there been? Was she involved with the wrong kind of man right now and couldn't extricate herself?

Naw. Susan didn't act like she was involved with anyone, but he still couldn't rule out his premise.

Susan met his gaze, subtly aware of his thumb stroking her wrist. Strange sensations wended through her, and strange thoughts, as well. This wasn't the way it was supposed to be. Ric Ramsey was just a candidate to play the role of Shane Orr. She wasn't supposed to become emotionally involved with him. But forces beyond her control were sweeping her in that direction, and she needed to stop them. After all, she hadn't heard the report from her friends yet, but despite the fact that her acquaintance with Ric was far too short to be absolutely certain of him, she knew in her heart that her friends would find nothing wrong.

Wrong?

There was nothing wrong about this man.

Not his striking looks, not his lean and fit body, not his personality, not his values, nor his dreams.

Not one blasted thing.

And if she allowed herself to think of Ric in any other light than a platonic arrangement, he could turn out to be as wrong for her as Jerry Westphal had been. She'd thought she'd known Jerry. What did she know about Ric? Susan picked up her napkin and fanned herself again.

Ric released her hand, swung his leg over the chair, and stood. He's leaving, Susan thought, disappointed as she watched him stand. He caught her hand again and pulled her to her feet. He stood inches from her, a mere breath away, and a throbbing tension thrummed inside her. When his head lowered, she closed her eyes.

"Susan," he said, his voice husky and low.

"I... " She was about to say that they shouldn't do this, but she wanted his kiss and had been expecting it all evening.

"Suse," he repeated.

The gravelly tone of his voice sent shivers down her spine. At the touch of his mouth on hers, she nearly went crazy. The kiss was soft and warm and light. His hands framed her neck, searing her already overheated body. He lifted his head and placed kisses on her eyelids. Susan drew in a shaky breath.

"Susan."

His voice had changed to a velvety softness, and it seduced her. Seconds later she felt the pressure of his mouth on her parted lips. She melted into him, loving the plundering touches of his tongue. Her knees weakened and she linked her hands around his neck while his hands slid to her shoulders. He pulled her body to his and sought deeper possession of her mouth. His hands inched down to her hips, and Susan felt his aroused body against hers. She moaned.

"Hmm. You taste so good," Ric said, coming up for air and combing a finger through her hair. "Beaujolais and cappuccino mix well. Kiss me, Susan. Kiss me the dynamite way you did last Sunday."

"What?" She quivered from the knowledge that she'd aroused him, but she didn't understand what he was referring to.

"Kiss me, Suse, like before. Take me up that mountain."

Not sure what it was she'd done last Sunday, Susan kissed his cheeks, his nose, his eyelids, letting her mouth slide to his ears. He tipped his head, giving her better access, and she teased his ear with her tongue. Her hands grew urgent, running though his hair until at last her mouth found his again.

In a frenzied attempt to please him, she rolled her lips back and forth, probing and tasting his mouth. Chemistry drove her to respond. As her fingers curled into the back of his collar, greedy with hunger, she continued to devour him. The ocean literally roared in her ears, and she felt as if she were shakily balanced on the edge of some precipice. Then sapped of energy, she fell limp and clung to him.

Ric supported her, lowering his head and planting a feathery kiss on her forehead. *God bless her, Sunday School had done it again.* Taken him skyward and then some. Frustration gripped him, and he gritted his teeth against the desire to explore more of her body. He nudged her legs apart with his knee and curled her hips into his body.

"I can't stand this," he murmured into her ear.

Ric reached for her again, rocking his lips over her warm moist ones. His insides burned and desire streaked through him. He couldn't understand how this very proper brunette could evoke such wild sensations in him, but she did, and he couldn't hide how she affected him. Loving the feel of her breasts pressed against him, he could barely think. Bells rang in his head. Gradually, he became aware that Susan was nudging him away.

"The phone, it's ringing," she said in ragged breaths.

Refusing to give her up, he held her fast and looked down at her. Her wide open eyes were dazed and luminescent. He wished she'd ignore the phone. "Don't you have an answering machine?"

"Aunt Kitty didn't believe in them, and I haven't gotten around to uh—" Her heart skittering, she pulled in a deep breath. "No. I'd better answer it." Finding the will, she pushed him away, dashed to the counter, and lifted the receiver. "Hello."

"Susan, dear, how are you?"

Susan gulped air, her gaze meeting Ric's sultry eyes. "Mother, how are you?"

"Fine, dear. I waited until the rates dropped to call you."

Susan nodded and glanced at the clock. "Oh, yes, it's after eleven there, isn't it?"

"You sound out of breath, dear."

"Out of breath?" Susan heard panic and uncertainly in her voice, and she tried desperately to listen to what her mother was saying while all the time she watched Ric like a mountain hawk.

Her mother mentioned something about the newspaper while Ric straightened his clothing and grabbed his windbreaker. He was leaving. Suddenly something her mother said caused her to jerk her head.

"What did you say, Mother?"

"You wouldn't happen to have Shane's parents' address or phone number, would you?"

"Shane?" Susan asked, totally preoccupied with Ric as he walked toward her in what seemed like exaggerated slow motion.

"Your fiancé, Dear."

Susan caught herself before her mother started asking more questions. "No, I don't have it."

As Ric stood only inches away, guilt at her dishonesty caused her to grip the receiver tighter. Gently, he leaned over and kissed her cheek. The movement pulled his shirt tautly across his chest.

"*Besa el maestro,*" he said, tilting his head and tapping his index finger on his cheek.

Susan complied.

"*Buenas noches.*" He winked.

"*Buenas noches,*" she whispered. Her eyes followed his progress across the room until he disappeared from sight.

"What was that you said, Susan?" her mother asked.

"I was just saying good night to my Spanish teacher."

"That's nice," her mother replied.

Yes, it was, she thought, touching her fingers to her cheek.

Chapter Eight

Susan crawled into bed, set the alarm, and flicked out the tasseled boudoir lamp, her pulse ticking away like a time bomb. Two hours ago, just moments before Ric's kiss she'd been sleepy. Now she was wide awake, the cappuccino only partially responsible.

Scene after scene of the entire evening spun like re-runs before her. Ric diving into the pool to save Roberto, Ric in his devastating green briefs, Ric teasing her in front of Reverend Tate, and Ric patiently tutoring her in Spanish.

Lord help her, she was headed for trouble.

After he'd left, she'd finally convinced her mother that her engagement was unofficial, and that an announcement in the paper or attempting to contact Shane's family would be most improper. Then she laid the ground work for failure, telling her mother Shane might miss the reunion and anniversary party because of an assignment in the Middle East.

Before retiring for bed, she'd graded papers, and the entire time she'd searched for reasons to eliminate Ric as a candidate for her fiancé. None materialized. Funny how they'd drifted into a friendship so quickly.

Susan heaved her shoulders and sighed. How could she have been so lucky to pick such á great candidate? He was turning out to be more than she'd hoped for.

You like him. You more than like him.

Yes, she more than liked him. And she didn't know what to do about it. Wide-eyed, she stared into the darkness. It would never do to fall for this man. He was passing through Las Cruces, not to mention her life. In no time at all she'd be a blip in his past. But, Lord have mercy, he'd never be that for her. No, she'd never forget Ric Ramsey, even if their encounters ended this very minute and she never saw him again.

There was an exciting recklessness about him, and for the rest of her days she doubted she could look at a bartender without a smile crossing her face. She could visualize herself pulling her granddaughter onto her lap and chattering away about how she'd met this fascinating man named Ric Ramsey.

That scene faded, replaced by the reunion. Mary Ellen would just die if she saw Ric. But he might not agree to the plan. As she'd mused earlier, he was a traveling man on his way to somewhere else, and the longer they were together, the harder it would be to disentangle her emotions. She had an uneasy feeling that if he did agree to pose as Shane, life would never be the same again. She wasn't sure her heartstrings were up to dealing with another mistake.

He seemed so genuinely attracted to her, the chemistry between them so magical.

Don't kid yourself. That chemistry is probably a routine occurrence for him. Remember, he's a traveling man—a man on his way from here to there—from Las Cruces to Who-Knows-Where? Globetrotter was written all over his face. Words from a childhood book circled in her head like rhythmic railroad wheels clacking on tracks and making her drowsy.

From here to there and everywhere.

The nightlight in the adjoining bathroom cast a faint ray through the room, and Susan snuggled deeper into the covers. Seconds before sleep claimed her, she spied Ric's briefs hanging jauntily on one of the bedposts. The kelly green jockeys she'd scooped from the dryer.

Susan smiled.

"Hey Al, I'm taking a break," Ric called out over the raucous Friday night crowd. "Cover for me, will 'ya?"

Ric wiped his hands on a towel and tossed it on a shelf under the bar. He couldn't believe his eyes, but it seemed that nearly two months of surveillance was about to pay off. A man had come in, a man Ric swore looked like the one they had yet to identify in the photograph with Susan's handyman, the sinister looking guy who'd accompanied the Garcias on the day he'd tailed Susan to Juarez. Passing by the bar, the guy had headed to the room where the band was playing. It had been a piece of dumb luck that Ric had spotted him.

Ric walked across the wooden floor to the entrance of the dance hall, dodging around people as he went. It was nearly midnight and the place was packed. Five and six people crowded around tables that could barely accommodate four. Smoke hung thickly in the air, and the band whacked away at a medley of Garth Brooks hits. Narrowing his gaze, Ric sought his quarry while he reviewed what he'd learned so far.

During the past two weeks, he'd ridden his motorcycle by the Garcia house at midday, and he'd even driven down their street a couple of nights after he'd gotten off from work. On two different occasions he'd sacrificed his sleep, rising at dawn, to tail Angelina and Juan Garcia to their jobs. Angelina worked as a maid at a motel, and Juan worked as kitchen help in a Tex-Mex restaurant. If they were getting rich from selling drugs, there sure was no indication of it from their lifestyles. Of course, that all could be a well-planned cover.

With no spare agents to spell him or infiltrate where the Garcias worked, Ric was helpless. Any number of people could have approached Angelina or Juan Garcia on the job. If his buddy, Johnny, hadn't been working at Judd's and killed nearby, Ric would have quit his job and applied for one at the Tex-Mex Restaurant.

Disgruntled, Ric slid his boot back and forth on the floor. He could be getting the cart before the horse, too. He'd found no evidence that Juan Garcia was doing anything illegal. All they had on Garcia was his monthly trips to Juarez, courtesy of Susan Stewart. Ric took a step further into the darkened dance hall and leaned his shoulder against the archway.

And why did Garcia drive off with Susan's car once they'd crossed the border? Ric rubbed his chin. He'd sure like to know the answer to that one. If there was another trip to Juarez any time soon, he hoped the Agency would provide more personnel to assist with surveillance on both sides of the border.

Ric cursed the dimly lit room and crowded dance floor. It was nearly impossible to pick anyone out in the crush of people. He was positive the guy who'd walked into Judd's was the one in the photograph. While casing the Garcia's neighborhood, he'd discreetly shown the picture to some of the kids, but no one knew the guy. Either that or they weren't telling. Not wanting to stir up a hornet's nest or scare the guy off, Ric had stopped asking around and had given up more sleep to stake out the neighborhood, instead. But the guy had been a no-show until he spied him tonight. Ric shouldered his way around a group of people blocking his view.

There he was, hovering by the band.

Less than a minute later the band took a break, and the man and a guitar player walked toward an exit behind the stage. Ric patted his shirt pocket, checking for his cigarettes. He'd given them up three years ago, but he'd taken to carrying them at Judd's. They came in handy as an excuse to take a break and observe the parking lot from time to time.

Ric slipped through the exit and hugged the stucco wall of the building. Adjusting his vision was no problem. The parking lot was lit about as dimly as the dance hall had been. Frozen in place, he hid in the shadows and slowly turned his head one hundred and eighty degrees, searching for the men. A match flared to his left. Ric shifted his gaze to that direction and stealthily crept closer.

"When?" Ric heard the guitar player ask in Spanish.

"Fifteen days from now," the tall, gaunt man answered, his Spanish pronunciation not as sharp and clear.

"That's a week earlier than usual," the guitar player commented.

"There's been several shipments and the merchandise is piling up." The man flicked his ashes from his cigarette onto the ground.

"Will you be going with them?"

"I'll let you know. Tell your uncle three Sundays from now." The tall man clapped the guitar player on the back, then sauntered through the parking lot.

Ric wanted to follow him, but the guitar player hadn't moved. About the time the man reached the edge of the parking lot, a car drove up and stopped. Tossing his cigarette to the ground, the man jumped in, and the car sped away. A second later the guitar player re-entered Judd's.

Ric sagged against a parked car. It had been too dark to distinguish the make of the car or see the license plate. Damn, but he wished he had more support. Taking a cigarette from his pocket, he crumpled it in his hand, letting the shreds fall to the ground. A quiver of rage shot through him. That man might have been responsible for Johnny's death. His conversation with the band member definitely reeked of some kind of clandestine deal. First thing tonight he'd check out who the guitar player was.

Steady, Ramsey, he counseled himself. The meeting he'd witnessed could have nothing at all to do with Johnny's death, but whatever it was, something was scheduled for three Sundays from now. That'd be one Sunday he wouldn't be spending with Sunday School. Or would he? Since the guy was definitely the same man who'd accompanied Susan and the Garcias to Juarez, he just might find himself tailing her again.

Damn.

Ric balled his hand into a fist. Just when he'd begun to feel so sure of Susan, so positive she wasn't involved, this sleaze shows up.

Don't waver, his conscience nagged.

She was an ethical woman. She'd been outraged to discover that a man she'd loved had sold drugs to kids, and Ric was equally convinced that her former boyfriend, Jerry Westphal, was exactly that—former. The disgust on her face and in her voice told him there was no way she could still be involved with him.

But where the hell did she fit into this bizarre situation? Ric drew in a long, frustrated breath and kicked a stray pebble across the parking lot. Were they using her as a decoy to keep him occupied? That didn't make sense. The minute he'd seen her, he'd grown suspicious. Besides, she'd led him to Garcia. Not very smart on their parts, unless they wanted him to find out about Garcia. Nah! He was crediting them with more cunning than they deserved. He should stick with his instincts. If there was a connection, if Sunday School was involved in something illegal, it must be without her knowledge. He'd stake his life on that.

Sunday School.

Lustrous brown hair slanted over her left eyebrow and big, chocolate brown eyes snuck up on him. Visions of her sweet face had hounded him all week. Duty and desire. An incompatible twosome where she was concerned. Sunday School had cast a spell on him. Losing perspective while undercover was damn unprofessional and risky. Dumb, too.

Ric kicked at another pebble and glanced at his watch. His break had already stretched to ten minutes. He'd have to return to the bar soon, but he couldn't stop thinking about Susan. For the past five days he'd been inclined to believe his involvement with her was strictly personal. But now if she ended up driving to Juarez with this crowd, she'd be back on his list of suspects. And maybe that would be a good thing. Because if Sunday School was on the up and up, they were headed for a relationship. He could feel it in his bones and other places, and he wasn't sure he was ready for it. Not the type of involvement Sunday School implied.

Why the hell had she sought him out? After all, Judd's wasn't the most respectable place in town. Was she looking for an affair? Did she understand that he had dreams and plans and they didn't include a woman in Las Cruces?

Halt there Buddy, his inner voice commanded. *Just what do you call the streak of jealousy that surfaced when she was talking about Jerry Westphal? Detachment?*

Convicted by his conscience, Ric shook his head and walked toward the door. Since he wasn't ready to examine his feelings and he sure as hell couldn't figure out why she'd singled him out, he'd use the excuse that the verdict wasn't crystal clear about Sunday School as a reason to continue seeing her. Such as he planned to do the day after tomorrow, this coming Sunday in fact.

And tomorrow he'd call Drew Matthews at the Agency. They had a lot to discuss.

"How ya doing?" Ric called over his shoulder, letting the wind carry his voice back to Susan.

She nuzzled closer and shouted against his helmet. "Fine."

Ric chuckled. *Sure she was.* She was a quaking mass of Jello, but he gave her high marks for her pretense. When he'd suggested they ride his motorcycle out to the balloon site, she hadn't blinked an eye, but the lacing and unlacing of her fingers just before she'd mounted the bike revealed her fear.

Yet she'd gone through with it, and he was damn glad. If he had to rise at seven in the morning bleary-eyed from less than five hours sleep, compensation was in order. And Susan's hips snuggled up to him was a mighty fine reward. Having her legs tucked in behind his was none too shabby either. This time she'd covered them up with tailored khaki slacks and red tennis shoes. The woman owned enough tennis shoes to wear a different color every day of the week.

Heading west down the road to where the balloonists were congregating, Ric lifted his face into the wind. A beautiful, hot, sunny day, and despite having learned only yesterday that the guitar player was Juan Garcia's nephew, he was in a good mood. He'd deal with that tomorrow. As for today, no matter what doubts cluttered his mind, he was determined to hold them at bay and enjoy what promised to be a full day spent with Susan.

He especially looked forward to the days end and what it might bring.

Like climbing that mountain again.

Susan curled her head against Ric's broad back. Here she was. On the road again, back on his Honda, pushing her adrenaline to the limit. She might not be fond of riding his bike, but she was very fond of the position it put her in. Ric turned off the main road, and a veteran by now, she leaned in the direction of his turn. The trip was mercifully short, and he soon cut the engine, bringing the bike to a halt and dismounting.

"Nice tush, Senorita," he whispered as he undid the chin strap of her helmet.

And so was his. An image of Ric in his briefs danced before her. She felt her face grow warm. Would that tempting vision never leave her? And then she remembered his briefs still hung on the bedpost of Aunt Kitty's bed. Her bed now.

Blinking away the provocative pictures, Susan concentrated on the sight before them. A sight that belonged on a postcard. Three colorfully striped balloons were already airborne while three more were preparing to leave. The brilliant colors against the azure blue sky and coppery mountains in the distance were breathtaking.

"Last chance to back out," Ric teased as they approached Horace Brown and the two men helping him assemble the balloon.

"Are you kidding? I've been wanting to do this since I moved here. Of course, if you're suddenly having second thoughts about taking the flight, you could wait—"

"Not on you life, Sunday School."

"What did you say?"

"Nothing." A scowl creased his face and his eyes flicked back and forth as if he were put out with himself.

Minutes later the balloon rose and gradually began to drift with the wind. Quiet peace surrounded them, so quiet, she imagined you could hear a human heartbeat hundreds of feet below. Susan pointed over the rim of the basket. "Look there's Old Mesilla." The ancient Spanish town, once a crossroads through the mountain passes, came into view.

If she remembered anything about this adventure, apart from Ric and the balloon's glorious floating sensation, it would be the awesome quiet. So quiet a horse's whinny and a cowboy's comforting voice drifted skyward with amazing clarity.

She reached for her camera hanging around her neck. Snapshots of the balloon ride and the rodeo later this afternoon weren't the only reason she'd brought it along. As she leaned over the basket and aimed her camera, Ric gallantly held onto her hips. A ripple of pleasure paraded up her spine nearly causing her to drop the camera. After taking her pictures, she handed the camera to Horace and asked him to snap one of her and Ric. Now if Ric disappeared from her life, she'd have evidence he once existed.

"Now I know how Aladdin felt on his magic carpet," she commented, nestled in the circle of Ric's arms as they posed for Horace. Poised as they were like a cloud in the sky the poignant lyrics of Disney's song from the movie, 'Aladdin' hummed inside her. She'd taken Roberto and Rosalita to see it, and now as she studied the thorny mesquite and yucca plants below, the palette of earth colors dotting the cliffs and mountain bluffs, she felt as if she too, saw a whole new world.

"There's the Rio Grande." She gestured with her hand.

"Doesn't look like much," Ric remarked.

"Even on the ground it's almost dry." Just like her throat whenever he was near.

Ric draped his arm around her shoulder and gave her an affectionate squeeze. He'd taken off his sunglasses for the picture, and looking into his eyes, she swore she could read his thoughts. With the wind blowing her hair away from her face, she stood on tiptoe and kissed his cheek.

"What's that for?"

"For sharing this ride with me." For more than she dared say.

His heart-twisting smile stole her breath away. One of those dangerous kinds of manly smiles she'd come to associate with him. As if they'd been transported to their own private world, she stood helplessly still. Sharing this with him made it extra special, and she realized yet another memory had been forged in her brain. From this day forth balloons and Ric would be forever entwined.

In response to the quiet whoosh of the burner, Susan lifted her head to watch the bluish-orange flames shoot into the interior of the balloon. Seconds later the balloon responded, ascending to meet with a curtain of air that sent them ever so subtly in a different direction.

An hour and half later much to her dismay, Horace vented the balloon, allowing air to escape. With a skip or two they played hop-scotch with the land, until he set them back on the ground. Yards and yards of rip-stop nylon slowly deflated while she and Ric helped gather it together. Right on cue the chase crew chugged into view, veering off the road onto the desert and pulling close to where they'd landed. One man carried a cooler. Flipping it open, he handed a chilled split of champagne to Ric.

"A tradition," Horace explained, "in honor of your first ride."

"Nice tradition," Ric replied, uncorking the bottle and pouring champagne into two small goblets. "To a memorable day." He clicked his goblet against hers, then smiled from the corner of his mouth, his gaze settling on her lips. "Think I'll start a tradition of my own."

He pulled her into his arms and kissed her. Long and hard, not giving her a chance to protest. She wouldn't have anyway. Perhaps he knew that. Her quick surrender was his proof. Uneasiness skittered up her spine on a collision course with the rush of pleasure shimmying its way down. Sparks were certain to ignite when they met.

Ric stepped away, then extended his hand to Horace. "Thanks for the ride." He flicked his wrist and checked his watch. "Come on Suse, we have a rodeo to catch in El Paso. Let's head back to your house and pick up your station wagon."

Lost in her daydreams and entranced by the heart-stopping moments they'd shared, she fell into step with him as he gently propelled her toward the chase car and the second part of a day she'd never forget.

Settled into their seats in the air-conditioned arena, Ric looked over the cowboys below. The balloon ride had been everything he'd expected and far too short to suit him. He'd have appreciated it more if he hadn't had to rise at the crack of dawn. But being with Susan was worth it.

"Watch this next rider," Ric said minutes later, draping his arm around her shoulder. He'd been studying the rodeo program and listening to the chatter of the people around them. "From what I hear, he's the favorite."

A runty-looking steer barreled out of a chute about the same time as a roan horse and rider came out of another. Horse chased steer while the rider worked his rope. A buzz of anticipation stirred through the small arena. The spectators watched closely as the rider started to twirl his rope into a loop.

"Watch the teamwork between the horse and rider," Ric instructed.

"Can *you* do that?"

"Rope calves?" He helped himself to some popcorn from the half empty box they shared.

"No, I meant can you make a lariat like that?"

"Used to. Reckon I still can."

"What's that in the cowboy's mouth?"

"A piggin string. It's a small piece of rope to tie three of the calf's legs together. Hotdog! He's got him." His gut suddenly tightening, Ric shifted his gaze and stared into space.

Susan saw the loop drop around the calf's neck. The horse halted and backed up as the rope tightened around the calf. Responding to the crowd excitement, she clapped and cheered, drawn to the drama as the cowboy raced against time. Seconds later he dismounted, wrestled the calf to the ground, and tied three legs together. When the loud speaker announced the cowboy's time, shouts and applause filled the indoor arena.

Having followed the action with rapt attention, she slanted a glance at Ric. He wasn't clapping. He sat still, his mouth clenched, no humor in his eyes. Once before up on the mountain she'd seen a similar look cross his face and had been puzzled, even alarmed. Perhaps because she hadn't known him well. But this time there was no icy glare or sardonic twist to his mouth. As if he'd communicated his thoughts, in one swift second she knew what haunted him. The past melded with the present, and the rider had become his brother.

She reached over and covered his hand. His fingers laced with hers, and she tightened her grip. He met her gaze, sad gray eyes holding her brown ones, and she wished she could do or say something to ease his pain. For endless moments their gazes transmitted silent messages.

"You're thinking about your brother, aren't you?" With his gaze still riveted on her, he nodded. "It's going to be all right, Ric."

"Damn right." He gave her hand a reassuring squeeze. Once he became a lawyer, he was going to lock up every drug dealer he prosecuted, so kids like his brother could grow up to be like this cowboy or whatever it was they dreamed of being. For a time when he'd been an agent, he'd fought the battle that way. Now he felt an urgency for this temporary assignment to end and to begin the next phase of his life. But he had a double score to settle first.

His brother's and Johnny Montoya's.

"Do you think your brother might enjoy going to a rodeo some time?" Susan quizzed.

Aw, Sunday School, what am I going to do about you?

The woman was not only clairvoyant but a saint. Tommy never seemed aware of much in his life, but damn, a rodeo might get through to him, might please him. Why hadn't he thought of that? Because he'd been too busy playing cops and robbers and studying law, and because he lacked the sensitivity of this woman sitting beside him. This long legged brunette who he'd once thought wasn't his type. Damn, but he wanted to kiss her and tell her—

W*hat, Ramsey? Tell her what?*

Susan watched Ric's eyes light up and a smile brighten his somber features. Contentment rushed through her. And then she knew by the twinkle in his eyes what he planned to do right here in the arena in front of hundreds and hundreds of people. As his face inched closer, she tipped her head, her breath catching in anticipation. The people around them faded as Ric's mouth brushed across her lips. She closed her eyes and leaned toward him. His hand reached up to the side of her neck and pulled her closer to deepen the kiss. His kiss was slow and thorough. Her mouth throbbed beneath his, and she felt the impact clear down to her toes.

She inched away. “Ric, the people—” Her voice fizzled out as he nibbled on her lower lip, catching it between his teeth.

As he worked his mouth from one side of her lips to the other coaxing them open, the people faded to oblivion. His mouth tasted of butter and popcorn, and her heart galloped faster than the horse and rider chasing after the calf below. She wanted his kiss to go on forever, wanted to wrap her arms around his waist and feel his hardened body pressed against hers. She wanted more. She wanted him.

And then she heard them—the whistles, claps, and catcalls, and she knew by the degree of heat in her cheeks that she was redder than a setting New Mexico sun. Ric lifted his mouth from hers, a hint of embarrassment on his face. It only endeared him to her more.

Before he righted himself in his seat, he whispered into her ear, “You’re the best, Suse. When I take Tommy to the rodeo I’d like it if you’d go with us.”

Stunned, Susan went breathlessly still. *Not fair, Ric, not fair.* Her harmless quest for a fiancé was about to backfire on her. There was something more than a burgeoning friendship between them. Something more than chemistry and goosebumps.

She was falling for the man she planned to ask to pose as her fiancé.

Susan picked up the rodeo program and fanned herself.

Susan’s station wagon sped west on the interstate. Randy Travis’ voice crooned from the car radio, barely audible over the hum of the air conditioner. As the orange rays of the setting sun challenged her vision, Susan lowered the visor and glanced at the clock. Nearly six, and they were about five miles out of Las Cruces. Affectionately, she glanced across to her right and the sleeping man beside her.

To Ric.

He’d offered to drive her wagon to El Paso, and she’d let him, but as the rodeo drew to a close, she could tell from his glassy-eyed look and his yawns that lack of sleep was catching up with him. Her own energy level rapidly dwindling, she rubbed the crook of her neck and eased the station wagon onto the exit ramp. It had been quite a day. A day of intimacies. Three Sundays ago she’d have told herself she was getting to know him, interviewing him for an important role. But now?

Her feelings for Ric were getting mixed up in what was supposed to be a straight forward business arrangement. And she didn't know him well enough to gauge how he felt about her. At times she swore she could read his thoughts, but it could be sheer physical need on his part. Despite his tender invitation to include her when he and his brother attended a rodeo, the man spelled '*temporary*'. Turning into her driveway, she stopped alongside Ric's motorcycle.

She unbuckled her seat belt and leaned toward him. The tips of her fingers tickled the side of his throat. "Wake up, sleepy head, we're home."

Suddenly, his hand clamped around her wrist, and he bolted awake, slamming against the confines of his seat belt. His iron grip tightened, and Susan cried out in pain. He muttered something unintelligible, then yanked her imprisoned wrist and forced her to tumble onto his shoulder.

"Ric, stop, let go, it's me." Shaken, she tried to pull free.

"What?"

"My hand, let go!" His now-open eyes had a menacing look to them, like a predator preparing to devour his victim. As her heartbeat kicked into overdrive, she shoved harder, breaking free.

"My God, Susan! I'm sorry." The groove by the side of his right cheek deepened. He reached for her hand again, his fingers gently stroking her skin as he examined her wrist. "Did I hurt you?"

"It's all right." She trembled. "You must have had a nightmare." Avoiding her gaze, he looked away, and she could have sworn he flinched.

"Something like that," he mumbled, chilled by what he'd done. His sleep had been deep, and roused from it, he'd reacted like he did when he was under attack. "Sorry, Suse." He lifted her wrist to his mouth and kissed it. "Promise me you won't do that again."

Do what? Wake him up that way? That implied he'd be sleeping in her presence again. Strangely, the new Susan liked the sound of that.

But not the old Susan. Curiosity consumed her. Confused by Ric's violent behavior, the old Susan grew wary. Even suspicious.

Chapter Nine

Ric smiled.

Something downright homey about watching a woman work in her kitchen, he mused, his gaze trained on Susan's petite tush as she bent over to get some cheese from the refrigerator. His eyes followed her every movement from the counter to the refrigerator and back again, taking particular note of the pull of her khaki slacks each time she bent over. She seemed quite at home in the kitchen, which was a unique experience for him. Most of the women in his past had shunned the kitchen with a passion.

He'd offered to help, but she'd insisted he sit at the table and simply keep her company. Soup, sandwiches, and coffee, she'd said. Lots of coffee. A fan of Colombian, she'd brewed enough to make Juan Valdez proud.

Kind of nice to have someone fussing over you, caring whether you'd stay awake on the drive home.

Jeeze, he must be getting old. A beautiful, warm, desirable woman flitting around him and he had all he could do not to fall asleep in his chair.

The sudden memory of how he'd manhandled her jolted through him. Sleep deprivation must have been responsible. Susan's touch had interrupted an episode he'd been reliving about a drug dealer who had tried to knife him. He'd beaten the guy to a pulp, and Lord help him, he could have done it to Susan, too.

"Here we go." Susan carried a tray of food to the table. "Grilled cheese sandwiches and soup." She set his bowl in front of him. "Maybe we'd better skip the Spanish lesson tonight. I'm a little bushed, myself."

"Good idea. Don't think either of us could concentrate." Thunder intruded. "A storm's coming."

"That remains to be seen." Sitting down, she stirred her soup with her spoon. "The weather out here has a habit of thundering and making out like we're in for a whopper of a storm, and what do we get—nothing more than a fantastic display of heat lightning and nary a raindrop."

"All bark and no bite, huh? It did that in San Angelo, too,

but something tells me this one is no false alarm."

"Feel it in your Apache bones, do you?"

Ric snapped his fingers together. "Son of a gun, you missed my rain dance when you went to powder your nose."

"That I would have liked to have seen." Ric dancing around, exposing his charms. Painted quite a picture. "Sure you don't need to repeat it?"

"Not necessary. The weather forecast I turned on for a minute or two before coming into the kitchen cinched my prediction." He winked, taking a bite of his sandwich. "Maybe another time, Senorita."

"A rain check?" She winked back.

"A promise."

Dinner was quiet and relaxed. They sat at the table companionably recounting their day. Susan started stacking their plates when she realized Ric had been right about the weather. The wind picked up and the sky darkened. The combination of the rain and Ric's fatigue ruled out another scene of Ric in his briefs and the temptation to join him in the pool. His briefs! She stopped clearing the table and rose.

"Sit," Ric jumped to his feet. "You put supper together. Least I can do is clear up."

Susan pasted another gold star by his name. Fatigue tinged his voice, yet he still insisted on helping. "Okay, but how about one more cup of coffee in the living room before you go home. Might be better to wait until the storm blows by."

Ric shrugged and rinsed the plates. "Another cup sounds fine, and as for the storm, it's no big deal. I'm waterproof. This one probably won't last that long." As he loaded some of the dishes into her dishwasher, he glanced over his shoulder. "I said sit, Woman." Though his tone was firm, his lips quirked to a crooked smile. "I'll pour our coffee when I'm done."

"No, I have to go get something." As she raced from the room, heat engulfed her cheeks again. For nearly a week now his briefs had adorned her bedpost, nightly capturing her attention just before she flicked out the light.

In her bedroom she snatched his briefs off the bedpost, not at all certain she wanted to part with them. Thinking it might be awkward to just come out and hand them to him, she stuffed them into a large brown envelope, stopping to run a comb through her hair and freshen up. By the time she returned to the living room, Ric sat on the couch, two mugs of coffee on the sofa table in front of him. She sat down and set the envelope next to her mug.

"I'll probably leave as soon as the storm dies down," Ric said.

That wasn't what he wanted. He eyed her, then the sofa. Struggling with a sudden surge of desire and skeptical of his ability to keep it under control, he raked a hand through his hair. He shouldn't allow himself to become entangled with her. He needed to remember there was a lot more to Susan Stewart than met the eye. Why had whatever power that might be sent this woman into his life at this particular time? He wasn't ready—

Ready to what? Ready to commit to a woman. Committing to a cause had never been a problem. But to a woman? To Susan? When his sleep-fogged brain cleared he had a heap of thinking to do.

"Good," Susan said, her gaze still glued on the package. "I mean I'm glad you're going to wait till it stops raining."

"It's been a hectic week," he commented. He'd spent almost every waking minute staking out or trailing the Garcias. "Guess I could stand a few minutes down time."

"I'm tired, too. Tomorrow's a school day, and Wednesday is the kids last day."

"Bet the kids are happy about that."

"A couple of us teachers are, too. It's a chance to recharge our batteries." Susan grinned. Neither wanted the evening to end, and both were too tired to do more than exchange inanities, scintillating conversation beyond their ability right now.

"And just how much time do you plan to take off?" Ric stretched his arms, trying to loosen a kink in his back. "My guess is none."

"Actually, I plan to take a week off in July, fly home to Pittsburgh." Great opening to bring up Shane Orr, but she sensed Ric was too beat to deal with such a complicated subject. Lord knows, she was.

"Good, you deserve a break, but I bet the rest of the time you plan to tutor kids like Roberto and Rosalita."

"Yes I do." That he'd remembered their names amazed her.

"How many?"

"About ten in all."

"Here?" He paused, seeming to weigh his thoughts. "If it's

here you might need liability insurance, especially with the pool."

She smiled at his lawyerly concern. In a peculiar way it sounded like he cared for her. "No, not here. Transportation's a problem for the kids. There's a church in their neighborhood, and the priest offered me space on Mondays and Thursdays."

"And if I know you, you're doing it for free."

She nodded.

"Thought so. Too bad I didn't have you for a teacher, though I doubt it would have helped."

"Sounds to me like you didn't much care for school," she said, keying in on his comment.

"There was always a million things I'd rather have been doing. School grew on me, or rather the importance of an education did. I still wake up some nights in a cold sweat thinking I have an exam the next morning and I forgot to study for it."

"Is that what happened in the station wagon?" Lines at the sides of his brow knitted together. "You woke up from a bad dream," she clarified.

He took a long, thoughtful swallow of his coffee and set down the mug. "Something like that."

"One of those bad memories from the service?"

"Yeah. Sort of."

Realizing he had no intention of elaborating, she searched for something to say to break the awkwardness that had descended on them. Vibrant electricity had existed between them all day. Now uncomfortable bouts of silence replaced it.

"I'm sorry it happened, Suse."

"Like you said, you've had some bad experiences." She remembered the jagged scar she'd seen on his back, and a sliver of apprehension darted through her. Ric could be exasperatingly uncommunicative at times, and darned adept at steering the conversation in another direction. His life. His right, she supposed.

Ric rubbed his chin. "It doesn't happen often, only when I'm overly tired and drift into a deep sleep."

"And when someone tickles you awake in the middle of a nightmare." Lightning struck and the lights flickered off. She started to rise for a flashlight when they flickered back on.

"Rain's coming down hard now," he remarked.

Susan tossed her head and smiled. Just as she'd predicted

he'd changed the subject. The skill should serve him well when he started practicing law. "From the sound of the it, we could be getting our eight inches for the year all in one night."

A deluge howled outside and her never-been-baptized umbrella sat idle in her purse, although she was beginning to suspect it served more as a psychic charm rather than to ward off raindrops. The new, unpredictable side to her behavior toyed with the idea of grabbing the umbrella and dashing outside to christen it, but the weary look on Ric's face dissuaded her.

Ric jammed his hands in his pockets, then withdrew them. Susan's questions made him uncomfortable. He wondered what she'd think if he ever shared his past with her. Not the kind of tales she heard in church. He stretched his feet out in front of him, his gaze by chance spying an assortment of baskets stacked in the corner of the living room. Jeeze, the woman was addicted, a regular pack rat.

"It's kinda cozy to cuddle with your girl in a rainstorm," he said.

"Sort of like being in a cabin during a snowstorm."

"I forgot. You're a Yankee." His eyes dropped to the envelope on the table. "What's in the envelope?"

Susan's gaze followed his. She silently stared at it. "Uh—your undershorts."

"My—"

"You left them here and—"

"And you didn't want me to be walking around bare assed for another week," he teased.

"No." She gazed at his killer smile. "Of course, I assumed you had others."

"A whole drawer full."

And probably in every color of the rainbow. Tension returned and the blossom of a blush heated her cheeks. In a matter of seconds poses of Ric clad in six different briefs, each a different shade, joined the memory of him in his kelly green ones.

A naughty look crossed his face, and he sent her a lopsided smile. "Say, Suse, speaking of snow-covered cabins in the mountains, how about we do some mountain climbing?"

Mountain climbing? What was it about Ric and his fixation for mountains?

He reached out and took some strands of her hair between

his fingers. "I've heard there's lots of mountains around Pittsburgh."

His voice set loose a liquid warmth inside her stomach, and the touch of his fingers on her cheek caused her to shiver.

"Every Yankee woman deserves a taste of Texas hospitality."

"Every Yankee woman?" She challenged the teasing glint in his eyes.

"Well, maybe only the one in my arms." He pulled her into the circle of his arms and kissed her.

This kiss was different, more gentle yet intense. His lips brushed over hers, tender and coaxing. A lover's kiss, silky sweet, it urged her to respond. Ric's fingertips caressed the hollow of her neck, and Susan gave a shuddering sigh, then without a moment's hesitation invited his tongue into her mouth. As he explored it, she linked her arms around his neck and scooted closer to him. His fingers began to massage the back of her neck. When his hands dropped to her hips, pressing her to him, she heard her voice turn husky and whisper his name.

He released his hold on her. She felt his hands slowly move upward, drifting over her breasts and journeying on to frame her face. Those soulful gray eyes stared into hers, his finger pausing at the pulse point on the side of her neck. His fingers lingered on her skin, his touch every bit as stirring as his kisses. Her pulse throbbed like his speeding motorcycle, and she let out a slow breath in an effort to quell it, fearing he could sense how much she was coming to care for him. The glow in her eyes probably gave her away. Even though she was totally incapable of viewing them, she could feel their sparkle.

"Suse— " he said, his voice pitched low.

Their lips touched, and she was lost again, lost in a world of spinning colors. Why did this man have the power to arouse her so easily? She sighed, breathing in his piney fragrance, savoring the involuntary groans triggered deep in his throat. She became aware of the slow journey of his hands as they retraced their path down her neck, over her shoulders, and coming to rest at the side of her breasts. As his hands gently caressed them, all she could do was burrow her hands in his thick mat of hair, fling her head back, and enjoy the sweetness of his touch.

"Kiss me again, Suse," he urged.

And Susan complied, at first nipping his lower lip with her teeth. Her mouth covered his, and their tongues met while his fingers unsnapped her bra and beguilingly traced circles around her breasts. Seconds later he pulled his mouth free, and pushing her down on the sofa, placed a kiss on her breast. If she'd been looking for excitement and adventure, she'd found them, but she was in the market for a fiancé not a brief affair. From the satisfied groan in Ric's throat, she sensed they were both hovering on the threshold of something she wasn't prepared to cross. At least the old Susan wasn't, and the old Susan seemed to have reasserted herself, berating her for being irresponsible and rash.

"Ric," she whispered, pushing her hand against his chest.

"Umm—"

He remained still, and she pushed again, nuzzling her lips against his ear, unable to resist tracing his lobe with her tongue. "Ric."

"I know," he answered, yet didn't move, his lips a breath away, their warmth fanning her face.

"Please." She nudged his solid chest again.

"Yeah, yeah, I know," Ric mumbled, cradling her head to his chest.

The phone helped her. It jangled shrilly in their ears. "We need to stop."

"Yeah, the phone." He flopped back against the arm of the sofa. "Answer the damn thing, Suse."

She clutched her blouse together and dashed into the kitchen. "Hello," she hastily said into the receiver. "Oh, Mother. What? Yes it's hot down here. Very hot." As she watched Ric tuck his shirt into his pants and walk toward her, Susan lifted her hand and fanned herself. "In fact, I'm roasting." With Ric around, her air conditioning bill promised to be outrageous. As Ric lazily strode closer, a disarming grin pasted on his face, she held her hand over the receiver.

"Your mother?" he quizzed, raising an eyebrow.

Mesmerized by his tousled hair and bedroom eyes, she drew in a tremulous breath and nodded. As she tried to listen to her mother's conversation, her gaze remained locked on Ric's compelling face,

"I think we've done this before. Your mother has impeccable timing. *Besa el maestro*," he hoarsely whispered, slanting his left cheek downward.

Susan stood on tiptoe and brushed her lips across his cheek. He quickly turned, capturing her mouth. A whimper escaped her lips when he withdrew. Seconds later he waved, disappearing through the kitchen door.

"Did I hear someone, Susan? Is someone there?" her mother inquired.

"Yes." She gulped. "He just left."

"Was it Shane, dear?"

Susan paused, cocked her head, and crossed her fingers. Why not? "Yes, Mother. It was Shane."

Ric draped his wet jacket on a hanger and hung it in the shower stall. Stumbling back to his bedroom, he shed his clothes, pulling on a dry pair of red skivvies. They reminded him of Susan, Susan and her beet-red face and skittish smile, and of his green skivvies in the envelope still sitting on her coffee table. He'd forgotten to take them with him.

Dead on his feet, he rubbed his chin and lay on the bed, his arms propped under his neck and his ankles crossed. *So Ramsey, you had your day with her and now you're more involved with her than you were twenty-four hours ago.* So much for remaining professionally aloof. Aloof had flown the coop ever since a dark-eyed brunette in a skirt that hid too damn much of her legs had come sashaying up to him. No point in lying to himself. This was not a woman he'd walk away from and forget. For days now he'd sensed that Susan was the woman he'd been waiting for.

He knew the signs. He was falling in love with Sunday School.

And he knew it was wrong to let his emotions become involved with a potential suspect, but God help him, she tempted him. From the tip of her toes to the top of her head, everything she said and did endeared her to him, and he didn't know what he was going to do about it.

Tread water, he supposed. Go with the flow until there was no doubt about her innocence. The very thought that she might not be sent chills across his skin. She was his Sunday School, and she was innocent. His heart told him so. Like he'd told himself over and over, if there were a connection, it had to be under coercion or because someone was using her without her knowledge. And he damn well had to find out what she knew even if she didn't know what she knew.

Yeah, he liked the last hypothesis. It suited Sunday School to a T.

But until she was in the clear or someone relieved him of this assignment, telling her how he felt was out of the question. The air conditioner rattled against the window frame. Ric shook his head and grunted. He'd be glad when he could pack up and leave this dive, live in a decent place, a place with a jacuzzi.

A jacuzzi with Sunday School in it.

"Aren't you glad you came to Judd's tonight?" Robin quizzed Susan.

"I don't know about Susan," Pam interrupted, "but I am. Haven't had a good look at Ric Ramsey since the last time we were here."

"And he's worth looking at." Zestful enthusiasm flowed from Robin's voice.

Looking at Ric behind the bar and taking note of how his thick brown hair curled at the collar of his black shirt, Susan blushed and agreed. The dark color gave a dangerous aura to his appearance.

Pam spoke behind her hand. "So, Susan, now that you know Ric is on the up and up, that he actually graduated from the University and that he grew up in San Angelo, when are you going to ask him?"

"Not here." Uncomfortable, Susan shifted in the booth. Not with all the noise and music and everyone looking on, especially her two overly enthusiastic friends.

When Pam and Robin had brought her the good news about Ric on Monday night, she'd been eager to contact him, but reaching him remained a problem. He'd never given her a home phone number. She didn't even know where his trailer was. And phoning him at Judd's just wouldn't do. As he'd left the other night without making plans to see her again, she'd jumped at Robin's suggestion that they come to Judd's to celebrate the end of the school year.

If she could wrangle a moment alone with him, she'd invite him to dinner this coming Sunday. That's when she'd finally get around to asking him to pose as Shane Orr.

"Susan." Robin's voice brought her back to the present.

"This coming Sunday. I hope to ask him Sunday. That is if he drops by."

"The reunion isn't that far away now, is it?" Robin asked.

"No. Only three and a half weeks."

"If you'll just watch the way he looks at Susan, there's no doubt that he'll accept." Pam sighed. "Too bad I don't have a reunion and a make believe fiancé to come up with. I sure wouldn't mind dancing with him."

"Speaking of dancing, they're about to start the line dancing lessons." Robin's lips curved at the corners. "Eat up. After all, staring at Ric Ramsey isn't the only thing we came for. We're here to celebrate Susan's last day of school."

"I don't know about you, but I came just to look at him." Pam's eyes sparkled as she spoke.

At Pam's comment Susan became aware of how nearly every female in the room cast Ric a lingering look. A possessive pang shot through her stomach. As she slipped out from the table and followed her friends into the dancing area, Susan walked by Ric and nodded. He nodded back, their gazes momentarily connecting. No surprise that pinpricks soared through her body. She touched her fingers to her temple, wishing she had a fan, and walked on.

Ric heard Susan's honey-sweet laugh above all the other noise in the room, and his lips twitched into a grin. She and her two friends weren't sitting all that far away from him. He'd noticed them the minute they'd entered the bar, almost dropped the beer mug he'd been about to fill from the tap. She hadn't been back to the bar since the night of her flat tire. Could she be here because of the Garcia's? Naw, not with her two friends in tow. So what was the occasion tonight?

Not that he minded feasting his eyes on her.

That was the problem. Since she'd arrived, he could barely concentrate on what he was doing, had almost screwed up the Margarita he'd just made, catching himself a second before he'd laced it with rum. The state he was in, someone could pass drugs right in front of his nose and he wouldn't notice a thing.

But something he very definitely noticed was Susan in her

long, denim skirt and navy tennis shoes. Someone was going to have to teach that woman how to dress properly. Such as boots instead of those colorful shoes she paraded around in, and jeans that hugged her hips, like the ones she'd worn the day they'd ridden up the mountain.

Ric spent the next twenty minutes suspended in frustration. He could only see a small part of the dance hall from his vantage point, and he knew that line dancing didn't necessarily involve a partner. It wasn't until he heard the instructor announce over the microphone that she was going to teach them the two-step that Ric's anxiety level rose. He endured the next few minutes as much as he could, but when music from the jukebox replaced it and there was no sign of Susan, he'd reached his limit.

Damned woman. She gave him no peace night or day. Some crusty cowboy could be pawing her this very minute. And if anyone was going to be pawing her, it was going to be him.

"Hey, Al," he called, beckoning to one of the waiters. "I'm due a fifteen minute break. I'll pay you twenty-five dollars if you'll let me stretch it into twenty-five and cover for me." Ric slipped two bills from his wallet.

"Twenty-five for ten extra minutes?" Al grinned and took the money. "Must be some hot chick."

Ric grimaced. She'd better not be. This crowd was too rough for her. She didn't belong here.

Ric rounded the corner and uneasily eyed Susan. "Your Cheating Heart" belted from the jukebox, and, just as he thought, some young buck was dancing with Sunday School, holding her too damned close. He glowered at them until one of Elvis' dreamy ballads started to play. Jealousy pricked him into action. In two shakes he walked up to them and tapped the guy's shoulder.

"Hey," Ric drawled, pulling Susan into a conventional dance position.

"Ric!"

"I'm taking a break," he mumbled into her ear. "Your next twenty minutes are mine."

"Yours?"

"Yeah." He tightened his hold and tried to control the jealousy railing inside him. It was probably written all over his face.

"Something wrong?"

"Not now. This is my kind of song—nice and slow." He didn't go in for those high-filuting dance steps that kept partners apart. The two-step he could tolerate now and then. Give him the slow dances—the kind where you pulled the woman's hips into your belly.

Susan looked up at his softened expression and snuggled deeper against his chest. The way she felt tonight, the next twenty *years* of her life were his for the asking. Cuddled against him, she had little trouble following him as they barely moved on the crowded floor. His left hand released hers and wandered into her hair. Whenever they did manage to take a step, his legs brushed against hers from thigh to calf. Susan closed her eyes and trembled.

"You all right, Suse?"

"Yes," she answered breathily. "I'm fine."

"Well, I'm not."

His answer surprised her, and she inched away and tilted her head. There was a half smile on his lips, but so much more in his eyes. They were dark, smoky, heavy-lidded, and sensuous. "What's wrong?" she asked, almost sure she knew the answer.

He stopped dancing. "It's hot in here."

She was burning up, too, and she sensed from his manhood pressed against her stomach that he was suffering from more than heat.

"How 'bout we go outside?"

"Yes." Her answer was a ragged whisper. Outside, alone, she could invite him over to her house on Sunday.

Ric stood inches from her and fought his frustration. He looked down at her and caught himself wishing they were somewhere else. The way she'd melted into him had been his undoing. That and his damned imagination. This craziness had to stop. The trauma of dealing with her was interfering with his assignment, even though she was tangled up in his assignment. Go figure how he was going to solve that one. Somehow managing to remember his purpose for being at Judd's, he cast a furtive look around the room.

As he took her hand and snaked through the maze of people, leading her behind the platform and to the door that opened onto the parking lot, he saw the guitar player watching them. Let him, Ric sneered. Pedro Garcia was Juan's Garcia's nephew, and he'd deal with both of them another time. Right now he had more important things on his mind. Once outside, he held Susan inches from him, the combination of the moonlight and streetlights illuminating her face. His gaze slid down her face to her throat and to the swell of her breasts.

"Suse."

The gravelly need in his voice held her captive. He bent closer, inch by inch, his face lowering. Susan watched him dip his head and touch his lips to hers. Soft and gentle, they rocked across her own in sweet seduction. Roughly, fiercely, as if he was out of control, Ric deepened the kiss. With a gasp, she absorbed the delicious sensations, and wiggled against him.

"Suse, Suse," he murmured against her lips, breaking off his kiss. "I didn't know you were interested in dance lessons."

"Doesn't hurt to broaden your horizons." She waited for his reaction, and when his jaw fell open and a trace of shock appeared in his eyes, she winked.

"I can broaden your horizons for you."

That he could.

He stroked her cheek with his thumb. "Did you come here to see me?" he asked, stroking her cheek with his thumb.

"Yes, but don't get conceited. We were celebrating, too."

"Celebrating?"

"No more school, no more books—"

"—no more teacher's dirty looks," he finished for her. "You're welcome to send me a dirty look anytime."

"Is that right?"

"Yes ma'am." He patted her bottom tenderly.

"Actually, I wanted to ask you over this Sunday."

"Oh, our Spanish lessons."

"That, and there's a festival in town—booths, crafts, and food." She was running out of time. She needed to ask him if he'd pose as Shane as soon as possible. "I thought we could do the lesson, go to the festival, bring home some food, and eat it around the pool."

"Sounds good. This Sunday, you say?" Ric paused. His curiosity aroused, a premonition gnawed at him, and he had to know the answer. "Sunday's fine, but how about the next one? Want to tackle another Spanish lesson then?"

"I'd love to, but I have to go to Juarez ."

Dammit Sunday School. Damn, damn, damn. He'd been

hoping she wasn't going. "Juarez again? You go there a lot."

"My yard man is counting on me taking him."

I bet he is. He and that other gorilla.

"He doesn't have a car," Susan explained. "He and his wife have family they need to visit over there."

Sure they do.

"His family doesn't have the money or transportation to come visit him," she went on to explain, sensing an uneasiness in him. Was he jealous of her spending time with others, or was she imagining it? "The Garcias always bring lots of items from the states for their family, and I think they bring them some money, too. It's the least I can do for them," she said with quiet justification.

Bless Sunday School's heart. Ever the do-gooder, they'd pulled the wool over her eyes and were using her. He was sure of it, and relieved, too. Damn relieved. "So what time do you want me to pick you up?"

"How about we do our lesson at three, and then go the festival around four?" She swallowed then looked him in the eye. "Be sure and bring a swim suit."

He liked the sound of that. It hinted that they'd both be in the water. He especially like the vision of her in a bikini. Glancing down at her long skirt, he supposed he wouldn't get that lucky. "I think you still have my skivvies at your house."

A flush crept up her neck and spread over her face. "Yes, I do, but—"

He got a kick out of teasing her. With her head angled down, her hair obscured one side of her face. "But you'd rather I wore a bona fide swimsuit." At her nod, he smiled. "Good. I'll be there by three, swimsuit in hand. Now where were we?" He flicked his wrist to the light. "Oh, yeah, I've got ten more minutes. Come here, Miss Stewart.

Pulling her back into his arms, he closed his eyes and reclaimed her lips.

Chapter Ten

Ric parked his bike in the McDonald's parking lot, marched over to the black sedan, and opened the door. Pulling it shut, he reached for the foil-wrapped hamburger, sitting between him and the other occupant of the front seat. He took a bite and faced José Vella.

"So what's up that warranted me driving from Las Cruces?" he asked José.

"We've had word that someone's been snooping around in Austin and San Angelo asking about you."

"Damn," Ric swore.

"You tell anyone you had connections there?"

"One person, but anyone could have—"

"Who?" José interrupted.

"Susan Stewart, but she couldn't have conducted an investigation." Ric rubbed his chin. Seemed he was always tired. Was it the hours that this job demanded combined with his age, or was it emotional stress?

"The Stewart woman could have told someone else who had the means to launch an investigation," José suggested.

"It could have been an idle remark she made to someone," Ric shot back, taking another bite of his hamburger.

"And it could have been deliberate."

"Anyone could have been suspicious and checked me out. Maybe someone at Judd's."

"Maybe." José's eyebrows rose in cadence with his cryptic reply. "But the inquires were confined to San Angelo and Austin. They didn't bother to check any further into your past. Do the math, Ric. It adds up."

Uncertainty flashed through Ric. He'd forgotten that when he'd fed Susan the information about himself, he'd done it to see if it would filter back to him. That was when he'd suspected her. Now...

"There's more."

"What?" Ric asked, refusing to accept José's conclusions.

"We've identified the dude in the photo."

"The one I saw come into Judd's?" Ric creased his brow.

"Yes. He's Hector Mendez, a card carrying member of the

Ortega Cartel—a low level lieutenant, a runner and an arm twister."

Ric whistled.

"So, it looks like this may be the man Johnny Montoya stumbled across," José speculated. "The Agency is pleased. You still think this Stewart woman is crystal clean?"

"Yeah." But doubts were resurfacing. He didn't want Sunday School involved under any circumstances, but who else knew about Austin and San Angelo? Who else could have triggered those inquires? "You have everything set for next Sunday?"

"A veritable army on both sides of the border. Neither you nor Miss Stewart and her party will be able to sneeze without us knowing. What are you gonna do?" José queried.

"Don't know. Right now I'm winging it. I may wangle a ride in the car with them. Does the Agency plan to arrest them?"

José gave him a quick nod.

"All of them?" Ric asked before José could speak.

"All of them. At the border on their trip back."

"I'm positive the woman's innocent." Ric swore under his breath.

"You're not going soft, are you? Remember Johnny Montoya."

Yeah, he was going soft, and yeah, he remembered Johnny. Ric clenched his teeth. He owed it to his buddy to find his killer. But where did that leave him with Sunday School?

Ric rode his motorcycle back to Las Cruces, a permanent scowl pasted on his face. God help him, he didn't think he could watch when they arrested Susan. He could visualize those big brown eyes of hers staring at him in bewilderment, silently questioning why the authorities were detaining her.

And how is she going to feel when she learns you set her up?

Not bloody likely to ask him over for Spanish lessons. Not bloody likely to ask him for anything.

Ever.

Ric walked a step or two behind as Susan wended her way from booth to booth examining the crafts on display at the festival. Tension walked with him as it had the entire duration of their Spanish lesson prior to coming here. Though he resolutely refused to believe Sunday School was a knowing participant in the drug ring, shards of unease scraped through him.

The news that someone had checked up on him put him on guard. Someone might be out there right now watching—someone who might suspect or even know he was an agent. Before he'd left the trailer, he'd slipped a knife into his boot for precaution. Things were coming to a head. A week from today it would be over, and he wondered if Sunday School would hate him when she'd learned who he was. Ric shivered. Nothing ever went smoothly. She could be injured—

"Oh, Ric, look," Susan's voice rang out, mercifully breaking into his unpleasant thoughts. "Look at this turquoise jewelry." She stared at the array of bracelets, earrings, necklaces, and rings, picking up a piece now and then.

Ric grinned. He never could understand women's fascination with jewelry nor how inordinately expensive the trinkets could be. As far as he was concerned, the festival was an expensive version of a flea market. He watched her try on a ring, holding it aloft and admiring it.

Susan looked at the price tag and immediately slipped it off her finger. "Story of my life," she remarked. "Champagne tastes on a Coca-Cola budget."

Frugal when it came to herself and generous to others, Saint Susan gave money away almost as fast as she made it. Money couldn't be responsible for her involvement in this case. And the Agency hadn't turned up any large debts charged to her. Had Westphal, her old boyfriend, contacted her and played on her sympathies? Susan impressed him as someone who'd be an easy mark for a sob story.

From his stance several feet away he watched her move on to the adjoining booth of baskets. That should keep her occupied, but he was wrong. A minute later, like a little girl whose nose was pressed against the glass plate of a candy store lusting after a delicious piece of chocolate, she was back again, eyeing the ring. He admired her will power when she stepped away a second time and shook her head as if mentally arguing with herself.

While she wandered back to the baskets, Ric walked up to the booth and checked the ring. She was right. The price was highway robbery, but she was worth it. The thought that the ring would be something for her to remember him by appealed to him. Hopefully, in time her memories would improve, for he sensed that after next Sunday her opinion of him might suddenly be less than charitable. He fished out his wallet and credit card and minutes later pocketed the ring.

He started off in the direction he'd last seen her, eager to surprise her with the ring. Spying her hot pink umbrella, the one that fashionably matched her tennis shoes, he quickened his pace, then suddenly froze in his tracks. Two men and a woman were chatting with her. He recognized them immediately.

Juan and Angelina Garcia, and the notorious Hector Mendez.

Ric's gut knotted. He hated seeing them anywhere near Susan. While trying to decide whether to barge into their cozy gathering or step back out of sight and observe them, Susan spotted him.

"Over here, Ric." She gestured to him.

Dammit, Sunday School, this might not be the best of ideas. He squared his shoulders and walked toward them, his eyes narrowing as he cautiously watched the two men by Susan. "Hey," he muttered, coming abreast of them.

"Ric, this is my yardman, Juan Garcia, and his wife, Angelina."

Ric shook hands with them.

"Ric is a bartender at Judd's," she explained to the Garcias.

"That so," Juan Garcia remarked. "My nephew plays guitar there."

Ric nodded, his gaze still riveted on the other man. "Yeah, I know who he is." The man beside Juan stared back at Ric, his eyes cold and hard, his face impassive.

"I'm Carlos Garcia, Juan's cousin." He extended his hand to Ric.

You're Hector Mendez, and you're lying through your teeth, Ric thought as he shook the man's hand. Their gazes met, and Ric clearly read a warning in Mendez' icy stare.

"Well, it was pleasant seeing you, but we have children wandering all around here and need to gather them together." Juan gently nudged his wife to move. "We'll see you next Sunday, Senorita Stewart."

"Sunday," she repeated as they walked away.

No doubt about it. Garcia and company were hell-bent in getting away. Ric slanted his hat lower. Six o'clock in the afternoon in mid June was too damn hot for parading around this festival. "They the folks you drive to Juarez?"

"Yes, they are."

"Susan."

"Yes?" A frown curved her lips downward.

No doubt his serious tone puzzled her. Time to get down to business, he supposed. He stirred some dust with his boot toe. "It's been awhile since I've been to Juarez. Mind if I tag along?" *Say yes, Sunday School, say yes.*

"You want to go?"

"I'd miss not seeing you next Sunday."

Susan's heart cartwheeled. So, she'd been right last Wednesday, after all. He did care for her, and he was jealous of her time. Was it possible her fantasy might come true? As silence spiked between them, she met his piercing gaze. He gave her a sexy wink. His ability to change moods so quickly surprised her. When he'd been speaking to Juan's cousin, she'd been taken aback by the grim look on his face.

Despite her confusion, Susan suddenly wished they were anywhere but this hot, crowded place. It was far too public for the thoughts racing through her head. "I'd miss you, too. I'd love for you to come along. In fact, I'm getting to hate the trip, but I know the Garcias so look forward to it. I'll probably bore you with shopping."

"That's okay." She probably would, but he planned to slip off and follow the Garcias and Mendez. From what he'd learned, there'd be plenty of agents around to hitch a ride with if he needed one. "Great then, it's settled. I'll be glad to help out with the driving if you want."

His decision to accompany her had been totally spontaneous. Smarter to follow her separately, but strange vibrations traveled up and down his spine—instincts that Mendez and Garcia suspected him—prickly sensations that warned him Susan could be in danger. Fierce protective feelings demanded he be with her.

"I don't know about you," he said, inching closer and lightly placing his palm on her shoulder, "but I could sure jump in a pool right about now."

She wasn't averse to the idea either.

Searing heat that always appeared wherever Ric touched her blazed through her blouse to her skin. Images of them together in the pool followed. Susan automatically fanned herself. "Sounds good to me, too."

She peaked under the brim of his hat into his imploring eyes. Whatever was bothering him earlier seemed to have blown over. "How 'bout we stop and pick up a basket of chicken on the way?"

Basket, he snickered to himself. Knowing Susan, it would probably end up stashed somewhere in her house. Maybe that's what the grubby thugs had enticed her with. A lifelong supply of baskets!

He'd gotten lucky!

It might not be a bikini, but Susan's bathing suit held other compensations—high cut legs and a low cut back. He hadn't been able to keep his eyes off her, especially her legs, the whole time they'd been eating. And something was bothering the lovely Miss Stewart. She'd been fidgety and jumpy throughout the meal as if she was uncomfortable and flustered about something, rarely making eye contact with him.

What are you hiding, Sunday School? His survival instincts told him he had to find out, but a sinking feeling in his stomach deterred him. He didn't want to be proven wrong about her. "You okay, Susan?"

"Yes, I'm fine." She didn't look at him.

Ric's hawk like eyes caught her shiver. "You're not cold, are you?" She couldn't be, not with the temperature in the high nineties.

"No, not cold. Something gave me the willies."

Damn, it didn't sound good. He decided he'd better check out some things. "You know much about Juan and Angelina Garcia?"

"The Garcias? Not really. He worked for my aunt about a year before I came. The house and yard had gotten too much for her to handle. I do know they have six children, and that he's a hard worker and dependable."

"Is he illegal?"

"No. I pay his social security. Why do you ask?"

"Don't know." He shrugged. Now *he* was having trouble meeting *her* gaze.

Curiosity covered her face. Damn, but he was getting rusty at this and unprofessional, especially around Susan. He let his eyes linger on her legs a while, admiring her firm calves and thighs. “Just had a hunch, and I’m glad I was wrong. Know anything about the other man?”

“Carlos Garcia? He always comes with them when we drive to Juarez. He’s a cousin, I think. He’s quiet. Now he’s someone who definitely gives me the willies.”

I’m with you there, Sunday School. I’m with you there. “Yeah, he did have a skuzzy look to him.”

“What’s with all the questions?” Her eyes clouded with confusion. “You think Carlos Garica’s an illegal alien?”

“Nah. Just my overactive imagination and too many spy novels.” He had no proof, but he strongly suspected Carlos Garcia, aka Hector Mendez, was the sonofabitch who’d killed Johnny. Ric leveled his gaze at Susan. “Guess with all the trips you take, you’ve had to put up with being checked at the border a time or two.”

“So far, I haven’t been stopped.” As if she found his questions strange, she angled her head and frowned.

“Lucky you. I was stopped once.”

“I’ve heard it can be a real hassle. Maybe they always pass us by because the Garcias’ usually bring some of their children with them, and we look harmless enough.”

And Hector Mendez counted on that, Ric thought.

“Sometimes they ask about my purchases and want to see them, but they never examine the whole car. I keep wondering when they will. I wouldn’t mind if the border patrol stopped all of us, all the time,” Susan remarked. “The thought of smuggling sickens me, especially drugs.”

Ric let out a lungful of air. Okay, so he was on the mark about Susan’s disgust for drugs. But if she wasn’t a criminal, then what the hell was behind her agitation? “Suse, what’s bothering you?” He knew damn well what was bothering him.

“I—” Her fingers fidgeted with her bathing suit strap. “I need to talk to you.”

As he looked into her worried eyes, Ric felt his stomach sink down like an elevator.

“I have sort of a confession to make.”

Aw, hell. He sensed he wasn’t going to like what he heard. *Blast it, cough it up.* This beating around the bush was driving his nuts. “Go ahead, Suse.”

“You see—” Susan looked down at her feet.

How could she possible explain this to him? She was still working up the courage to ask him to pose as her fiancé, and then when she looked at him, she was lost, especially when she let her gaze trail the dark hair swirling down his tanned chest to his swimsuit. His black swimming briefs hung low on his narrow hips and were little improvement over his skivvies.

She raised her head to find him staring at her. "I know this is going to sound silly, but well, I've kind of stuck my neck out over something. I mean you'd think I'd have more sense, more self esteem at my age. I just can't figure what came over me. Anyway, I have this high school classmate, Mary Ellen Hathaway, you know the kind who's so perfect she never gets a hangnail. Well, when she called about our reunion, it just slipped out that I was engaged."

"Engaged!" His head jerked up. Shock flitted across his face.

"Actually, I'm not. It was a lie." She shrugged her shoulders in a helpless gesture and let out a long sigh. "I never lie, and I don't know why I said it—probably because I never intended to attend the reunion. But before I could undo it, Mary Ellen told my mother, who immediately became ecstatic, and then before I could explain it to her, my sister and brother called with news of a big anniversary party in my parent's honor just days after the reunion, and one thing led to another, and there I was scheduled to fly to Pittsburgh with Shane."

"Who the hell is Shane?" Ten volumes higher than normal, Ric's voice ricocheted across the patio.

"Shane Orr is my imaginary fiancé."

"Your what?"

"Fiancé. I know it sounds foolish, but then I got to thinking why not go to the reunion? Why not get someone to pose as Shane? Why not make my mother happy for a few weeks? After all, as soon as it was over, I could easily kill him off since I'd imagined Shane was an undercover agent."

Ric sputtered and coughed. "Did you say undercover agent?" He watched Susan nod her head, but doubts remained. By God, maybe she was working for the opposition. Was she trying to get a rise out of him, discover if he was an agent? Her story was too incredible to be true. Ric studied her, thoughtfully rubbing his chin as if her bombshell made perfect sense to him. On second thought considering Sunday School, it did.

"Yes," Susan answered. "I imagined him as an undercover

agent. It's not that I couldn't get a man. I probably could, but I needed one in a hurry, and not just any man. Advertising in the newspapers would never have done."

"Newspapers?" Perplexed, he watched her twist her beverage glass round and round in her hands, nervously applying pressure to it. Certain it would crack under the strain, he removed the glass from her hands. "What was wrong with the newspaper?"

"All kinds of men could have answered."

"Answered what?" He was beginning to think Sunday School belonged in a padded room.

"My ad."

"For an undercover agent?"

"For my imaginary fiancé who was an undercover agent."

Ric swallowed audibly. No way she could know about him—could she? This wasn't some kind of test was it? Naw. Just a coincidence. A damned uncanny one. Unsettling seconds passed, and Susan shakily met his gaze, which he imagined was every bit as bewildered as he was.

"Ric, the reunion is three weeks away, and I was wondering ..." She paused and swallowed two deep breaths. "I know this is going to sound totally off the wall. I mean if you had been the one to ask me, I'd be as flabbergasted as you are. But anyway, here goes." She crossed her fingers. "I was wondering if you'd be willing to fly to Pittsburgh and pose as my fiancé."

Too stunned to speak, Ric sat there. He pressed his lips together to keep from smiling. He thought he'd heard everything until now.

"I'd pay your expenses."

Pay his expenses! Just exactly what was she proposing? "Let me see if I have this right. You want me to pose as your fiancé—three weeks from now you say?" His gaze left her face and drifted down her body to her legs, then back up to her face. *Lord help him, he was actually considering it.*

"Yes. I know it's short notice, but the minute I saw you I knew you'd be perfect for the part, only you were a stranger. I wanted to get to know you before I asked you."

"You mean to say that's what all our dates have been about? Getting to know me well enough to ask me to pose as your fiancé?"

"It started out that way, but—"

"But, what, Suse?" He sensed he had her on the ropes. She was ruffled and jumpy, but mostly adorable.

"Oh, Ric, I don't care whether you pose as Shane or not. It was a stupid, fairy tale fantasy, and it's not important. What I really care about is you. Us. And what I feel for you is more important than playing some silly old role. Just forget it."

And how am I supposed to do that?

Susan sighed, her long-lashed eyes focused on his shoulder. "I don't want to spoil what we have, or at least what I think we have."

"And what's that, Suse?"

Susan grew tongue-tied. There it was—the big question. She knew the answer, but if she told him, would he turn and run—run from commitment? His tone almost defeated her. Almost. But she was determined. She crossed her fingers and looked him in the eye for several long seconds. "It started out that I was just going to ask you to pretend to be my fiancé, and somewhere along the way I found myself falling, found myself in over my head." She rose from her chair. "This wasn't such a good idea."

She walked away, turning her back to him. As she clutched her arms across her chest and stared down at the blue water in the pool, she fought hard against the insecurity building in her. Seconds later she sensed him behind her, felt his breath on her ear. His arms surrounded her, and he pulled her back against his body.

"I'm falling in love with you, too, Suse."

"Wh-at?" Her voice cracked.

"Yeah. It happened so fast it spooked me."

She spun around in his arms and looked up at him. "I kept telling myself it was too quick, but I couldn't fight it, though I guess at my age putting a timetable on things is foolish. Oh, Ric, forget what I said. I'll go and face the music myself. It's what I deserve. 'Bout time I was responsible for my actions," she rambled on, then paused, tapping a forefinger against her lips. "Though having Shane killed may not be such a bad option. I know, I know," she argued with herself, "more lies, but better that than asking you to do anything so childish and dishonest."

Ric flinched. He still couldn't be honest with her, but he was utterly convinced she had nothing to with the drug ring. He almost laughed out loud when he remembered how he'd suspected her, and all the time she'd been sizing him up for some make-believe character she'd dreamed up. A small chamber of his brain continued to caution him to be wary, but the mist in those shimmering eyes of hers told him otherwise.

And what's more she was blushing and fanning herself—dead give-aways she was telling the truth.

Damn, how he wished he could tell her the real reason he'd come to town. Ric cocked his head, quickly processing what lay ahead. His assignment should be concluded next Sunday, and when it was over, he planned to explain to the authorities how Susan had been used without her knowledge. After that his calendar was clear. There'd be nothing more to hold him here. Except Sunday School. The idea of spending more time with her appealed to him. Of course, once she found out he was an agent, had used her and had been unable to prevent her arrest, it could turn out to be the shortest make-believe engagement on record.

"I'll go, Suse. I'll do it." Jeeze, he must be bonkers. "Who knows, the Pirates might be in town, and I could catch a game," he teased.

"You'll go? To Pittsburgh? Oh, Ric you mean it?"

"Yeah, I do." Some life he'd had. No home, no roots, no one to care about. No one to care about him. This woman, whom he didn't want out of his life, wasn't making him do a damn thing he didn't want to do. He tightened his arms around her waist. She was soft and warm in the circle of his arms, and a wayward tear slithered down her cheek. He bent his head and captured the solitary tear with his lips.

"Hey, Suse."

"Mmm?"

He placed his index finger under her chin. "Remember how during our conversations about you being engaged you got uptight. Was this the reason?"

"Yes. Even though I knew it was totally irrational, I kept wondering if you knew."

Ric breathed a sigh of relief. The mystery was solved. Damn glad it didn't have to do with her ex boyfriend, he could only hope that once they rounded up the Garcias the mystery of her involvement would be solved as easily. He cupped her face and brushed his lips over her mouth. "How about a swim?"

"Now?"

"This very second." With his arms wrapped around her, he edged them over to the pool. He'd been itching to get her into the water from the moment he'd seen her swimsuit. While she linked her hands behind his neck, Ric yelled, "Geronimo," and cannonballed their joined bodies into the pool.

They surfaced, and Susan clung to Ric as they both treaded water until they could stand. Her nipples tingled with pleasure from the pressure of his chest, and his hands sliding over her hips caused her pulse to quicken. His mouth found hers, his firm lips parting her own, and she probed his mouth with her tongue, ending the kiss when she heard vibrating groans deep in his throat.

Ric inched away from her, still holding her. His fingers glided upwards and tightened around her shoulders. "I've been wanting to get you wet and in my arms all night."

She looked up at his gray eyes that were shining with intensity. It was dark now. Both the pool and patio lights illuminated his face, and his bone-melting smile penetrated her very being.

"Dance with me." His voice was low and sexy as she curled in closer to him, her legs touching his.

"Here?"

"Here," he huskily repeated as his thumb grazed her collarbone.

"What about music?"

"You mean you don't hear it?"

Taken with his teasing tone, Susan slanted a glance up at his face. "All I hear is an Indian War Chant."

"Naw, that's my heart, booming to the beat." He wrapped his arms around her waist again and two-stepped her through the water, humming the tune of 'When the Saints Come Marching In,' into her ear and occasionally filling in the lyrics when he knew them.

"That's not what I'd call romantic." She rubbed her nose against his, then laced her hands behind his neck.

"The lady wants romance. How 'bout "The stars at night are—"

"Deep in the heart of Texas," she said, singing with him as he twirled her in the water. "Keep trying, Ramsey."

"I intend to." He dipped his head and feathered butterfly kisses on her eyelids.

"This is New Mexico, not Texas."

"Don't know any New Mexico love songs and besides you're messing around with a good ole Texas boy."

Finally, he started to croon the poignant ballad Elvis Presley had made so popular, the one they'd danced to at Judd's, and Susan's breath caught in her throat. She felt him rest his chin on her forehead, and as she swayed in his arms desire invaded every corner of her body. Dancing with him to that tune had nearly decimated her, but now with his wet skin bonding to hers, the torment was unbearable. She shuddered.

"Cold?" he asked, absorbing the quivers of her body. This was the second time tonight she'd done that.

"Only on the outside."

"Know what you mean." Stroking his hands up and down her back, Ric guided her in slow swaying dance steps. "You're the singer, Suse—"

"Me?"

"Yeah, in the choir."

"How'd you know?" She wedged a hand between them, then pressed both her palms flat against his solid chest. His sleek, wet, solid chest. "Did I tell you?"

"Must have. Sing us some dance music."

She couldn't remember whether she'd told him she sang in the choir or not. At this point she couldn't remember much of anything, not with his hard thighs pressed against hers. Her repertoire wasn't all that extensive. A hymn was out of the question and after Ric's husky rendition of 'Love Me Tender', so was a steamy torch song. She searched her mind for a song she knew the words to, settling on one she'd sung last summer when she'd been recruited to sing in the church production of hit show tunes. "How 'bout Memory from *CATS*?"

"Go for it, Suse. Sing me a love song."

Susan took a steadying breath and began to sing. At least she thought she was singing. The ferocious beat of her heart drowned out the lyrics for her. Gamely, she rallied and heard her voice tremulously recite the words in the song that told of being left alone with nothing but memories of a golden day in the sun. *Those were words to choke on.* She'd had a number of special days with Ric and despite what he'd said, there were no guarantees he'd hang around Las Cruces. The very thought of him saying good bye any time soon left a lump in her throat. She continued to sing, coming to the final words of the song, words that promised hope of a new day dawning.

Was there a future for them beyond the Shane Orr masquerade?

As if he could read her thoughts, he drew her tighter against him and began to whistle in accompaniment. She finished the song and their wet bodies stood breathlessly still, toe to toe, neck to neck, skin to skin.

"I want you," Ric murmured into her ear.

Susan squeezed her eyes shut. "I want you, too, but ... "

He traced her trembling lips with his finger. "But you take making love very seriously. So do I."

"Once, long ago, when I was young, young and naïve, I made a stupid mistake." She'd paid for her foolishness and vowed to repent. "I abandoned my faith, the way of life I'd chosen for myself. And—"

"And you don't sleep around."

"Not even with men I care very much about." Her eyes fluttered open.

"And not with a guy you've only known a few weeks."

Moved by his understanding, she trembled when his fingers trailed to the hollow of her neck. A hot fiery ache leaped inside her. With Ric, her will power grew fragile, her resolve nearly stripped away. He had only to touch her and it was like being fried under the hot New Mexico sun. "That's not to say I'm not tempted, that desire doesn't flare up."

"I know, Suse. This guy from your past. Do you still have feelings for him?"

"Jerry? If you're asking do I love him, no. But I guess I do feel sorry for him."

"Good. I don't want you getting the wrong idea about me. I'm in for the long haul. I'm committed, want to see how we feel about each other a couple of months from now. Have to admit my knees are a little shaky. I lack a lot experience in this."

"You?"

"Yeah. From what you've said, you're not sexually active, but you've given your heart away a time or two. I never have. It's always been no strings for me. But not this time. I'm in love and there's more to love than sex."

She believed him. She trusted him. She loved him. "Oh Ric."

"And baby, the way we burn each other up, sex between us is one thing I'm not worried about. There are ways, you know—to give each other pleasure. "

His hands moved over her hips. “Show me,” she whispered.

He led her from the pool and toweled her dry, his palms torturously lingering on her calves and thighs. Susan’s world spun with anticipation. He swept her into his arms and carried her to the bedroom, the entire time his sultry gaze never leaving hers. As he strode to the bed, Susan glimpsed his skivvies hanging like a trophy from the bedpost and stiffened.

Terrific!

“What is it, Suse?” He followed the direction of her gaze and threw back his head and chuckled. “Kinda like the way you’ve decorated. Suppose I donate the pair I wore tonight and you can hang it on another post.”

“What color?”

“Red.”

Red was good, matched her face if her burning cheeks were any indication of the color of her skin this very minute.

“And I wouldn’t mind contributing some more.”

“Promises, promises.”

“I’ll show you promises.” His eyes danced with deviltry.

He let her body slide down the hard length of his, fusing his hips to hers until her feet landed on the floor. He lowered his head and gently slid his lips over hers, barely touching them. Inching downward, he glided his tongue to the hollow of her neck and down to the vee between her breasts. A strange wildness ran through her as his knuckles brushed over the underside of her breasts.

“You’re beautiful,” he whispered, “and I promise to make this as beautiful for you as I can.”

Susan could barely whisper a response. The slow journey of his heated gaze from her toes up to her eyes pulled the breath from her.

He stretched out beside her on the bed and drew her into his arms. “Your skin is warm.”

“I know,” she murmured through her very parched throat. As Ric pushed the top of her swimsuit aside and lowered his mouth to the tip of her breast, the need building inside her intensified. He took the mound into his mouth, and when she could stand it no longer, she trembled under his sensuous touch. As if worshipping her body, his hands roved everywhere and a symphony of agony rumbled through her.

“Oh, Ric.” She tangled her fingers through his hair.

A hunger that had burned inside man since God had given him Eve blazed through Ric as he fought for control. He wanted to remove her swimsuit, but he knew if he did he'd be lost. He wanted her, wanted her long slender legs wrapped around him, wanted to be lost in her honey warmth. But he wanted more from her and with her—a lifetime he hoped.

And he admired her value system, admired her grit as she was driven to the edge of desire every bit as much as he, yet refused to compromise her principles. She'd be a woman he could always trust. A strong woman who wouldn't bend when life sent troubles hurtling their way. His mother would approve of her even though Susan wasn't Catholic. His former partner would have too. Yeah, Johnny would have liked her. Sunday School was a gift he damn well hadn't earned, and just the thought of losing her cut him to the heart. He wouldn't do anything to risk it.

If she could be strong, so could he.

He watched her body toss with frenzy when he slid his fingers past her thighs and inside her bathing suit. Soft noises murmuring in her throat drove him wild. Temptation gnawed at his stomach, then crept down to his loins. Her skin was hot. His hotter. Heat and dampness enveloped them both. He drew on his skills, caressing her trembling thighs with his fingertips, teasing her, till Sunday School in one blazing breathless moment gasped his name and crested into what he judged to be a hell of a charismatic experience. Aching to possess her, to ride the tidal wave of passion surging through her, Ric let loose a string of silent obscenities and clamped down on his inner pain.

Her incendiary response tested his will power. She was his for the asking, but he'd made her a promise. He knew if they went any further her conscience would leave her no peace, not to mention the hell his own would put him through. For now the pleasure he'd unselfishly given her would have to be enough. He rolled to the side keeping one arm around her shoulders. She cuddled her back into him, their legs tangling together.

"That was beautiful, Suse. You're beautiful."

"It's never been so—"

"So explosive," he finished for her. Kissing the nape of her neck, he rolled away.

"Don't go." She lifted her hand to his muscled shoulder, running the backs of her fingers across his skin.

"I'm not going far, not when you touch me like that."

She playfully traced his scar then kissed it. "This must have hurt," she said, dragging the tips of her fingers over it, wondering how violent his past had been, speculating where the future would take him, and wishing with all her might that the love that flowed between them tonight could last forever.

"Yeah." A hooded look sheathed his eyes. "Got it a long time ago."

"The service again?"

"Yeah." His eyes gazed at her hungrily. Rising from the bed, he sauntered to where his jeans lay and rummaged through the pocket. Her gaze followed him and eagerly focused on his bronzed body when he returned moments later.

"I bought this earlier today—a token of how I feel." He reached for her right hand, his large one swallowing hers, and tried the ring on two of her fingers before sliding it over her middle one.

She gazed down at the turquoise ring. "It's gorgeous." She hugged and kissed him. "How did you know—"

"I watched you drooling over it at the festival. Guess since I'm your unofficial fiancé, this is your unofficial engagement ring."

"I love you," she tremulously whispered.

"Love you, too, and Suse..."

"Mmm." His guarded look puzzled her, a look reminiscent of the one she'd seen the first time they'd kissed up on the mountain. Did he have misgiving about their arrangement? Well she did, too. She'd live out the reunion fantasy, but she'd level with her parents.

"I—uh—" he stammered. "Whatever might happen, trust me. Now *Besa el maestro, rapido.*"

"*Rapido*?"

"*Sí!*"

As Susan brushed her lips across the column of his throat, she felt his pulse skitter beneath her mouth. Wanting to stay warm and safe like this forever, she sensed Ric was troubled about something. Something he wasn't ready to share, yet he'd said he loved her. Her imaginary fiancé actually loved her.

Even more incredible, the bet had taken on a life of its own.

Chapter Eleven

"So far, so good," Ric muttered the following Sunday as he and a fellow agent drove through the streets of Juarez. They were tailing Juan Garcia and Hector Mendez who were headed back to the appointed rendezvous with Susan.

Thinking back, Ric recounted the day. The ride down to Juarez had been tense but uneventful. Angelina Garcia and the Garcia children had been noticeably absent when he and Susan had picked up Juan and Hector. Though Ric had thought that odd, he'd shrugged it off. The telling glare in Hector Mendez' eyes had been far from friendly. During the entire trip to Juarez, Ric had felt a hole smoldering in the back of his head.

Once or twice when he'd glanced in the right outside mirror, he'd seen a late model brown Chevrolet following them. He remembered there'd been a brown Chevy tailing them the day he and Susan had driven his bike up into the Organ Mountains. Maybe these thugs had been watching Susan more carefully than he realized and noticed him with her. That could explain the inquiries into his past. He'd kept a watchful eye on the car, but knowing that there were dozens of Agency cars on their tail, not to mention others already stationed across the border, Ric hadn't been concerned.

Just as always, Susan had turned over her station wagon to the two men after she'd driven into the heart of the city. Ric had stayed with her, not wanting to leave her alone with Garcia's so-called relatives until he was assured that she was under heavy surveillance. Then he had excused himself, telling her shopping wasn't his bag and he'd sit on a bench or do some exploring. Instead, he'd walked around the corner and hopped into a car of a fellow agent who'd been in radio contact with other agents following Garcia and Mendez.

For the past three hours he and numerous agents in other cars, had waited patiently outside a house with an attached garage. No need to speculate that Garcia and Mendez were busy secreting drugs into Susan's station wagon. Five minutes ago the wagon had emerged from the garage. When they crossed back into the states, the trap would spring shut on the two men. The case would be closed, Johnny Montoya's killer caught, and Ric could get on with his life. He only hoped Sunday School would understand when the agents swarmed the car. If everything went as well as it had been going, he should be able to shield her from any suspicion.

As they traversed the congested streets of Juarez, the car in front of them commanded Ric's attention. "Slow down and turn here," he cautioned the agent behind the wheel. "I want to beat them to the rendezvous and this is a short cut."

Ric breathed a sigh of relief as the driver of his car pulled up at the shopping center where he was supposed to meet Susan. He'd made it back before Mendez and Garcia. As he left the car, his gaze anxiously shot to Susan. He took a step in her direction and halted. She was chatting away with two young American women.

Two attractive women, and all too familiar.

He'd seen them before. While he continued to study them, he noticed that Susan's Mexican escorts still hovered around her, no doubt waiting for Garcia to reappear. They were in for a surprise. As soon as he and Susan, along with Garcia and Mendez, drove off in Susan's station wagon, Mexican agents would surround and arrest them.

Edgy and knowing why, Ric patted the gun tucked inside the waist of his jeans. With a sense of curiosity and caution, he approached Susan. He didn't like the unexpected appearance of these women.

"Ric," Susan called out. "Perfect timing. Mr. Garcia should be here any minute."

Any second, Ric silently amended, sneaking a look at his watch. "I see you made some purchases," he remarked, standing in front of her. "Don't tell me, baskets."

"One of the packages is. Oh, these are my friends from Las Cruces, Pam and Robin. They told me they might follow us into Juarez today to shop." Susan paused. The real reason they'd come was because they'd wanted an excuse to meet him, but she wasn't going to tell him that.

"Friends?" Ric's brow wrinkled. "Oh, yeah. Think I saw you two at Judd's with Susan."

"Nice to meet you." Pam shifted her packages and extended her hand.

"Susan told us that you agreed to help her out," Robin said, shaking his hand also.

"What?" Ric stared blankly at them, not sure he understood. From the corner of his eye he saw Garcia and Mendez get out of Susan's station wagon and walk toward them. "Help her out?" he asked, his attention on Mendez and not on what he was saying.

"You know," Robin said, "about posing as Shane Orr, the undercover agent."

"Agent!" Hector Mendez roared as he joined them. "Did she say undercover agent?"

Ric squeezed his eyes shut and muttered a curse. *Damned interfering females!*

"No," Susan said, spinning on her heels to face Juan Garcia's cousin. "He's not—"

"Shut up, Senorita Stewart." Hector placed a gun at Ric's ribs and nodded to the other men hovering around. "Take care of those two women," he yelled to his cohorts, then turned to Juan Garcia. "Help me get these two into the station wagon."

A prickling sensation rushed up Susan's spine. "But—"

"I said shut up, Senorita, or I'll put a bullet through this man's ribs," Hector sharply commanded, hostility pulling his face into ugly lines.

She froze. The low chill of his voice left little doubt that he meant what he said. Why did Carlos Garcia have a gun poked in Ric's back? Ric slammed his body against Carlos' arm, but Carlos brutally kicked Ric in the back of his knee, forcing him to stumble. She heard the pistol click and drew in a ragged breath. "No," she moaned.

"And you, Ramsey, don't try any heroics. After I shoot you, I'll shoot the woman." He reached under Ric's blue chambray shirt and tossed a gun to the ground.

Susan's eyes opened wide as frisbees. Ric with a gun? Her gaze sought Ric's. Rage blazed in his dark eyes as he met her frightened ones. The cords in his neck tightened, and she backed away, all set to run, but Juan Garcia grabbed her wrist and yanked her to her station wagon. As she heard Pam and Robin scream, Juan rudely shoved her into the back seat and climbed in after her.

Pushing Ric in front of him, Hector walked around to the driver's side and opened the door. "You, into the front," he ordered Ric, the gun still riveted on Ric. As Hector slid behind the wheel, he tossed some rope back to Juan. "Tie the Senorita's hands and then Senor Ramsey's or whoever he is."

"Please," Susan pleaded, gazing into the cold, black eyes of the man who held the gun. "Why are you doing this? It's all a mistake, a dreadful mistake. Ric isn't an agent. Mr. Garcia, tell your cousin that it was just make-believe, a foolish joke."

"I'm not laughing, Senorita," Hector growled before Juan could speak, "nor am I taking any chances."

Susan twisted away and lunged for the door, but as Juan pulled her back, she saw Carlos Garcia pistol whip Ric in the head. A strangled scream made its way through her vocal chords. "Don't, don't—oh, Ric."

"If you don't want your friend to bleed all over your car, sit still, Senorita," Hector warned her.

"Good, Lord, he's bleeding already!" Terror flashed before her eyes. "Ric! Ric! Are you all right?" She tried to lean forward to get a better look at him, but Juan finished tying her hands and pushed her back.

"Let her go," Ric spit out, succinctly adding a sting of epithets.

"He's right, Hector, let Senorita Stewart go," Juan chimed in.

"Hector?" Susan exclaimed. "I thought your name was—"

Susan stopped in mid-sentence, watching in helpless horror as Hector chose that moment to deliver another blow to Ric's skull, knocking him unconscious. He raised his gun to Ric's head as Juan leaned over the seat to tie Ric's hands.

"Lady, if you don't shut that mouth of yours, your boyfriend will pay for it." Hector narrowed his gaze, focusing it on Juan. "You shut up, too. I haven't figured out what we're going to do yet."

"She may be right. The guy might not be an agent," Juan interceded.

"It's too late to bother whether he is or he isn't. He smells like one to me."

"Why should it matter whether Ric's an agent?" Susan piped up. Hector turned and glared at her. "Unless... " Her jaw dropped. Dawning came to her, and she slumped down in her seat. Fear washed over her, and she wasn't sure which rattled more, her heart or her teeth.

Hector reached across to the back seat and stuffed a handkerchief into Juan's hand. "Put a muzzle on the bitch, will 'ya? I'm tired of telling her to keep quiet." Hector put the station wagon in gear and scanned the area. "With those two

American women screaming like coyotes, they're sure to attract the police. Our best bet is to hope we can cross the border before the police start looking for us," he said to Juan as he turned the key in the ignition and gunned the motor.

Susan frantically pushed her tongue against the gag, then looked at Ric's bleeding head. The sight made her skin crawl. This was a nightmare. These men were deranged. She couldn't believe that Juan Garcia would do this to her. What was he involved in? Drugs? Had Juan and his cousin been using her all this time to smuggle drugs into the country? How could he have conned her so? Feeling gullible, she hung her head. Then anger took root, and she nudged her chin upward, heaving a strangled sigh through her gag.

Poor, Ric, she thought, her gaze drifting to his head.

It was her fault.

All her fault that he'd become entangled in this mess and was now bleeding to death on her front seat. If he hadn't accompanied her today, none of this would have happened. Worse still, she could lay everything at her doorstep. Ric's life was threatened because she'd childishly invented Shane Orr and foolishly asked Ric to pretend to be an undercover agent. And if that wasn't enough, she'd shared her news with Pam and Robin. Why, of all the times she'd come to Juarez, did they have to follow her today? Now these goons thought he was an agent.

Susan flinched, immediately regretting her exasperation with her friends. The last image she'd had of them was being surrounded by a menacing phalanx of men, and as Hector had driven away she'd heard them screaming. Though her friends had invited themselves into the predicament, she felt responsible for them, too. At the moment she had enough guilt in her to take responsibility for the ills of the world.

The late afternoon sun slanted in through the window by Juan Garcia. It was a gorgeous day, a Sunday to remember. A day when happy, ordinary things were going on in many people's lives, people who at this very moment were blithely riding by, totally unaware of what was happening to her and Ric. Suddenly, she wanted to know the date. If this was her last day on earth, it seemed important to know the date that would be chiseled on her gravestone. It was late June, nearly July, it was—June 29th.

Don't think about it, she told herself. Think about the past few days and how alive Ric has made you feel, but her pep talk did little good. After a brief prayer, Susan tested the rope, twisting her wrists back and forth. Much to her surprise, she discovered that Juan hadn't tied them tightly. Perhaps she could work herself free. Hope bubbled inside of her.

Okay, Susan, your prayer has been answered. This is no time to panic. You have a job to do. You got Ric into this mess, and you'll damn well have to get him out of it. If she could just get free, she could reach her purse and ...

And grab the umbrella, then knock Hector senseless.

Holy Hannah, where had that brainstorm come from? Her gaze was drawn to her purse and the hot pink umbrella inside it. It was as if the umbrella was trying to tell her something. She didn't know what, but the idea of using it definitely energized her.

Quietly, she set to work on the ropes again.

Regaining consciousness, Ric tasted the blood oozing down from his temple to his lips. He shook his head. Jeeze, what a mess! He gritted his teeth against the buzz rumbling in his head. Agents had surrounded them, but everyone had been frozen in place not wanting to jeopardize his or Susan's life. This wouldn't have happened if it hadn't been for those women. He'd had a premonition that they spelled trouble. And now he'd put Susan's life in danger. That was why he'd opted to accompany her in the first place—in case Mendez tried to use her as a hostage when the border guards challenged them and asked them all to step from the car.

Freaking, inept idiot, he'd bungled this one badly. Another sign that he'd been right to retire, but not at all comforting under the circumstances. His jaw ticked. He dare not push this creep too far, or he'd hurt Susan. Susan. Sunday School and those long silky legs of hers. And so typical, she'd worn one of those long skirts of hers and white tennis shoes. She must have run out of colors. One thing for sure, she'd run out of luck.

He glanced down at his bound hands. Running his hands over her legs had been a taste of heaven—a taste he wondered if he'd ever sample again. Would they both live to climb that mountain again?

If you keep your head about you, you both will, Buddy.

He looked out the window, noticing they were nearing the border. Mendez had to know the guards would be ready for him. Did he intend to barrel his way through? If he did, the guards were bound to shoot out the tires.

And then what?

Hostage time with Susan the prime candidate.

He had to get her out of the car. Something told him Garcia wasn't a hardened criminal. Something he'd heard in the man's voice revealed a concern for Susan. God, he hoped he had Garcia pegged right.

Ric angled his head to the side, letting his gaze slide to Mendez while glimpsing into the back seat. Damn, they'd gagged Susan. He shifted his gaze to Garcia. The man stared back at him. Looking Garcia dead in the eye, Ric flicked his gaze toward Susan and then back to Garcia. Beads of perspiration dotted Garcia's forehead as he nodded. Ric let out a sigh. He'd guessed right. The man had no taste for violence. Garcia would help him save Sunday School.

Ric faced forward. Cars were lined up ahead of them. Mendez would have to bring the wagon to a halt, and when he did, Ric would distract him. Then Garcia could help push Susan out of the car. That's all he wanted. Susan out of this car.

Mindful of Susan's faith, he called on the Lord to spare her, then before attempting to communicate with her, Ric checked Mendez. Mendez seemed aware that he'd regained consciousness, but unconcerned, the thug kept his eyes glassily trained on the road ahead. This time Ric turned so he could face Susan, who sat directly behind him. The lump in his throat grew larger.

Aw, Sunday School.

Her eyes were like two luminescent moons with large dewy tears pooled in them. He ached to blurt out the truth about himself. If he didn't make it, she might always suspect he'd used her, not believe he loved her. Slowly, she met his gaze. He saw her gulp for air as she forgot to breathe through her nose and struggled with her gag. He clenched his bound wrists, wishing he could tear the gag from her lips and pound his fists into Mendez's slimy face.

He exchanged the same eye gestures with Susan as he had with Garcia, tipping his head ever so slightly in the direction of her door, waiting until he saw understanding glisten through her tears. She half closed her eyes in response and immediately opened them, trust in him evident in her gaze. There was an earthy sensuality to her simple gesture and despite the dire situation, Ric felt a tug at his heartstrings along with a powerful pull in his loins.

With nothing but his eyes he sent a thousand messages to her. Profound emotions vibrated through him, and they stared at each other, memorizing each others face. Her eyes mirrored his feelings, and he was loathe to let go of her gaze, but sensing his time to act was limited, he winked at her and mouthed the words, 'I love you'.

This is it.

Good bye, Sunday School. I hope we both make it.

A second later he turned and faced the windshield. Slamming his left foot onto the brake and using his head as a spear, he rammed his body into Mendez.

Everything happened simultaneously or so it seemed to Susan. The station wagon came to a screeching halt, sending Juan Garcia and her crashing forward against the front seat, since neither of them were wearing seat belts. She tasted the metallic drops of her blood on her tongue as the gag slipped from her mouth. On another level she was remotely aware that Ric and the man in the front seat were struggling. The sight of a gun whipped across her vision.

"No, no," she shouted, thrusting her bound hands into her purse. As if knowing what was expected of it, the hot pink umbrella jumped into her hands. She raised the weapon and smashed it down in a frantic karate chop onto the man's extended arm. A bullet exploded like a deafening roar, and Susan screamed, petrified Ric had been shot.

A second later Juan Garcia pushed her down on the seat, unlocked her door, shoved her out onto the street, and tumbled out on top of her. "No, no, no," she railed. "Ric." She mustn't leave Ric.

Susan hit the pavement without being able to protect herself. Her arms and face stung from the abrasions. By the time she managed to shimmy and wiggle out from under Juan Garcia's body, scores of men surrounded her, their guns drawn and pointed at both of them. Her ropes had loosened and fallen from her wrists, and as she tried to sit up, she heard the sound of tires digging into the roadway. She watched in horror as her station wagon spun around and raced in the opposite direction. Ric was in the car, and he might be wounded.

When a man holding a rifle took aim at the fleeing wagon, she froze. “No,” she yelled, a fierce protection for Ric’s welfare showering over her. Every muscle in her body tensed, yet somehow she found the power to rise to her feet and charge into the rifleman’s body. “Don’t shoot,” she pleaded, knocking him onto his butt.

Hands grabbed and held her.

“She must be part of the gang. Get her off me,” the rifleman ordered. He stood and took aim again. “Too many people and cars in the way,” he muttered.

Someone slapped handcuffs around her wrists, and frustrated tears filled her eyes. “What are you doing? I’m not a criminal. You have to stop that station wagon.”

“We’re trying to, Ma’am.”

She heard the crash. Everyone heard it. There were too many people in her line of vision for her to see, but she noticed the shocked expressions on their faces. “What happened? Tell me what happened,” she urged as tears streamed down her face.

“The station wagon spun out of control and fell into the Rio Grande,” someone answered.

“Oh, please God, no.” Then something snapped inside her. “You’ve killed him, you’ve killed, you’ve killed him,” she raged in incoherent gasps.

Spots flashed before her eyes. This couldn’t be happening. Hadn’t happened. Her mouth grew dry, her stomach queasy. A fuzziness settled over her eyes. It was more than she could bear. Susan fell to her knees, foul-tasting bile creeping up her throat. A moment later she fainted.

Chapter Twelve

Concentrate, Susan.

Smile.

Nod.

She'd been walking around the banquet room, table-hopping, visiting old classmates for the past thirty minutes, but her heart hadn't been in it. The smile on her face was stiff and artificial. She shouldn't have come. Even the excitement of seeing old friends couldn't chase the blues away.

Ric Ramsey.

Always it was Ric—thoughts of him dragging her down into the doldrums.

Carrying her champagne glass with her, Susan walked over to the circle of people gathered around Mary Ellen Hathaway. Just as she'd predicted, Mary Ellen was holding court. The moment she joined the group Mary Ellen pounced on her, inquiring after her fiancé. Susan looked upon it as part of her penance to deal with Mary Ellen.

"Shane couldn't come. He's had an accident," Susan point-blankly explained, fingering her turquoise ring.

"Really?" Mary Ellen's voice dripped with disbelief and sarcasm.

"He was injured in the line of duty," Susan emphasized.

In her mind there was a symbiotic relationship between Ric and Shane, and as long as Ric was alive, she couldn't find it in her heart to kill Shane off. Ric might not be an agent, but he did exist and he had been injured. Severely. And she wished to heaven she knew where and how he was.

"What a shame," Mary Ellen said, her voice reeking with false sympathy. "We'd been so looking forward to meeting him."

Susan was grateful when someone else caught Mary Ellen's attention. She tried to chat with other classmates but had difficulty hearing what they said. She was part of the conversation, and yet she wasn't. Mechanically, she nodded her head, made appropriate comments now and then, and listened to the tape of songs that had been popular during their high school years play in the background.

But memories pressed in.

Memories of a tall Texan. She'd dreamed about him being here even before she'd met him, dreamt about them dancing at the reunion. As always, his smile would warm her. He'd hold out his hand, wrapping it around hers. Tingles would travel up her arm. He'd kiss the back of her hand and curl her into his arms. Romantic music would play. Lights would sparkle and highlight his deep-set eyes. She'd snuggle into his embrace like she belonged, and they'd glide across the dance floor. Suspended. Floating. The back of his knuckle would graze her cheek, and he'd pull her to his chest, pressing her to him. It would be glorious and alive. They'd be the center of attention, dancing as they had in the pool.

She'd lift her face and...

He'd lower his, lower and lower, his fingers sliding up to the base of her throat and...

His mouth would lay claim to hers. Rapid-fire sweetness would burst through her and then ...

Susan flinched. Someone had asked her a question. "Las Cruces," she answered, wiping a tear from her eye and walking to the shadowy edge of the banquet hall.

She missed Ric. Where was he? What had happened to him? How badly was he hurt? Why wouldn't anyone tell her? She felt as if she'd been given a run-around. And if that wasn't enough gloom and doom, she'd lost her umbrella. Must have happened when she'd changed planes in Dallas. Her loss spelled someone's gain.

The umbrella was magic. She was convinced of it. To this day, she'd swear it had communicated to her moments before she'd used it on Hector Mendez.

Susan scanned the room. As turnouts go, it was a good one. There'd been close to two hundred students in her class, and easily half of them were here tonight, along with a collection of spouses, escorts, and friends, all jammed into the hotel banquet room. While everyone around her continued to talk, Susan gradually became aware of a hush spreading across the room. Heads turned, including Mary Ellen's, in the direction of the entrance.

Obviously someone important had arrived. The sea of people between her and the entrance parted. From the corner of her eye she saw someone slowly making his way to where she stood. She turned.

Ric!

My God, it was Ric! Her bottom lip trembled, and for a moment every heartbeat in her body shut down.

It couldn't be!

For the past two weeks she'd been trying to learn the extent of his injures and where he was. This had to be someone who looked like him. It had to be. It was an optical illusion. It was—

Ric.

Oh yes, it was Ric, and he was on crutches. Butterflies traveled from her stomach and collected in her throat. Was he all right? Unable to move, she heard voices around her, saw him walking towards her in slow motion, but she couldn't move.

She stood there absorbing every inch of him. A blur of happy tears welled in her eyes, and she bit her lip. He looked delicious, like an icy sherbet, clad in blue trousers, a nubby white jacket, with an electric blue shirt and yellow tie. Every bit as ruggedly handsome in this outfit as he'd been in jeans and a T-shirt, his presence filled the room. Her gaze dropped to his legs. He wore one shoe, his other foot covered with a sock and wrapped in a cast.

A mere twenty feet from her now. He stopped, their gazes met, his gray one holding hers, refusing to let her look away. While they searched one another's eyes, two eons passed. Maybe three?

"Ric." The words tore from deep in her throat, and breathless and flustered at last, she broke free from the invisible bonds that had held her in place. She ran to him and his arms, crutches extended, opened to welcome her. "Ric, it's really you."

"You mean Shane, don't you, Suse," he whispered, giving her a crooked grin.

"What?" Lovingly, she scanned his face, noticing a few cuts and bruises. "Oh, Shane, yes of course" She skimmed her fingertip over one of his bruises. "Are you all—"

"Later, Suse, later. First things first."

His arms spanned both his crutches and her waist, crisscrossing behind her back and drawing her into his thighs. Held firm, crushed to his lean, muscular body, she felt the solid barrier of his cast. As she melted into him, Ric slanted his mouth across hers. His lips were warm and firm, instantly branding her mouth and creating fluttering sensations inside of her. She flattened her palms over the lapels of his jacket, reveling at the feel of his solid chest, and delighted to be in his arms after all the anguished hours she'd spent worrying about him.

The kiss was over far too soon to suit her and was no where near as intimate and satisfying as their kisses usually were. It left her yearning for more. As Ric lifted his head, she heard the twittering comments from the crowd and sensed he'd broken it off to spare her embarrassment. He eased her to his side, placing his hands back on his crutches.

"Ric was my cover name," he explained to those gathered around him. A wry smile tugged at his mouth. "She gets confused sometimes."

She gave him a dirty look. "You came, you're actually here," she mumbled, still incredulous that he was standing next to her.

"I promised I'd come."

The softly spoken words turned her veins to putty, and she choked with emotion. Overcome with the need to touch him, Susan slipped her trembling arm through his. "Are you all right? Where did they take you?"

"Classified." He winked to those nearby, then lifted a hand to finger a lock of her hair.

"Oh, of course," Susan answered, pleased at how readily he fell into his role. "It's just that when I couldn't reach you and didn't know the extent of your injuries, I was so worried, the car crash, you know," she rambled incoherently.

Their conversation was inane, far too public, and not at all what she really wanted to say to him. Her gaze flickered over him again. Were there other cuts to match the jagged scar low on his back? "How are you, *Shane*," she asked, finding it difficult to keep up the charade. She wouldn't be satisfied until she could explore his muscular body and discover for herself how extensive his injuries were.

"I'm fine. I missed you," he whispered into her ear.

"Me, too."

"Car crash?" Mary Ellen's voice stridently intruded as she and others formed a circle around Susan and Ric.

"I was on a case," Ric swiftly replied, his gaze slicing into Mary Ellen. "The car I was in spun out of control and down an embankment."

"More like a ravine," Susan clarified, her eyes misting with tears at the memory.

Mary Ellen's gaze narrowed to an accessing frown as she stared at the man next to Susan. "So you're—"

"Shane," Ric broke into her words, propping himself on one crutch and extending his hand. "Shane Orr, Susan's fiancé."

For the past two hours, throughout dinner, throughout the introductions, throughout the acknowledgments, speeches, and awards, Susan had been in agony. Most especially when the class president had led a toast in honor of her engagement to Shane. She'd wanted to crawl into the woodwork and disappear. Ric had been wonderful, masterfully handling whatever situation arose—especially when Mary Ellen made a snide remark about Susan not having an engagement ring.

"Yes she does," he'd firmly insisted, lifting their linked hands onto the table. "I gave her this turquoise ring. Neither of us cared about diamonds, did we, Suse?"

"Uh, no." She gazed down at the ring, poignantly remembering when he'd slipped it on her finger. At the time they'd pretended it was an engagement ring, and now in an ironic make believe way, her dream was coming true. If Ric only knew how deeply she wished their engagement was the real thing.

"'Course, if you want a diamond, I'd be glad to get you one," Ric said huskily.

Susan felt Ric's hand tighten on hers. "No, that isn't necessary." She met his gaze straight on. "You're all I need."

As the evening wore on, there'd been other agonies as well, such as the fact there hadn't been a moment for her and Ric to be alone. The women fawned all over him, many of them confiding to her how strikingly handsome he was, and the men monopolized him in conversation, especially Ralph Kuzak, who was a detective with the Pittsburgh Police Department.

She had to give Ric credit. He talked a good game, and he seemed to possess a noticeable talent for spinning a yarn. The imaginary cases he drew out of the air and the way he related the incidents with such vivid realism had her almost believing he'd actually been an undercover agent. He was charming and witty, an excellent conversationalist, revealing skills that would serve him well in the court room, and he commanded so much attention that there were times when she wondered just whose reunion it was—hers or Ric's.

Though her classmates might have kept him preoccupied, he'd never left her side. Except for when they'd been eating or she'd been fanning herself with her napkin, their fingers had been entwined the entire time. But she wanted more. There was so much she wanted to ask him, to tell him, and she ached to run her fingers over every inch of him. She wanted him all to herself.

Constantly, she'd look at him and blink her eyes in wonder, still unable to believe he was actually here. It was a miracle. And the fact he'd remembered to come, that he'd kept his promise to pose as Shane—she could never thank him enough for that, considering that he must have had to struggle through some serious pain and injuries to get here.

The band cranked up and most of the couples sharing the table with them drifted off to the dance floor. His gaze drifted to her feet and lingered. She followed his stare. "What?"

"Just checking. Thought you might be sporting a pair of sequined tennis shoes. Sorry, Suse, dancing's out." He patted his cast. "'Course we could just stand there and lean against each other." He winked, his smile growing mischievous. "I wouldn't mind that at all."

And neither would she.

"That's all right, Ri..., Shane," she said, catching herself. She'd been tripping over his name all evening. She, the one who'd devised this whole scheme seemed to have more trouble remembering to call him Shane than he did. "Actually, I'd rather go somewhere and talk."

"I was hoping you'd say that. I booked a room here." The corners of his eyes crinkled. He rose from the table, balancing himself on his crutches. "Let's vamoose. I've got a lot I want to talk to you about."

And so did she.

With the eagerness of a teenager minutes away from receiving his driver's license, Ric sat down on the edge of the bed and placed his crutches on the floor. "Come here, Suse." He'd taken pleasure in watching her all evening, but the memory of their kisses and the way she'd felt in his arms had left him aching with desire. He loosened his tie and opened the top two buttons of his shirt. "That kiss downstairs was a sorry excuse for a welcoming. This cast has a nasty habit of interfering with what I'd like to do, but I think I can improve on that kiss."

Susan stepped between his legs. "I kind of like this cast. Lets me know where you are and limits your access to the opposite sex."

"That could apply to you, too."

"Uh uh," she murmured, "cause I don't plan to let you out of my sight, and I think I can adapt to that cast. Just watch me."

"With pleasure, Ma'am."

As Susan snuggled into him, careful not to jar his leg, he pulled her onto the bed. With her body stretched beside his, he molded his lips to hers. His tongue sought entrance and plumbed the inner recesses of her mouth. Ric stopped, took several steadying breaths, then kissed her again and again, his lips stealing down the length of her throat.

Susan feathered her hands over his cheeks, tenderly tracing his cuts. "Oh, Suse, what you do to me," he groaned, raw frustration evident in his voice. "I hate to stop, but I want to clear some things up before we go any further."

He gritted his teeth, seeking the will power to harness his powerful need. A chain reaction born of desire was about to rage out of control, and if he didn't think it was so damn important to tell her who he was, he wouldn't have stopped them. Tensing every muscle, he brought her hands to his lips and kissed them. "Later, Suse, later, and that's a promise."

"Just like your promise to come to the reunion as Shane."

"You can count on it." He drew in a long, deep breath. Those big, dewy eyes of hers were weakening his resolve. "Guess I'm not as strong as I thought I was. Right now, I'm just damn glad to be here." He propped a pillow behind him and sat apart from her.

His words tugged at her heart and her conscience. "Ric, I've been up a wall with worry over you these past couple of weeks. Over and over I see your car tumbling off that cliff."

"It's nice to know you cared. I missed you something terrible, too, and I was worried about whether you'd been injured."

"I'm fine. They took us to a hospital, and once we were released, there was an endless stream of Mexican Police, Texas Police, and American Special Agents questioning us. Once or twice I had the feeling they suspected us of being part of the drug ring and were going to arrest us."

"Us?"

"My two girlfriends and me."

"Oh, yeah," he said, remembering what Drew Matthews had told him, remembering that the Agency hadn't been convinced of her innocence until he'd come out of his coma and set them straight.

"Not that I blame the authorities," Susan continued. "After all, I suppose I did look suspicious when I attacked the agent who was taking aim on the tires of my station wagon."

"You lunged at a guy with a rifle?" At her nod, he snickered. "Why, you little hellcat." He remembered she'd been the one who had prevented Hector from shooting him. "You saved my life, Suse. The bullet from Hector Mendez's gun only grazed my leg."

"Thank God, but I was frantic. It was twenty-four hours after your car tumbled down the ravine before I got back home, and no one would tell me where you were. The next few days I called every hospital, every Agency, every police station I could think of. Finally, someone connected with the Drug Agency told me you were alive and that the other guy—"

"Hector Mendez."

"Yes, Hector Mendez was dead." She shivered "They kept a tight lid on where you were and what had happened. It was a whole week before a small article appeared in the paper stating that Federal agents had cracked a drug smuggling ring in Las Cruces, and all the while I was convinced they were lying to me about your condition. I think they still thought I was involved."

"I'm sorry, Suse. While I was unconscious, the Agency didn't know what to think." Ric almost grinned, recalling how his superiors had described Susan as a woman who needed a hurricane named for her after the way she'd hounded them about his welfare. "I'm sorry they put you through that." He took her hand in his.

"Don't be. I'm the one who's sorry. I'm the one who contributed to making Hector Mendez think you were an agent. I'm the one responsible for getting you mixed up in this mess." Tears welled up in her eyes and she paused. "When the authorities wouldn't tell me where you were, I began to fear they suspected you of impersonating an agent—or that they thought you were part of the drug ring. I must have contacted the police daily, trying to make them listen to me, trying to tell them that you weren't. I tried to explain how the misunderstanding had come about."

"I know."

"And they thought I was crazy."

"I know."

"And Ric, it was crazy. It was a silly, nutty idea asking you to pose as my fiancé."

"I don't think it was." He leaned over and kissed her brow.

"You don't?"

"No, I don't, and I'd like to talk to you about that."

She frowned, pensively tilted her head and shook it, her expression clearly confused. "What did you mean when you said you know. What did you know?"

"I knew you'd hounded the police or the Agency daily. According to Drew Matthews, you gave them one big migraine."

"You knew!" She jumped to her feet. "How?"

"Well, not at first. I was in a coma for about four days, but when I came out of it, the Agency filled me in on all your phone calls."

"Agency? Ric, they didn't have you in a prison hospital, did they?"

"No, Suse, they didn't have me in a prison hospital," he answered in a patient tone.

"Where did they take you?"

"Houston for the first week, then after I came out of my coma they flew me to Washington."

"D. C.?" Her eyes narrowed. Suspicion filled her voice.

"Yes. Sit down, Susan." He patted the bed beside him.

"They flew you to Washington, D. C.?"

She sounded so perplexed he had to smile. "Yes, for debriefing, reports, all that red tape stuff... " He hesitated. The moment of truth had arrived, and he wasn't sure how she'd take it. "Sit down, Suse," he repeated, relieved when she finally did. "The truth is I am an agent, or at least I was."

"You're an agent?"

"I was D.E.A. for five years."

"You were D.E.A.. I-I ... don't believe it."

"It's the truth. On my Apache heritage, I swear to it. The scar you saw on my back is a living souvenir." He looked her dead in the eyes. "I left the Agency three years ago, but the past few weeks I've been on temporary assignment helping them crack a drug ring."

Susan held his gaze for several seconds and began to chuckle. Then her chuckle broke into gusts of laughter. "The joke's on me, don't you see?"

"See what?"

"I dreamed up that you were an agent while all the while you really were one. When I asked you to pose as my fiancé and explained to you that he was supposed to be an agent, you must have had a hoot."

"I admit at first when you mentioned the idea, it gave me a jolt. I wondered if you knew I was an agent and were trying to get a reaction out of me. Back at the beginning when I met you, I wondered—"

"You had me under suspicion, didn't you? I was a suspect. Even after the accident, your cohorts thought I was part of the drug ring, didn't they?" An energy built in her voice. "All the time I thought you were interested in me and you were only—"

"No," he said with forceful vehemence, refusing to let her finish. He brushed back a wisp of hair from her eyes and lowered his voice. "It was never pretend. Maybe I suspected you on our first date. I'd been waiting for someone to make contact with me, and you made a big production of it with that flat tire—"

"My flat tire was legitimate."

"I know that now. Hell, by the second time I was with you after I'd followed you to Juarez—"

"You followed me to Juarez."

"And to every blasted basket shop in the city. It was my job. A good buddy and former partner of mine had been killed at Judd's weeks before that. Look, Suse, there's not a deceitful bone in your body. Maybe I didn't have any proof to back up my hunch, but by the second time we were together, I knew you couldn't be a drug dealer, not when I saw the way you loved kids and heard about how you hated drug dealers. But I couldn't figure why you'd approached me, at least not until you explained your fiancé scheme to me."

"I'm so embarrassed."

"Don't be. I had trouble sorting everything out myself. When the Agency informed me that Hector Mendez was a known drug runner and I saw how he and Garcia were tied in with you, the only way I could accept it was to assume they were using you, which it turned out they were. But never,

never did I use you. If I was guilty of anything it was being very unprofessional concerning you. Even though I was convinced you were innocent, I knew I wasn't supposed to become emotionally involved, but I couldn't help myself."

"You couldn't?" At his decisive shake, she added, "You weren't faking it?"

"Lady, if that's what you thought—" He broke off his anger.

"No, I never thought that, Ric. Not at the time, but just now when I realized I was a suspect—"

"I told you two weeks ago I loved you. I still do."

"I love you, too." Her heart was bursting with happiness.

"And I'd very much like to be your real fiancé."

"What?" Susan caught her breath. Had she heard him right?

Ric cocked his head. He'd spent hours in the hospital, waiting, hoping for this moment. "I want it all, Suse, family, kids, roots, a jacuzzi."

Just his luck, there was a jacuzzi in his hotel bathroom, and he had a damn cast on his leg. Yeah, he thought, returning to his main premise, he wanted Sunday School for his wife even if it meant their house would be overrun with baskets. He could handle that as long as it was a package deal.

"What do you say, Susan? Will you marry me? I don't know where I'm going to live. I've applied to the district attorney's offices in Las Cruces, San Angelo, and Houston—"

"Yes," she breathlessly interrupted him. "Yes, to anywhere in the country as long as we're together." She started to giggle again.

"What's so funny about marrying me?"

"I'm laughing about my bet with Pam and Robin. Not only does it appear that I've won, but it's completely backfired."

"What bet?"

"Uh oh." She rolled her eyes. "Don't get huffy."

"I'm not getting huffy."

"That first day I saw you in Judd's, I was telling my friends about how I'd spouted off to Mary Ellen Hathaway about having this dynamite fiancé who was a secret agent. I'd just about decided to kill him off when they bet me I could ask you to do it and successfully pass you off as Shane Orr. And they were right. You were magnificent tonight, pure dynamite."

"You approached me on account of a bet—"

"At first, yes, but the more I got to know you, the more I

discovered how much I liked you. I fell in love with you, and by the time I got around to asking you, I was secretly wishing it could be for real."

"It is now."

"Yes, it is. Ric, I felt so sure about you that I was ready to ask you to be Shane long before Pam and Robin got back from their trip to Austin and San Angelo to check you out."

"Check me out! You mean it was those two who were nosing into my past?" He threw back his head and laughed. "And here we thought since you were the only one I'd told about my past that you'd unintentionally passed it along to Garcia. And all the time it was those two whacky women."

"They're not whacky."

"That's debatable. They're the ones who sicced Hector Mendez onto me." Ric arched his brow. "One of them doesn't happen to own a brown Chevy?"

"Pam does."

Ric snapped his fingers. "It was them up on the mountain, following us, wasn't it?"

"You saw them?"

"Just barely. You did a pretty damn good job of distracting me."

"That's what you meant every time you referred to climbing a mountain, isn't it? It's about our first kisses the day we rode your motorcycle up the mountain."

"You're kisses surprised me. I kept wanting to see if you could repeat the performance."

"And did I?"

"Yes, Ma'am. Right now I'm torn between introducing your parents to their daughter's fiancé or climbing that mountain again."

She kicked off her shoes. "Well, a gal sure can't climb a mountain in heels." She peered at him through a fringe of lashes and impatiently tapped her lips with her fingertip. "Besa la maestra."

He leaned over and brushed his lips across her mouth. "I intend to, for the rest of our lives and over every blessed inch of your beautiful body." Especially her legs. "Te amo, Sunday School, te amo."

"Sunday School?"

"Forget it. Right now I'm dying here."

Susan arched an eyebrow. He'd called her that once before.

One of these days she'd get to the bottom of it, but not now. "So, Agent Ramsey, you want to go mountain climbing?"

"Yes Ma'am. Strap on your hiking boots—or should I say tennis shoes—and take me up that mountain."

AUTHOR'S NOTE

There I was sitting under the dryer in the beauty parlor, rifling through a woman's magazine, when, WHAM BAM, an article on flirting jumped out at me. The more I read, the more my mind began to hum. By the time the dryer clicked off, I'd mentally outlined three chapters and scribbled notes on every scrap of paper I could find in my purse. My writer's juices were flowing, and from the way I behaved I'm sure everyone looked askance at me much the way the hero of this story finds himself looking at the heroine. Months later FIVE STEPS TO FLIRTING was completed.

Regarding the birth of the second story found in this book, Sherry Cobb South, author of several Young Adult novels, asked her critique group to suggest catchy titles for her soon to be published novel. My contribution was, THE BET THAT BACKFIRED, and though it wasn't chosen, I couldn't shake loose of it. Despite the fact I was working on another story at the time, the title demanded a story of its own. After developing the plot, outlining the novel, and watching the story unfold, I renamed the story SUNDAY SCHOOL AND THE SECRET AGENT.

My first love is writing modern day fairy tales, and that's what I have created here. I hope these stories bring a smile to your face and allow you to suspend rock-hard reality, cast your worries aside, and escape into the fantasy world of romance and frivolity.

AUTHOR BIOGRAPHY

Gail Kennedy is a transplanted Yankee who loves the South and football with a passion. Shortly after moving to Mobile, (many moons ago), it blew her mind to discover her great grandfather had resided there one hundred years earlier. Not only did he join the 12th Alabama and fight under General Lee, but miraculously he survived the entire war. It had all been a hush, hush, family secret... but that's' another story—a story perhaps she'll write one day.

By the way, did I mention she loves football, especially college ball. An English major with a degree from Tufts University and a Master's Degree in Early Childhood Education from the University of South Alabama, she remembers writing her first book in second grade, and (dating herself) recalls playing with paper dolls—creating fantasy worlds for them. Now that her dream has come true, she pinches herself daily to make sure it's real and not one of those intricate plots her mind weaves at the oddest of moments, such as waiting in long check-out lines, driving as a passenger in a car, weeding the flowerbeds, or sitting in waiting rooms.

A senior citizen, having the time of her life launching a new career, married to her college sweetheart, and mother of three children, she's never given up believing love makes the world go round and invites you to journey with her while she escapes into the world of make-believe.

And don't forget football. Start a conversation about it and you'll see what I mean.

TM

To learn more about us visit our web site at
www.laughingowl.com